Praise for the previous novels of

LORI WILDE

"Romantic, funny, sexy, and poignant. I loved this book."

Kristin Hannah for *The First Love Cookie Club*

"Delicious details, a small town full of memorable characters, great dialogue, and humor all combine to make this a highly enjoyable tale about two people who find healing—and each other."

Booklist (*Starred Review*) for *All of Me*

"Sexy and a hoot. . . . A delicacy that really hits the spot."

Romantic Times BOOKclub for *License to Thrill*

"Lori Wilde has created a rich and wonderful story about the charm of small town life combined with the power and passion of first love. Delicious!"

New York Times bestselling author Robyn Carr for *The Cowboy Takes a Bride*

"Full of colorful characters . . . as satisfying as a glass of lemonade on a hot day."

Publishers Weekly for *The Cowboy Takes a Bride*

By Lori Wilde

A Cowboy for Christmas
The Cowboy and the Princess
The Cowboy Takes a Bride
The Welcome Home Garden Club
The First Love Cookie Club
The True Love Quilting Club
The Sweethearts' Knitting Club

Available from Avon Impulse

The Christmas Cookie Chronicles:
Carrie
Raylene
Christine

LORI WILDE

A COWBOY *For* CHRISTMAS

AVON
An Imprint of HarperCollins*Publishers*

AVON BOOKS
An Imprint of HarperCollins*Publishers*
10 East 53rd Street
New York, New York 10022–5299

ISBN 978-1-62090-593-7

Printed in the U.S.A.

To Michael Lee West,
one of my favorite authors
and my dearest new friend. Bake on, sister.

Special Acknowledgment

Writing a book takes a lot of research. I must thank two people who helped me learn about military benefits and how sometimes military families can fall through the cracks in the system and end up without support when their loved ones die in combat. To Colonel Tom Fossen USAF and Army Captain Jessica Scott, who is also a phenomenal writer in her own right. Thank you from the bottom of my heart.

Chapter One

When she got right down to it, Lissette Moncrief's infatuation with cowboys was what *really* started all the trouble.

There was something about those laconic alpha males that stirred her romantic soul. Their uniforms of faded Wranglers, scuffed cowboy boots, jangling spurs, and proudly cocked Stetsons represented rugged strength, fierce independence, and a solemn reverence for the land. Their stony determination to tame wild horses, mend broken fences, and tend their families made her stomach go fluttery. Their cool way of facing problems head-on, no shirking or skirting responsibilities, weakened her knees.

A cowboy was stalwart and steady, honest and honorable, stoic and down-to-earth. At least that's what the movies had taught her. From John Wayne to Clint Eastwood to Sam Elliott, she'd crushed on them all. She loved Wayne's self-confident swagger, Eastwood's steely-eyed ethics, and Elliott's toe-tingling voice.

When she was sixteen, Lissette and her best friend, Audra, had sneaked off to see a fortune-teller at the Scarborough Renaissance Fair in Waxahachie. Inside the canvas tent, Lady Divine, a pancake-faced woman in a wheelchair, spread spooky-looking cards across an oil-stained folding table. She wore dreadlocks tied up in a red bandana, and a flowy rainbow caftan. On the end of her chin perched a fat brown mole with long black hairs sprouting from it like spider legs. The tent smelled of fried onions and the farty pit bull–terrier mix stretched out on a braided rug in front of her.

Lady Divine studied the card alignment. She tapped her lips with an index finger and grabbed hold of Lissette's tentative gaze, but she didn't say anything for a long, dramatic moment.

"What is it?" Lissette whispered, gripping the corner of the cheap greasy table, bracing for some horrific prognostication like *You have no future.*

"Cowboy."

"What?" Lissette thrilled to the word.

"There's a cowboy in your future."

"Will he become my husband?"

"Only time can say."

Eagerly, she leaned forward. "Is he handsome? What's he like?"

"Dark." Lady Divine's voice turned ominous.

"In personality or looks?"

"This cowboy will influence you deeply. He brings great change."

"In a bad way?" She knotted a strand of fringe dangling from the sleeve of her jacket.

Lady Divine shrugged. "What is good? What is bad? Who can know? You can't avoid this cowboy. He is inevitable."

The fortune-teller continued with the reading, but Lissette absorbed none of the rest of it. She was so stunned by how the woman had zeroed in on her cowboy infatuation. Later, she and Audra had dissected the woman's uncanny prediction. They were in Texas, after all. The likelihood of running across an influential cowboy at some point in her future was far above fifty-fifty. Not such a mystifying forecast in that context.

Most people would have blown off the reading, dismissing it as nothing more than the slick pitch of a smarmy woman who made her money telling gullible people what they wanted to hear, but for a girl besotted with cowboys, the fortune-teller's prophecy had not only mesmerized Lissette, it also set her up for heartache.

If she hadn't been convinced that a cowboy was her future, she would never have ignored the warning signs. If she hadn't romanticized Jake into a modern-day version of John Wayne, she wouldn't have married him. If he hadn't sounded like Sam Elliott on steroids, she wouldn't have heard the lies he told her. If she hadn't duped herself into thinking that he was the second coming of Clint Eastwood, she wouldn't have had a child with him. If she hadn't swallowed the cowboy mystique hook, line, and sinker, she wouldn't be here in Jubilee, Texas, the cutting horse capital of the world, dealing with this new, life-shattering situation all by herself.

Then again, how could she regret anything that had given her a son?

She glanced at her two-year-old, Kyle, who was seated in the grocery cart. Unable to draw in a full breath, she ran a hand over Kyle's soft brown curls as he sat in the grocery cart eating cheddar Goldfish crackers from a lidless sippy cup decorated with images of gray Eeyore. Cheesy yellow crumbs clung to his cupid bow lips and there was a grape juice stain on his light blue T-shirt.

Genetic nonsyndromic autosomal recessive progressive hearing loss.

The words were a mouthful that boiled down to one gut-wrenching truth. Kyle was slowly going deaf, medical science could not cure him, and it was all her fault.

It turned out both she and her late husband, Jake, unwittingly carried a recessive connexin 26 mutation and poor Kyle had lost the genetic lottery. So said the audiologist, geneticist, and pediatric otolaryngologist whose Fort Worth office she'd just left with the astringent smell of cold antiseptic in her nose and a handful of damning paperwork and referrals clutched in her fist.

Deaf.

Such a frightening word. It sounded too much like "dead."

Deaf.

Her poor, fatherless baby.

Foggy as a sleepwalker, Lissette pushed her grocery cart down the baking products aisle of Searcy's Grocery, past an array of orange and black cupcake sprinkles, candy molds in the shapes of ghosts and pumpkins, and gingerbread haunted house kits.

Her lips pressed into a hard line, resisting any stiff attempts she made to lift them into a smile for fellow shoppers. Misery bulged at the seams of her heart until it felt too swollen to fit inside her chest. It beat, as if barely stitched together, in halting ragtag jolts. A sense of impending doom pressed in on her, hot and smothering.

It couldn't be true that her child was losing his hearing in slow, agonizing increments, never to be reclaimed. She had to seek a second opinion.

A third.

And a fourth if necessary.

But with what? Consultations did not come cheaply.

Swallowing back her pain, Lissette refocused on her goal of shopping for baking supplies. That was the answer to her money troubles.

Searcy's was the only locally owned supermarket in Jubilee, the cowboy-infused town that Jake had settled her in four years ago before he first shipped off to the

Middle East. In the beginning, she'd embraced the place, the community, the culture, the cowboys, but then, bit by bit, her eyes had been opened to the truth. Cowboys were like everyone else. Some good. Some bad. All fallible. It had been a mistake to romanticize a myth. No man could give her a fairy tale. She understood that now and she was determined to provide for herself. No more depending on a man for anything.

The store, with its narrow aisles, sometimes felt like a womb—comforting, cozy, communal—but today, it felt like a straitjacket with the straps cinched tight. Maybe it was the candy pumpkin molds, but an unexpected nursery rhyme popped into her head.

Peter, Peter, pumpkin eater, had a wife and couldn't keep her. Put her in a pumpkin shell and there he kept her very well.

"Da . . ." Kyle gurgled with the limited vocabulary of a child half his age. "Da."

Shoppers crowded her. She needed to get to the flour, but Jubilee's version of two soccer moms—i.e., Little Britches rodeo moms—stood leaning against the shelves gossiping, oblivious to those around them.

Lissette cleared her throat, but the moms either ignored her or didn't hear her, something she'd grown accustomed to as the middle child, bookended by more attractive, gregarious sisters.

"Um," she ventured, surrendering a smile. "Could one of you ladies please hand me a ten-pound sack of cake flour?"

"Did you hear about Denise?" the shorter of the two women asked the other as if Lissette hadn't uttered a word. "She up and left Jiff for a man eight years younger than she is."

"Get out! Denise? No way."

"I tell you, losing all that weight went straight to her

head. She thinks she's God's gift to men now that she can squeeze into a size four."

"My cousin Callie is single and searching," the taller one mused. "I wonder if Jiff's ready to start dating."

Feeling invisible, Lissette sighed and bent over, trying to reach around them to get to the flour, but the ten-pound bags were on the bottom shelf. The woman with the single cousin had her fashionable Old Gringo cowboy boots cocked in such a way that Lissette couldn't reach it.

Normally, she would have stopped at Costco for a fifty-pound bag when she'd been in Fort Worth, but those big bags were so hard for her to lift, and besides, she'd driven the twenty-six miles back to Jubilee in a such a fog she didn't even remember leaving the medical complex.

She straightened. It was on the tip of her tongue to ask the women to kindly step aside when a ten-year-old boy on wheeled skate shoes darted past, almost crashing into Lissette's elbow. She jumped back and gritted her teeth, anxiety climbing high in her throat.

Kyle was staring at her, studying her face.

Calm down.

She was on edge. Kyle would pick up on her negative energy and that was the last thing he needed. If she thought her morning had been lousy, all she had to do was imagine what it felt like to her son—poked and prodded and unable to understand why.

It hit her then, how confusing life must be when you couldn't hear, how much communication you missed. Then again, in some regards, that might be a blessing. Did she really need to hear about Denise and Jiff's crumbling marriage? Her own marriage had been filled with so many thorns that the occasional sweet bloom couldn't make up for all the painful sticks.

"Da." Kyle raised his small head, his usual somber expression searching her face through impossibly long eyelashes—Jake's eyelashes—as if seeking an answer to the silent question. *Why can't I hear you, Mommy?*

Why hadn't she suspected something was wrong? Why hadn't she realized that her baby could not hear? Why had it taken a nudge from her best friend, Mariah Daniels, for her to make a doctor's appointment?

She'd been angry at first when Mariah said, "It's funny that Kyle doesn't respond when you ask him to do something."

Lissette told herself Mariah was jealous. Kyle was so much quieter than her son, Jonah, who was six months younger. But then she started noticing how Kyle watched her hands more than he watched her face, how he never cared for toys that made noise, how his language skills lagged behind Jonah's, and how he often seemed so willful, never listening when she cautioned.

Her chest tightened. Her son hadn't been ignoring her. He wasn't willful. He simply had not heard her warnings. At times, she'd been so impatient with him. She pressed her lips together, her throat clogged with shame and regret. How could she have been so clueless?

"Sweetie," said a tiny elderly woman with a severe, blue-tinged bun piled high on her head and tortoiseshell glasses perched on the end of her nose. She wore a lumpy floral print dress that scalloped around saggy calves and didn't quite hide the tops of her coffee-colored, knee-high stockings.

"Yes ma'am?"

"Would you mind reaching that box of powdered milk on the top shelf for me?"

Lissette forced a smile. She wouldn't be rude like the rodeo moms. Mariah Daniels was five-foot-one, so even though she wasn't particularly tall herself at five-foot-five, Lissette was accustomed to retrieving things off top shelves. "The blue box or the red?"

"The blue, please."

Lissette had to stand on tiptoes to reach it, but she got the box down.

"Bless you, my dear. Be proud of your height."

"I'm not that tall."

"To me, you're a tower." Her blue eyes twinkled. "And who is this little man? How old are you?" she asked Kyle.

Busily eyeing the baking chocolate, Kyle crunched a Goldfish and did not respond.

The elderly lady bustled closer. "Are you two years old? You're about the same size as my great-grandson. You look like you're two years old."

Kyle did not react.

The woman cocked her head like a curious squirrel. "Is something wrong with him, sweetie? He's not answering me."

A dozen impulses pushed through Lissette. The defensive part of her wanted to tell the woman to mind her own business. The "nice girl" started thinking of a delicate way to explain. Her shell-shocked psyche curled the words *He's deaf* around her tongue, but she couldn't bring herself to say it out loud.

Not yet. Not when she hadn't even practiced saying it in private.

Instead, she completely surprised herself by blurting out, "His father got blown up by an IED in Afghanistan on the Fourth of July."

The gnomish woman stepped back as if Lissette had slapped her. She gasped and put her hands to her mouth. "Oh my Lord, you're that poor young widow that I read all about in the *Jubilee Daily Cutter*. Oh sweetie, I'm so sorry. I know exactly what you're going through."

You have no idea what I'm going through, Lissette wanted to scream, but she kept her taut smile pinned in place. "Thank you."

"I'm so sorry," the woman repeated and patted Lissette's forearm, and then a tear trickled down her wrinkled cheek. "I lost my boy in 'Nam."

"I . . . I . . ." Lissette stammered. She could not imagine—never wanted to imagine—losing her child. She clenched her jaw, unable to find the right words.

The elderly woman dug into a purse the size of Vermont and came up with a crumpled tissue clutched in arthritis-gnarled fingers. "They never did find his remains." She pressed a knobby knuckle against her nose, blinked through the tears. "Johnny Lee's been gone forty-four years, but I think of him every single day. He was only eighteen when the Lord called him away. Just a baby. My boy."

Their gazes locked. Two mothers united in loss.

Lissette squeezed the woman's shoulder. "Is there anything else I can get you from the top shelf?"

The great-grandmother dried her eyes. "Why, thank you for the offer, sweetie. I am running low on baking soda."

"Big box or small?"

"Small. There's nothing big about me." Her congenial chuckle was back, but her faded gaze stayed caught in the past.

Lissette handed her the box of soda.

The woman raised her chin. "I'm going to tell you what I wish someone had told me. Don't try to be brave. Don't hold it all in. I know the grief is immense, but don't fight it. Cry hard when you receive bad news because that's how you will make way for tears of joy. When you can accept your losses and forgive your mistakes, then you can embrace a happy future."

The woman turned and vanished so quickly that for one startling second, Lissette wondered if she imagined the whole exchange.

Accept your losses.

It was a strange thing to say. It felt like surrender. Lissette was familiar with surrender. She was, by nature, accepting of the circumstances she found herself in. It was far easier to give in than to put up a fuss.

When Jake had told her that instead of quitting the army as he'd promised, he reenlisted and was going back to the Middle East, she had not only accepted it, she'd been secretly relieved. It was something she would never admit to another living soul, because when he was home on leave Jake was restless, moody. He had frequent nightmares and he would get up in the middle of the night and disappear without a word.

Sometimes he wouldn't come home for days at a stretch. He never told her where he went and if she pressed for an explanation, he'd grow surly and curt. It had been easier to tiptoe around him. She suspected he might be having an affair, although she tried not to think about it too much.

Fearing he was suffering from post-traumatic stress, she'd suggested counseling, but Jake yelled at her and even put his fist through the wall, proving to her that he did need therapy. She'd been afraid of his rage and she'd backed down, never knowing what was going to set him off or what he was capable of. He was no longer the charming cowboy who'd swept her off her feet, but she was loyal to the bone, and she kept hoping that once he was back home for good, eventually he'd heal and they could become a real family.

The gossipers were still hogging the flour shelf. She took a step forward, cleared her throat, and opened her mouth, determined to ask them to please move, when the store's public address system crackled.

"Attention shoppers!" announced the store manager. "It's Searcy's five for five. For the next five minutes, any five items on the baking products aisle will sell for five cents. You have from three P.M. until three-o-five to get your purchases and check out. On your mark, get set, go!"

Before the announcement finished, the baking goods aisle flooded with customers. A sea of shoppers pushed against her, tossing her farther from the flour as they snatched and grabbed at everything in sight.

Okay, she'd go for the vanilla. It was right behind her. She spun her cart around, but a handholding young couple with matching facial piercings and tattoos halted right in front of her.

Hands locked, they stared her down. The young man had a Mohawk. The girl's hair was Barney-the-Dinosaur purple with glow-in-the-dark neon green streaks. Neither said a word, just glowered in simpatico, their gazes drilling a hole through Lissette. Apparently, they wanted her to move rather than force them to let go of each other's hands so they could continue on their way undivided.

Fine, Sid and Nancy. Let it never be said I stood in the way of punk love.

Lissette tried to maneuver her cart off to one side, but people jostled each elbow and the cart wouldn't roll. Some sticky crap stuck to the wheels. Flustered, she picked the cart up and tried to eke out a couple of inches.

"Hey!" complained a woman she bumped against who was tossing a handful of garlic salt bottles into her cart. "Watch where you're going."

"I'm so sorry," Lissette apologized.

The amorous duo wrinkled their noses at her, turned, and stalked back the way they'd come, never letting go of each other in the about-face, even though they had to raise their coupled hands over the heads of other shoppers.

Ah, true love. Once upon a time she'd been that young and dumb.

Someone stumbled against her. Someone else smelled

as if they'd taken a bath in L'Air du Temps. Simon and Garfunkel's "The Sound of Silence" trickled through the music system. The irony was not lost on Lissette.

Claustrophobia wrapped around her throat, choked her. She broke out in a cold sweat. She stood frozen, wishing the floor would open up and swallow her whole so she didn't have to deal with any of this. She would have unzipped her skin and stripped it off if she could have. Her hands shook. Panic clawed her chest.

It took everything she had to curb the urge to abandon the grocery cart and sprint like a madwoman to her quaint Victorian home in the middle of town. Grab Kyle up, clutch him to her chest, tumble into the big, empty four-poster bed, and burrow underneath the double-wedding ring quilt that her mother-in-law, Claudia, had made.

She ached to go to sleep and wake up to find this whole thing was just a wickedly bad dream—Jake's death, the fact that he left his four-hundred-thousand-dollar life insurance policy and his one-hundred-thousand-dollar military death gratuity benefits to a half brother she never knew existed, and now today's striking blow of learning that Kyle was going deaf.

Her son would never be a concert musician. Never speak three languages. Never hear the sound of *his* children's voices.

She'd been utterly shocked when she'd learned her husband had not named her his beneficiary. Then bone-deep anger. Followed by marrow-chilling dread when the government informed her that because she was not his beneficiary, she and Kyle were no longer eligible for Jake's VA benefits. Nor would they be able to receive any monies under the Survivor Benefit Plan or Dependency and Indemnity compensation because, in violation of a direct order from his commanding officer, Jake had been killed while returning to a village trying to save orphans in the line of fire. Willful misconduct, the Army called it.

She'd taken out the only health insurance she could afford—a catastrophic policy with a massive deductible. None of today's medical expenses would be covered, or any further expenses, until she hit the ten-thousand-dollar annual threshold.

The only thing she knew for certain was that the money she'd been anticipating to provide for her and Kyle would not be forthcoming. Beyond a tiny nest egg in an untouchable retirement account, Jake's cutting horse, and her Queen Anne Victorian, she had only five thousand dollars left from the money the army had given her to bury Jake. If he hadn't told her numerous times that he preferred cremation to burial, she wouldn't have had even that small sum.

In this real estate market her house was more liability than asset. The only thing she had of any worth to sell was Jake's cutting horse and the accompanying horse trailer, but she just hadn't made herself go through the motions yet. She had to do something and soon. Today she'd worked out a payment plan for the medical services Kyle had undergone, but this was only the beginning.

"Damn you, Jake," she whispered. "For treating us this way. Damn you for refusing to get help and killing what little love we had left."

It struck her then that she couldn't really remember what Jake had looked like. Big guy. Strong. Muscled. Smelled like protein. John Wayne swagger. But that was it.

They'd been married for four years, but he'd been in the Middle East for a big chunk of that time. If she broke it down into consecutive days, they probably hadn't been together more than six months total. She'd had his child, but she'd known nothing about the secrets he kept tucked away under that Stetson. She never asked about the war. She believed in letting slumbering dogs alone. Besides, she hadn't really wanted to know what horrors he'd seen. The things he'd done.

Ostrich. Sticking her head in the sand.

But now? She had to do something to stretch her budget.

What bothered her most about losing the money was that the mysterious half brother had never shown up. He didn't call, nor had he even written to express his condolences. You would think five hundred thousand dollars would at least earn a sorry-your-husband-got-blown-up-in-Afghanistan-thanks-for-the-money card.

"I'll help you as much as I can, Lissy," Claudia said, but her mother-in-law was little better off than she was.

Lissette's own family was upper middle class, but their investments had gotten caught in the real estate crash and they were cash strapped as well. Besides, whenever her parents gave her money, there were always strings attached. So far, she'd been too proud to ask them to help, but she was going to have to get over her pride, and accept the strings. She had a part-time job making wedding cakes for Mariah's wedding planning business, The Bride Wore Cowboy Boots, but her salary barely covered her mortgage.

Which was why she was at the grocery store.

Survival.

On the way home from Fort Worth, an idea had occurred to her. Cowboys had been her downfall, but clearly she wasn't the only one mesmerized by the fantasy. Why not take advantage of her infatuation? Do what you know, right? Add cowboy-themed baked goods to her repertoire to supplement her wedding cake business.

Her mind had picked up the idea and run with it. Pastries straight from the heart of Texas made with indigenous ingredients. Velvet Mesquite Bean Napoleons. Giddy-up Pecan Pie. Lone Star Strudel. Bluebonnet

Bread. Mockingbird Cake. Chocolate Jalapeño Cupcakes. Prickly Pear Jellyrolls. Frosted sugar cookie cutouts of cowboy boots and hats, cacti, longhorn cattle, spurs, and galloping horses.

Even though it meant going out on a limb with her remaining five thousand dollars, she'd grasped at the idea. It gave her something to think about besides Kyle's diagnosis. But now that she was here amid the five-minute-sale madness, the idea seemed stupid. Throwing away good money.

What else was she going to do? Baking was all she knew. It wasn't as if she possessed the skill set for anything else.

Bake.

It was an edict. She fixed on the word.

Bake.

Something comforting. Something sweet. Something lifesaving. Cookies and cakes, doughnuts and cream puffs, strudels and pies. Salvation in pastries.

Bake.

Kyle dropped his sippy cup, arched his back, let out a screech of frustration. One high bounce off the cement floor sent Goldfish splashing up and down the aisle.

A woman behind Lissette let out an exasperated huff and pushed past her, crunching Goldfish underneath the wheels of her cart.

Kyle wailed, made a grasping motion toward the scattered crackers.

The gossiping women still hogging the flour shelf glared at her.

Yes, I'm the villain.

Finally, they turned and stalked away.

About time.

Kyle howled, tears dripping down his cheeks. Lissette

snatched the sippy cup from the floor, and then thumbed through her purse for more Goldfish crackers, but the bag was empty.

Get the ingredients and get out of here. He'll calm down in a minute.

Ignoring everyone else, she started grabbing what she needed. Let's see. Cake flour, check. Pure cane sugar, check. Vanilla, vanilla. Real vanilla. Not that fake stuff. Where was the real vanilla?

She searched the shelves, going up on tiptoes and then squatting down low, pawing through extracts and flavorings. Almond, banana, butter, coconut. No real vanilla. Dammit. The budget-conscious shoppers had wiped it out like locusts. Now, she'd have to drive to Albertson's on the other side of town.

Couldn't one simple thing go right today?

C'mon, c'mon there had to be one bottle left.

Without real vanilla, she couldn't start her new baking project. Without her new baking project, she couldn't afford to get Kyle the best deaf education. Without getting him the best education, her son's future was indeed bleak.

Oh, there was so much to think about! She had no idea where to start. The medical brochures and jargon only confused her more. She knew nothing about deafness. She'd never even met a deaf person. How could she help her child? The pressure of tears pushed against her sinuses and an instant headache bloomed, throbbing insistently at her temples.

She couldn't let her son's life be destroyed. She *had* to get that damn real vanilla.

But the cupboards were bare and Kyle was shrieking.

"Ma'am, ma'am," a pimple-faced stock boy in a Black Keys T-shirt came over. "Your baby is disturbing the other customers. Can you please take him outside?"

Harried, Lissette looked up from where she crouched, the floor strewn with baking products and crushed Goldfish crackers. It was all she could do not to let loose with a string of well-chosen curse words. The mother inside her managed to restrain her tongue. She stood, wrapped her arms around her sobbing child, and tugged him from the cart.

Head down, she rushed toward the front door.

"Would you like a sample of Dixieland cinnamon rolls?" called a woman at the end of the row dishing out samples.

Lissette spun to face her, Kyle clutched on her hip, his face buried against her bosom. "I bet it's made with fake vanilla, isn't it?"

The woman looked taken aback. "I . . . I . . . don't know."

"That's what wrong with the world," Lissette said. "Fake food. Nobody knows what they're eating. We're all getting artificial, prepackaged garbage dished out by corporate marketing departments—"

Stop the rant, Lissette. This woman is not the enemy. Canned cinnamon rolls are not the enemy. Fake vanilla is not the enemy.

Three months of anger and shock surged to a head. For three months she'd been at loose ends, not knowing where her future was headed, but there in Searcy's Grocery, just weeks from Halloween, everything she'd ignored, tamped down, and shut off, erupted. She stormed from the store, leaving slack jaws hanging open in her wake.

Her heart slammed against her chest with jackhammer force. Her negative energy flowed into Kyle. He fisted his little hand in her hair, yanked, his hopeless shrieks piercing her eardrums.

Calm down, calm down.

But she'd lost all ability to soothe herself.

Bake. The no-fail solution to runaway emotions. Bake. How could she bake without real vanilla?

Get real vanilla.

It was a nonsensical edict. Of course it was, but the command stuck in her brain. She made it to Jake's extended-cab pickup truck. She'd wanted a Prius and this was what she ended up with. The key fumbled at the lock, but she finally wrenched the door open and got Kyle buckled into his backward-facing car seat.

By the time she slid behind the wheel she was only breathing from the top part of her lungs. Her diaphragm had shut down, paralyzed, seized. Puff, puff, puff. Short, fast pants swirled through her parted lips.

Hyperventilating.

Real vanilla, whispered her mammalian brain.

Go home, commanded her last shred of logic.

She started the engine, put the truck into reverse, and stamped her foot to the accelerator. Her worn leather purse rocketed to the floorboard, sending the contents scattering—makeup, hairbrush, wallet, plastic Happy Meal toys.

Dammit! She reached down for her purse.

Instantly, she felt a jolt, heard the jarring crunch of bending metal, tasted the wiry flavor of alarm. She lifted her head, saw a big red pickup truck filling her rearview mirror, and realized she'd just hit someone.

Chapter Two

Rafferty Jones had a simple goal. Find a certain woman. Deliver what he'd come to Texas to deliver, do what he'd promised, and then get out of Jubilee before things turned dicey. He wanted to be long gone when that happened.

Because they would turn dicey, of that he had no doubt.

He was not usually a procrastinator, but now that he'd driven the streets of Jubilee, which were overrun with horse trailers and dually pickup trucks like the one he drove, he was suddenly uncertain about his mission.

It felt too familiar here. People in Stetsons and Wranglers and cowboy boots were the majority not the minority. In L.A. he was the oddity. In Jubilee, he was part of the scenery. Country music played from shops on the square instead of rap or hip-hop. The air smelled of fresh harvest. Folks waved and smiled as if they knew him.

As if he belonged.

Instead of driving straight to the address clipped to the papers on the seat beside him, Rafferty decided to stop at the grocery store. He knew he was stalling, but he hadn't eaten anything since Tucumcari except a small bag of peppered beef jerky. He wasn't a big fan of greasy truck stop fare or fast food. A can of tuna and crackers washed down with V–8 juice sounded just about right to him. Throw in a couple of bananas for dessert and he was good to go.

Searcy's Grocery looked homegrown. It should do the trick.

He pulled his old Dodge Ram diesel into the lot and out of nowhere—*wham*—a late-model Ford extended-cab pickup truck bulleted backward out of a parking space and clipped his left front fender.

Dammit.

He put his aging Dodge into park, and swung his gaze to the driver of the Ford.

She was a pretty woman with an agitated expression on her thin face. Not beautiful, but nice-looking.

She turned her head and their gazes met.

He saw it then. That haunting vulnerability he seemed fatally attracted to. Her skin was pale, her eyes wide, her pink bottom lip pulled up between straight white teeth.

Unexpected fear seized him. He couldn't express why or in what way, but his gut sensed she could do him serious harm.

Blow off the damage, back up, and drive away. Now.

Too late.

She was opening her door, and swinging to the ground. She wore a long-sleeved white cotton shirt over a blue denim skirt that made her look all of eighteen. The hem swished against the top of black knee-high boots. A mass of wavy, brown-sugar hair tumbled down her back. He couldn't help noticing the wedding band on her left hand. She was married.

Disappointment arrowed through him.

Why the hell did he care? His romantic relationships always seemed to end in a messy tangle. Besides, he was only in town for one day.

All you'd need is one night with her.

But something told him that one taste of this woman would never be enough and damn if he didn't have an urge to run his fingers through that cascade of thick hair. It looked incredibly soft. Good thing he'd noticed the ring before he said something glib and flirty. The last thing Rafferty needed was an angry husband punching his lights out for lusting after his woman.

"I am so sorry." She kneaded her forehead. Distress glazed her green eyes and the worry lines creasing her brow furrowed deeper than a crunched fender.

That was his first clue that she was having a really bad day.

Watch it. No sympathy. Don't cut her any slack. Pretend she's a hairy, knuckle-draggin' steelworker.

"It's my fault. I wasn't paying any attention to where I was backing."

He wasn't going to argue. She had plowed into him. "No, you weren't."

Okay, he was being unrelenting, but it was his only defense against her wide-eyed upset. Rafferty hardened his jaw. He wouldn't be feeling forgiving if she were a six-foot, two-hundred pound guy.

But she wasn't.

The woman moved forward, spied the damage to his truck, and groaned. She splayed her palms against her lower back. "I'll pay. Let me just get my insurance information."

"Hold up a minute." He reached out and rested a hand on her slender shoulder. Big mistake. His body reacted instantly. Lightning-quick, he dropped his hand. *Think of something else besides how good she smells. Horses. Think about horses.*

"What? What?" She blinked as if seeing him for the first time.

"Are *you* okay?" Rafferty asked, unable to stop his dumbass self from caring.

"Fine, fine." She looked harried, distracted . . . *fractured.*

Do not go there. It's not your duty to fix her life.

A thin wail came from the backseat of the Ford. There was a kid in the truck. Double damn.

"What about your baby?" Rafferty arched an eyebrow.

Her mouth formed a startled O. She pivoted and rushed to her child.

Rafferty followed, even though he had no idea why.

Clucking a soothing noise, she removed a toddler in a blue T-shirt who was kicking hard, arms flailing. He seemed more mad than hurt or scared.

Like any good mother, she examined him thoroughly in spite of the squirming and squalling. "Hold still for Mommy," she pleaded.

The boy bucked against her, snorting in loud frustration.

Rafferty stepped closer. "Hey there, little britches," he said, and gave the boy a stern but gentle look. "Ease up on the volume."

The toddler's gaze fixed on him. His mouth clamped shut and he quieted, his eyes filling up with Rafferty.

"He needs a nap," the woman apologized. "And he misses his daddy."

"Traveling man?"

She jerked her head up. "Huh?"

"Is his daddy a traveling man?"

Her face darkened and her jaw tightened. "My husband . . ." She trailed off, her voice distant, but strong. "Died in Afghanistan."

Damn. There was a lot of that goin' around.

"I'm sorry, ma'am." He tipped his Stetson. "It wasn't any of my business."

She hitched the boy on her hip and turned back to stare

at their two trucks kissing back fender to front, but the foggy sheen to her eyes told him she wasn't seeing the slight damage. Was she thinking about her husband?

He shifted uncomfortably.

"Let me just get my insurance information," she repeated and tracked around the front of her pickup to get to the other side. Rafferty trailed behind her. He couldn't make himself not notice the sweet sway of her hips.

She opened the passenger door and tried to one-hand the glove compartment open. The toddler started whimpering again.

"You want me to hold him for you?"

She pressed her lips into a grim line, shook her head. A fall of brown-sugar hair slanted across her cheek.

"I don't mind helpin'," he offered.

"I've got it," she snapped.

Rafferty raised his palms. He knew when to back off. This one's nerves were wiredrawn and he had a feeling it was not just because of the smashup.

She half leaned over, one side pressed against the seat, the child tucked in the crook of her arm, and dug through the glove compartment. Papers flew every which way—receipts, fast food napkins, computer printouts of MapQuest destinations.

"I know it's in here somewhere," she mumbled.

The kid was tuning up, working out his lungs.

Rafferty met the boy's eyes, laid a finger over his own lips.

The toddler stilled.

The woman's head jerked up and she thrust the child toward him. "Fine. Hold him."

Rafferty's arms wrapped around the boy, who looked surprised to be there. He studied Rafferty's face with the astuteness of a miniature cop.

In the meantime, the child's mother was still rooting

around in the glove compartment and muttering under her breath. "I found the old one, but it's expired. The new one has to be in here somewhere."

"Could it be in your purse?" Rafferty asked, trying to be helpful.

Their vehicles were blocking the back end of the parking lot and a few people had already thrown them irritated glances. If he wasn't holding the baby, he would have gone ahead and moved his truck.

"No, no, my husband always puts it in the glove . . ." She trailed off, her shoulders slumped, and all the fight seemed to go out of her. "I didn't pay the car insurance." She gulped visibly. "I forgot to mail it in. The stamped envelope is setting under a pile of correspondence on the table in the foyer."

"Look, it's okay. Don't worry. I'm insured."

"It's not okay. It's not okay. It's not." She pounded a fist against the dashboard and then burst into tears.

Women's tears did not scare Rafferty. Not when he'd grown up with a mother who was emotionally more child than adult, not when he'd practically raised his younger sister and brother all by himself.

"Hey," he soothed, the center of his chest pinching oddly. "It's just a crumpled fender. Nothing to cry over."

"It's not the damn fender." She glowered.

"I know. I know." He shifted the boy onto his other hip and reached for one of the fast food napkins that had fluttered to the seat.

Stop it. You know how you get. It's not your job to solve her problems.

His fingers accidentally brushed her arm.

She drew back, alarm running across her face. Belatedly, she must have realized what he was after, because she accepted the napkin he offered, pressed it to her eyes. "I'm sorry."

"You've been through a lot. Losing your husband—"

"It's more than that." She sobbed softly. "He can't hear, he can't hear."

Rafferty was confused. "Who?"

She waved at the baby.

"Your son?" he asked, just to clarify.

"He's going deaf."

Sympathy yanked at him. Because of his deaf ranch foreman, Guillermo Santo, who never allowed his lack of hearing to slow him down, Rafferty knew that from the boy's point of view, deafness wasn't the end of the world, but the news had to have been a sharp blow to the mother. He started to tell her about Guillermo, but stopped himself. He shouldn't get into her business.

"Ah, hell," he mumbled, not knowing what else to say.

"I just found out today and there's nothing the doctors can do to stop his hearing loss. He'll be completely deaf by the time he's five." She shredded the napkin with anxious fingers. "I haven't told anyone yet. I can't bear to tell anyone."

"I get that."

"I can't stand to listen to their questions, see the pity on their faces."

"'Course not. You need time to absorb it yourself." The toddler had fallen asleep in Rafferty's arms, curled up against his chest; the pressure of the little boy's head weighed heavily against his heart.

"He'll never be able to identify birds by their calls or hear a football coach holler out plays or listen to his wife tell him that she loves him." Her voice cracked again as a fresh round of tears sprang to her eyes. She swiped at her cheeks with both hands.

Jesus, just walk away, Jones.

But how could he do that? He had her boy in his arms. He reached out to her then, pulled her from the truck, and just held her there in the parking lot. The child in one arm, the distraught mother in the other.

Rafferty was instantly aware of everything about her—the softness of her skin, the sound of her ragged breathing, the pressure of her breasts poking against his ribs. Trapped. He felt trapped, and yet underneath it was another, completely opposite feeling.

Contentment.

On the street, a pickup truck with a throbbing bass passed by. A breeze gusted shaking autumn leaves from a nearby elm tree. Dark clouds bunched overhead. An elderly man and woman crossed the parking lot, arms linked, holding each other steady.

Rafferty shifted his gaze back to the woman in his embrace. Her crisp white blouse smelled of spray starch and the neckline dipped into a modest V revealing just the barest hint of cleavage. Sexy in an innocent way. Above her collar hung an opal stone suspended from her long, slender neck by a fine gold chain. Her skin was smooth and creamy pale. She was not a woman who wandered out into the sun much, and the contrast to his own tanned skin was stark.

"I'm sorry," she said. "This is stupid. I don't usually . . . This isn't . . . *me*."

"Shh. It's okay," he said. But it wasn't okay and they both knew it. With her son's diagnosis, her life had changed forever.

Shoppers skirted the fender bender, staring goggle-eyed, taking mental notes, drawing erroneous conclusions about them. Nosy Roseys. Ogling. The downside of small-town living.

The woman's hands curled into fierce fists. "I'm about to implode. I can't take any more. Not now. Not on top of everything else."

The October breeze ruffled her hair over his shoulder.

She smelled like cinnamon rolls—sweet and warm and yeasty. Spray starch and cinnamon rolls. A homey kind of scent he had not grown up with. She dropped her forehead against his neck. Through the open collar of his western shirt, he could feel her soft breath feather the hairs on his chest.

"I'm so furious at my husband for leaving when I needed him most."

"That's understandable." He rubbed her back, hurting for her in an alarmingly empathetic way.

She tilted her chin up. "Is it? Is it really? Or are you just trying to make me feel normal?"

"What's normal?"

"I have no idea." She laughed mirthlessly, but he felt her body relax. She pushed her fingers through her hair, ruffling the thick honeyed strands.

"Listen. Forget all about this fender bender," he said. "Your truck is fine and I have insurance to fix mine. No harm, no foul. You go on home, put your baby to bed, have a hot soak in the bathtub, eat something healthy, and then turn in early. You'll feel better after a good night's sleep."

His advice sounded lame. How could he offer advice to a woman who'd lost her husband prematurely and violently and then just found out her child was going deaf? He could tell her that the boy would easily adapt to what she saw as a handicap. Guillermo considered his deafness no different from eye color. Just part of who he was. She needed time to grieve and let go of the image of what she thought her son might be, but Rafferty wouldn't tell her this. Eventually, she'd come to understand it for herself.

"I can't let you do that." She stepped from the circle of his arms. "I'm so embarrassed I broke down like this in front of you."

"Think nothing of it. I'm a stranger in town. You'll

never see me again. You can pretend I was sent by your guardian angel to help you through a bad day."

"I like that idea. Thank you." She gave him a slight smile. She had gorgeous lips. Right out of a man's fantasy.

"Will you be okay to drive?"

"Yes." She nodded, reached for her son.

He passed the boy to her. "You'll get through this and one day you'll be happy again."

"Right now, that sounds like a pretty impossible promise."

"Just hang in there."

Platitudes.

He knew it as surely as she did, but now they were at the awkward stage. She'd shown him—a stranger—too much raw emotion. They'd touched in an intimate gesture saved for close family and friends. Plus she was probably feeling like she owed him gratitude she didn't want to owe. That would make anyone feel uncomfortable.

Get away from her as quickly as possible and leave her to her sorrow. She wasn't his responsibility. But Rafferty had a hard time walking away from anyone in need. Like it or not, it was just the way he was wired.

You can't save the whole world.

"Thanks," she said. "For being so understanding. Usually, I'm not this high-strung."

He got a glimpse of the steel magnolia in her as she straightened her shoulders and raised her chin. "I believe you."

Rafferty waited while she secured the boy into his car seat once more and settled herself behind the wheel. Hang those people tooting their horns at him to move his vehicle. Slowly, he sauntered back to his truck. He climbed in, started the engine and with a sharp screech of metal, backed up, separating his truck from hers.

She slid on sunglasses, hiding her weary eyes, and waved at him as she left the parking lot.

That was it. She was gone. Out of his life.

He should feel happy right? Instead of disquieted. Shrugging off the feeling, he took the parking spot she'd vacated and tried not to think about her, but his shirt was still damp from her tears and his collar smelled of her.

Pleasing. Sweet. Special.

The crowded store was packed with moms who'd just picked their kids up from school and were swinging by for groceries on their way home. Seeing those kids with their mothers made him think of Amelia and how he'd never had a normal childhood.

When he was small, before the other kids came along, Amelia called him her snoopy little bodyguard because he quizzed the men she dragged home. He wanted to know who they were, what they did for a living, and why they were with his mother.

Amelia would laugh, make excuses for him to the men, then give him two dollars and tell him to go down to the corner store to buy a Nutty Buddy for them both. He'd protest because they hadn't yet had dinner and Amelia would say in a high voice that tinkled like glass tapped with a spoon, "You can't count on anything in life, Rafferty, so eat dessert first."

By the time he got back from the store, Amelia and the man of the day would be in her bedroom making thumping noises. He'd sit in a chair in the hallway licking his Nutty Buddy while hers melted. Eventually, the bedroom door would open, the man would leave, and Amelia would stagger out rumpled and smelling funny. She'd pick the melted chocolate and nuts off the puddle of ice cream and then lick her fingers. She'd wander into the kitchen, pour a glass of red wine, then collapse on the couch in her filmy pink housecoat, stare out the window, smoking Virginia Slims and reciting melancholy lines from her favorite movie, *Doctor Zhivago.*

To this day, Rafferty hated both Omar Sharif and Nutty Buddies. But Amelia was better now. Finally, one of the numerous rehabs he'd gotten her into had worked. She was taking her medication, staying sober, and doing well.

Family.

What could you do? They not only affected who you became, but the choices you made. Like it or not, you couldn't escape your DNA. Family marked you with indelible graffiti and weighted you with the freight of permanent memories. Good, bad, indifferent, and everything in between. Blood branded you. Claimed you. Broke you down to the most basic level.

Which brought him back full circle to the reason he was here in Jubilee. Family pulling at him from both ends. He thought of the brown-sugar haired woman in the Ford pickup truck and hoped she had family to help her. She was going to need it.

Thank God, he hadn't gotten her name and phone number. Otherwise, he might have been tempted to call and check on her.

Rafferty fisted his hands. People often didn't want his help. He had a hard time wrapping his head around that one. He'd been accused of thinking he had the answers to everyone else's problems, but when you saw someone heading blindly off a cliff, didn't you have some kind of responsibility to stop them from taking the plunge? Did that make him a know-it-all?

He tucked the questions to the back of his mind, bought tuna and crackers and V–8 juice, and took it back to his truck. He sat there in the parking lot eating and practicing what he was going to say to the person he'd come to Jubilee to see.

Excuse me. You don't know me but . . . No, that sounded

lame. Hell, he'd had fourteen hundred miles to come up with a good intro and he still couldn't think of the right way to break the news.

He finished his meal, dusted off his hands, and consulted the map to his destination. He'd studied it a dozen times during the drive to Texas, but now that he was so close, he got a sick sensation in the pit of his stomach.

Just get it over with.

Mentally, he shook himself, started the pickup, and headed for the X spot on the map a mile away. He flipped on the radio. Barenaked Ladies were singing, "If I Had a Million Dollars." Lighthearted. He could use a dose of that in spite of his situation.

The closer he got, the tighter anxiety's grip on his spinal column grew. His sense of honor prevented him from simply mailing what he needed to deliver, along with a letter of explanation. It's what most people would have done, but he couldn't do that. He'd made a promise. This deserved a face-to-face meeting. Even if it made his palms sweat.

He entered a tree-lined neighborhood filled with old homes built around the turn of the twentieth century. Lots of flowers and big sturdy oaks. White picket fences and window flower boxes. Two-acre lots. Roomy, welcoming, the whole damn works. Totally opposite of his arid horse ranch outside Los Angeles.

How different would his life have been if he'd grown up here? How different would he have been?

Useless. Such thoughts. He'd grown up on the streets of old Hollywood in a variety of squalid apartments. Amelia, who'd once been an extra in a couple of B movies, was convinced she'd make it as a star as long as she didn't let her kids get in the way of her ambitions. But booze, men, and drugs? Oh yeah, those came before anything—children, career, her health.

Self-medicating. She'd been self-medicating. Trying to ease the pain of her bipolar condition. He understood it now, but back then? He'd been one resentful kid.

He glanced at the map. The house he was looking for turned out to be a three-story Queen Anne Victorian with a gated archway on a corner lot. Rosebushes, devoid of flowers this late in the season, grew in wild profusion along the fence line.

Rafferty cut the engine and sat staring at the front of the house. An American flag fluttered from a holder that was positioned underneath the eaves. A toddler's Big Wheel in camouflage colors was parked to one side of the uneven cement driveway that meandered away from his view to the back of the house. A sack of horse oats lay propped up against the side of the house.

An odd swell of panic struck him and he blew out his breath. He felt as if he'd stumbled across a Norman Rockwell family blindsided by war. *Dammit, Jake, why did you have to go and get your stupid self killed and leave me behind to pick up the pieces? Messy shit, this.*

Story of Rafferty's life. Cleaning up after everyone else. He hadn't even had time to grieve the brother he barely knew and now here he was about to face the Widow Moncrief.

What was he supposed to say? Sorry your husband left his money to me instead of you? It didn't matter. He was giving it back. He couldn't keep the money, no matter how much he could use it. Rafferty had never in his life taken something that didn't belong to him and he wasn't going to start now.

What would Jake's wife say to him? How would she react? Would she tell him stories about his brother? Would they become friends?

In your dreams, bastard boy. You don't belong here in Norman Rockwellville. Fractured or not.

Family loyalty. Why did it mean so much to him? Especially when it didn't seem to mean anything to anyone else. Maybe that was it. Maybe that's why family loyalty meant so much. He'd never really had it. He was searching for the glue that would finally make him stick.

Don't believe for one second that you'll find it here.

The next few minutes were not going to be easy. Nothing to do but get through it.

Suppressing a sigh, Rafferty climbed from the truck and started up the steps, knowing in his heart that no matter what he did, there could be no mending the past.

He paced the porch, gathering his courage. *C'mon. Just do it.* Finally, he raised his hand, rapped on the door.

A long moment passed. The wait was killing him.

He knocked again.

From behind the door, he heard movement. He braced himself, but even so, he was not prepared for what he saw when the door opened.

Because he found himself staring into the pretty green eyes of the woman from Searcy's parking lot.

Chapter Three

A panicky sensation twined around Lissette.

The cowboy she'd smashed into must have changed his mind about letting her off the hook over the fender bender because here he was on her front porch. Maybe he'd called his insurance company and they told him to hunt her down and hold her accountable. Beware of handsome cowboys making promises. She'd known his behavior had been too good to be true, but she couldn't blame him. She'd been in the wrong. Nothing to do but offer to make installment payments for the damage to his truck. Another pothole slowing her down on her journey of building her business to provide for her son.

Behind him, the clouds gathered darkly, smelling of rain. Thunder grumbled. A whisk of wind shook red leaves from the oaks in the front yard, sent them scraping across the porch. A cool draft rushed past her.

The cowboy was still dressed in those snug-fitting Levi's and scuffed cowboy boots and Stetson. His body was hard and lean. He worked outdoors, a real live cowboy, even though his license plates had identified him as being from California.

He was taller than she remembered. Not as tall as Jake,

but close. Shadows fell across his face, making his beard-stubbled jaw look as if it had been chiseled from stone. His cheekbones were high, sharp, and in this light, foreboding. A shiver passed through her, stirring the prickly awareness lighting up her nerve endings.

A cowboy. Not another cowboy. Why did he have to be a cowboy?

You live in cowboy country. What do you expect?

Involuntarily, she took a step backward, then immediately regretted it. She didn't want him to think that he held the upper hand, even if he did.

His dark chocolate eyes narrowed. "You," he said, sounding surprised. "It's you."

"Me," she confirmed, mildly amused. If he hadn't expected to find her here, then he hadn't come looking to make her pay for his dented pickup, but if he wasn't here about the fender bender, why was he on her front porch?

Silence stretched out long as a lonesome highway.

Their eyes hitched up like a truck to a trailer and they studied each other warily.

Lately, life had come at her in a hazy blur of pain. As a defense mechanism, she numbed herself against sensation, but right here, right now, everything dropped into distinct, pinpoint-focus. She could finally *see* again. What had before seemed unfathomable was now fraught with clarity and before he said another word, she suddenly knew exactly who he was.

Finally, he glanced at a note clipped to the papers in his hand that were an identical copy of the government papers she had tucked into a drawer. "*You're* Lissette Moncrief?"

An icy blade that had nothing to do with impending rain, knifed her. The haunted expression on his face, the throbbing at the hollow of her neck, her husband's insurance papers crumpled in his broad masculine fingers, the hairs rising on her forearm all fused into this crystal-clear moment.

She brought a hand to her chest. Words jammed up. She opened her mouth. Closed it. Finally stuttered, "Y-yes."

In excruciating slow motion, he swept off his cowboy hat, held it over his heart like he was about to recite the Pledge of Allegiance. His thick, whiskey-colored hair, creased from the mold of his Stetson, curled up along his scalp. He swallowed hard, his Adam's apple pumping up, and then slowly drifting down. "My name is Rafferty Jones."

Yes. Here he was at last. Jake's illegitimate half brother showing up three months too late.

Her hand grasped the side of the door and it was all she could do to keep from slamming it in his face. How screwed up was it that fate had sent her plowing into him in Searcy's parking lot? The clarity cracked into a mosaic of confusion. Nothing in the world made sense.

Ice slicked her from the inside out. A hundred unexpressed emotions locked up her throat, clicking closed a hundred tiny padlocks. She couldn't speak. This was the same man who'd stolen her money.

It wasn't your money and he didn't steal it. It was Jake's life insurance and death gratuity to do with what he wished and apparently he wanted his brother to have it over you and Kyle. Honor that. Accept it. Move on. You don't need Jake's money. You can take care of yourself.

"May I come in?" he asked, his eyes somber. "I came to pay my condolences."

"A bit late, don't you think?" Okay, that was bitchy. She didn't know anything about his circumstances or what was in his heart.

His eyes never strayed from her face. She couldn't remember the last time anyone had studied her so intently.

These days most people—at a loss for the right words or afraid that widowhood might be contagious—avoided catching her eye. It would only get worse once Kyle's condition became general knowledge.

It was refreshing, his unrelenting stare. She held his gaze. Didn't waver.

"I'm sorry I couldn't have come sooner," he said. "I've been in Australia for three months on business, and it wasn't until I got home last week that I found . . ." He tightened his grip on the papers. "This."

"You didn't know Jake was dead?"

He shook his head. "Not until I opened this letter from the army upon my return home. Who around here would tell me?"

Lissette fingered her bottom lip. "The army didn't call? E-mail?"

"No."

"Why not?"

His shoulders lifted. "I dunno. Must have slipped between the cracks. Government bureaucracy at its finest. My phone number is unlisted and I'd gotten a new e-mail address. Whatever the snafu, they simply sent this letter, a copy of Jake's papers, and the check."

A doleful expression flickered across Rafferty's face so briefly she wondered if she'd imagined it.

It occurred to her then that his loss was fresher than hers. She had already come to terms with Jake's demise. Honestly, she'd been alone so much of their marriage that she scarcely missed him during the course of her day-to-day life. While she had mourned her husband and the tragedy of his passing, their marriage had been crippled for a long time, and it was only with his death that she'd begun to realize the extent of it.

But Rafferty was still adjusting to the news. Then again, how well had he even known Jake? Her husband had never mentioned his half brother to her. Claudia claimed never to have heard of him. If the brothers had any kind of a real bond, why hadn't Jake ever told her about Rafferty?

"I'm sorry," she said sincerely. "That's a terrible way to find out."

Neither Rafferty nor Lissette spoke. They stood breathing in the heaviness of the moment, more cloying than New Orleans humidity in August.

What to do? She could rise to the occasion, invite him in, and discover what he wanted, or she could give him some excuse and send him on his way. She twisted the doorknob in her hand. The urge to swing it closed was strong, but she could see the pain on his face, even as he struggled to hide it.

"Come in," she said finally, stepping aside and wondering all the while what she was letting herself in for.

The stranger conscientiously grated his boots against the scraper before stepping inside.

"Please, come into the kitchen. Bad news goes down better with coffee and crumb cake," Lissette called over her shoulder as she led the way.

Stetson still clutched in his hand, he followed her. "Where's your boy?"

"I put him down for a nap."

Rafferty moved with the lanky, loose-limbed gait of a natural cowboy, as if he was more comfortable on horseback than on foot. His dark eyes scanned the room, the tight, masculine lines of his mouth at once both comforting and unnerving. A mouth that seemed to say, *I'm a man you can count on. Trust me.*

Lissette blinked, seeing the room through a stranger's eyes. The kitchen housed commercial-grade appliances, two large convection ovens, a state-of-the-art refrigerator, and dishwasher. Stainless steel glistened and everything smelled of organic cleaning products. Three wooden bar stools were tucked up to the backside of the marble-slab cooking island.

Her parents had paid for her kitchen renovations as a lavish Christmas present the previous year when Texas laws had changed to allow cottage-industry bakers to operate from their homes as long as certain conditions were met. Before the law passed, Lissette had been forced to lease space from a commercial bakery in the nearby town of Twilight, to make the wedding cakes she sold through Mariah's wedding planning business. The renovations were another reason she was reluctant to ask her parents for money. They were still paying off the loan for the project.

"Have a seat," she invited.

Rafferty pulled out a bar stool. The wooden legs scraped against the terrazzo floor. He settled his cowboy hat on the seat of a second stool.

Lissette turned to grind coffee beans. Soon the rich smell of freshly crushed French roast filled the room and the only sound between them was the gurgle of the coffeemaker.

Rafferty perched awkwardly on the stool, as if he were just waiting for an excuse to fly away. He tilted his head, studied her hands.

Feeling self-conscious, she tucked her arms behind her back. "So," she began, searching for something to say. "You're Jake's half brother. I never knew about you."

He nodded as if that did not surprise him. Strong, silent type. The cowboy type. Someone she should stay away from.

"But you knew about me?" she asked.

"Not much," he admitted. "Just your name. Jake sent me your wedding announcement."

"But not an invitation?"

"No."

"Don't you find that strange?"

"No."

"Why not?"

He shrugged. "I'm the skeleton in the closet."

"You're younger than Jake."

"By four years."

"That makes you twenty-nine."

Another nod.

"Me too," she said for no reason. "I'll be thirty in January."

"You look much younger." He spread his palms out on the island, the backs of his tanned hands startling against the white marble. His nails were clean and clipped short but his knuckles were crisscrossed with small nicks and scars.

Her face heated at his straightforward comment. "It's not just Jake. No one around here has ever talked about you. That fact in and of itself is quite odd in a small town where even the brand of laundry soap that people use is up for public discussion."

Slowly, he drummed his fingers against the marble, producing the simple duple meter of a funeral march. The beat sent a shiver over her. He shrugged again, circumspect. Nothing at all like Jake.

She felt like a cotton shirt twisted dry by the old-fashioned wringer that decorated her mother-in-law's screened sun porch in retro country chic. Knotted up. Tense. "When did you learn who your real father was?"

"I always knew. My mother didn't hide the fact that my father was married with a family in Texas and he wanted nothing to do with us." He kept up the drumming. "Who knows? Maybe that's why I became a cowboy. To impress him."

Lissette tried to imagine what that was like. Knowing

that your father wanted nothing to do with you. A rush of sympathy washed over her for the little kid that he'd been, growing up without a dad. It killed her soul to realize that her son would never know his father either. It wasn't fair. For Rafferty or Kyle.

"Did you ever meet your father?" she asked.

Rafferty shook his head.

"I never met him either." She moved to pour up the coffee in matching blue earthenware mugs. "Gordon died before Jake and I met. Everyone says he was a die-hard cutting horse cowboy. Real alpha male."

"So my mother tells me. I guess that's why she fell for him."

"And the wedding ring on his finger didn't stop her?" She slid a mug in front of Rafferty, stepped back to lean against the kitchen counter, putting distance between them. "Sugar? Cream?"

He placed a hand over his cup, indicating black coffee was fine with him. Lissette stirred two spoonfuls of sugar into her mug.

"My mother is what she is," he said evenly, no judgment in his voice.

"Why didn't she demand Gordon provide for you? She could have forced him to pay child support."

"I don't know."

Perplexed by his calmness, Lissette pushed a strand of hair from her eyes. "Didn't she ever think about what she was doing to you?"

"Good coffee," Rafferty mused, and took a long sip.

To hell with the coffee. She settled her hands on her hips, unexpected fury digging into her. "I don't understand why your mother would do that to you."

He shifted, said nothing for so long that she thought that he wasn't going to answer. It had been rude of her to ask. It was none of her business. She stared out the window, saw a sparrow perch on the rooster weathervane Jake had installed, and wished she could take the question back, because she understood all at once that her anger had nothing to do with Rafferty or his mother.

Finally, he said, "I love my mother, but she's bipolar. She's much better now, with the right medication, but when I was a kid . . ." He let his words trail off. His eyes stayed impassive, unreadable, giving no clue as to how he felt.

"I . . ." She swallowed, traced an index finger over the countertop. "I'm not going to say I'm sorry for what you've gone through because I know how wearing other people's pity can be. But you've done well for yourself in spite of your childhood."

"I've done well *because* of it," he corrected. "If my mother had been strong, I wouldn't have had to be. She made me who I am."

How could he not be filled with rage and pain? How did a person get to such lofty acceptance? She bit down on her thumbnail. Why couldn't peace come in a powder that you could stir in your coffee like sugar and drink it up?

"So how and when did you first make contact with Jake?"

His unflinching gaze met hers. That head-on look told her that this man did not shy away from trouble, but neither did he go searching for it as Jake had. "Jake came to California looking for me after Gordon died. It was the summer he turned twenty."

"That would have made you sixteen."

"Yep. To me, Jake was superhero. Larger than life. Over the top. He did everything in a big way."

"That's Jake," she said. Stopped. Corrected. "Was."

She saw it, the first glimpse of raw emotion on his face. Loss. Regret. But then it disappeared like smoke up a chimney. "What was that like? Meeting your half brother for the first time?"

"I was excited," he said. "It felt good to have someone looking out after me for a change."

"How long did he visit you?"

"The entire summer."

"Your mother didn't mind that he stayed so long?"

"He paid room and board. She liked that. Jake kept trying to talk my mother into moving. The neighborhood was so rough that gunfire woke us up more nights than not. Finally, before Jake left, he rented an affordable apartment in a safer part of town and moved us all in. He paid up the rent for two months, but of course, after that, Amelia couldn't make the payments and we ended up back where we'd started."

Lissette didn't know what to say, so she just opened the lid of the cake plate, cut off two slices of crumb cake. "What were you doing in Australia?"

"Making a film."

"You're an actor?" That surprised her. It wasn't that he wasn't good-looking enough to be an actor, because he certainly was. He just seemed too down-to-earth for such a quixotic career. Then again, what did she know of him?

"I train horses for the movies. I have to be on set every day."

"Is there a lot of money in that?"

"I wouldn't say a lot, but I do all right. I work on three or four movies a year. It covers the bills."

A low rumble of thunder crackled overhead. She glanced out the window again. A black cat ran across the backyard in a fine-mist drizzle. Another long silence stretched between them. They looked everywhere but at each other. The red light on the coffeemaker glowed. The kitchen clock ticked loudly. The crumb cake dissolved into sweet moistness on her tongue, but she barely tasted it.

"Jake called me from Kandahar," Rafferty murmured.

"What?" she asked, not certain that she'd heard him correctly. "When?"

"It was just days before he was killed. He hadn't called me in five years."

Distressed, Lissette inhaled audibly. Jake had called Rafferty from Afghanistan, but he had not called her? She hadn't even gotten more than a couple of e-mails from him during the three weeks after his arrival in Kandahar for his tour of duty until the time the death notification officers had shown up on the Fourth of July to break the tragic news.

At the time, she'd thought Jake's silence was nothing more than a symptom of their deteriorating marriage. Now, with what Rafferty was telling her, she couldn't help wondering what else had been going on in Jake's head.

"What . . ." She moistened her lips, braced herself. "What did he say?"

Rafferty winced, but he didn't mince words. "Jake must have seen something pretty damn bad. He wouldn't talk about what had happened. Just that—"

"What?" Her throat convulsed.

His gaze seared hers. "Are you sure you want to know?"

She lifted her chin. Did she? Her stomach quaked. Her hand was glued to the cake plate. She braced herself. "Yes."

Rafferty pressed a palm to the nape of his neck. "He said that he shouldn't have come back to Afghanistan, but that when he was home in Jubilee, he tried so hard to be what you wanted him to be, but he simply couldn't do it."

"Wh . . ." Air got trapped in her lungs. "What does that mean?"

"After being in the Middle East he couldn't live a regular life. Being a husband, a father, and the thought of going to work at a normal job. It was—these were his words—too stupefying."

Her cheeks burned as if he'd slapped her with two open palms. Her mouth worked but no words came out. She'd suspected as much. When Jake was home he seemed so distant. And yet, when he talked about Afghanistan, his eyes would light up and his muscles would tense and he'd grow restless with excitement. As if he was addicted to war. When she'd seen the movie *The Hurt Locker*, she remembered thinking, *That's Jake. To a T.*

She shifted her gaze to an aloe vera cactus in the windowsill. It needed watering. Grateful for something to do, she moved to fill a cup with water. Why had she prodded Rafferty to talk about his conversation with Jake? Really, what did it matter at this late date?

"Jake said he didn't fit in here anymore," Rafferty went on. "And that he only felt real when he had a gun in his hands. He said war was a bigger high than bull riding."

An involuntary squeak escaped her. She dropped the cup she'd used to water the plant into the sink and plastered hands over her mouth. *Please, please, stop talking.*

Rafferty's voice gentled. "He hated that he would rather be at war than with you and your son. He was very conflicted about it."

His words were a visceral punch to her organs because a part of her knew it was true. In spite of his cowboy roots and his first career as a bull rider, Jake had been a natural-born soldier. A warrior. Once he'd found his element, he couldn't be happy anywhere else.

Jake's rugged rawness was what attracted her to him. He'd been different from anything she knew. But when he was home from battle, well, he'd done dumb, dangerous things. Chicken drag racing. Drinking too much. Getting into fights. Other things she didn't know about for sure, but suspected. Pushing the envelope. Living on the edge.

Finding any way that he could to work up a head of adrenaline. The down side of a brave man.

Recklessness.

Rafferty's gaze followed her as she moved about the kitchen, dishrag in her hand, wiping down counters that didn't need cleaning.

What did he think of her? Did he believe that she wasn't interesting enough to keep her husband home? Dull Lissy? She wondered it herself.

"I tried to talk to him about what he was going through, but Jake said there was no way I could understand." Rafferty paused, blew out his breath. "He was right."

Lissette briefly closed her eyes, battled back the self-pity that threatened to overtake her. "Why . . . why didn't he tell *me* any of this?"

"He didn't want to hurt you," Rafferty said kindly. "He loved you, but he had demons that he couldn't shake."

"Did he . . ." She cleared her throat. "Do drugs?"

Rafferty made a face. "It wouldn't surprise me."

A shiver ran through her. Lissette hugged herself, dropped her gaze to the floor. She wished Rafferty would go. She couldn't deal with this. With him. Not now. Not on top of the awful news she'd gotten about Kyle.

"I've scared you." Rafferty's voice softened. "I didn't mean to scare you."

"I'm not scared," she lied, and raised her chin. "I know that war damaged Jake in an irreparable way."

"I'm still trying to wrap my head around the fact he's gone," Rafferty murmured.

"Poor you." Why was she being so horrible? Was it because she was hurt and scared? She caught herself. Apologized. "I'm sorry, that was uncalled for."

"Completely understandable under the circumstances."

"I don't need for you to cut me slack. Be an ass. I can take it on the chin."

"Why would I do that to you?"

Jake would have. He believed in the cruel-to-be-kind approach to helping someone get over something. He had a forceful, oversized personality. Whenever he'd walked into a room all the attention immediately shifted to him.

But this man wasn't Jake.

There wasn't much resemblance between her husband and his half brother. The strong chin was the same, inherited from their father. Jake had his mother's dark brown hair, but Rafferty's hair was lighter. Whiskey-colored. Jake had been taller, broader. Rafferty was leaner, wirier, just a hair under six foot.

Rafferty reached into his shirt pocket and took out a folded piece of paper. "I brought this to you."

"What is it?"

"Jake's life insurance and death gratuity check." He pushed it across the marble slab counter toward her.

With her index finger, she pushed it back at him. "It's yours. Fair and square. You owe me nothing."

"It's not right. You were his wife. He's got a child he should have provided for." Rafferty thumped the check her way. "Take it."

"He wanted you to have it for some reason. It's not my place to question Jake's motives." She swirled the damn check in his direction. "He called you, not me."

"Maybe he just forgot to change his beneficiary and it's nothing but a clerical oversight."

"I don't think so." Lissette folded her arms, shook her head. "Jake was very deliberate about stuff like that."

"Don't be stubborn, woman. You need this money more than I do. I don't have a deaf child to educate."

Lissette pressed her lips into a hard line, struggled hard not to cry. She was not going to cry in front of him again. She was tired of crying. What good did it do? "Don't you dare feel sorry for me you . . . you . . . California cowboy."

"Is that supposed to be an insult?" He lowered his eyelids, flicked her a hard stare. There was something sultry in his eyes. The way he looked at her. Like a slow simmer rolling into a boil.

The look shot straight through her. She shivered again. Tightened her arms around herself. "If I intended on insulting you, I would have called your paternity into question."

"Ah." He smiled lightly, but his tone was barbed. "There it is." He was staring at her so hard, she could scarcely breathe from the pressure of it. "I'm a bastard. Go ahead. Let's get this out in the open. Your father-in-law screwed my mother and, ta-da, here I am." He spread his arms wide.

Her emotions churned, raw and achy. They were taking the circumstances out on each other when neither of them was to blame for what other people had done. They were caught in the middle.

She softened, relented. "You've been carrying that around a long time, haven't you?"

"Hey, now I'm the one who doesn't need *your* pity."

She exhaled. "Why are we getting angry with each other? This was none of our doing. Not the cheating, not the leaving of great sums of money, not the dying in a war."

"But we are the ones left to pick up the pieces."

She folded the check and stepped around the island. The closer she came to him, the shallower his breathing grew. Her breathing was none too confident either.

Lissette leaned over.

Felt Rafferty flinch.

His masculine scent got tangled up in her nose. He smelled of horses and cotton and leather. She gulped. What was she doing so near him?

She dropped the folded check into the front pocket of his shirt. In the process her hip bumped lightly against his side. It was all she could do not to leap back at the accidental contact. She pretended it hadn't happened.

The muscle in his jaw jumped. He was doing some pretending of his own. He clenched his hands into fists on the tops of his thighs.

"Take the money." She patted the check through his shirt pocket. She could feel the hard muscles of his chest.

He went stock-still.

Her pulse skittered.

"I can't just go back to California and leave you here by yourself. Not with your son the way he is. You'll need support."

"I'm not alone." She tossed her head. Pride wouldn't let her admit how scared and lonely she felt. "I have friends, my parents are in Dallas and Jake's mother is nearby."

"Claudia," he said roughly.

That surprised her. "You know Claudia?"

"I know her name. My mother took it in vain a time or two."

Lissette smiled. "Probably not as much as Claudia cursed your mother. Claudia looks prim and proper, but when she's angry that woman can cuss a blue streak. Although she never once spoke your name. Not even when we found out about Jake's bequest."

"What did she say when she found out?"

"She refused to talk about it."

"You didn't ask her about me?"

"It was easier to let it go than to pin her down. I didn't want to get cursed at." Not that her mother-in-law had been anything but warm and welcoming to her, but Claudia was the kind who preferred to sweep problems under the rug and pretend they didn't exist. Lissette understood the impulse. She didn't like conflict either.

Their eyes met and they both laughed. It was an uneasy, weird laugh, but it broke the tension.

"I wouldn't feel right, keeping this money," Rafferty said. "Not when your son is going to have medical bills."

"It's my problem, not yours. I want to handle things on my own. Prove that I don't need some man to take care of me."

"Take the money," he commanded.

She folded her arms under her breasts. "Jake left it to you."

"And I want you to have it."

"Well, I don't want it." She folded her arms over her chest. "Now if you'll excuse me, it's been a long day and I have some calls to make."

He didn't move, and for a long moment, she thought he wasn't going to leave.

She held her breath, uncertain of what to do next.

Finally, he got to his feet and settled his cowboy hat on his head. "I'm goin' for now," he said. "You need time alone and I respect that. But this discussion isn't over. Not by a long shot."

Chapter Four

Was she being stubborn about accepting the money?

Lissette closed the front door behind Rafferty and went to check on Kyle.

Heaven knew she needed the money, but something in her bristled at taking the check from him. Maybe it was petty anger with Jake for shutting her out. Maybe it was because she did not want to be beholden to Rafferty in any way. But mostly, Lissette wanted to cultivate her independence.

She would soon be thirty and she'd never done anything solely on her own. She'd gone from her family's home in Dallas to college at Southern Methodist University studying to become an art teacher. During her junior year, when she was twenty-one, she'd found her true calling when, just for fun, she took a cake decorating class offered by a local craft store. After that, she was hooked.

She'd persuaded her parents to let her drop out of SMU and they'd funded pastry school at Le Cordon Bleu College of Culinary Arts in Dallas. She'd graduated two years later with an associate's degree in pastry and baking arts. At the age of twenty-three, she'd gone to work for the Dallas Hyatt Regency that her father managed. He often joked he was indulging Lissy's foray into food fantasy. Her parents had always assumed she was merely playing at being a pastry chef and that she'd quit once she found a husband. After all, as they'd told her, she was their sweet, passive child who never rocked the boat. She wasn't cut out for a high-pressure career.

Two years later, she met Jake at a party she'd been catering through the Hyatt. He'd been the guest of honor, a sendoff by buddies because he'd just joined the army after his retirement from bull riding. A friend of his had been killed in the Middle East and he felt a strong sense of duty. She still recalled his reasoning for joining the service in his late twenties. It should have been an omen of things to come.

"I want to fight. Really get my hands dirty," he'd said. "Be part of the action. I've already wasted too much time fooling around with bull riding. It's time for me to cowboy up and do the right thing."

In her naïveté, she'd admired his willingness to do a job that other men shied away from. What she'd seen as honorable self-confidence had turned out to be self-destructive arrogance. He liked playing protector because he enjoyed control. Not a bad quality in a soldier, but that trait had a darker side.

He'd written to her during his training at Fort Leonard Wood in Waynesville, Missouri, and when he returned, he'd proposed. Giddy at having snagged herself a handsome cowboy, she'd accepted. He'd been assigned to Fort Hood in Killeen and whenever he got leave, he would drive up to see her. He was exciting and cowboy-staunch. He made her feel special. She wasn't around him enough to see the chinks in his armor until it was too late. They married after having known each other less than three months.

Their wedding took place at the Hyatt Regency where they'd met. Not long after that he was sent to the Middle

East. Lissette had been willing to stay in Killeen while he was gone, but Jake had said, "You're too special for that. We'll buy a house in my hometown. Jubilee's halfway between Killeen and Dallas, and my mother will be there to help you get settled in."

On one level, she'd liked living in Jubilee. It was an interesting town. She got along well with her mother-in-law and she quickly made friends, but because she had not lived on base, she missed out on the military culture. She'd never become part of the close-knit group of army wives.

Now, she wondered if there had been another reason Jake hadn't wanted her to stay in military housing. Had he believed she was too fragile for it? That she couldn't handle the pressure? But she knew she was stronger than most people believed her to be.

Kyle was lying on his back, his eyes closed. He looked so peaceful. Her heart tugged. Was she being stupid by turning down the money? Yes, it might be nice to make it on her own, but Kyle's well-being was more important than her pride. She should be grateful that Rafferty was an ethical person.

God, she hated feeling like this. Vulnerable. Wounded. She knotted her fists, channeling the helplessness to anger. Determined to fight back. She might be down, but she damn well wasn't out.

A photograph of Jake sat on the dresser. She crossed the room to pick it up. She'd taken it not long before Jake's last deployment. It had been in the late spring, the mimosa trees blooming in an ecstasy of sweet pink. In the picture, her husband was pushing Kyle on a park swing. Her son's head was thrown back and he was laughing gleefully. Happy. Kyle had been happy.

Too bad that she and Jake had not. She'd stayed in the crumbling marriage for the sake of her son.

Lissette pulled her bottom lip up between her teeth and traced an index finger over Jake's face. The expression was one she'd seen many times. A smile tinged his lips, but there was no joy in it. Smiling simply because he thought it was expected of him—a man playing the role of father, but not really feeling it.

Until now, she'd accepted the false smile. Pretended she hadn't seen the emptiness in his eyes. But she could no longer deny it. Jake had been haunted. He'd never been the same after going over there. And then to get himself killed while willingly disobeying orders. Saving those orphans had been heroic and she would never take that last unselfish act from his memory, but she had to wonder about his deeper motivation. Had he subconsciously harbored a death wish?

What had he seen? What had he done? How much darkness had he hidden from her?

She'd asked these questions of herself before, but she'd been too scared to ask the questions of him. In all honesty, she hadn't wanted to hear the answers.

No rocking Lissy's safe little world.

Well, Jake had rocked it to the core and the aftershocks were still coming.

And now there was Kyle's diagnosis. This was one truth she would not, could not run from.

She might not be able to change circumstances and she couldn't undo the past, but there was one thing she could do. Make the best possible future available to her son.

And in order to do that, she needed money. No more wasting time. She had to start putting her plans in action as soon as possible.

"Well, Jake, what now?" Rafferty sat in his pickup truck parked outside Lissette's house. Rain came down slow and steady, dotting his windshield with precipitation and misting the air gray, causing the streetlamps to flicker on prematurely.

When Jake had called him back in June, just before Rafferty left for Australia, he'd said some disturbing things. Some of which Rafferty had told Lissette. He regretted being so frank with her. She had suffered enough. But he felt she'd deserved the truth.

The one thing he had not told her was that Jake had made him pledge that if he didn't come back from Afghanistan, Rafferty would make sure that his wife and son were taken care of.

Of course he'd agreed. Jake had saved him once and he'd do anything for his older brother. When he found out about Jake's bequest, he thought maybe that's what he meant. Give Lissette the money. But why not just make her his beneficiary in the first place? Why use him as the middleman? Then the truth of it hit him all at once.

It's not about the money. He wanted you in Jubilee to pick up the pieces of the mess he left behind.

Honestly, Rafferty had not expected Lissette to reject the money. She needed it. She had a child to raise. A child who would need specialized schooling.

Lissette was both proud and stubborn. She didn't want pity or sympathy. She just wanted to make her own way in the world. He understood that impulse. He had some pride issues himself.

And he liked seeing her fight back. When he was a kid, he would have given anything if Amelia had been strong enough to stand on her own two feet. She'd had no one to depend on, and as a result, she'd leaned on him hard. From the time he was very young, four or five, it had been like he was the parent and she was the child. He put her to bed when she got drunk. He locked up the apartment at night. He brought her aspirin for her hangover.

Rafferty chuffed out a heavy breath. He probably

should have just left the check on the counter and driven away. Reality would have brought her to her senses eventually and she would have put it in the bank.

But there was that promise he'd made Jake. To look after Lissette and Kyle, and right now, she needed a whole lot more than money. She needed an attentive ear to listen and a shoulder to cry on and someone to help her with the boy until she had time to absorb what was happening to her.

He should be that someone.

Only one problem. A surprising problem he would never have anticipated in a hundred years.

He was attracted to her.

In a way he hadn't been attracted to a woman in a very long time, and that was wrong on so many levels. She was vulnerable and hurting and his half brother's widow.

The rain drummed down while he dithered. He needed to find a motel, make some plans, and figure out how to convince her to let him help without robbing her of her pride, dignity, and independence.

He was just about to start the engine and drive away when he saw her come out of the side door. Her head was ducked under a big black umbrella. She had on wader boots, and Kyle was on her hip. She rushed toward the detached garage that was just behind and to the left of the house.

She disappeared from his view for a few minutes. Curiosity kept him where he was. She reappeared without Kyle and the umbrella, hurrying toward the sack of oats slumped against the side of the house. It was a fifty-pound bag, and while it had been sitting under the eaves, it was damp.

She bent, tried to hoist the oats onto her slender shoulder. Unceremoniously, the sack ripped open, spilling oats all over her and the ground. She let out a curse and looked ready to have a meltdown.

Rafferty was out of his pickup, crossing the yard in five quick strides. "It's okay," he called. "Don't cry over spilled oats."

She tossed her arms in the air. "What am I going to do? Just what the hell am I going to do, Rafferty? Jake's horse needs tending and that was the last bag of feed. I've got to drag my son out in the rain and I'm covered with oats and . . . and . . ."

He saw the struggle on her face. She was trying hard not to cry. "It's gonna be fine, Lissette. I'm here. We'll go to the feed store. Get more oats. Feed the horse. All you have to do is let me help you."

"I hate this," she said vehemently. "I hate not being strong enough or tough enough to take care of things on my own."

"Everyone needs a helping hand now and again," he said smoothly.

"Even you?"

"Even me. Now come on. Let's get the hell out of the rain."

Claudia Moncrief had been waiting all day for her daughter-in-law's call. The longer she went without hearing from Lissy, the more anxious she grew. To calm herself, she puttered in her backyard fall garden, harvesting turnips, onions, and pumpkins. When the rain began, she simply slipped into an old yellow rain slicker and went back at it.

Her cell phone was tucked in her back pocket. She had to stop herself several times from being the one to call. She did not want to be a meddlesome mother-in-law, but she was concerned. Lissy had told her she had an appointment with specialists at Cook's Children that morning, but she hadn't been specific about the time or the reason.

Claudia suspected for some time now that there was something wrong with her only grandchild. She feared autism, so she'd kept her mouth shut. When Lissette's best friend, Mariah, had spoken up, Claudia had been relieved. She didn't have to be the bad guy. And it wasn't as if she felt strong enough to broach the subject. She was still fragile. She'd just recently stopped lying in bed all day, praying for release from her suffering. Jake had been her only child, and she loved him more than her own life.

Grief spilled over her in waves. It hit like this. Quiet at times, and then *wham*. It was a two-by-four upside the head. She ducked her chin to her chest, rocked down onto her knees in the wet soil, and sobbed.

She had always feared Jake would die young. It was a thought no mother ever wanted to entertain, but it had nibbled at the back of her brain for years. He had been bold from the beginning. Climbing like a Sherpa to the top of the kitchen cabinets before he could even walk.

Fearless.

As a boy, he'd had a horrible habit of running into the street without looking both ways first. He liked to jump from the roof of the house, and if he got hurt, he would laugh it off. Her pediatrician told her that he had a high pain tolerance, which, combined with his daredevil nature, had starting turning her hair gray before she was thirty. Now her hair was completely silver.

When Jake was in those odd in-between years on the bridge from childhood to adolescence, he'd started drawing dark images of war—bloodied and embattled soldiers with severed limbs, exploding bombs dropped on villages, daggers and cannons and guns.

Always guns.

As a teen his fascination with guns grew, they were

joined by wild bulls, fast cars, and even faster women. Claudia had been so grateful and relieved when he'd brought Lissette home to meet her. Her only concern was that quiet Lissette would be flattened by her son's oversized personality. Lissy had been good for Jake. Settling him by at least some small measure. On the other hand, she wasn't so sure that Jake had been good for Lissy. She was so wary at times and hesitant to make decisions on her own for fear Jake would disapprove. Her daughter-in-law's reticence only seemed to deepen the longer the marriage went on.

But Claudia admired Lissette's kind calmness. Her ability to remain impassive in situations where other people got overexcited and reactionary was a true gift. It's how she had survived life with Jake. He'd been a war ship. She'd been the rolling sea.

Claudia didn't know where her son got the darkness. Her new-agey sister, Carol, said that maybe the trouble was left over from a previous life, but Claudia didn't believe in reincarnation, even though part of her found the idea appealing. Second chances. It was a provocative notion, but what was the point if you couldn't remember who you'd been in a previous life? How could you correct past mistakes if you couldn't remember them?

For the most part, she was an optimistic person in spite of all the curveballs life had thrown her way. The death of her first baby, born three months premature. These days, they probably could have saved Robbie. But back then? She shook her head. Three months in the NICU, looking like a naked baby sparrow, hooked up to tubes and monitors. Such a tiny, precious thing. All that suffering and then she'd still lost him.

She'd been so thankful when Jake had come along a year later to ease her grief. For years, she believed her life was perfect. She had a handsome cowboy husband

and a healthy baby boy and then one awful Christmas Eve she discovered Gordon had sired a son by another woman when he'd been on the cutting horse circuit out in California. Claudia's happily-ever-after had come crashing in on her.

It wasn't even the cheating that ate at Claudia so fiercely. Gordon had always had a revved-up sex drive and a wandering eye and she understood what problems that combination could cause when he was on the road alone. Before Jake came along, she'd traveled the circuit with him, but once she had the baby, her son had become her entire world.

No, it wasn't so much the affair as the fact that Gordon had two sons while she had only one. He'd not only cheated on her, but he'd cheated by having a child without her. Jake's birth had been difficult, resulting in her having to have a hysterectomy. Even though Claudia longed for more children, she couldn't have them. So she showered love on Jake. But part of her couldn't get over the fact that she was no longer a real woman. Empty. Wombless. Barren.

Gordon vehemently denied that the child was his, but Claudia knew the truth. It had eaten at her, dark and festering. And then she'd gone and done a horrible thing. The big, nasty awful that earned her a place in hell. She'd done what she had to do to protect Jake. She had not regretted her actions when she'd done it, but with the passing of time came wisdom. Hindsight stirred the edges of her secret disgrace into bloodred remorse.

She pretended to believe Gordon that the baby was not his and she never told him about her big awful sin. They repaired the tatters of their marriage as best they could and moved on. Neither one of them ever spoke of Amelia Jones and her son again, and for the most part, she put it out of her mind and life returned to normal.

Twelve years ago, Gordon had been kicked in the head by a wild quarter horse he'd been trying to tame and he'd died of a brain hemorrhage on the way to the hospital. Then when she lost Jake on the Fourth of July, she lost her direction. Lost both her heart and her soul in one fell swoop. If it hadn't been for Lissette and Kyle, she might have done the unthinkable.

She'd been completely stunned a few weeks later when she learned Jake had left his life insurance money and death gratuity benefits to Amelia Jones's son, although she offered no explanation to Lissette. She had even pretended that she had no idea who Rafferty Jones was. That lie ate at her, but she hadn't been strong enough to face her daughter-in-law, especially when she could not understand why Jake had cut his wife and child off from the money that rightfully belonged to them. And without thinking what the consequences would be for Lissy and Kyle if he were killed, Jake had disobeyed a direct order and gone back to save orphans in jeopardy. She was so fiercely proud of him for that. His last act had been completely unselfish, but she was furious at the government for calling Jake's supreme heroism willful misconduct and by that designation, denying Lissy and Kyle survivor benefits.

Now there was something terribly wrong with her grandson. Was this delayed retribution for her despicable actions? Was this life extracting a cruel payback?

"Please," she prayed, even though she was no longer certain God listened. So many of her prayers had gone unanswered. "Please, let Kyle be okay. It's not his fault. None of it. Don't take things out on him."

"Claudia?"

She jerked her head up, swiped uselessly at the tears rolling down her cheeks with the rain-covered sleeve of her slicker.

Her next-door neighbor, Stewart English, had pushed

open her backyard gate and stood there, umbrella in hand, wearing faded blue jeans, battered old cowboy boots, and a long-sleeved navy blue T-shirt identifying him as a member of the Jubilee Fire Department. His wife, Linda, had died the year before. Cancer. They'd been married thirty-four years. Had three kids. Claudia and Linda had been best friends.

"Stewart." She forced a smile. "How are you?"

"It's raining. You're gardening in the rain."

"I know."

"I brought you some bread." He held up the loaf of bread wrapped in a plastic bag. "Made it myself in the bread maker that Ben's wife bought me for Father's Day. First time I hauled it out of the box. It's pretty good. I made two loaves."

Claudia got to her feet, stripped off her gardening gloves. "That was sweet of you."

The yeasty smell of fresh, hot bread drifted across the yard toward her in spite of the scent-dampening rain.

"Brought butter I churned myself."

"You churned it yourself? Now that is quaint."

Stewart wore a ball cap embossed with the same emblem that decorated the pocket of his T-shirt. He was bald underneath the cap. He was one of those guys that once his hair started falling out, he'd taken the shears to his whole head, simply going with it instead of fighting nature. Up until the day he died at forty-nine, Gordon had had a full head of brownish-blond hair.

"Gemma's on this back-to-nature kick," Stewart explained, speaking about his oldest daughter. "She's bought her own Jersey milk cow. Gives me all this fresh milk. Far more than I can drink. I had to do something with it. Gotta tell you, it's the best butter you'll ever taste. Warning, it's addictive."

To keep her figure, Claudia had given up excess carbohydrates a long time ago, but the bread did smell good and she'd lost twenty-five pounds since Jake died. Why not indulge? It might take her mind off the fact that Lissy hadn't called. "Would you like to come in?" She inclined her head toward her back door.

"Nah, can't. Hope's got me hooked up on some blind date." Hope was Stewart's youngest child. "I'm not interested in dating, but you know kids."

She nodded. "The things we do to please them."

Stewart's eyes met hers. "You've been crying."

"Who me?" Claudia forced a laugh. "No, no. It's those winter onions I've been grubbing out of the ground."

Stewart screwed up his mouth in an expression that said he didn't believe her, but he didn't say anything.

"So," she said, as the rain dripped steadily onto his umbrella. "Who's the blind date with?"

"Piano teacher," he said. "From Twilight. She gives lessons to Hope's kids."

The neighboring town of Twilight lay thirty miles southwest of Jubilee, and the two communities had a natural rivalry.

"Well, at least she's musical. Music is nice."

"I don't think it's going to be a love match," Stewart went on. "The fact that I'm tone deaf will probably be a deal breaker."

"Don't pass judgment. Give her a chance."

"Oh-ho, this sounds like the pot calling the kettle black to me," Stewart said. "I remember when Linda tried to fix you up with her cousin Larry and you wouldn't even consider it."

"Larry sold vitamins through multilevel marketing, for heaven's sake," Claudia said. "I couldn't get involved with a guy who could fall for a glorified pyramid scheme."

"Touché." Stewart smiled. "FYI, Larry declared bankruptcy last year. You dodged a bullet."

She smiled, glad for Stewart's distraction.

"How's Lissette?" he asked.

Claudia drew in a deep breath. "She's hanging in there."

"I heard she had a fender bender in Searcy's parking lot this afternoon."

"What?" Alarm pushed through her. "Where did you hear that?"

"Mailman."

"Oh my goodness." She pressed a hand to her chest. Why had she been so hands-off? Lissette needed her and she'd been here grubbing in the garden in the rain feeling sorry for herself. "Is she okay? What about the baby?"

Stewart touched her arm. "It was just a fender bender, Claudia. She's fine."

"How can you be so sure?"

"C'mon. You know the gossip mill. If she'd been hurt you would know about it."

Why hadn't Lissy called? "She might be hurt. Maybe she hit her head and got a headache and she went home to lie down and got a brain bleed like that poor actress Natasha Richardson."

"You're letting your imagination run away with you. There's no point jumping to conclusions. Don't get upset until there's something to get upset about."

She knew Stewart was simply trying to comfort her, but she didn't need to be told how to feel. Why was it that men always negated a woman's feelings? They thought they were being tough, but Claudia suspected it was really because emotions scared the hell out of them. She bit down on her tongue to keep from saying something tacky.

"Why don't we go in the house and call her," Stewart said. "That should put your mind at ease."

"I need to see her."

"Tell you what, you change your clothes and then I'll drive you over."

"Okay, okay," she said, her pulse thready.

Stewart followed her into the mudroom, where he took the bread and butter from her arms and set it on the kitchen counter. She kicked off her muddy shoes and, trailing water, padded through the house to the bathroom.

She had an awful feeling that something was terribly wrong. She exhaled with the weariness of a woman who'd been through bad times and knew things could always get worse.

Claudia took a hot shower, got dressed, and by the time she wandered into the living room, she was feeling better. Stewart perched on the edge of the recliner, thumbing through the TV channels. He'd turned on the lamp.

"Anything good on TV tonight?" Claudia asked.

He shrugged, looked embarrassed. "I like *Survivor*."

"The girls in bikinis," she guessed.

"Nah, it's the whole Robinson Crusoe thing. Always been fascinated by the idea of being stranded on a deserted island. Not that I mind the eye candy." He chuckled. "But it's the survival element that intrigues me."

Claudia clasped her hands in front of her. "I'm sorry for losing it."

"Completely understandable. You've been through more than anyone should ever have to go through."

The phrase *losing a child* went unspoken.

They studied each other in the light from the lamp. Stewart had nice eyes—kind, intelligent, forgiving.

"Are you ready to go?" he asked, dangling his car keys from his finger.

"Thank you for doing this," she said, and then totally shocked herself by going up on tiptoes and planting a light kiss on his cheek. His masculine skin was pleasantly rough beneath her lips.

Stewart ducked his head and moved toward the door like someone had set a house on fire. "It's nothing," he mumbled.

Good God, Claudia, what were you thinking?

She cringed. It had been a totally innocent gesture but now she understood it had been a grave mistake. Something between them shifted instantly. Their neighborly relationship had been knocked off kilter.

The streetlamps were coming on and the rain had eased off. Stewart escorted her over to his driveway, helped her into the passenger seat of his Lincoln Town Car with comfortable leather seats. When he got in beside her, she realized it was the first time she'd ever been alone in a car with him. It felt weird. Particularly after that stupid, meaningless kiss.

Why had she kissed him?

Neither of them said a word on the short drive over to Lissette's house. Claudia couldn't bring herself to look at Stewart, just kept her gaze averted out the window. Why was she even letting him drive her? She should have driven herself.

Except her stomach was shaky. From worry over Kyle? she wondered. Or the kiss? Maybe it was both. Her lips tingled from the contact. Good grief, she was being so silly.

You're not fifteen. Forget the kiss. Keep your mind on what matters—your daughter-in-law and your grandson.

Stewart pulled up to the adorable Victorian home painted a beguiling sage green. Claudia's gaze fixed on the red dually pickup truck parked at the curb. The front fender was dented in. Lissette had company. An uneasy feeling settled over her. Who did the truck belong to?

None of your business, you nosy old woman.

That's when she noticed the California license plate.

Claudia sucked in her breath. California. The state where Gordon's illegitimate son lived.

Dizziness swirled her head. Could it be he? After all this time?

You're jumping to conclusions. That's a big leap.

She shifted her gaze to Stewart. He was glancing at his watch, and she remembered belatedly that he had a date. Suddenly, retreat felt far safer than knocking on Lissette's door.

"I've changed my mind," she said, tamping down the dread filling up her lungs. "Please, take me back home."

Chapter Five

Awkward silence rode with them on the three-mile trip out of town.

Lissette drove. Rafferty wasn't comfortable in the passenger seat. He was used to being in charge.

John Wayne Boulevard meandered past a feed store, a horse vet, and a shop that sold fancy masonry stone, potbellied woodstoves, metal windmills, deer feeders, dog kennels, and stock tanks. A rambling limestone building had a sign bragging: "Best Handmade Furniture in Texas." They breezed past a Western wear clothing store, a tractor supply, and two places that sold horse trailers. There was the First Horseman's Bank of Jubilee and a tiny newspaper office called the Daily Cutter.

That odd feeling of belonging stole over Rafferty again. If he could have custom made a town to fit his personality, Jubilee would have been it. How much of Gordon Moncrief's DNA had marked him? Where else would he have gotten such a longing for a town he'd never been to?

Lissette branched off John Wayne Boulevard, took Farm-to-Market Road 730. Rafferty glanced over at her. In spite of clunky wading boots and the tension pulling at her lips, she was an attractive woman.

Absentmindedly, her fingers moved up and down over the steering wheel as if she were playing piano keys and producing a soft unhurried rhythm. Her hands moved smooth as water, savoring the texture of leather beneath her fingertips. It was a sensual movement even though he was certain she did not intend it that way.

She was as cool as clouds on a hot summer day—a balm for heated skin. Except Rafferty was suspicious of clouds. Clouds could be all fluffy and inviting one minute, providing respite from the sun, but they could turn on you in a second. Dump gray rain on your picnic. They could harbor lightning, hailstones, tornadoes—all kinds of trouble. Just like today. Wet autumn clouds had blown in out of nowhere, saturating the countryside in sodden grayness.

He let his gaze travel down the column of her long neck to the slope of her slender shoulders, and even, yes, damn him, to the swell of her breast. The long-sleeved, button-down white shirt partially camouflaged nature's generous gift, but he could tell she would rock a bikini.

His gaze drifted back to those fingers, still moving over the leather steering wheel wrap. Clearly she was unconscious of the slow tempo she'd set up, staring out through the windshield, but Rafferty was certain the restless habit was a relief for her, perhaps a contrast to her whirling mind, an attempt to slow down her mental process.

She turned her head and caught him staring at her. He whipped his gaze forward. She pulled up to a twenty-acre plot of land strung with barbwire fence where a lone quarter horse waited in the field. At the sound of the truck engine, the horse lifted its head and started moseying toward the red pole barn.

"I'll get the gate," Rafferty volunteered, and hopped from the truck.

He unlatched the gate and swung it open so she could

drive through into the pasture. Lissette parked and got out. Rafferty closed the gate. Kyle was asleep in his car seat. Rafferty reached for the umbrella on the floorboard and opened it up as he softly closed the passenger side door so as not to awaken the boy.

Side by side they headed toward the pole barn through the slog of mud. She'd been smart to wear waders, even though they made a sucking sound with each step as she plucked her feet upward. His cowboy boots would need a thorough cleaning when this was over.

They stepped into a particularly thick morass and when Lissette trudged forward, her left boot stayed rooted in the quagmire.

"Oh!" she exclaimed as the submerged boot jerked her backward. Arms flailing, she grabbed at his elbow with both hands.

The wind snatched the umbrella from him, tossing it over his shoulder. He struggled to maintain his balance, to keep Lissette from falling into the mud puddle.

"Whoa," he exclaimed. "Whoa there."

But gravity had other ideas and Rafferty lost the battle.

Lissette tumbled onto her butt in a graceless heap, momentum dragging him down on top of her.

The next thing Lissette knew Rafferty was straddling her. His knees plowed into the mud on either side of her waist. His crotch settled right against her navel, only the material of her cotton blouse and his blue jeans between them. He looked as startled as she felt. As if he too had just had the air knocked from his lungs.

Disoriented, she gaped up at him. A hot, sensual, searing sensation streaked through her lower abdomen. She'd never experienced anything like it.

Cool mud oozed at her back. She was barely holding herself up on her shoulders, trying to keep her head from getting slimed along with the rest of her. Her knees were bent, revealing to the world at large what kind of panties she was wearing—whimsical, yellow, polka dot boy-cut panties. Her personality might be understated, but when it came to lingerie, Lissette let her freak flag fly.

She tried to reach around and tug the hem of her skirt down, but Rafferty Jones was an immovable object.

"Are you okay?" he asked, not seeming to realize she was trying to effect some kind of dignity here. His gaze drifted as he assessed her, lingering on her mouth before sliding down her neck to fix on her breasts. His eyes narrowed and a slight smirk tugged at his lips.

Good grief, he was ogling her!

That's when she realized one of the buttons on her blouse had popped open revealing a lacy yellow bra that matched her panties, and Rafferty had noticed.

"Get off me!" she snapped, more embarrassed than angry. Her mud-encrusted fingers flew to do up the button.

"Polka dots." He grinned. "I'm a big fan of polka dots."

"Got a thing for Minnie Mouse, do you?"

"Love of my life."

"Get off," she repeated through clenched teeth. Okay, now she was just irritated. She knew he couldn't help seeing her bra, but he could help grinning like a loon about it.

"Hey, you're the one who pulled me down on top of you," he pointed out sensibly.

She pressed her muddy palms against his chest and shoved.

His laughter rolled out across the pasture as he tumbled off her. She tried to scramble to her feet, but the mud refused to let go.

Somehow, Rafferty managed to stand, damn him for being more nimble. He put down a hand to help her up, even as he continued to chuckle.

"Stop laughing. It's not funny."

"It's sort of funny."

"No it's not. I'm covered in mud. You're covered in mud. We're going to ruin the interior of the truck."

"Mud washes off," he said philosophically. "Take my hand."

She didn't want to take his hand, but she couldn't seem to extricate herself on her own. Blowing a strand of hair from her eyes, she glared and sank her palm into his.

A quiver shot straight through her body. She tried to deny it and let go of his hand as soon as she was steady. She looked everywhere but into his bemused brown eyes.

His pants were covered in mud from the knees down, but she'd fared much worse. She could feel ooze caking her back from her shoulders to her feet, and her blouse was smeared with mud from where she'd buttoned up.

Primly, pretending nothing at all had happened, she lifted her head. "You can stand here making like a hyena all night if you wish, but I'm going to feed the horse."

"Hang on a minute," he said, taking hold of her elbow. "Let me help you get some of that muck off."

She opened to her mouth to tell him she was just fine, that she didn't need his help, but before she could get the words out, he was running the back of his hand over her fanny, scraping off the gunk. A picture of what they must look like to someone passing by, both of them covered in mud, Rafferty trying in vain to clean her with nothing but his hand, finally struck Lissette's funny bone.

Laughter erupted from her throat, spilled into the gathering twilight. A nearly full moon broke through the cloud covering as it started its journey up the sky. The vapor lamp above the pole barn flickered on, shining a purplish glow over them. Rafferty's laughter joined hers and soon they were holding on to their sides and every time they looked at each other they dissolved into fresh gales of giggles.

It felt strange. Laughing like this.

She couldn't remember the last time she'd laughed so hard. Long before Jake had died. When had she stopped laughing?

Didn't matter. She shouldn't be laughing like this. Today, she'd learned her son was going deaf and there was nothing she could do to prevent it. Nothing funny about that.

A clump of clouds slid in front of the ascending moon, blunting the light, turning the horizon the color of ashes. Somewhere, frogs sang to the rain gods. She could hear Rafferty's breathing—short, shallow, same as her own.

Their laughter died away and this time, when their eyes met, she could make out the faint lines tugging at his mouth. His handsomeness was stunning. She watched him run a palm over his five o'clock shadow, heard the soft rasp of whiskers.

Her body started trembling and his arms went around her. She did not want to cry. How nutty to be laughing one minute, crying the next. But it felt so good to rest her head on his shoulders, feel his grip tighten on her waist. Hear him whisper, "It's going to be okay. I promise, it's all going to be okay."

She clung to that promise even as she realized he did not have the power to offer such assurances. She swallowed back the tears, swiped at her eyes, even as she knew she was streaking her cheeks with mud. It was too late to worry about that.

Too late for so many things.

"We need to feed Slate," she said, stepping away from him.

Rafferty dropped his arms, looked as uncomfortable as she felt. How could she both want him near and wish he'd disappear? Reconciling the two feelings seemed impossible. She did not know him, but she wanted to.

Futilely, she smoothed her skirt, squared her shoulders, and moved toward the stallion waiting patiently underneath the shelter.

Rafferty went around to the back of the truck, took out the bag of oats they'd bought at the feed store, and carried it to the metal barrel with a clasp closing mechanism that stood in one corner of the pole barn. "Is that where you store the oats?"

She nodded.

"Who normally loads the barrel up for you?" he asked.

"I'm not a china doll, Mr. Jones," she said, hearing the snippiness in her voice. Why was she being disagreeable? They'd just had a good laugh together. Then again, maybe that was why. She wanted to get things back on formal footing. They were getting too damn cozy. "I don't know what you must think of me."

"Rafferty," he corrected easily. "I am your brother-in-law, after all."

Yes. Her brother-in-law. She'd do well to remember that instead of noticing how even mud couldn't hide the fact that his butt looked good in jeans.

Rafferty took the ring clasp off the barrel, opened the bag of oats with a pocketknife, and dumped them in. He found a metal scoop on a shelf and poured oats into the feed trough. The horse nuzzled Rafferty's elbow.

"Hey there," he cooed, scratched the stallion's nose. The headlights from the truck were directed at the interior of the pole barn, illuminated the damp evening. "He's curious and unafraid," Rafferty told her. "It's a good quality in a cutting horse. How old is he?"

"Three, I think."

"Right age. Has he ever competed?"

"Jake had been training him whenever he was home and he'd planned on showing him in the Fort Worth cutting horse futurity this year. He'd already paid the entry fee. Of course that was before he reenlisted."

"Does the horse have papers?"

"Yes." She waved a hand. "Somewhere."

Rafferty ran a hand over the stallion's flank. The animal continued calmly eating his food. He wasn't skittish. "Hmm."

"Hmm what?"

"He's a good horse. You could get a tidy sum for him."

"Selling him is on my to-do list. How much do you think I could get?" She didn't know why she asked Rafferty's opinion. She could have thrown a ripe peach underhanded in any direction and hit a cutting horse cowboy who would have willingly given her an assessment.

Rafferty shrugged. "All depends on his genetics. Plus a well-trained cutting horse will sell for more than one who isn't trained. If he's won a purse or two, that would increase his value as well."

She poked her tongue against the inside of her cheek. "How much would it cost me to have him trained?"

"Somewhere in the neighborhood of three to four thousand."

Lissette gulped. "That's an exclusive neighborhood."

He shrugged. "A good friend might do it for less."

"Too rich for my blood. Unless I was certain I could recoup the investment when I sell him. My focus is bringing in as much money as I can, not laying it out. Could I make the money back on him?"

"Maybe not. These things are iffy."

For a minute, the only sound they heard was Slate munching oats and the frogs' raucous croaking.

"If you could find Slate's paperwork, that would help me come up with a ballpark figure for you," Rafferty said.

"I don't want to put you to any trouble. I know you need to get on the road. It might take hours to find the paperwork."

"You givin' me the bum's rush?"

"You have your normal life to get back to."

"Neither of our lives are going back to normal," he said.

They stood there in the blue-white beam of the truck's headlights, muddy and tired. She saw the weariness in his eyes now that she hadn't paid attention to before. His emotional burdens were different from hers, but burdens all the same. She reminded herself that Jake's death was still fresh for him.

A long moment ticked by. The breeze gusted against her damp clothes. A yellow wedge of misty moon shoved a window through the bunched black clouds peeping coyly over Rafferty's shoulder. A green glow, the color of dolce verde gorgonzola, flickered gently across his face. His features held an impassive lightness. Firm, yet laid-back. Thoroughly alpha in appearance, but underneath an appealing, quiet kindness.

"Do you have a place to stay the night?" she asked before she even realized she was going to ask it.

"No."

"I've got . . . You could billet in the garage apartment. It's a bit junky, but it has a bed with a good mattress." Why was she doing this? She couldn't believe she was doing this. Offering the garage apartment to him for the night.

"Billet?" His lips curved slightly upward.

"Military term I picked up from Jake. It means sleeping accommodations." She shrugged as if the offer was no big thing. As if she wasn't feeling the disturbing and wondrous undercurrents flowing back and forth between them. "There's no point in getting on the road tonight in the rain or spending money on a motel room."

"Thanks," he said. "I appreciate the offer."

He smiled at her. Calm, steady, trustworthy. Why then did she feel like she'd just stepped off a cliff with a blindfold on?

On the return ride to Lissette's house, with the truck seats protected from their muddy bodies by empty feed sacks and the horse blankets he'd found inside the pole barn, Rafferty's mind was racing. Seeing the cutting horse had given him an idea. He was beginning to hatch a plan to give her the money without Lissette knowing she was taking it from him. The scheme would allow her to maintain her pride and independence and still let him live up to his promise to Jake.

Trouble was, it meant staying in Jubilee for the next several weeks.

Even bigger trouble, he realized he *wanted* to stay.

When he was a kid—particularly when things were bad with Amelia, which in those days was more often than not—he would lie in bed at night and fantasize that Gordon Moncrief would come for him and whisk him away to a better life in Texas. He had an old atlas and he'd looked up Jubilee, circling the town with a red pen. He promised himself that eventually, he'd make his way there, seek out his father and his real home, leave L.A. far behind.

When Amelia found the marked-up atlas, she'd laughed at him. "Give up the dream, kid. Gordon Moncrief doesn't give a tinker's damn about you. I'm the only parent you get."

Her comment hit him squarely in the solar plexus because he'd known it was true. Gordon would not be galloping to his rescue. It was up to Rafferty to save himself, to save his mother, to save the day.

Always saving the day. Lone Ranger Rafferty.

But after years of never hearing from Gordon, he'd completely shelved the dream, and then out of the blue Jake had suddenly shown up, appearing like a superhero in Rafferty's moment of greatest need. Jake was the new

Lone Ranger and Rafferty had eagerly accepted the role of Tonto.

Exhilarated to have someone to look up to, he'd fallen for the unexpected big brother like a pound puppy hungry for adoption. Rafferty swallowed back the memory.

Jake had never told Lissette about him. Why not? Had Jake been that ashamed of him? Rafferty had so many questions. Could he unearth the answers in this town and finally lay the past to rest? It was a new goal, this inner quest he'd buried since childhood. Get in touch with his roots. Find out where he came from. Resolve his issues from the past so he could completely let them go.

A new question arose in his mind. Was he simply using Lissette as an excuse to stay in Jubilee and find out more about Gordon? About Jake who'd disappeared from his life as quickly as he'd entered it? Or maybe—and this was probably it—did he simply prefer the handy excuse of digging up old history to facing the fact that Lissette stirred him in a way he hadn't been stirred in a long time. Stirred him enough that he was searching for reasons to linger?

In a way he did not want to be stirred, especially not by Jake's widow. It was wrong.

But after she killed the truck engine and looked over at him, her cheeks smeared with mud, her big eyes peering into his, a slow, indigo spark ignited deep in his belly, sending unreasonable desire spreading throughout his bloodstream, melting his reason.

He unbuckled the shoulder harness, leaned deliberately toward her. She was looking at him with a wavering smile that plucked her lush lips up, then tipped them down, then yanked them back up again.

Lissette started to say something and that's when he reached out to touch her cheek.

Kiss her.

The thought rolled through his mind like an unwanted melody. Her chin set hard and her eyes grew even wider and he saw it in her face—the same wanting that sank him.

It was hard to think through the delicious smell of her, the earthiness of mud on the top layer, the wizardry of yeast and cinnamon and brown sugar underneath. Amelia had never baked. To him, baking seemed an angelic skill, more akin to magic than science. Mix up some ingredients, add some heat and time, and *voilá*, an accomplished baker could create something that made the whole world seem brand-new.

He leaned closer.

Every impulse in his body urged him to kiss her. He ached to taste her flavor, to lay claim on her sweet mouth. He wanted to press his lips to the hollow of her throat, lick the steady beat of her pulse. He was feeling something powerful here, something too powerful to act upon. This was dangerous territory and Rafferty was a cautious man.

Her lips parted slightly.

From the backseat, the boy whimpered, waking up. Rafferty could not hear, did not want to hear. His fingers traced Lissette's skin and his own lips parted.

She hissed in air.

A quiet noise by most anyone's estimation, barely audible, but combined with the uncertainty in her eyes, the gentle flare of her nostrils, it was deafening—a whisper hiss loud enough to cut through the indigo heat like a whetstone-honed pocketknife—but instead of smothering the flames, that slight sound let in a back draft of shame, concern, agitation, and the spine-stiffening quake of reality. A definite, don't-cross-that-line sound, with his history on one side of it and all his hopes for the future on the other, a sound like the blister of plastic tossed recklessly onto a campfire.

A moment of utter silence followed while he forcefully swept aside the mental embers and instead of kissing her as he'd intended, rubbed away a smudge of dried mud from her petal-soft skin.

"Dirt," he mumbled, pulling his hand back and rubbing his index finger against his thumb. "You've got dirt on your cheek."

"Oh," she murmured, and her hand went up where he'd just touched. "Thank you."

They kept staring at each other.

"We both need a bath," she said, and even in the darkness of the cab, he could see her blush.

"Yeah," he said, remembering what it had felt like straddling her in the muddy pasture. Rafferty felt himself grow hard and he quickly glanced away, grateful for Kyle, who whimpered again. "I'll get him out of the car seat. You go on inside the house and take a shower," he offered.

"That's okay, I can handle it."

There it was again, her prickly pride. "You don't have to prove anything to me."

"What does that mean?"

"I know you can take care of your boy. If you let me help it doesn't mean that you can't take care of him on your own."

She ducked her head, stuck the truck keys into her purse. "I can't afford to grow accustomed to having a man to depend on. I don't want to grow accustomed to depending on anyone. Not anymore."

He barely caught what she said, decided to pretend that he hadn't heard it. Ignoring her words seemed safer than exploring what they meant or how they made him feel.

"Go on in the house," she said, and opened the door to get out of the truck. "You can strip off in the mudroom—" She halted abruptly as the feed sack she'd been sitting on stuck to her backside and chunks of falling mud clattered against the floorboard. "Good grief, what a mess. I'm the one who needs to strip off in the mudroom."

Strip off.

The words branded into his brain as his imagination spun pictures of Lissette in her yellow polka dot underwear. Rafferty moistened his lips, banished the image.

Her feet touched the ground and she reached around to peel the feed sack off her backside and then with an unexpected chuckle, she tossed the sack into the corner of the dark garage. "I'll deal with that tomorrow."

"Go on," he said. "Get yourself cleaned up. I'll give you a head start so you can leave your clothes in the mudroom, and then I'll bring Kyle in and entertain him in the kitchen while you take a shower."

Shower.

A vision of Lissette standing naked under steamy hot water replaced the polka dot picture. His throat tightened.

"I really can't let you do that. Kyle is my responsibility." While she opened the back door to retrieve her son from his car seat, Rafferty got out and went around to her side of the truck.

He noticed how her soft hair shone in the glow of the dim garage lighting. His gaze slid to the hollow of her throat. She was still wearing that pretty opal necklace. Had it only been since that afternoon that he'd first met her? Time warped and he had an odd sense that he'd known her for years. He was a practical man who did not believe in magical things like fate or destiny or soul mates, but this easy familiarity unsettled him.

"You know," he drawled, slowing down his speech in the hopes of slowing his pulse. "Our relationship will go a lot easier if you stop fighting me on every little thing."

"We don't have a relationship."

"But we will. I'm Kyle's uncle. Now that I've met him . . . met you . . . I don't want to go back to the shadows."

She opened her mouth as if she was about to argue, but shut it again.

"I've been meaning to tell you that my ranch foreman is deaf. We've worked together for ten years. I might be able to offer you some insight into the condition."

"Know a lot about deafness, do you?"

"I'm proficient in sign language, yes."

"Really?"

"Really, now say thank you, Rafferty, and go take a shower."

She looked like he'd just thrown her a lifeline when she was going down for the third time. "Thank you, Rafferty."

"See," he said. "Was that so hard?"

Hard.

Poor choice of words considering what was going on in his body.

"Go on." He motioned her toward the house. "I've got the boy."

She nodded, headed toward the house. Halfway there, she stopped and glanced back at him.

Rafferty had Kyle in his arms by then, the boy's little hands clutching his collar. "Move, Mama Hen. All is well here."

A bemused smile crossed her lips. For a split second she actually looked happy. *He'd* made her happy. He smiled back, but she ducked her head and hurried into the house, and that's when he knew he was going have to be very careful. Because he liked her.

Too damn much.

Chapter Six

A sexy cowboy was showering in her guest bathroom.

Lissette allowed that erotic image to flit through her head as she sat at her bedroom vanity blow-drying her hair. Kyle lay stretched out on his belly near her feet, legs swinging back and forth in the air as he ran the wheels of a red plastic fire engine over the hardwood floor. Above the sound of the blow dryer, she heard the hot water pipes vibrating inside the walls, the downside of owning a hundred-year-old home.

Rafferty. A stranger. Naked.

She thought of that moment in the cab of the truck when she had been almost certain that Rafferty was going to kiss her and she had just sat there, a small part of her *wanting* him to kiss her. Was she that hungry for a man's attention? Seriously, was she that messed up?

Thankfully, she'd been wrong about the kiss. He'd simply wiped mud from her cheek. Ha! So much for her silly ego.

She blew out her breath. If her neighbors knew she was thinking such things they would be scandalized. Some might say she shouldn't care what others thought of her, and she wished she had feathers so she could let opinions slide off her like water off a duck's back, but the truth was she treasured her social community. She'd found a home here in Jubilee and she hated upsetting the status quo.

This attitude used to bamboozle Jake. "Stop trying to please everyone, Lissette. Please yourself, dammit."

But when she dared to voice a strong opinion around him, he'd dismiss it out of hand—unless it was something he wanted or agreed with. To keep the peace, she'd learned to read his desires and reflect them back to him. She'd cut off pieces of herself in order to be with him. Denying what she needed just to avoid stirring the pot. Since he'd died, she felt a wondrous awakening as if anything was possible if she was brave enough to dig deep and do the work to find out what it really was that she wanted. She hadn't dared yet take those steps and now Kyle was in trouble and she no longer had the luxury of self-exploration. Her son came first. Always.

She was grateful for Rafferty.

Yes, grateful. Because for several miraculous minutes this evening—most notably when Rafferty had straddled her in the mud—she'd forgotten that her little boy was deaf. He'd gotten her out of her mind, lifted the heavy fog that had engulfed her since learning of Kyle's diagnosis.

But the tiny respite had passed. Vanished along with the fleeting attraction she'd felt for Rafferty during those insane seconds. Reality was back, big and ugly. She had to call her parents and Claudia and give them the sad news. Her gaze traced over her son. He looked so perfect. How could he be broken?

Impossible, and yet she knew it was true. No amount of denial or diversion could change the fact that Kyle was losing his hearing.

The same anguish that had hit her that morning was

back and packing a mind-numbing wallop, desperate and dark, plucking at her like fingers on guitar strings coaxing out a mournful melody.

She flicked off the blow dryer, set it aside, and absentmindedly ran a brush through her hair. Her gaze shifted to the bedside clock. It was almost eight P.M. Kyle's usual bedtime, but he'd napped extra long today and she'd have a tussle if she tried to put him to bed now.

At loose ends, she glanced over at the phone. Claudia would be beside herself with worry. Why hadn't her mother-in-law called already? Lissette hadn't told her parents that she was taking Kyle to the doctor, so she could get away with breaking the news to them tomorrow, but she had to phone Claudia tonight. She knew her mother-in-law. Claudia wouldn't sleep a wink fretting over her grandson.

The water went off.

Unbidden, she pictured Rafferty getting out of the shower, toweling off, and—

What would Claudia think if she knew Gordon's illegitimate son was in her house naked?

Lissette got up from the vanity. One problem at a time. Right now, she needed to get Rafferty squared away in the garage apartment. "Kyle . . ."

He can't hear you. How long will it take for you to get that through your head?

She wiped her fingers across her lips, and then bent down to pick up her son. It was sticky in here, humid from her shower and the rainy evening pressing against the old windowpanes, but it was more than clamminess that sent a slight sickness sinking into her belly. Kyle's diagnosis did that, the memory of that black moment when the doctor had explained about his hearing loss.

Had it only been that morning? It felt like a thousand

years ago. When she'd awakened today she'd been one person. Tonight she was someone else entirely.

The mother of a deaf child.

The memory brought the overwhelming guilt and despair back, the utter sense of helplessness. She closed her eyes, pressed her lips to her son's temple. "Mommy loves you no matter what."

On the lower floor a door closed. Rafferty. She had to deal with him.

Settling Kyle on her hip, she went downstairs.

Rafferty stood outside the guest bedroom looking out of place and uncomfortable. His damp hair was combed back off his forehead and he wore a fresh pair of jeans and a Los Angeles Rams T-shirt. He was barefoot. Lissette had never thought of toes as sexy before, but Rafferty had very sexy toes—long, lean, well groomed. Just like the rest of him.

Lissette's heart gave a strange little hop. She raised her gaze from his feet to his face. He tilted his head, looked a bit bashful at her assessment. Feeling pretty embarrassed herself, she walked to the linen closet at the end of the hallway, did a one-handed fumble for fresh sheets and a pillow, and loaded up Rafferty's open arms. Kyle's solemn little eyes rested on him, not missing a single beat.

"C'mon," she said, and led him through the kitchen.

In the mudroom, Rafferty put on his boots while Lissette slipped her bare feet into a pair of rubber flip-flops she kept at that back door. They went out that way, instead of tracking through the kitchen to the French doors, and around the side of the house to the driveway.

The backyard flood lamp was on, lighting their way to the garage apartment. She guided him up the wooden steps to the outside door. She paused, stood on tiptoes to retrieve the key hidden at the top of the door facing. She and Jake had talked about fixing up the apartment and renting it out, but he had decided that he didn't want her dealing with a renter while she was here alone, so the place was little more than a storage room. Although Jake had come out here a few times to watch football whenever she and her friends used the house for the Jubilee Co-op meetings. She pushed open the door and flipped on the light.

The apartment was a three-hundred-square-foot room layered in dust. Storage containers—filled with a variety of household overflow from Christmas decorations to old clothes to outdated electronics—were stacked almost to the ceiling. There was an ant trail from the door to where the bed was positioned in front of a garage-sale chest of drawers with a portable television set resting on it. In one corner stood a college dorm–sized refrigerator that wasn't plugged in and a small porcelain sink. Behind a second door lay a half bathroom, sink and toilet but no showering facilities. There was an intercom system that Jake had installed in the wall so Lissy could call him from the house if she needed him for something.

One large window looked out over the back of the house. From that vantage point, Rafferty would be able to see her when she was in the kitchen.

Thank heavens he was going to be here for only one night.

"This'll do fine," he said, and carried the fresh linen to the bed.

She was suddenly hyperaware that she was in her pajamas and housecoat. "I better go," she said. "I have to call Claudia and tell her about Kyle."

"Not an easy task."

"Coming on the heels of Jake's death, it's going to be a kick in the teeth." Lissette sighed. "I wish I could protect her a little while longer."

A mirthless smile lifted his lips. "You really like her?"

"She's been nothing but good to me."

"Rare mother-in-law." His expression was noncommittal, but there was something sarcastic in his tone.

Lissette bristled. "She's a good woman."

"I didn't say she wasn't."

They looked at each other. More tension between them because of stuff other people in their lives had done. She supposed she couldn't blame him for his attitude. From his point of view Claudia was probably the enemy, but today of all days, she'd used up her allotment of empathy on herself.

"Do you plan on telling her about me?" His gaze never left her face.

Kyle squirmed in her arms. Lissette shifted her weight. "Not until you've gone. There's no point in hurting her any more than she's already been hurt."

"So, it's not a totally open relationship."

Irritated, but not knowing why, she scowled at him. "Look, don't get me involved in your twisted family dynamics. I'm just the innocent bystander here."

He took a step toward her and it was all she could do not to back up. He was a very masculine man. "You mean that you want me to stay the Moncriefs' dirty little secret?"

Lissette gulped. "That's not what I mean at all."

"Sure it is. But don't worry. I'm used to being everyone's dirty little secret."

Oh hell, she'd hurt his feelings. That wasn't how she'd meant it, but with exhaustion weighing down every cell in her body she had trouble finding an apology.

"That's not what I meant. I'm just . . . this is all . . ." She waved a hand at Kyle's ear. "I'm hanging by a thread here."

He looked chagrined. "You're right. The hard feelings are all mine and they have nothing to do with you."

She exhaled audibly and it was only then that she realized she'd been holding her breath.

"It's been a long day for both of us."

She nodded, unable to speak. The empathy was all his now and Rafferty's eyes overflowed with it. One minute he was rubbing her the wrong way; the next, she wanted nothing more than to melt into his arms. Why did she have to have such a thing for cowboys?

"Everything has changed forever," she whispered. Kyle rested his head on her shoulder, slipped his arms around her neck.

"Yes."

"I would wish that I could go back to yesterday and stop time forever so that I would never have to know what was going to happen to Kyle, but if I did that . . ."

"What?" he prompted.

It would mean I would never have met you.

What kind of irrational thing was that to think? She didn't want to think it, but it coiled in her mind, tripwire tight and ready to spring.

"Why not just go back to the Fourth of July and stop time before you heard about Jake?" he asked.

Why? Because her marriage had been in trouble. Because she'd been miserable and she'd had no one she could tell the truth. Even a whispered word to her close friends about how emotionally damaged Jake had become and it would have gotten back to Claudia one way or the other. She couldn't have risked it.

After Jake's death, she'd felt as if someone had slipped a key into a lock, opened a door. She was a bird with an open cage door and the wide world beckoning to her and she couldn't spread her wings and fly, terrified that instead of taking flight, she would hit the ground hard.

Rafferty's hot eyes were still on her face. It was unsettling, this chemistry between them.

"You'll get by," Rafferty murmured softly. "You'll make a new life. Kyle will adjust."

"How can you be so sure?" she whispered.

"Because you're rock solid."

"How do you know that? You don't know me."

"I can see it in your face, in the set of your shoulders, the way you cradle your baby and because my mother wasn't solid or strong or dependable. It feels rough now, but you've got the right stuff, Lissette."

The way he spoke her name—the name she'd never much liked—as if it was the most beautiful name in the world, raised goose bumps on her arms.

"I don't feel strong. I feel like a dandelion. Blown every which way by life's winds," she confessed.

"Flexibility is what makes dandelions so strong," he said. "They have several ways of reproduction—through seed, through pollination, through buds, even through taproots. You can't keep a good dandelion down. They look delicate and ephemeral, but they are as resilient as any plant on earth."

She had to laugh at that. "They're pesky weeds."

"Beauty is in the eye of the beholder." He took her hand and drew her gently into his arms.

The gesture was too intimate, she knew it, but she didn't stop him. He held her close, Kyle cocked on her hip. She could feel the steady beating of Rafferty's heart. They stood there, the three of them, in that cramped garage apartment, drawn together by circumstance and sorrow.

She'd let him hold her earlier that day, but that had been in a public parking lot. In private, their embrace held added weight and a new dimension of possibilities that scared the living hell out of her.

She stiffened in the circle of his arms and immediately, he released her.

"Lissette," he whispered her name again, breathing butane on the embers.

Her hands were trembling. So were his.

"It's late," she said.

"Yes." He nodded, fully agreeing.

"I need to go."

"Yes."

"Good night." She brought her palm up to Kyle's head, drawing strength from touching him, grounding herself. First and foremost, she was a mother. It trumped everything.

"Good night," he echoed.

As quickly as she dared with Kyle in her arms, she turned and left the apartment, clattering down the stairs, rushing across the damp yard toward the safety of her house. Once inside, she bolted both back doors.

Not to keep Rafferty out, but to keep herself locked securely in.

It was almost ten P.M.

Claudia paced her bedroom, cell phone clutched in her hand. She'd been willing the thing to ring ever since Stewart had brought her home from Lissette's house. The longer it went without ringing, the more upset she grew.

Whose pickup truck with the California plates had been parked in front of her daughter-in-law's house? Could it be? Was it . . . ? Rafferty Jones?

Was that why Lissette hadn't called? Was she entertaining Gordon's illegitimate son? She could only imagine the things he might be saying about her. How much did Rafferty know about the awful thing she'd done?

Claudia closed her eyes. Remembered the moment still so fresh in her memory. How rage had shaken her hands. How jealousy and hatred tasted like peppered vinegar.

How that narrow corridor had smelled like sweat, garbage, and the sickly sweet odor of marijuana.

She'd gone to ugly lengths to protect her own son, to stake a solid claim on her husband. She'd been unable to absolve herself. How could she expect Lissette to understand or forgive her? Then again, it wasn't Lissette's place to forgive her. Rafferty Jones was the one she'd wronged.

Unable to bear thinking of her past mistakes, she finally made up her mind to call Lissette. Swallowing back her self-loathing, she punched in her daughter-in-law's number.

"Hi, Mom," Lissette answered on the first ring, "I was just about to call you."

From the first moment they met, she and Lissette had hit it off. When her daughter-in-law first started calling her Mom Moncrief, Claudia had been so pleased. She considered Lissette the daughter she'd always longed for. After a while, Lissette just dropped the Moncrief part and started calling Claudia Mom. Every time Lissette said it, a warm glow of happiness lit Claudia's heart and she bragged to all her friends about the close relationship she had with her daughter-in-law.

Except not tonight. Something was different. Something was wrong. Lissette sounded so weary, wary.

A heated flush of apprehension coursed through Claudia's body. Dread squeezed her stomach. Had her greatest fear come to pass? Was it indeed Rafferty Jones's truck parked in front of her daughter-in-law's house? Had she learned the terrible truth about Claudia? Would Lissy stop loving her because of it?

Dear God, no. She couldn't bear that. Not on top of everything else. Why, oh why hadn't she told Lissette the truth when they learned Jake had left his life insurance money to Rafferty?

Claudia could barely breathe. "Lissy, are you all right?"

"No." Lissette's voice was high and stringy. She sniffled.

"Are you . . ." Oh dear, oh dear, what had happened? Claudia's insides froze icy. "Crying?"

"It's Kyle," Lissette whispered.

Claudia sat down hard, missed the edge of the mattress, and tumbled to her butt onto the floor. "*Ooph.*"

"Mom? You okay?"

"What's happened to Kyle?" Claudia could hear her own voice shattering like crisp peanut brittle under an angry fist. Here she'd been selfishly worried about her own past misdeeds when Lissette had been laboring under the weight of something bad.

"He's . . . It's why I didn't call you . . . I didn't know how to say it. Couldn't bear to say it out loud."

Claudia rubbed her stinging rump—she'd gotten a bit bony down there—concentrating on the physical pain as a way to blunt the emotional turmoil that she knew was coming. A hundred horrible thoughts raced through her brain.

Leukemia. Autism. A brain tumor.

"What is it?"

"He . . ." Lissette hiccupped. "He's going deaf."

"What?"

"Kyle is losing his hearing."

"Oh," Claudia said. She had a split second to process the information and then relief rolled through her. Thank God! It wasn't autism. Or cancer. They would get him hearing aids and teach him to read lips and look into surgery. This wasn't the end of the world. They could be proactive. Do something about this. Fix her grandson. "Well, okay then. We can handle this."

"The hearing loss is progressive. Nonreversible. It's genetic," Lissette whispered.

"No one in our family is deaf," Claudia said, feeling defensive.

"I'm not pointing fingers. Apparently, your family carries a recessive gene for deafness, as does mine. It takes two parents who carry the recessive gene that creates this form of deafness," Lissette explained. "Jake and I were a perfect storm for producing deaf children. A bad genetic match."

"You were good together," Claudia said staunchly.

"No," Lissette whispered, and Claudia knew she was not talking about just genetics now. "No, we were not."

A stony silence, punctuated by Lissette's harsh breathing, settled in her ear. Every elongated second was torture, ticked off by a range of emotions too complicated to express, all shades and hues of dark bleakness.

Jake was her son. Her baby. Her only child. Pain and sorrow burned through her then, stoking unexpected anger that Claudia hadn't known was nibbling on the edge of her brain like some kind of bloodthirsty zombie.

"You were perfect together," Claudia snapped, frantic with despair. "Jake took damn good care of you—"

"Don't go there," Lissette warned, her tone suddenly deadly.

Alarm spread through Claudia. "What do you mean? Jake was—"

"I can't do this right now."

Claudia fought off the ugly brain-eating zombie whispering nasty things. *Jake didn't take good care of her. He wasn't a good husband or father. He was broken. Something inside him wasn't quite right.* No. No. She refused to hear it. "My son bought you a beautiful home. He—"

"Claudia, I'm warning you. Not another word or I'll hang up this phone."

Taken aback, she snapped her mouth closed. Lissette *never* interrupted, had never spoken to her like this. Normally, she was agreeable, easygoing. A real sweetheart.

Lissette always made her feel comfortable, welcome, and she readily accepted Claudia for who she was.

Ah, but she doesn't know the real you. She has no clue exactly what you're capable of.

While part of Claudia was startled by the change in her daughter-in-law, another part of her sat up and took notice. Lissette was setting boundaries, asking for what she needed. Claudia respected that, wondered where Lissette's gumption had come from. She was proud of her, even as her feelings were hurt.

This wasn't Lissette's fault. She was in pain over Kyle's diagnosis and she was letting her own grief drive a wedge between them.

"I'm sorry," Claudia apologized immediately. "So sorry, Lissy."

"I know, I know. Let's not point fingers. It's just the way it is." Lissette sounded so controlled under the circumstances. How could that be? "Something we have to accept."

"I'm coming over right now. I'll make you a cup of tea and we'll—"

"No!" Lissette commanded. "*Do not* come over here right now!"

The sharpness of Lissy's voice staggered her. "I drove by your house earlier." *Don't say it! Don't say it!* "There was a truck parked in front of your house with California plates."

"Yes."

Another long silence stretched between them. What did Lissy know? What had Rafferty told her? Claudia couldn't bring herself to mention his name. "You don't want me to come over?"

"No." Blunt. Hard.

"When?"

Another long moment passed; finally Lissette said, "I've got a wedding cake to deliver tomorrow. Kyle will be with the babysitter. After that, I'll come over and we can hash this out."

Hash this out? It sounded so ominous. The zombie hissed, *She knows. Rafferty's in Jubilee and he's told her everything. That's why she's being so tough with you.*

You're jumping to conclusions. You have no proof that it was Rafferty Jones's truck parked in front of her house. None at all. But her gut knew. Knew it as surely as she'd known Jake was destined to die young. Her chickens were coming home to roost. Hadn't she just been waiting for it all these years?

"I have to go," Lissette said. "Good night, Claudia." Then she hung up the phone.

Claudia sat on the floor, holding the dead phone, her heart lurching. Lissy had called her by her first name.

The dial tone set up a deafening racket.

Not Mom.

The unraveling of their relationship had started. Claudia hugged her knees to her chest and broke into inconsolable sobs.

Chapter Seven

No more self-pity, Lissette vowed. She was done with that. Pity was a waste of energy. Kyle didn't feel sorry for himself. Why should she? This was a challenge, a hurdle, but she refused to let her son's affliction define either one of them.

She was a warrior mom, going into battle against helplessness and despair. They would get through this one day at a time, one step at a time. They would be happy again. She'd started the healing process last night. She'd talked to Claudia even though the conversation had turned weird. Today, she would go see her mother-in-law in person. Then she would call her parents, but first she had to deliver a wedding cake. It was going to be a long day. Just thinking about everything she had to do made her bones ache.

One step at a time.

After tossing and turning, barely sleeping, she finally got up an hour earlier than her normal six-thirty. Even when she had managed to sleep, bothersome dreams crowded in on her. Disturbing, off-kilter dreams where she and Claudia and Jake were desperately searching for Kyle, who'd gone missing. Then somewhere in the middle of the dream they'd entered a war zone. Claudia disappeared in a bloody ambush and Jake morphed into Rafferty, who found Kyle whole and healthy eating cowboy cookies in Lissette's kitchen. In her dreams, she'd thrown herself into Rafferty's arms and he'd kissed her.

Hot and passionate.

His mouth fired a domino effect that began in the center of her stomach, spreading out in rolling waves. He tasted like heaven, sweet and warm and delicious. She hungered for more.

For a dozy second, happiness had poured over her like warm syrup and then she woke with a start.

Dream. It had been nothing but a dream.

To dispel the strange achiness weighing heavily in her lower abdomen, she started making cinnamon rolls. Thank heavens Rafferty was leaving today. Once he was gone, she could set about finding a new normal for her life.

After she put the cinnamon rolls in the oven, Lissette went to the commercial-grade refrigerator and started taking out the wedding cake she'd baked on Thursday evening. The cake was made up of four tiers and she would transport them in four separate boxes and assemble them once she got to the reception hall at Mariah and Joe Daniels's ranch. The wedding was at ten, but she needed to have the cake set up by nine.

She glanced at the clock. Six forty-five. She had plenty of time. She put the coffee on to brew and went to peek in on Kyle. He was still sound asleep so she tiptoed back to the kitchen before realizing there was no reason to tiptoe. Sadness caught her low, hard, and vicious. She closed her eyes.

Don't think about it. Not now.

She needed something else to focus on. Her mind obeyed and replaced her worries about Kyle with a vivid picture of what had almost happened in Rafferty's apartment last night. They'd come within inches of kissing.

Don't think about him either. Keep your mind on baking. Think about your business. The Texas-themed baked goodies. What recipes do you want to use? How do you intend on getting the word out? How are you going to finance the expansion?

The oven timer went off. She took out the cinnamon rolls and put them on the sideboard to cool. A knock sounded at the French doors that led to the back patio.

Rafferty.

She motioned him inside.

"Mornin'," he said, bringing in the smell of the outdoors with him.

"Hi," she replied, feeling suddenly shy. "Would you like breakfast before you get on the road?"

He paused. "We haven't finished talking about money."

She squared her shoulders, met his gaze. "I'm not taking Jake's life insurance money and I don't want to discuss it anymore. The topic is closed."

In her mind it was a done deal. The money was Rafferty's. She might want it, and wish that Jake had left it to her instead, but the truth was that he had not. At first, she'd felt hurt, shocked, betrayed, but as the months had gone by, she'd come to see it as a hard life lesson. She was responsible for herself and her son. Yesterday, Kyle's diagnosis had stirred up the feelings again, but today her conclusion was the same. It might be nice to be handed a pile of cash, but it wouldn't teach her anything about how to take control of her own financial future.

And Lissette was ready to be in the driver's seat. She'd taken a passive role for far too long. No more going where life's current took her. From now on, she was taking the helm in navigating the river of life, and she was determined to set an example for Kyle. With his hearing loss, he was going to face many challenges. If he saw her bravely making her way in the world in spite of the struggle and coming out triumphant, it would teach him to never give up until he achieved his goals. At this point taking the money would dismantle all her good intentions. She simply could not afford to accept it. Too much was at stake.

Instead of arguing as Lissette expected, Rafferty nodded. "I got that. I wanted to talk about Slate."

"What about him?" she asked warily.

"Before you say no, just hear me out."

She folded her arms over her chest and noticed he had a tiny half-moon scar over his left eyebrow that she hadn't seen before. "I'm listening."

"The Fort Worth cutting horse futurity begins at the end of November. If you enter Slate and he puts up a good showing, you'll be able to sell him for a much higher price, and who knows? He could even advance to the next level and earn you a bit of extra money. You said that Jake had been training him and that he had already paid the entry fee for this year."

"Yes, but that was before he decided to reenlist in the army."

"There's no reason to let the entry fee go to waste."

True enough. "That sounds good, but you said it would cost me three or four thousand dollars to train him. That money is earmarked for expanding my bakery business. I can't do both. The bakery is my future and this thing with Slate is a total gamble."

"Not if I help you. Slate's a good horse. I was just out at the acreage looking him over again."

She wasn't sure she heard him correctly. "You're offering to train the horse?"

"It's what I do for a living."

"Don't you have someplace to be? A ranch to run? A movie to make?"

"I'm in between movies. My ranch foreman handles the day-to-day operations on my ranch. I can take some time off. Let me do this for you."

"Don't feel guilty on my account because Jake gave you the money. I absolve you of all guilt. Go back to California guilt-free."

"It's not guilt," he said. "I have my own reasons for wanting to stay awhile in Jubilee."

"Had you planned on staying for a while before you got here?"

"No," he admitted.

"Why the change of heart?"

"Meeting you and Kyle, I—"

"We don't need you to feel sorry for us." She bristled.

"I don't feel sorry for you." His eyes were on hers, steady as the sun.

"No?" She felt oddly breathless.

"I feel sorry for me. For the father I never knew. For the brother I lost. For the childhood I never had."

"Oh."

"Look, you won't take the money, at least let me do this. It goes against my sense of honor to walk away leaving you and Kyle high and dry."

"We'll be fine."

"I know you will." He looked one hundred percent sincere. "There's no question of that. But don't let pride override common sense. Jake left you the cutting horse. Let me train him and then sell him for you after the futurity is over. It'll do wonders for my ego."

"Ego, huh?"

Rafferty's lips curled in a smile. He was particularly handsome when he smiled. "I want to prove that I'm as good a horse trainer as my father. Better even."

How could she deny him the opportunity? Especially when it benefited her.

"You can pay me with free room and board while I'm here. How does that sound?"

It was so tempting, but dangerous as well and there were Claudia's feelings to consider. "I suppose we could try it for a few days. See how it goes. Trial basis."

His shoulders relaxed. "Okay."

"Would you like a cinnamon roll?" she asked, pushing back the baker's spice rack to make room for the saucers she took from the cabinet.

Her mother had given her the rack for a bakery school graduation present. The hand-carved wood rack was from Williams-Sonoma, a store she could not afford to shop in. The squat glass jars held rich, dark cocoa powder, vanilla sugar, whole allspice, cloves and nutmeg and ground Saigon cinnamon.

"Sounds good," he said. "Smells good too." He came closer until Lissette was hemmed in between him and the corner of the kitchen cabinet. "*You* smell good. Like cinnamon candy."

"It's not me." She held up the spice jar marked "Cinnamon" in block lettering.

"Nope, it's you."

She raised her wrist to her nose. He was right. She did smell of cinnamon.

"It's my favorite spice."

Was Rafferty flirting with her? He didn't seem the flirty type, but she could swear he was flirting with her—the look in his eyes, the closeness, his friendly tone, the compliment. This was why it was dangerous to have him around. Even if he wasn't flirting with her, she was imagining it. Wanting it.

"Here." She shook off the feeling—if he was going be staying here, she couldn't have any of that—and pushed a cinnamon roll toward him. "Help yourself to the coffee."

"Da." Kyle stood in the kitchen entryway in his diaper, pointing at Rafferty. "Da."

"Don't read anything into that sound," Lissette said quickly. She didn't want Rafferty thinking that Kyle was calling him daddy. "It's about the only thing he says." She wiped her hands on a cup towel, moved to pick up her son. "Hey, little man, do you need a dry diaper?"

"What do you feed him for breakfast?" Rafferty asked. "I'll get it ready while you change him."

"You're too helpful, you know that?"

"And you're looking a gift horse in the mouth."

"The Trojan horse was a gift."

"Do you want me to leave?" He inclined his head toward the door.

Did she? "No," she answered truthfully. "I'm just . . ." She searched for the right words so as not to hurt his feelings.

"Cautious. I get it."

"Kyle loves Cheerios. No milk. He eats them dry."

"Where do you keep the cereal?"

She hoisted Kyle onto her hip, nodded toward the pantry.

Rafferty retrieved the cereal box. "Got a little plastic bowl?"

"His Elmo bowl is in the dishwasher."

"Gotcha."

She took Kyle into his bedroom to change him. He squirmed the entire time. When she was done, she put him down and he immediately toddled back into the kitchen ahead of her, clearly fascinated with Jake.

Rafferty had found the bowl and poured up half a cup of Cheerios into it. He squatted down in front of Kyle, gave him a big smile.

Kyle reached for the Cheerios, but Rafferty set the dish

on the table out of his reach. Her son grunted in frustration.

What was Rafferty up to? Lissette stood in the doorway watching him.

Rafferty formed a circle with his right hand, and then slowly and distinctly enunciated, "Cheerios."

Kyle cocked his head, studied first Rafferty's hands and then his face.

Rafferty picked up the dish again, then repeated both the sign and the spoken word.

Immediately, Kyle made a circle with his hand in imitation of what Rafferty had done, along with puckering his little mouth into the shape of an O.

"Good boy!" Rafferty exclaimed, ruffling Kyle's hair and rewarding him with the bowl of Cheerios.

Her son beamed up at him.

Surprised joy squeezed Lissette's throat. She splayed a palm over her chest. Her son had just communicated in rudimentary sign language!

"Are you okay?" Rafferty asked.

Overwhelmed, she nodded, unable to speak.

"Should I put him at the table?"

She motioned toward the dining room table chair topped with a red plastic booster seat.

Rafferty guided Kyle to the table. Lissette turned away, pressed her lips together tight, laid a hand over her mouth. She blinked, busied herself with taping up the boxes filled with the tiers of the wedding cake.

After he had Kyle situated, Rafferty came over to rest a hand lightly on her shoulder. "You sure you're okay?"

"Thank you," she whispered. "I can't tell you how hopeful it makes me feel to see him picking up sign language so quickly."

"It's going to get better," he promised, his touch at her shoulders tightening into a reassuring squeeze.

She quelled a strong urge to lean against him. It was

too much, this contact, their swiftly growing closeness. She stiffened and he responded instantly, dropping his hand, backing off.

"Well," he said. "I have some calls to make. Find out who I know that might be interested in buying a first-class cutting horse."

"Thank you," she repeated.

He headed toward the door, stopped when he got there, turned back around. "Lissette?"

She met his gaze but couldn't read what he was thinking. "Yes?"

"Where's Jake buried? I'd like to visit his grave."

"It's going to get better, I promise," Mariah said, and slung an arm around Lissette's waist when the wedding was over. It had been a ten A.M. ceremony with a reception brunch, and the bride and groom had just left. A few friends and family members lingered in the reception hall, which had been converted from a horse barn, visiting and catching up.

Since she was contract labor and not an employee, Lissette usually didn't hang around once she got the cake set up. But that morning after she arrived, she'd told Mariah about Kyle's diagnosis and Rafferty's appearance in her life. They hadn't had much of a chance to talk beforehand, so she stayed afterward, needing her levelheaded friend's take on her situation.

"I know." So as not to give in to self-pity, she started pulling the white lace slipcovers off the chairs and folding them into neat squares. "I don't think it was such a smart idea for me to let Rafferty stay in the apartment while he trains Slate to compete in the futurity."

"Why not?"

"You know how I am about cowboys." Lissette waved a hand. "They're my fatal attraction."

"Are you saying you're attracted to him?"

"Yes. No. I mean, I could be, and that's what's so scary."

"You're not going to fall for him just because he's a cowboy. You're not that shallow."

"A cowboy who's staying in my backyard. I don't get why he's willing to do this for me. He doesn't owe me anything."

"He probably just wants to help."

"I don't want to feel beholden. Not to him. Not to anyone. Not anymore. Is that crazy?"

"Not crazy, no." Mariah shook her head. "But everyone needs help now and again and this certainly qualifies as one of those times. It doesn't mean you're weak or helpless. Honestly, I think it's kind of sweet that he feels protective of you. Especially since staying here in Jubilee is bound to stir up some negative blowback for him."

"You mean Claudia." Lissette patted the slipcover flat and added it to the pile she was accumulating.

"That's going to be a sticky wicket."

Lissette groaned and covered her face with a hand. Telling her mother-in-law about Rafferty was not going to be fun. "I know. How did I get myself into this situation?"

"Hey, you haven't done anything wrong."

Lissette glanced over her shoulder to make sure no one was in earshot. "I had a sex dream about him."

"Who? Rafferty?"

"Shh."

Mariah looked slightly shocked, but she rushed to reassure her. "It's just a dream, Lissy. It doesn't mean anything."

"It's that stupid cowboy fantasy I've had since I was a teenager. You'd think after things didn't go so well with Jake I would have gotten over it." She snatched up another slipcover to fold. "That's it. I'm going to tell him I made a mistake this morning. I don't need his help selling Slate. Joe or Cordy or Brady would be happy to help me find a buyer. Why did I agree to his scheme?"

"What's the difference if Rafferty helps you or one of your friends?"

"You're right." She gritted her teeth. "I hate being a damsel in distress."

"Men like to feel needed, Lissy."

"Well, he can feel needed somewhere else."

"It's not about Rafferty, is it? Not really."

Lissette slumped down into one of the chairs she'd just stripped of its slipcover. "No," she admitted. "I just don't want to get into another situation like I was in with Jake. He took control and I followed. I don't want to repeat that pattern."

"Rafferty's not Jake. Just give him a chance. And besides, he's not going to be here forever. His time in Jubilee is limited. Cut yourself some slack. Let him train the horse. Hell, bring him to our monthly poker game next Friday. What's the worst that could happen?"

At two o'clock that same afternoon, Rafferty stood on the banks of the Brazos River that ran a serpentine path between the twin towns of Twilight and Jubilee. The river divided the two counties, Parker to the north, Hood to the south.

The October wind blew against the water, whipping up moody whitecaps. Dead leaves fell from the red oaks. They skittered across the asphalt of the empty boat ramp, dry and thin as old bones. Numb gray clouds bunched, threatening to pepper the muddy ground with more rain, and the air smelled briny.

He breathed in the bitter, brittle, brown flavor, jammed his hands into his pockets, and hunched his shoulders. He thought about going back to the truck for his denim jacket but decided not to bother. It felt good, this bracing blast.

A mourning dove cooed from its perch on the highline wire overhead. Far off in the distance, a drilling rig pounded steadily, echoing a hard, steely tempo up and down the river. This part of the country sat on the Barnett Shale, the largest producible reserve of natural gas in the United States. No boats traversed the waterway. No cars passed on the bridge. No one anywhere. In that moment it felt like the loneliest place on earth. And this was where Claudia and Lissette had left Jake. Cremated him. Scattered his ashes. Walked away. Without even a tombstone to mark his passing.

Unexpected resentment rapped on his chest. He didn't know where the feeling came from, but by damn, there should be some kind of monument to honor a fallen solider, some testament to the fact that Jake had existed. He got the feeling his brother hadn't been the best husband or father in the world, but he had mattered, and however briefly, Rafferty had known him, he'd loved him.

"It was Jake's wishes," Lissette had said as he'd stood in her kitchen that smelled of cinnamon rolls. " 'When my time comes, cremate me and don't make a damn fuss. No military brouhaha. No ceremony.' Those were his exact words."

The wind mussed his hair and Rafferty finally gave in and retrieved his jacket. He wandered back down to the water's edge, sat on a large, flat, smooth river rock. The stone was cold, even through the seat of his jeans, and he was glad for the warmth of his jacket. He watched bits of flotsam whirl and twirl down the river.

"Well, Jake," he said, "you sure screwed the pooch. You went back to war when you could have walked away. Left that sweet wife of yours alone. Abandoned your boy. Now he's gonna grow up without a daddy. You don't get how tough it is for a boy without a dad. But I do."

Great. Now you're sounding like a Lifetime movie of the week. Poor you. Suck it up, Jones.

"Still can't believe you left a woman like Lissette," he mumbled. "She's something special. Didn't you know that?"

In his mind's eye, he saw Lissette as she'd looked that morning in the kitchen, a flowered apron tied in a perky little bow around her narrow waist, her busy hands boxing wedding cakes. Those slender, delicate hands produced such smooth, graceful movements. Those hands kneaded and mixed, cut and shaped. And the things she baked—crumb cake and cinnamon rolls—tasted like sugary magic on his tongue. He figured love was like that, created from the heart, sweet and unexpected, like Lissette, drawing him in with the scent of cinnamon and home.

Home.

Nostalgia for something he'd never had drifted over him. But this was not his home. He didn't belong here. He knew that, but stupid thoughts keep crawling through his mind, unwanted and forbidden.

He liked the hint of sassiness in Lissette that reared its head at unexpected times. As if sass were a little-used muscle and she was trying to sneak in a workout. There was something innately compelling about the brown-sugar-haired, warmhearted, single mother that got to him, something that had nothing to do with their current situation. He would have been attracted to her under any circumstances. She possessed an unconscious grace, a quiet, enigmatic sexiness, and a pair of sorrowful green eyes that, when she turned them on him, made him forget his own name.

Guilt crept in then for the way he was feeling about his dead brother's wife. Desire. He wanted her. It was completely wrong. Make no mistake. He knew it, but he wanted her all the same.

Biology. Chemistry. Grief. His habit of falling for women in need. He liked being the one that other people ran to when they were in trouble. Although it always seemed to backfire on him in one way or the other. Any or all of those excuses were true, but in the end, they were simply excuses used to rationalize the sleepless night he'd spent thinking of Lissette and the kiss he'd wanted to steal.

One smart thing. That was the one smart thing he'd done. Or rather, hadn't done.

If he hadn't promised Jake he would take care of her, if he hadn't hatched this scheme to train Slate and enter the cutting horse in the futurity just so he could secretly purchase the stallion from her as an anonymous buyer to save her pride, he would have already been on the road back to California.

The sound of a truck engine drew his attention to the boat ramp where his pickup was parked. So much for solitude. He hadn't made much headway into his conversation with Jake. Hadn't even touched on the gratitude he felt for the way his half brother had saved his ass from prison on that long-ago summer day.

He couldn't make up his mind whether to just stay here or get in his pickup and clear out before the other vehicle showed up. In his hesitation he ended up in the middle of the road, halfway between the rock and his pickup when the other truck came into sight.

It was a familiar black extended-cab pickup with tinted windows.

Lissette.

Chapter Eight

She should have expected Rafferty to be here. Why hadn't she expected him to be here? But honestly, she hadn't even known that *she* was going to be here, coming to the river where they'd scattered Jake's ashes had been a spur-of-the-moment impulse.

Lissette had paid Mariah's babysitter Ruby an extra twenty bucks to keep Kyle for a few more hours while she had a long talk with Claudia. It would be easier; she rationalized, if Kyle wasn't there to stir the emotional pot.

On the drive back to Jubilee, she'd toyed with the ring on the third finger of her left hand. It was time to take it off. She'd only worn it this long because of Claudia. The love she'd once felt for Jake had long disappeared, replaced only with sadness for the lost hopes and dreams and the waste of it all.

That's when an idea had taken hold inside her. Toss the ring into the river. Say good-bye once and for all. Close the book on that chapter of her life.

"Oh, Jake." She sighed. "How did we get here? Once upon a time we had such stars in our eyes." Or maybe it had just been she. In her infatuation with cowboys in general and Jake in particular, she hadn't seen things clearly.

And now here was another cowboy standing in the middle of the boat ramp, staring at her with hungry eyes.

A chilly thrill lifted the hairs on her arms. Rafferty was so sexy! Part of her wanted to throw the truck into reverse and shoot out of there, but how would that look? She forced a smile, parked the truck, and got out.

"Hey," she said a little breathlessly as she rounded her vehicle.

"Hey."

They exhaled simultaneously.

"Where's Kyle?" he asked.

"Babysitter's. I have to go talk to Claudia in person."

Rafferty's gaze searched her face, his eyes attentive as if he was trying to figure out every thought that went through her mind. She wasn't accustomed to this kind of masculine attention. It made her nervous.

And grateful.

Gratitude was the dangerous part.

He bowed his head against the gusting wind, the early afternoon sun slanted over his shoulder. He wasn't wearing his Stetson and his mussed hair curled down the back of his neck. He hadn't shaved that morning and her fingers twitched to trace over the dusting of dark stubble.

He lowered eyelashes as long and thick as Jake's and Kyle's. Something all three Moncrief men had in common. Gorgeous black lashes. Those lashes softened the fine lines at the corners of his eyes. Lines that said he'd brushed up against the hard side of life too soon and too often. On any other man, that hardness would be intimidating. But he wore it like a badge of honor, not a weapon. He made her feel safe.

Something else to worry about.

"You came out here to pay your respects to Jake," she said.

He nodded. "You too?"

"I came—" She halted abruptly, not sure she should tell him the truth, then decided, no, she was just going to say it. "To say good-bye to him one final time."

Clouds passed over the sun, casting them in shadow. "One final time?" he echoed.

Silently, she reached up, removed her wedding ring, and slipped it into her pocket. "I'm tired of pretending."

In the muted light, Rafferty's whiskey-colored eyes darkened, glinted with meaning she couldn't read. Was he upset with her? The taut planes of his face remained impassive. The man kept a tight rein on his thoughts, but of course, he was a cowboy. It was the nature of the beast.

She lifted her chin. "Our marriage was over in our hearts, if not officially, long before Jake shipped off for his last tour. I've only worn the ring this long for Claudia's sake. She was under the delusion that we had the perfect marriage."

Lissette braced herself. Waiting for his anger or his judgment or both.

Instead, he nodded toward a dirt path leading through a forest of nearby public land. "Would you like to take a walk?"

"Yes," she said simply.

He put his arm out, but didn't touch her, rather ushered her toward the thicket, his hand stirring up the air behind her. She could feel him as surely as if he had placed a palm to her back. An involuntary shiver passed through her. Why did she overreact every time he came near her?

"You're cold," Rafferty said, and the next thing she knew he was shrugging out of his blue jean jacket and draping it around her shoulders, leaving him wearing a blue chambray work shirt with the sleeves rolled up a quarter turn. His scent wrapped around her, warm and masculine.

She didn't need him to take care of her and here she

was hugging his jacket around her, pretending she was chilled from the weather and not his proximity. "Thanks. It turned out cooler than I expected. I should have brought a jacket. Odd time of year in Texas. Hot one day, cold the next."

"No problem."

But it was a problem. A very big problem. In the exchange, his knuckles grazed her hand. Her body heated at his touch and she felt her nipples tighten. What was this? A dozen different emotions pelted her—anxiety, attraction, guilt, irritation.

Yes, he irritated her.

They tramped around a fallen log, passed through a cedar copse, their feet crunching crisply on fallen leaves. The wind bit their cheeks. They could no longer see the river, but they could hear it rushing softly toward Lake Twilight.

"Where are we going?" he asked.

"Huh?" For a second, she thought he meant metaphorically, and then realized he was speaking literally. "I don't know." She laughed. "You invited me for the walk."

"This isn't my stomping grounds. I have no idea where this path leads."

"We'll run into a fence soon. A ranch borders the public property. Why?"

"I like to know where I'm headed."

They were walking side by side. She cast a glance at him. "You're the opposite of Jake. He liked to be surprised. When we went on trips he refused to make reservations. He said it killed the spirit of adventure. We ended up staying in some gawd-awful places because of it. On our honeymoon in Corpus Christi, we forgot it was spring break and we ended up sleeping on the beach because there were no rooms to be had."

"Jake was a spontaneous guy."

Lissette couldn't help wondering if he had known Jake better than she had. "We got sand fleas."

"You were a good sport to go along with it."

"I have a tendency to get caught up in whatever tide I find myself floating in and Jake was a tsunami. There was no denying him."

"That's not necessarily a bad thing."

"What?"

"Going with the flow."

"It is if you lose yourself. Jake was a storm who blew through my life," she whispered, feeling terrible because she did not mourn her husband the way he deserved to be mourned. Although the tragedy of his death hurt and saddened her, a shameful part of her had been quietly relieved that the waiting and worrying was finally over. She could at last move on. "He left me breathless and broken."

Rafferty did touch her this time, the tips of his fingers gently pressing against the middle of her spine.

"I'm okay," she said.

"You're amazing. You know that."

She gave a half laugh. "I'm nothing special."

"Stop it." His face turned fierce and the harshness in his voice startled her. "Stop hiding your light under a bushel. You're exceptional, Lissette Moncrief, and it stuns me to think you don't realize that."

She brushed a lock of hair from her forehead. "If I'm so exceptional why did—" She bit down on her bottom lip, stalked ahead of Rafferty.

"What?" He halted.

She stopped, turned back to face him, hauled in a deep breath, and there in the quiet of the forest, she said the words out loud to another human being for the first time. "He was having an affair."

"Jake?"

She nodded, pressed her lips together. Jake had been

the father of her son. A man she once loved until war changed him into a stranger she no longer recognized.

"How do you know?"

"I saw his truck parked outside a no-tell motel."

"He could have been there for another reason."

"It wasn't the first time."

"Lissette," he murmured. "I'm sorry."

"Why?" she said lightly, because it no longer hurt. "This has nothing to do with you."

Rafferty shifted his weight. "He left your money to me."

"Hey, better you than his mistress." She didn't mean to sound bitter, because she really *wasn't* bitter. Just stating facts.

"Tell me more about your business," he said.

She was glad for the change in topic and they started walking again. She told him her plans for the cowboy-themed bakery and all the things she needed to do to make the business a success.

"I could help with that," he offered. "Loan you a little money to get going. Even if Slate wins a purse, it won't be for several weeks."

"We've already discussed this."

"I'm not talking much. A few thousand. Just so you don't have to pinch pennies."

She was about to say no, but she really did need some help if this was going to work. Was Rafferty the right person to borrow money from? "I'll think about it."

"Just say the word and the money is yours."

She reached the barbwire fence before he did, stopped, and turned to find him standing right in front of her.

"End of the road," she said.

They were face-to-face, her back to the fence, Rafferty's shoulders hunched, the sleeves of his blue Western shirt billowing in the wind. He was shielding her, protecting her from the brunt of the cold breeze blowing off the river. She swallowed, uncertain what to say or do next.

"It's peaceful out here." He took a step closer.

"Quiet."

"I like quiet." He rested a hand on the fence post beside her. The muscles in his wrist flexed with tension and his eyes were murky. He had the same look on his face as he'd had last night when they were together in the cab of her truck. The tips of his cowboy boots almost touching hers.

He did not move.

His scent, however, encroached on her. His jacket weighing heavily on her shoulders. He smelled good. Sexy and masculine.

Lissette was suddenly hyperaware of everything—the raspy sound of their comingled breathing, the tingling sensation shooting through her nerve ends, how the material of his jeans stretched across powerful thighs. How his brown eyes actually had sumptuous flecks of gold in them. She thought of honey crisp apples dipped in rich caramel—sweet and tart and gooey delicious.

A strong physical urge pushed through her with an intensity she'd never felt before. Desire. Yearning. Lust.

As irrational as it seemed, her body wanted his. *You just want to feel something again. That's all.* She was feeling plenty of things right now. Plenty scared.

"Lissy," he murmured.

The way he spoke her nickname, so low and rhythmic and gentle, loosened something inside her head. Turned off the faucet of logic or turned on the spigot of capriciousness. The part of her that had been fighting to keep breathing, to put one foot in front of the other, to pick up the pieces of her tattered life, evaporated, and she was left with no defenses, no ramparts.

She was vulnerable, raw, open. So stupidly open to even the smallest glimpse of peace.

"I'm so sorry," she said. "I have to go."

Then before she did something incredibly stupid like allow him to kiss her, she ducked her head and rushed away.

On the way to Claudia's house it occurred to her that if a bystander had seen her and Rafferty together—meeting on the boat ramp, taking a walk, Lissette rushing back with her cheeks flushed and looking guilty—he would have assumed a rendezvous. It hadn't been a tryst but it would certainly look that way to an outsider.

She pulled into Claudia's driveway and stared at the ranch-style bungalow. Her mother-in-law was not going to be happy when she learned Rafferty was in town, working for Lissette, and living in her garage apartment.

By nature, Lissette found conflict uncomfortable, which was the reason Jake had always gotten his way with her. She hated to fight. Disagreements made her feel as if she was being attacked. For the most part, she had trouble taking a stand. She could usually see both sides of an argument. Plus a small voice at the back of her head often whispered, *Why put in your two cents' worth when no one listens anyway?*

Jake used to teasingly call her a fence sitter. "Hey Lissy," he'd ask, "what's the view from the fence?"

One memory from her childhood stood out crystal-clear. When she was three or four years old, she'd gone shopping with her mother and sisters. It was winter and they were bundled in coats. As they crossed the Target parking lot, Brittany, her older sister, was showing off, twirling her sparkly baton and bragging about how she was the prettiest girl in her class. (She was too.) Her mother pushed Samantha in a stroller, and clung to Lissette with her other hand. Across the parking lot, glittery pinwheels, advertising a sidewalk sale, spun gaily in the cold breeze, looking bright as a rainbow.

The spinning entranced her and one thought centered firmly in the front of her mind. *I want it.* Her desire was so clear. She thought of nothing else, but she wanted that pinwheel. She broke away from her mother's hand and dashed for the display.

Car brakes squealed. Her mother screamed her name. A horn honked so loudly in her ear that Lissette startled, snapped from the mesmerizing pinwheel trance. She stared quivering into the hot, yawning, bug-splattered grille of a tangerine-colored sports car that had halted just inches from her nose.

Her mother reached her, fell to her knees, scooped Lissette into her arms, and squeezed her so hard against her chest that she couldn't breathe. The rough material of her mother's tweed coat scratched Lissy's cheeks, already raw from the cold weather. She tried to separate from her mother, struggled to breathe, but the harder she moved against her the more difficult it was to catch her breath. Her mother's distress became her own.

"Don't ever, don't ever . . ." her mother wailed.

A man got out of the orange sports car. "She just darted out in front of me. Zip, like a lightning bolt."

"You almost killed my child," her mother screamed, still squeezing Lissette with every ounce of strength she had in her. "She could have died."

Lissette felt she could either keep struggling and have the life squeezed out of her or go limp into her mother's arms. She let go, stopped fighting to breathe, accepting what was, and when her mother finally released her, she felt strangely disappointed.

She shook off the memory, and bracing herself for the conversation she'd been dreading all morning, Lissette tapped lightly on her mother-in-law's front door, and then pushed it open and stepped over the threshold. "Knock, knock," she called.

"Lissy?" Claudia's voice drifted thinly to her from the back room.

Her mother-in-law hadn't changed the house since Jake was in high school. A coatrack made of deer antlers stood in the foyer, a yellow rain slicker hanging from one of the horns.

Lissette ran a hand over the paneled wall as she walked down the corridor. "Where are you at?"

"Bedroom."

Claudia didn't sound right. Concerned, Lissette made her way to the back bedroom. The door was ajar, and before she even pushed it open, apprehension closed over her.

Nudging the door farther open with the toe of her boot she realized for the first time that she was still wearing Rafferty's blue denim jacket. It was too late to take it off now. The sleeves hung below her fingertips. Involuntarily, she curled her hands into self-conscious fists.

She stepped into the room and smelled an aroma she did not normally associate with her mother-in-law.

Alcohol.

An empty bottle of Merlot rested on the oak hardwood floor. On the bedside table sat a glass with a few swallows of red wine left in it. From the old-fashioned record player in the corner, Billie Holiday sang the blues. It was the middle of the day and Claudia was drinking?

"Are you sick?"

"Does heartsick count?" Claudia sat in the middle of her bed in her nightgown, her eyes red-rimmed and a box of tissues beside her. Spread out in front of her lay photographs covering every inch of the duvet. There were pictures of Lissette and Kyle, snapshots of Claudia and Gordon when they were young, but predominantly, the photos were of Jake.

Jake as a newborn swaddled in a powder blue blanket. Jake on his first birthday, diving into a chocolate cake and wearing nothing but a diaper. A four-year-old Jake holding a fishing pole in one hand, a three-inch sun perch in the other. A similar photograph a year later, Jake holding a front tooth in one hand, a dollar bill in the other, and wearing a wide, gap-toothed grin. And as he grew older there was Jake with a broken arm. Jake with a broken leg. Jake with a black eye. Jake with stitches in his forehead.

Oh, Claudia. Lissette's heart twisted. "Mom, how long have you been in bed?"

"All day," she declared, hiccupped loudly, slapped a palm over her mouth. Laughed.

"Have you eaten anything?" Lissette moved aside some of the photographs and sat down on the end of the bed. Her gaze fell on the picture of her and Jake at their wedding. They were both grinning like fools, but even then, there was something about the untamed look in Jake's eyes that troubled her now. Why hadn't she seen it then? Quickly, she glanced away.

"I'm not hungry."

"You gotta eat something. Let me fix you some soup." Lissette started to get up.

Claudia grabbed her. "No, stay here. Tell me about Kyle."

She sighed. "Maybe this conversation should wait until you feel better."

"I feel fine."

"You've been drinking."

"So." Her chin-length silver bob was mussed flat in the back from the morning spent in bed. "I'm over twenty-one."

Lissette hesitated.

"Talk. I'm fine," Claudia insisted.

Slowly, in excruciating detail, she told her mother-in-law everything that the doctor and audiologist had told her the previous morning. How was it possible that only one day had passed since she'd received the terrible news?

Claudia sat there looking like she was about to come unraveled. Where was the strong-willed woman that Lissette usually leaned on?

Her mother-in-law's shoulders shook. Her chin trembled. She was quaking all over. Her head bobbing from the force of her sorrow. Lissette felt it. Claudia's grief. Deep in her bones. The same way she'd immersed into her mother's distress on that long-ago day in the Target parking lot.

It tore clean through her. She moved closer, scrunching pictures between them, and wrapped her arms around her mother-in-law.

Claudia clung to her. Sobbed. "First we lose Jake and now . . . and now . . . poor little Kyle is going deaf. It isn't fair, dammit. Life is not fair."

"No one ever said it was," Lissette said calmly.

Suddenly, Claudia reached out and grabbed Lissette's left hand. "You stopped wearing your wedding ring."

"I'm a widow. It's time to let go."

"It hasn't even been a year," Claudia protested. "Hell, it hasn't even been six months."

Maybe not, but their marriage had been emotionally over for quite some time. "He's not coming back," she said gently.

"I know that, I know that, but I thought you would honor his memory—"

"I have honored his memory. I still do." Lissette considered telling Claudia about her suspicions that Jake had cheated on her, but one glance in her mother-in-law's face and she knew she couldn't do it and there was no way she could tell her about Rafferty. Not now. Not while she'd been drinking. Claudia was hurting so badly.

Lissette lowered her tone, drew in a deep breath to

calm herself. "I have to do this for me, Claudia. I have to let go of Jake in order to be strong enough for Kyle. You understand that. I know you understand it because that's what you did for Jake when Gordon died."

Claudia shook her head. "No. Jake was twenty when Gordon died. It wasn't the same." She reached up to pluck at a metal button on Rafferty's denim jacket.

Lissette gulped, prayed Claudia wouldn't ask why she was wearing a man's oversized jacket.

"I'm afraid," Claudia whispered.

"Afraid of what?" Lissette leaned forward, touched her forehead to Claudia's. She smelled of talcum powder, roses, and Merlot.

She cupped Lissette's cheek in her palm. "That you'll forget Jake. That you won't tell Kyle who his father is."

"Jake gave me my son," Lissette said. "There's no way I can ever forget that. And you're going to be around to tell Kyle's children about his father. There's no way my boy is not going to know who his dad was."

"You mean that?" Claudia whispered. "You're not going to cut me out of Kyle's life?"

Lissette pulled back, looked her squarely in the eyes. "Now why would I do that?"

She shrugged, nodded at Lissette's bare left hand. "You'll meet a new man. Fall in love. Move away."

"No," Lissette said. "I'm not moving away. My home is here. My friends are here. *You're* here."

Relief and gratitude glistened in Claudia's eyes. "You mean it?"

"I'm expanding my business. If I wasn't serious about staying would I do that?"

"Expanding your business?"

"Kyle's got to have medical attention, therapy, special education classes. None of that is going to come cheaply. I'm planning on including cowboy-themed pastries. Then when that takes off, I hope to open a storefront in town."

Claudia brightened, wiped at her eyes with the back of her hand. "I think I *am* hungry now," she said. "But let's not have soup. I've got a pint of Häagen-Dazs butter pecan in the freezer. Grab it and two spoons and come tell me all about your plans."

Lissette smiled, patted Claudia's hand, got up, and wandered into the kitchen. They'd weathered that squall, but she knew the storms were far from over. Eventually, she'd have to tell Claudia about Rafferty.

Not if you send Rafferty away first. Avoid the pain altogether.

She opened the freezer door, stared unseeingly inside. Cold air blasted her face but at the thought of sending Rafferty away, her stomach turned hot and unsettled. He'd come out of nowhere, an answer to her prayers.

That's not good. You shouldn't depend on anyone else. This is your son, your bakery business. Ask Rafferty to buy Slate from you and then send him on his way. It's the best solution all around.

But he was, after all, Kyle's uncle. This might be the only time her son had a chance to know him. The boy needed a strong male role model. No denying that.

Where was that ice cream? Rooted to the spot, Lissette nibbled her bottom lip, couldn't see what was right in front of her.

If she didn't ask Rafferty to leave, then she had to tell Claudia before someone else did. As soon as word got out that he was living in her garage apartment, the town would be buzzing with the news.

Let's be honest, Lissette, whispered a subversive voice in the back of her head. *About the real reason you want to send him away. He makes you feel something you're ashamed of feeling.*

Yes. It was true. This afternoon at the river, she'd

nearly begged him to kiss her, and that was the true root of the problem.

She didn't trust herself around him.

Finally, she saw the pint of Häagen-Dazs, curled her fingers around the icy carton, the cold seeping into her skin.

Asking Rafferty to leave would be far easier than causing Claudia more emotional pain. Far easier than examining the real meaning of the world-rocking chemistry surging between them.

She had no choice. Rafferty had to go.

Chapter Nine

Whenever she baked, Lissette remembered what she'd been born for. Feeding people. Making them smile. Bringing a sweet taste of heaven straight down to earth.

In pastry school, her instructor had been a flamboyant Frenchwoman aptly named Madame Boulanger. "I believe in zee church of dessert," the raven-haired teacher, who could have been Cleopatra's twin, declared on the first day of class. Eyebrows arched high, nose in the air, hand placed dramatically over her heart, she went on. "If you are not at this moment a true believer, then you must quickly become a convert or you will fail my class. Only believers are allowed in *my* kitchen. Only the lovers of cake. If you do not love cake . . ." She made a slicing motion with her index finger across her throat. "You are dead to me."

Lissette broke from her normally reticent nature. She'd grinned, pressed her palms together in supplication, bowed her head, and announced, "Let us pray. Dear Cake that art in Madame Boulanger's kitchen—"

The rest of the class gasped, gaped, and it was only then that Lissette realized she'd come across as if she were mocking the Frenchwoman, but the truth was the exact opposite. She'd been so swept up by finding a teacher who loved baking as much as she did—and took it as seriously as a religion—that spirit had moved her to express her joy in an impromptu kitchen prayer.

Wincing, she'd raised her head, her mind frantically searching for an acceptable apology. How awful if she got kicked out of school on the first day.

Her fellow students stood goggle-eyed; some looked uncomfortable and embarrassed for her. Others appeared gleeful in their schadenfreude.

"What is your name?" Madame Boulanger demanded, hand on her hips.

"L-Lissette."

"That is a French name."

Lissette gulped, barely managed to eke out, "Yes."

"You." Madame Boulanger snapped her fingers. "Come here to me."

This was it. She was being dismissed. She was going to have to go home and confess to her parents she was a one-day washout. Hangdog, she'd shuffled over.

The instructor rested her hand on Lissette's shoulder. "For the rest of the semester, you are my favorite student." She turned to the other students, delivered them a hard glare. "The rest of you must strive to be as inspired by baking as Lissette." She pronounced her name *Lees-ette.*

Stunned, Lissette stood there blinking for a moment until it sank in that not only had she not been tossed from the class, but Madame Boulanger had just anointed her teacher's pet.

Madame Boulanger was from Lyons and frequently expressed heartfelt contempt for all things Parisian. She hated Paris as much as she loved bread. "Lyons," she loved to say, "is the true France."

She heaped special attention and privileges upon Lissette, and while Lissette had soaked up every bit of the knowledge the eccentric French pastry chef bestowed on her, Lissette's time at the Dallas Le Cordon Bleu College of Culinary Arts had been anything but pleasant.

Her jealous peers ostracized her, and for someone who liked making other people happy, she spent her days navigating stormy kitchen seas. They would sabotage her desserts, changing the temperature on the oven when she wasn't looking, tossing handfuls of salt in her batter behind her back, removing the labels from the extracts and replacing them with false ones.

To blunt her loneliness, she threw herself into baking and quickly excelled far past everyone else in the class. Which only increased her isolation. Still, she persevered and graduated with top honors.

"It is painful, being a great artist," Madame Boulanger whispered to her when she handed her a diploma. "You have a natural gift, Lissette. Do not waste it."

She had to wonder what Madame Boulanger would think of a Texas-themed bakery. Would she approve or turn up her nose and pronounce it beneath Lissette's talent?

Strive, strive, always strive for excellence. Her old teacher's favorite mantra popped into her head.

Which was what she was doing this very minute. Baking. For two reasons. One, to test out potential new recipes for her business, and two, to keep herself busy while she waited for Rafferty to return so she could tell him that he had to leave.

After polishing off the pint of ice cream with Claudia, she'd gone to pick up Kyle from the babysitter and she'd come home feeling restless and edgy. She knew the only cure was to get elbow-deep in pastry dough. Kyle had been wired after playing all day with Jonah, so even though it was late afternoon, Lissette had put him down for a nap.

She still hadn't called her parents or told her friends about Kyle's deafness, but she had at least talked to Claudia. One step at a time. Tomorrow. She'd tell her parents tomorrow.

Tonight, she had to ask Rafferty to leave.

As she mixed the ingredients, she practiced the speech in her head. *You're a nice guy. I really like you, but—*

A knock sounded at the French doors and she jerked her head up to see Rafferty cradling a stack of books in the crook of his arm. Feeling both apprehensive and stupidly happy to see him, she waved him inside with flour-dusted fingers.

He came in, clicking the door closed behind him. His Stetson was tipped back on his head, giving him a rakish appearance. He smelled of autumn and musty yellowed paper. Just looking at him made her breathless.

"Hey," he said. "Something sure smells good."

"Roast in the Crock-Pot, dinner rolls in the oven, and I'm working on a prickly pear cactus cake for dessert. New recipe." She might as well feed the man before she tossed him out. Unpleasant news went down easier on a full stomach.

"You can make cake from a cactus?"

"I can make dessert from anything," she bragged.

"Not the least bit cocky, huh?" His smile warmed her from the inside out.

"It's not cocky if you can back it up."

"I enjoy seeing you like this."

That comment had her dropping her gaze to the greased and floured pan she was pouring the prickly pear batter into. She hunched her shoulders against the weight of what she didn't want to tell him and concentrated on scraping the bowl with a red rubber spoon. The final bit of batter dripped teardrops into the cake pan.

He cleared his throat. "Lissette?"

Reluctantly, she set down the bowl and raised her chin. Her kitchen suddenly seemed far too bright with the evening sun glinting through the windows and the recessed halogen lights shining down on the white marble countertop. She'd wanted a cheery kitchen, but now it was almost blindingly dazzling.

"Hmm?" She wiped her hands on a kitchen towel so old the hem had started to unravel. A wisp of yellow thread dangled loose.

"Is something wrong?" His voice lowered.

"No, nothing wrong." She licked batter from an index finger, tried to ignore the tension pulling down her spine.

"You sure?" His gaze scorched her mouth.

She froze with her finger on her bottom lip.

He shifted the books in his arms, his gaze moving up to meet her eyes. "Lissette?"

"Whatcha got?" She nodded at the books in his arm, desperate for something to look at besides his face.

"I've been to the library," he said.

"Oh?" She felt faintly dizzy.

"I was doing some research on my lineage. Did you know the Moncriefs are quite an influential family in North Texas?"

"Wrong branch of the family tree. We aren't kin to those Moncriefs."

"So I learned. Story of my life." He turned and settled the books on the dining room table, then came into the kitchen with her. "But I checked out these books for you."

"You got a library card?"

He looked amused. "It was the only way they'd allow me take out the books."

"You had to give a local address in order to get a library card."

"I put down your address. I hope that's okay."

"Rafferty," she exclaimed, hearing her voice peak high on the last syllable of his name. "Now everyone in town is going to know you're staying here."

"I see." He stood incredibly still, not moving, not saying another word. The kitchen island was between them, wide and safe. He stepped around it, demolishing her safety zone. His boot made a soft but determined sound against the terrazzo. Not so secure now. Closer. Quite close.

Too close.

Habit twisted her hands around the cup towel, not just wiping off remnants of cake batter, but building a thin barrier between them. She hitched in a breath, trying to draw in air past the sparks of desire and shroud of misfortune that made her long for a man she should not, could not want.

"Come here," he said so tenderly it set her bones quaking. He reached out his hand and gently encircled her left wrist with his thumb and index finger.

She didn't resist. Let herself be led. Oh, why was she such a bendable dandelion? Swaying whichever way the wind blew? Why couldn't she have been born a sunflower? Thick and stalky. Following the light instead of getting caught in life's currents. Why was taking a stand and sticking to it so difficult for her? Why couldn't she be tough and bitchy?

But here she was, allowing Rafferty to lead her smooth and easy—as if they were waltzing—into the dining room. His calloused palm was so sweetly rough she fought against closing her eyes and committing the feeling to memory before she lost it forever.

Tumult.

Stop it. Stop it. Whatever you're feeling is just some weird reaction to finding out about Kyle's condition. It's sexual attraction or loneliness or a messy combination of both. It's a distraction. A dream. Nothing real. Nothing to bank on.

He let go of her hand, picked up a thin book with a green spine and cookies on the front cover, and put it in her hand. *How to Start a Cottage Bakery in Texas.* Another book. *How to Write a Business Plan.* Then another. *Your Road to Financial Freedom.*

The books weighted her arm, anchoring her to the spot. He'd been thinking of her. Checked out these books for her. Jake never read, much less went to the library. He had enough reading in school, he'd told her once when she tried to get him to read *To Kill a Mockingbird.* But Lissette loved books. She read to Kyle all the time.

Read.

To her deaf son.

Why hadn't she known?

The title of the next book Rafferty stacked on top of the others caused her heart to stumble. *Hearing Loss in Children.* There were two more books. One on baby sign language, the other book on American sign. Her knees trembled.

The last book on the table was another thin volume. Black with gold lettering. *The Poems of Charles Baudelaire.*

"What's that?" she asked.

He snatched it up, tucked it behind his back. Looked as embarrassed as if she'd caught him with a copy of *Penthouse.* "That's for me."

Bemused, she met his gaze for the first time since he'd brought her into the dining room.

"Poetry?"

"Reading poetry helps me relax when I have trouble sleeping."

"Okay," she teased, but she loved how incongruous it seemed—a rugged cowboy reading poetry. "If you say so."

"You've never heard of cowboy poetry?" he asked, eerily reading her mind.

"Sure."

"Stop smirking."

"Who me?" She couldn't stop smirking and she had no idea why.

"Just because I never finished high school doesn't mean I can't read. I did get a GED."

"I didn't mean anything by it. I'm sorry if you thought I was making fun of you. Thanks for the books. That was kind of you to think of me."

He shrugged. "Maybe black and white facts can help you see your way through this rough patch."

"That's why poetry doesn't fit," she said. "Not because you're a cowboy, but because you're a pragmatist."

He wagged a finger and his eyes crinkled at the corners. "You don't know me well enough to make that assumption."

She didn't know him at all. Lissette settled the books back on the table. "Thank you for the books. You're right. I need to make a plan. Both for the business and for Kyle."

"I hate seeing you struggle."

"I'll be okay."

"I have no doubt." His eyes burned golden in the slanting orange rays of the setting sun, slipping through the thin sheers covering the French doors.

This was it, the perfect time to ask him to leave.

She straightened her shoulders, forced her chin up, and met his eyes. "Rafferty."

"Lissette," he mocked, his tone lightheartedly somber.

"About this afternoon at the river . . ."

He took a step closer. Bent his head. His masculine scent stirred her in untold ways. "Yes?"

"It was . . . I was . . ."

"Special," he whispered.

"No. Yes. That wasn't what I was going to say."

"It's what *I* was going to say."

She put up a stop-sign palm. Universal sign language. *Don't come any closer.*

But he didn't stop. He took another step, and the next thing she knew her palm was touching his chest and she could feel his heart pounding rapidly through the cotton material of his shirt.

They stood there for so long. Just gazing at each other, Lissette's palm stop-signed against his chest. No talking. Simply staring in wonder at what was passing between them. The yeasty smell of home-baked rolls wrapping them in a snug hug of aroma.

And if Kyle hadn't started crying, they might have stood there until the very end of time.

Thirty minutes earlier Claudia had gotten a disturbing call from Peony Clark, a member of her book club and the weekend librarian at the Jubilee Public Library. They'd known each other for thirty-four years since they met at Lamaze class. Both of them had been husbandless at the time. Gordon was off on the cutting horse circuit, while Peony had just divorced her no-good husband because he wouldn't work. They'd become each other's coaches since they were the only two in the class not part of a couple.

"I didn't know Lissette had long-term, out-of-town company staying with her," Peony began right off the bat. She wasn't the sort to pussyfoot around a topic. "He's such a young, handsome man."

The truck with California plates.

Claudia's tongue stuck to the roof of her mouth.

"He came in to check out books on how to start a cottage bakery and what to do if you have a deaf child and a book of poems by some Frenchman."

Claudia bit down on a knuckle to keep from groaning out loud. There wasn't a shred of privacy in Jubilee. You checked out a book and ten minutes later the whole town knew about it.

"Do you know who he put me in mind of?" Peony mused.

"Who?" she whispered, hand to her throat.

"Gordon."

Claudia closed her eyes, tightened her grip on the phone. It *was* he. She'd feared as much from the minute she'd seen the truck parked in front of Lissette's house, but now she knew it was true. Rafferty Jones. And he was staying at Lissette's house?

She supposed she'd been in denial, thinking that Rafferty would never show up here. He had his money. There was no reason for him to come to Jubilee. As each day passed without him putting in an appearance, she began to breathe a little easier, but secretly, she'd been waiting. Dreading the inevitable. Eventually, everyone was going to learn about her awful secret.

After Jake died, Lissette had asked her about Rafferty, but she'd brushed off the question because she'd been too ashamed and too shocked by Jake's bequest to discuss it. Bless her heart, Lissy had just let it lie.

Peony, however, was not shutting up. "Is Lissy keeping company with him?"

"No," Claudia snapped. "Listen, Peony, I have to go."

"Okay, I just wanted to give you a heads-up, because he really is handsome and if he's staying with Lissy, people in town will start talking."

People like you.

"Thanks, bye." Claudia hung up.

Agitated, she grabbed up her keys from the cobalt carnival glass bowl resting on her hutch and headed for the garage. By the time she got to Lissy's house, nausea sat high in her stomach. The street in front of the Victorian was empty, but when she pulled into the driveway, she saw the plump rump of the red Dodge Ram dually. The same truck she'd seen before with those damning California plates.

She killed the engine, sat there for a long moment, drumming her fingers on the steering wheel. *Don't go in. Just go back home.* But she had to find out what was going on.

Twilight elbowed out the dying rays of the evening sun as Claudia edged toward the back patio doors. She stopped underneath the old elm tree when she spied Lissette standing in the middle of her dining room with a tall, lanky man who looked so much like Gordon that Claudia almost cried out.

Cupping a hand over her mouth, she stood watching, unable to move as her daughter-in-law put out her palm and Rafferty Jones took a step forward until Lissy's hand was resting at the level of his heart.

It was such an intimate scene, a man and woman gazing into each other's eyes, totally spellbound, like something from a romantic movie.

Oh God. Claudia's stomach roiled. She'd never seen Lissette gaze at her son with that blissed-out expression. It was a look of pure, unadulterated hero worship.

A vile reptile of jealousy slithered through her. Jealousy because Amelia Jones's son was alive and hers was not. Jealousy because Lissette was looking at Rafferty as if he hung the moon and painted the sky with stars. Jealousy because she feared losing the two things she had left: Lissy's friendship and her grandson.

On legs stiff as wooden picks, she spun around and stalked back to her car, barely able to breathe, her mind a jumble of past, present, and future, a future where she no longer had Lissy and Kyle in her life. Once her daughter-in-law found out what she'd done—

She broke off the thought, couldn't bear to think it. Rafferty had been so young. Maybe he didn't remember her? Hopefully, maybe, please God. But even if he didn't remember, she had no doubt that Amelia would have told him. Poisoned. Claudia had been so filled with poison when she'd learned about Gordon's indiscretion.

It hadn't been Rafferty's fault. None of it. And yet, she'd taken her anger out on that little boy. Nothing in her life shamed Claudia more than what she'd done twenty-seven years ago. She'd been crazy out of control. Madly in love with Gordon and jealous to the bone. Were there any worse sins than the ones committed in the heated rage of jealousy?

Cataleptically, she shot from the driveway, peeled off down the street as fast as she dared in a family neighborhood. Rod Stewart was on the oldies channel of the satellite radio declaring that the first cut was the deepest. Ain't that the damn truth? Not only the deepest but the widest as well, with pain that eviscerated your entire life.

She squinted to see through the windshield, and that's when she realized she was crying. *Again? Seriously, Claudia?* Here she was middle-aged, slipping rapidly toward senior citizen status, in prairie skirt and cowboy boots, ricocheting around Jubilee like a spent bullet.

Sometime later—she had no idea how long because she'd been traveling in circles, but she'd already driven through a Beatles triple shot including "Hey Jude," Bob Seger's "Old Time Rock and Roll," "The Weight" by The Band; Three Dog Night; The Who; and now the Rolling Stones were telling her that she was "Out of Time"—Claudia made it back to her side of town.

Even so, she was still trembling, fueled by jealousy, shame, regret, and bone-deep grief that she could not shed.

The sky was inky black, only a sliver of ghostly moon showed through the filtering clouds. Suddenly, she felt too exhausted to breathe. She pulled over on the side of the road, dropped her face into her hands, and sobbed for all that had gone wrong in her life. She'd been hurt and betrayed and she'd lost the two most important things in the world.

Her husband and her son.

And now poor little Kyle was going deaf and Lissette was drifting rapidly away from her with the man that

Claudia had cheated out of his birthright. Why, oh why had she done it? There was no taking it back. No unsaying it. No undoing the damage she'd done.

"Damn you, Claudia Marie Bonham Moncrief. Damn you to hell." She pounded on the steering wheel.

Fresh tears slipped down her cheeks. Suffering ripped through her. She closed her eyes, swallowed hard.

Just go back. Introduce yourself to Rafferty. Tell him what you did. Put it all out in the open. Apologize. Ask for his forgiveness.

Secrecy was what gave sins their power. Or so said her minister. But it wasn't so easy, confessing the most awful thing you'd ever done. Risk losing the love and respect of the daughter-in-law she loved as much as she would have loved her own daughter.

Claudia remembered the painful day Jake had learned about Rafferty. It was right after Gordon's funeral and he'd been going through his father's things and found the letter from that crazy buckle bunny Amelia Jones telling Gordon that he was Rafferty's father. Why had Gordon kept it all these years?

"Why didn't you tell me?" Jake accused.

"It was your father's private business."

"I had a brother! I could have known my brother! You kept me from my brother!"

"Your father said it wasn't true. I chose to believe him." She had lied bald-faced, still trying to salvage her relationship with her son.

He had stared at her as if he didn't know her, his upper lip curled into a sneer. "How could you have stayed with Dad knowing he stepped out on you?"

"I loved him," she said simply, and that part was true. "I loved him since I was eighteen years old. There wasn't a more beautiful sight in the world than your father on a cutting horse."

Jake had snorted, glared at her scornfully. "If that's love, then spare me."

"You don't know the first thing about love."

"Blind cow."

Jake had actually called her a blind cow. It still hurt, even now. Nothing had ever been the same between them.

The next thing she knew, Jake left town without a word and he was gone for the entire summer. He didn't call her, not once. She'd been frantic, but she'd suspected all along where he'd gone. When he came home, the only thing he'd said about it was "I found my brother. He's a good kid. I can't believe Dad never recognized him. Never left him any money. It's not right. It's not fair. And I'll never forgive you for not telling me about him."

Jake had never mentioned Rafferty to her again and for that she was incredibly relieved. But he was forever changed. Grew more arrogant. Harder. He threw himself into a bull-riding career. He did okay, but he was never great at it. But he was good-looking and had his pick of buckle bunnies who followed the circuit. Finally, as he got older, he realized he would never be a world-class champion. His best friend was killed in Iraq, and the next day, he retired from the rodeo and joined the army.

Right after that, he met Lissette, and for a while things were good again. But then he got sent to the Middle East and he fell in love with combat. She could see it in his eyes. Then when Jake was killed she'd been shocked to learn that he'd left all his life insurance money to Rafferty. Trying to make up for his father's mistakes, she supposed. But in the process, he'd made the same error Gordon had. He hadn't taken care of his own child.

Whose fault was that? Because of you, Gordon believed that Rafferty was not his son.

A hand rapped on her car window.

Claudia startled, glanced up. "Oh!"

It was Stewart, wearing a leather jacket and holding a motorcycle helmet underneath his arm.

She switched off the radio, peered into the rearview mirror, saw a Harley-Davidson pulled over on the shoulder of the road behind her.

He rapped again.

She rolled down the window.

His forehead creased in concern. “Are you okay?”

“You’ve got a motorcycle. When did you buy a motorcycle? Why did you get a motorcycle?”

Stewart shrugged. “Middle-aged crazy. Lost-spouse grief. Who the hell knows? But I always wanted a motorcycle, so why not? Who cares if I look like a fool? I only get this one life and I’m going to live it the way I see fit.”

“I did a terrible thing. A mean thing.”

“You?” Stewart sounded as if he didn’t believe her. “You don’t have a mean bone in your body.”

“Shows how much you know me.”

“I know you. I’ve lived next door to you for thirty years. You were my wife’s best friend.”

“I can be very mean.”

He laughed like she had said something earth-shatteringly funny. Little did he know.

“This is not humorous.”

“I didn’t say it was.”

“I’m an awful person.”

“You’re not,” Stewart disagreed. “We all have things we’re ashamed of.”

Claudia tilted her head up to look at him. The headlights from his Harley glinted off his bald head in a totally sexy way. “What are you ashamed of, Stewart English? Did you ever cheat on Linda?”

“No,” he said staunchly. “Never.”

“Then you’re one in a million. What do you have to be ashamed of?”

"Come for a ride with me and I'll tell you?"

"On your motorcycle?"

"On my motorcycle."

"I've never ridden on one of those things before."

"Perfect. It's time to lose your motorcycle virginity."

The virginity line should have offended her. If she were with her church group, she would have acted like she was offended. She was not offended. In fact, she wanted to giggle at the thought that she had any kind of virginity left. "I don't have a helmet."

"You can wear mine."

"What will you wear?"

"Might as well live dangerously. No one is getting out of this alive."

"Life sucks."

"Profound."

"Stop making fun of me. Life does suck."

"Sometimes it does. But not right now. Right now, in this moment, you have the possibility for a fine adventure if you'll just take it."

"I'm wearing a skirt."

"Wrap it between your legs."

"I don't know about this."

"It's not rocket science. You climb aboard, hang on."

She nibbled her bottom lip. Maybe something adventuresome would shake off the dark funk.

"Limited time offer." He held out his hand. "It's now or never."

Why not? What did she have to lose? What was the worst that could happen? She and Stewart get splattered all over the pavement in an accident. After all she'd been through that didn't seem so bad.

God, you're morbid today.

Yeah, well, she'd just discovered her only grandchild was going deaf and her husband's illegitimate son was staying at her daughter-in-law's house. And Lissette had stopped wearing Jake's ring.

"Claudia?"

"Yes, okay, I'll do it. Follow me home, I'll change and then we'll go."

"I'm afraid if I give you that much leeway you'll back out. Come now. Lock your purse in the trunk."

This was stupid. She should just tell him no, but she did not. She locked her purse in the trunk as he suggested and gave him her car keys since she didn't have a pocket.

He tucked her keys in the front pocket of his jeans and led her to the motorcycle. It was big and shiny with chrome. A right large mechanical beast.

Stewart strapped the helmet onto her head, and then got on the bike. She straddled the seat behind him, but was reluctant to wrap her arms around his waist, until he started the engine and she felt the growl of power. She'd better hang on if she didn't want to get thrown off.

Claudia slipped her arms around his waist was startled to realize how strongly muscled his torso was, even at fifty-nine. It felt so novel, touching a man again in such an intimate way.

The Harley took off and Claudia gave a little squealing giggle at the surging acceleration. She hadn't giggled in years. It made her feel giddy, girlish, and foolish.

You're too old for this nonsense.

Maybe so, but she couldn't resist the thrill that buzzed through her system and she found herself resting her helmeted head against Stewart's shoulder.

Stewart drove them through the darkness, faster and faster, until Claudia's heart was riding in her throat. *You shouldn't be here with your best friend's husband.* But Linda was dead. Like Gordon and Jake.

Gone.

The past was past, the future, murky and uncertain.

All she had was right now. Right this minute and she was clinging to the waist of a sexy, bald fireman, the sleeves of her sweater were flapping out behind her as they sped away into the night on a souped-up Harley.

If her neighbors saw them it would set off a gossip storm.

He drove around Jubilee Lake. It wasn't much of a lake as lakes went. Very small, filled mostly with cattails and water lilies. No good for swimming or boating. Mostly, it was a necking spot for young couples. What was it they called it now days? Canoodling? Or was that term passé too? Once you got beyond a certain age, it was hard to keep up. Time moved so swiftly.

The rising moon sent a shimmer of light reflecting across the water. Stewart pulled over to a spot underneath a large pecan tree. The pecans would be coming off soon. Next month. Maybe she'd come back and gather enough to make pecan sandies as a gift to Stewart to thank him for taking her motorcycle virginity.

"Why are we stopping?" she asked after he killed the engine.

He reached up to unsnap the strap from around her chin and lift the helmet off her head. "So I can do this."

He dropped the helmet to the ground and she was so lost in his eyes she didn't even hear it fall. The next thing she knew she was in Stewart's arms and he was kissing her like tomorrow might never come.

Chapter Ten

Rafferty stayed for the pot roast. He shouldn't have stayed, but the thought of eating alone in the garage apartment was too solitary to bear. He was accustomed to taking his meals with his ranch hands, or when he was on a movie set, with the crew. Before Dane and Heather had gone off to college, he'd tried to have a family meal at least once a day, and he missed the ritual with his siblings. Shared mealtime had a way of drawing people closer. That was the danger of eating with Lissette and Kyle.

The three of them sat at the kitchen table just like a family.

Connecting.

It was a damn scary thought. He'd just raised his younger siblings to adulthood, finally gotten his mother straightened out. For the first time ever, his life was his own. He could be selfish for once. Discover what it was that *he* truly wanted. He'd dreamed of such freedom for years.

Why then did he feel the urge to take on the task of shepherding his dead brother's family? A brother he barely knew. He couldn't seem to break the caretaking habit.

Throughout the meal, Rafferty used baby sign language to communicate with Kyle. Focusing on signing the names of food to his nephew—roast, potatoes, carrots, rolls, milk. It helped to keep him from thinking about how his chest still burned from where Lissette's palm had touched his heart.

His nephew.

Rafferty smiled across the table in the cheery lighting, the taste of roasted rosemary potatoes lingering on his tongue.

His nephew.

Rafferty's smile was both rueful and strangely satisfying because "his" was an ownership word that he had no right to use in conjunction with the boy. He didn't want to use it and yet the truth of it wedged in his brain.

Biologically, Kyle *was* his nephew.

When the whip-smart toddler beamed at him, bewilderment punched Rafferty in the gut. How could he feel something so complicated for a kid he didn't even know?

Not just the kid—Rafferty's gaze shifted to Lissette—but for the mother as well.

She smiled back at him, soft and sweet and inviting. Sitting there, a threesome ringing the table, they were like an old Frank Capra black and white movie playing in an almost empty theater, a nostalgic echo of an idealized past.

It's a Wonderful Life. Meet John Doe. You Can't Take It with You.

Bullshit. Whimsical bullshit. He didn't know why he was thinking like this, except his eyes linked with Lissette's and he thought, *I can make a difference here.*

Now that's just ego talking, Jones.

Lissette leaned over the back of her son's chair, a sheaf of brown-sugar hair falling over her neck as she reached around his shoulders to cut his roast into bite-sized pieces.

She rested her chin on the top of his head as she worked. The root vegetables smelled earthy, fragrant of autumn harvest, and it seemed to Rafferty that Lissette fortified her son with riches of the heart, perpetuating a timeless ceremony of maternal communion.

Kyle tilted his head back and looked up into his mother's eyes. She kissed his forehead and they laughed together, bonded in their tight cocoon of love.

Rafferty had never seen anything as special, as beautiful as that look from mother to son.

He felt like an interloper. He mumbled something about getting more sugar for his tea, got up, and walked into the kitchen, his heart suddenly pounding strangely. For what, he had no idea. Something rearranged inside him in the face of that unconditional love. He felt insignificant. Out of place. Unworthy.

And he realized a hard, inescapable truth. No one had ever loved him with that kind of pure, sweet fierceness.

On Sunday morning, Lissette went to church as usual, even though the last thing she wanted to do was go out among the community. So far she'd told only Mariah and Claudia about Kyle's condition. She didn't think either one of them would gossip about it, but she braced herself for sympathy and a barrage of questions just in case.

Nothing was different at the church, where most everyone wore Wranglers and boots and cowboy hats. The church was a plain wooden structure with a simple cross on the steeple. It was nondenominational, unless you counted the cowboy way of life as a religion.

But Claudia wasn't there. She usually sat with Lissette and Kyle and she never missed a church service unless she was ill. Had her mother-in-law been drinking again?

Lissette had thought about asking Rafferty to join them

for church but had quickly dismissed the idea. For one thing, she didn't want to have to explain the relationship to the world at large. For another, she still didn't know how to tell Claudia about him. Besides, he'd left before dawn and he hadn't come into the house to tell her where he was going. To train Slate, she'd assumed.

When she got home from church, he was back. As she unloaded Kyle from the backseat, he appeared on the stairs leading to his apartment, clutching a big brown paper bag.

"My turn to pay you back for dinner last night," he said.

"What?"

"I stopped by a place called the Mesquite Spit and picked up barbecue for lunch. I've also got a surprise."

A surprise?

She felt at once both wary and excited. What kind of surprise?

"Let's eat first," he said, and headed for the back door.

Intrigued, she followed him.

They ate in the kitchen. Lissette brought out the Sunday plates. When she was growing up, her mother used the good china for Sunday dinner, and she'd kept up the tradition, even though most of the time it was just she and Kyle.

Rafferty practiced sign language with Kyle again. Her son was picking it up amazingly fast. He remembered everything Rafferty had taught him from the day before. Maybe his deafness was not going to be as much of a hurdle as she'd thought. At least not from Kyle's angle. The audiologist had told her that children were resilient and adapted quickly. Much more so than adults.

They finished their meal and Rafferty insisted on helping with the dishes. Good-naturedly, he let Lissette tie one of her aprons around his waist so he wouldn't get his shirt wet. Instead of making him look domesticated, the dainty apron accentuated his craggy masculinity, calling attention to his muscular torso, strong sturdy legs, and hard, tight butt.

Lissette swallowed, hyperaware of him.

They stood side by side at the kitchen sink, Lissette washing the delicate china, Rafferty rinsing. On the floor behind them, Kyle sat stacking blocks.

Jake had never helped with the dishes. "Woman's work," he'd bluster in a macho tone of voice and disappear to putter in the garage, hang out with his friends, or watch sports on TV.

On more than one occasion, Claudia had apologized for her son's attitude. "I spoiled him," she'd confessed with a faint smile. "I wanted him to have a happy childhood, so I didn't make him do chores. I can see now where that was a mistake."

Lissette honestly hadn't minded much. Jake was a big, tough guy, after all, a cowboy and a soldier. Besides, she considered the kitchen her domain. Her haven. She really hadn't wanted him mucking around in it and she was used to not having him around. Whenever he was on leave, it disrupted her routine.

But it felt surprisingly nice to have Rafferty by her side, and she was glad she had not refused his help. The clink of silverware against the plates made a reassuring clang, and this peacefulness comforted her. Rafferty soothed like a cool balm on a hot sunburn.

She passed him a plate, and his big tanned hand wrapped around the delicate ecru china. The dishware had been a wedding present from her parents. It had survived longer than her marriage. He held the plate gently, rubbed it in a circular motion until it squeeked. She couldn't seem to stop watching his hypnotic movements.

For one jolting second, she remembered what it had felt like when his work-roughened fingers had rubbed mud from her cheek. She was immediately, outrageously turned on.

"What are your plans for expanding your baked goods business?" he asked, snapping her out of her trance.

"If I'm going to do this right, I need to be very practical about it. I was doing the wedding cakes part-time, basically just to help out my friend Mariah, who runs her own wedding planning business, but it's time I stopped playing around and got serious. So, besides coming up with the recipes, which is the fun part, I've got to set up a home office."

"You'll need a Web site, too."

"How do you know I don't already have a Web site?"

"I Googled you."

"You Googled me?" She wasn't sure how she felt about that.

"It was before I ever came to Jubilee," he said. "I wanted to get some idea what I was getting into, but you didn't turn up in a Google search. Which is good for privacy, but bad for business."

"I never had a need to advertise and besides, with Texas law you can't accept orders and payment over the Internet for goods baked in your home."

"But people could call you up to place orders. Or mail in an order form and payment."

"I think so. I'd have to look into the law."

"Plus you want to expand and open a storefront some day. You need a Web site."

"Great. One more thing on my to-do list."

Rafferty leaned over, reaching for a plate to dry, and his elbow accidentally brushed against her breast.

He froze at the same moment she sucked in a quick, sharp breath. The contact was not intentional. She knew that, but her body responded as if it had been a very deliberate attempt to arouse. Her nipples hardened and her stomach went sloppy soft and she forgot to breathe.

Rafferty backed up fast and looked like he was about to sputter an apology, but then he said nothing.

Ah, he was going to pretend it never happened. Good move. So would she. "Thank you," she murmured.

His eyes widened. "For what? The boob graze?" An unexpected sly grin played across his mouth and an impish spark lit his eyes. "My distinct pleasure."

She loved how he could surprise her, being so sweet one minute, a total guy the next. "Not the boob graze. I'm overlooking the boob graze. Unless you did it on purpose. Did you do it on purpose?"

"Depends," he quipped.

"On what?"

"Whether you liked it or not." The impish light turned sultry. This man possessed raw sexual power that he was purposely keeping sheathed. His gaze swept over her and he curled his fingers into his palms. Struggling, she realized with a start, to keep his physical urges in check.

Heat blistered her cheeks. She decided to ignore that comment and the hungry expression on his face. She wasn't adept at flirtation. Had never been good at it. She tossed her head. "I was thanking you for giving Kyle some attention."

His shoulders relaxed and he pressed his palms against his outer thighs. He'd won whatever internal battle had been going on in his head.

"It's no big deal," he said.

She squeezed the damp dishcloth she hadn't even realized she was clutching in her right hand. "Yes," she said. "Yes it is. You're teaching him sign language. That's huge."

"What kind of guy would I be if I didn't pass on what I know about sign language?"

"It's your ranch foreman that's deaf, correct?" she asked, steering the conversation far away from boob grazes and whether she liked them or not.

He rested his back against the counter, legs splayed and arms crossed. "That's right. Guillermo Santo. In fact, he's the surprise I was telling you about. I've set up a Skype session with him for one o'clock our time."

"Really?" How truly wonderful it would be to have a discussion with a deaf person. Hopefully, Rafferty's foreman could offer her insight into what life was like for the hearing impaired. She had so many questions. "That's so kind of him to agree and you for setting it up."

"Guillermo's a great guy."

"How does that work?"

"Skype or talking to Guillermo?"

"Speaking with Guillermo."

"Sign language. I translate. He prefers not to speak. He grew up in the Deaf community where oralism is discouraged."

"Oralism? Is that a real thing or are you just being dirty." She surprised herself by teasing him.

"Not that I can't be dirty under the right circumstances." He winked mischievously. "But in this case, I'm being serious. Oralism is the education of deaf students through the spoken word and lipreading. As opposed to manualism that advocates sign language."

"You were teaching Kyle both methods, weren't you?"

He nodded. "It's just a stopgap measure until you can decide which way you want to educate your son. I can't make that decision for you, but I wanted to communicate with him more effectively. Before we get hip deep into this, there's a lot to consider."

She dropped the dishrag into the sink, dried her hands on a cup towel, and turned to face him. "Like what?"

"Whether you want Kyle to learn sign language or not."

"Of course I want him to sign. Anything to help my son communicate."

"It's not as simple as that."

She cocked her head. "What do you mean?"

"Read those books I gave you. There's a lot to consider on how you want to raise Kyle. Guillermo was brought up in the Deaf community. He had a deaf mother. Most deaf children are raised in hearing families where no one else is deaf. The Deaf community historically has preferred sign language, but deaf children who are raised more integrated with society are taught to prefer lipreading. People have very strong opinions on both sides of the fence."

She kneaded her temple against a forming headache. "I've got so much to learn."

"You can handle it."

Lissette wished she were as confident in her abilities. "Is he . . ." She swallowed. "Does Guillermo lead a normal life?"

"He runs my ranch when I'm away. He's married, got two kids of his own. Best ranch hand I ever had. I'd trust him with my life."

While they finished the cleanup, they talked about Rafferty's ranch and his work in the movies, then discovered they shared the same favorite movie, *Old Yeller*. Neither one of them thought a movie date was complete without popcorn and a box of Sno-Caps.

"I loved the movies when I was a kid," Rafferty said. "It was the one place I could escape from my life. There was an old dollar theater down the street from where we lived. It had creaky wooden floors and dusty velvet curtains on the walls. I used to volunteer to sweep out the theater in exchange for free movie passes. I watched everything that came through there, even the titles in Spanish."

"I loved the movies too!" she exclaimed. "My mom

would drop me and my friends off at noon on Saturday at the multiplex and she'd pick us up at six. We'd spend the day watching movies. I haven't been to the theater in years."

"I don't go much either," he admitted. "Mostly it's for the premiere of movies my horses starred in."

"That sounds so impressive."

He shrugged. "It's just a job like any other."

"But you know movie stars."

"I've met them, sure, but we're not best buddies or anything. Remember I'm just the hired help."

"How did you get into that line of work?"

"I fell into training horses by accident. Never chose it as a career. Horses chose me. I love 'em. They're such sensitive, intelligent creatures. My mother was dating a guy who ran horse stables. This was after Jake had come to visit and he'd told me about Gordon, so I had horses on the brain. This fella was one of my mother's better companions until she screwed up that relationship. He took an interest in me. Hired me to muck out stalls. Even after he and Amelia broke up he let me hang around. I was good with horses right out of the gate. Horse sense is just one of those things you're born with, I guess, like musical abilities. One thing led to another and the next thing I knew, I was training horses for the movies."

"I bet you had a ton of girls chasing after you."

He looked sheepish. "Yeah, but I'm not easy."

"No?"

"After raising my bipolar mother and making a few relationship mistakes, I got pretty choosy."

"That must have been tough."

"Mostly, I had to learn that it wasn't normal to be the one to wake up your mother so she'd get to work on time and mix her hangover concoctions. I make a mean Bloody Mary."

"You've worked hard your whole life."

"That's not a bad thing. I'm not afraid of hard work."

"You never had a childhood."

"No," he agreed, but there was no acrimony in his voice. He didn't blame anyone. He simply accepted things the way they were. "What was your childhood like?"

"Normal. Happy."

"You were lucky."

"Yes. I was lucky then. Not so lucky now." Her gaze strayed to Kyle. She moved to the table to put the remainder of the barbecue along with the sauce in the paper bag and left it on the kitchen table so Rafferty could take it back to his apartment to have for later. *Will I ever be lucky again?*

He came over to her, lowered his voice. "You've had a very rough patch, but things are going to get better. Just you wait and see."

This strong sense of connection bamboozled her. He seemed to be able to read her mind. To understand her in a way she'd never quite felt understood. She barely knew him and she'd shared far too much with him over the course of the past two days. He'd arrived at exactly the wrong time in her life.

Or at exactly the right time.

"It's almost one," he said. "Do you have a computer we can use or should I go get my laptop?"

"I've got a notebook computer. We can go into the living room." She ushered Kyle into the living room ahead of her. Her notebook computer was sitting on the bookcase. She gave it to Rafferty, who set it up on the coffee table and readied the Skype session.

"How did you learn sign language?" she asked him.

"Guillermo taught me."

"That says a lot about you. Most people wouldn't have

bothered. They would have just hired a hearing ranch foreman."

"What Guillermo lacks in hearing, he makes up for in the way he handles horses. He's got a natural talent with animals."

"Just like you."

"It's how we bonded. Over our mutual love of horses."

Lissette sat beside Rafferty on the couch. Kyle balanced on her knee. Keyed up, she took a deep breath, trying to calm herself down. Something akin to stage fright bit into her. This was it. Her first step to shattering the invisible glass wall between herself and her son.

Guillermo Santo was a fortyish, stalky, black-haired Hispanic with somber dark eyes and perfect white teeth that flashed brightly whenever he offered up a smile. He wore a checkered Western-cut shirt and a battered straw cowboy hat. His hands moved at a speed so dazzling that Lissette had no idea how Rafferty kept up with him.

A sick feeling weighted the pit of her stomach. Sign language looked so complicated. How would she ever learn what it all meant?

You have to. For Kyle.

"Guillermo says he understands that what you're experiencing right now is very confusing," Rafferty translated. "But he wants to reassure you that this all will be old hat in no time."

Lissette smiled. Nodded. "Thank him for me."

Rafferty conveyed her message to Guillermo, and then to Lissette, he said, "What questions would you like to ask?"

Gosh, there were so many. She really didn't know where to start. She wasn't even sure what questions to ask. She felt clueless, in the dark, a total mushroom.

Kyle sat in her lap, mesmerized by the computer, his

gaze trained on Guillermo, watching every move he made.

In order for them both to see the computer screen, she and Rafferty had to sit close together, thighs and shoulders touching. If she hadn't been so focused on the Skype session, she would have come completely unraveled by the contact.

She tried not to be distracted by his body heat or just how firm his muscular legs were. He handled horses every day and it clearly kept him in tip-top shape. She gulped, disconcerted, and didn't look over at him.

"Lissy?" Rafferty said.

It felt too intimate. His use of her nickname.

"Uh-huh?" She croaked.

"What would you like to ask Guillermo?"

"Mmm," she said, determined to ignore the way her body hummed and tingled everywhere she was pressed against Rafferty. "What would be his number one piece of advice for me at this shocked, stunned, strung-out stage?"

He and Guillermo exchanged a conversation in sign language and then Rafferty translated for her. "It's not the end of the world. All the dreams you initially had for your son are still achievable, regardless of his hearing loss."

Learning this was an antidote to her despair. Guillermo was her angel of hope. She could see a glimmer of light, small and far away, but it was there.

"You must find the gift in having a child with hearing loss," Rafferty continued to interpret. "In searching for those gifts, your bond with your son will grown stronger every day and soon you will come to appreciate him for exactly who he is."

Lissette clasped both hands to her heart. "Tell him thank you for sharing his wisdom."

Kyle reached out to touch the computer screen. Guillermo waved at him. Her son laughed so loud he startled himself and looked back to see if Lissette had noticed.

Guillermo signed something to Kyle.

"What did he say?" Lissette asked Rafferty.

"He told him it's good to laugh."

"It is." She smiled at Guillermo.

The ranch foreman signed for a long time. He looked quite serious during the process. Kyle wriggled in her lap. Exasperated, she set him on his feet.

Rafferty signed back.

"What did he say?" Lissette asked.

"He recommends that you teach Kyle sign language over lipreading because he's so young and profoundly deaf. He believes that children who spend so much time learning to speak and lip-read are delayed in their academic development. Sign language is a deaf child's native tongue. Forcing a child to lip-read and speak is tantamount to stripping him of his identity, his community, and his culture."

Now, she understood the somber expression on Guillermo's face. Her decision on how to educate her son would impact Kyle for the rest of his life. It was not something to be taken lightly.

"I'll give his arguments serious consideration," she said.

Rafferty relayed what she said.

Guillermo shook his head. Signed something emphatically.

"I get the feeling he's unhappy with me," she mumbled.

"Not unhappy," Rafferty corrected. "Just concerned that since you are hearing, you're vulnerable to letting other hearing people sway you to their way of thinking."

"Thank Guillermo for his concern. I'll keep his advice in mind."

Rafferty translated. Guillermo's face softened and he nodded. They signed some more.

"What was that?" Lissette asked.

"Just ranch business," he said, but he looked a bit embarrassed, as if Guillermo had communicated something else that Rafferty was reluctant to share with her.

She narrowed her eyes and steely determination took hold of her. She was going to learn sign language, by God. She didn't like going through an interpreter, even one as helpful as the cowboy beside her.

An insistent tugging at her pants leg shifted her attention to her son. Kyle stood grinning up at her, his face, hair, and clothes covered in barbecue sauce. "Oh my goodness, look what you've been up to."

At that moment her telephone rang.

She jumped away from him, her gaze drifting to the cordless phone on the end table and the digital readout of the caller ID. She sighed. "It's my parents."

"Is that a bad thing?"

The phone rang again.

"No." She blew out her breath. "It's just that I haven't told them about Kyle yet."

"Ah," Rafferty said, and held out his arms. "Hand me the boy. I'll wash his face and hands."

"You don't have to do that."

"You need to have this talk with your folks. It might take a while and the young one is sticky. Give." Rafferty wriggled his fingers.

The phone trilled again.

Rafferty kept his arms extended.

In such a short time, she was already growing accustomed to his help. He was a guy you could count on. This wasn't good. It wasn't smart. Counting on him. She'd counted on people too much. It was time she counted on herself.

"I've got him," she said.

"Don't be stubborn."

Kyle grunted and unwittingly kicked her in the ribs as he leaned toward Rafferty's open arms.

The phone switched to voice mail. "Lissy, it's Mom. If you're home, please pick up. I just got the most distressing call from Claudia."

Rafferty arched an eyebrow, inclined his head in the direction of the phone, and took Kyle from her arms. "Talk to your mother," he said firmly, the total alpha male, fully in control.

With that, he left the room, her son tucked in the crook of his arm.

Leaving Lissette fuming, fretful, and flummoxed.

Just who in the hell did this audacious cowboy think he was?

Chapter Eleven

Rafferty sat Kyle down on the bathroom floor. He plugged the sink, turned on the faucet. He'd performed this same activity many times, taking care of his younger sister and brother. An old habit coming back to him like a good friend he hadn't seen in years.

He was trying not to think about Guillermo's parting message. *Be careful, boss. You know how you get with those helpless damsels.*

Mind your own business, Rafferty had signed back.

Lissette might be going through a rough patch, but she wasn't helpless. Any woman who could take such good care of a child all on her own—and let's face it, Jake hadn't been much help—had to be damn resilient.

That resilience was what attracted Rafferty. She wasn't like any other woman he'd ever known. She was tough, even if she didn't see herself that way. For instance, she hadn't automatically embraced Guillermo's strong opinion for sign language. Maybe that's why Guillermo had warned him. He saw Lissette's failure to immediately agree with him as a weakness, whereas in Rafferty's book, it took a lot of courage to stop and weigh both sides of an issue instead of plunging headlong into a knee-jerk response.

The way he often did. A knee-jerk response was how he'd ended up here in the first place. If truth be told he was the one not operating from a position of power. He'd let his heart rule his head when he decided to stay in Jubilee and train her horse. He was starting to regret his decision because he was getting too involved with her too quickly. Feeling things he should not be feeling.

Suddenly aware of the heat from the toddler's gaze, he glanced over. Kyle watched him, big eyes solemn. The kid had his mom's eyes. Rafferty stared back, unnerved by his intent assessment.

"Bet you're wondering what I'm doing here, huh?" He patted the stepstool, indicating Kyle should step up to the sink. "Don't think I haven't been asking myself the same question. The plan was to give your mama the money and then get the hell out of Jubilee."

Kyle pointed a chubby finger at him.

"Yeah, best-laid plans. I didn't count on your mama being in such trouble. Couldn't very well just turn my back on her, now could I?" Rafferty guided him up onto the stool.

A dollop of barbecue sauce was in Kyle's hair.

Chuckling, Rafferty dipped a washcloth into the water and scrubbed the boy's round little head. "It's gonna be okay," he said. "I promise. Your mama's strong. She's got your best interest at heart."

Unlike my mother.

That was unfair. Amelia had done the best she could. She couldn't help it that she had mental issues, but Kyle was lucky to have a grounded, stable mother like Lissette. One who would move heaven and earth to make sure his needs were met before her own.

Kyle held out both arms.

Rafferty gulped. He was getting too close, to this boy and his mother.

"You want me to pick you up?"

Kyle nodded as if he'd understood exactly what Rafferty had said.

"Look kid, I like you and everything, but I won't be around for long so it's not a good idea to get too attached to me."

Kyle didn't move. Just stood with arms outstretched.

"I'm seriously screwed here, aren't I?" Rafferty mumbled, and scooped the boy up in his arms. He was leaning down over the sink, guiding Kyle's hands into the water when Lissette marched in.

Rafferty cast her a sideways glance. A frown pulled her lips tight. The color was high on her cheeks. She lowered the toilet lid, sat down and crossed her arms over her chest. She was trembling all over.

Adrenaline kicked in. His pulse quickened. Fight-or-flight response. Part of him wanted to run, escape the bathroom's intimate confines. Another part of him wanted to double up his fists and do battle with whoever or whatever had upset her.

"I am so furious," she announced.

Rafferty stayed quiet, not sure how to respond. He busied himself soaping Kyle's hands with bar soap that smelled like green apples.

"Claudia called my parents and told them about Kyle. Can you believe that?"

"Maybe she didn't know you hadn't told them."

"She knew it the minute my mother answered the phone in a bright chirpy voice."

"That's an assumption on your part. Some people get cheery when they're depressed."

"What people?"

"I dunno," he finished lamely. "Some people, somewhere in the world."

"But not my people. Not in my world. Something bad happens, you aren't chirpy."

"Good point."

"I'm not just mad at Claudia either." Her left knee jerked up and down in a frantic rhythm, burning off nervous energy. "I'm pissed at my parents even more."

"Family can be irritating without meaning to be."

Lissette narrowed her eyes. "You're patronizing me. Stop it. Jake used to patronize me all the time. Pat the little lady on the head. Calm her down. Well, I don't need calming down. I have a legitimate reason to be upset."

"Not patronizing. Just playing devil's advocate."

"Well, stop that too. I want you on my side. Are you on my side?"

"I'm on your side."

"No matter what?"

"No matter what," he promised.

"Good. Fine." She stood up, paced two steps, ran into the wall, turned and plunked back down on the closed toilet seat again. "On a Sunday, my parents pulled strings."

"What kind of strings?"

"They got Kyle an appointment with some high-powered audiologist in Dallas for Monday morning."

"Your parents are that powerful?"

She waved a hand. "They know a lot of people."

"Maybe it's a good thing," he suggested. "Second opinion. Maybe you should keep the appointment."

"That's not the point. Of course I'm going to keep the appointment. I want the best for my son. The thing is that they interfered. They assumed I couldn't handle this on my own. They stepped in without my permission. They took over."

"They were just being concerned parents."

"My side. You're supposed to be on it, remember?"

"Right. How could they have been so awful?"

"Now you're making fun of me."

"Gentle teasing."

"This isn't funny."

"It's not." He nodded. "But you're going through a lot of turmoil right now. You're extra sensitive. Things seem worse than they really are."

She sighed heavily, gazed at her son with a woebegone expression. Rafferty ached to make it all go away, ease her suffering. "Do you want me to go with you to the appointment?"

"No," she said caustically. "I'm depending on you too much as it is. It's time I found my own way."

"There's nothing wrong with accepting help."

"There is if it keeps you from growing to your full potential."

"You feel stunted?"

She opened her mouth, her eyes filled with things she wanted to say, but she snapped her mouth shut after finally saying, "Does it really matter what I feel?"

Rafferty wasn't keen on discussing feelings either, so he didn't push her, instead gently scrubbed Kyle's sticky face with a washcloth. "You matter a whole lot to this little guy. And," he mumbled, "you matter to me."

She made a muffled sound, half pleasure, half alarm.

He turned to look at her over his shoulder and their gazes met for a long, electrified moment.

"Don't," she whispered.

"Don't what?"

"Say anything."

The bathroom was suddenly suffocatingly hot, the quarters too tight. He put Kyle down on the stool and bent over to dry the boy's hands. He cast a sideways glance at Lissette. A dewdrop of perspiration beaded on the little fingerprint-shaped canal between her nose and her upper lip.

Rafferty realized, with some satisfaction, that whatever this was he was experiencing, it was not one-sided. It pleased him to learn he wasn't the only one feeling strung out, strung up, strung along by attraction. He read it in her body language. Her hidden emotions revealed in her tense muscles, wavering smile, and shallow, rapid respirations.

Hell, his body was probably just as big a tattletale. His feelings sticking out like sharp points on a barbwire fence, giving off edgy clues to his state of mind, marking his weak spots, telegraphing his thoughts. He liked her. He wanted her. He was a big fool because of it too.

She wore a pair of loose-fitting jeans—he had the feeling she'd lost weight in the aftermath of Jake's death—and a blue flannel shirt with the charm of white lace edging the collar and the hem. Fluffy pink socks and the small silver earrings in the shape of Texas that decorated her delicate lobes accentuated her down-home country appeal.

Lissette looked both compellingly innocent and devastatingly sexy. The gentle goddess Persephone who saw only the best in life until Hades kidnapped her as his bride and the harsh reality awakened her from her stupor. He sensed that she struggled between her naturally optimistic outlook and the dark situation she found herself in. An internal conflict with the way she wanted things to be and the way they really were.

Hell, Jones, you just cast Jake in the role of Hades.

Jake. The war hero. Jake, the big brother who'd once saved his skin. He felt at once disloyal to Jake and infuriated with him for the way he'd treated Lissy. If she were his . . .

But she's not yours. She can never be yours, so squelch that thought right now.

"I'm not here to get in your way, Lissy," he said, straightening. "Or cause you trouble. All I want to do is help. You do know that, right?"

She nodded and for a long moment neither of them moved, as if a restrictive band had cinched around them, anchoring them to the spot.

Then Kyle reached out for him, his chubby little hands went around Rafferty's neck and he clung tight.

"Da." The boy rested his forehead at Rafferty's temple and patted his nose. "Da."

Rafferty melted.

Ah, hell. This was not good. Not good at all.

For the next week, Rafferty concentrated on training Slate. He loved his work and it was a good distraction. Helping him keep his mind off his feelings for Lissette. It also helped that Lissette and Kyle stayed in Dallas with her parents for a few days as she took her son to see a variety of specialists.

She came home on Friday, looking exhausted. He'd heard her drive into the garage and he'd come down the apartment steps to see if she needed anything. She offered him a sweet smile. He was a sucker for that smile.

Lord, he thought. *I've missed her.*

"How'd it go?" he asked.

"Exhausting. And the conclusions were all the same. He's going deaf and there's nothing that can be done. But in a way, I'm glad that's settled and over with. Now for the new tug-of-war. How best to educate him. Guillermo recommends teaching him sign language, and he is the only deaf person weighing in. While everyone else, my parents, Claudia, even the educators think lipreading and teaching him to speak are the way to go. The thing is I can't figure out why he can't do both, but when I say that, everyone seems to look at me like I'm crazy. They're pressuring me to pick. I've been told the faster I make a decision, the better off Kyle is going to be, but I hate making decisions under pressure. Especially one as important as this."

"Take your time," he encouraged.

"You're the only one who hasn't weighed in, the only one not pressuring me. Thank you," she said, "for giving me some breathing room."

"You'll come to the right decision in your own time."

"In the meanwhile, I'd like it if you continue teaching him both sign language and lipreading."

"You're not afraid I'm muddying the waters?"

"Right now, what you're doing for Kyle is the only thing that looks clear to me."

"Do you want me to watch him for you so you can take some time for yourself?" he offered, even though he knew getting more attached to the boy was just going to cause trouble down the road.

"Actually, I want to blow off some steam. My friends host a poker game one Friday night a month. They have a babysitter for the kids. Would you like to come along?"

He should say no. There was no point meeting her friends and getting invested in her community. He'd be on his way as soon he trained Slate for the futurity, but her smile was so beguiling, he couldn't turn her down. She deserved a fun night out. "Yeah, I'll come along."

They arrived at Joe and Mariah Daniels's Green Ridge Ranch right at six-thirty that evening.

"Penny," Lissette said as he pulled to a stop beside several other duallys.

"What?"

She chuckled. "In this day and age I should probably adjust it for inflation. Dollar?"

"Oh, you're asking what I was thinking."

"You had a faraway look in your eyes. Thinking of home?"

He slid a glance her way, felt a wicked grin creep across his face. "I was thinking about how sexy you look in those jeans."

"Rafferty!" Her cheeks flushed.

"I'm not going to apologize," he said, "because you *are* sexy as hell, Lissette."

"No I'm not. I'm a busy single mom of a handicapped child. I don't have time for manicures and hair appointments and—"

"Woman, look in the mirror sometime. Sure, you could use a little meat on your bones, but damn, you have some fine curves just as you are. You're young and vibrant and sexy as hell."

"You think I'm sexy?"

"I think it's sexy that you don't even realize how sexy you are."

He was saying too damn much. He'd promised himself he would not flirt or banter with her. Would not ogle or leer, but even a restrained man had his limits. He'd been watching her, enjoying the graceful way she moved, savoring the way she smelled. She was like a bit of sunshine mixed into his day. And he wanted her. Badly.

Rafferty clenched his jaw, tightened his hands on the steering wheel.

Lissette misread his hesitation. "Look, we don't have to go inside if you really don't want to be here."

"I want to be here."

"It's just that, well, you look like you're having some kind of inner struggle and losing the battle. I get the meeting-new-people thing. I'm shy too, at times. Jake brought me out of that somewhat, but to be honest, I'm just as happy sitting at home, baking or watching a movie, curling up on the couch with Kyle."

"They're your friends. We're not going to stand them up," he said, letting her believe that his inner struggle stemmed from introversion versus extroversion rather than the desire that flamed through him every time he was near her. Tonight she smelled of apricots. He wanted to lean over the seat and nibble the soft lobe of her ear to see if she tasted like the apricots he could pluck from the trees in his front yard.

Rafferty got out of the truck and started around to open her door for her, but she'd already hopped out and moved around to get Kyle out of his car seat. When she glanced up and saw him on her side of the vehicle, she looked surprised.

"Oh," she said. "You were coming around to open the car door for me."

"Sorry, habit."

"No reason to apologize."

"I've met women who claimed I set the feminist movement back twenty years when I open the door for them."

"You're in Texas now. Plenty of men open the door for women. We love our cowboys and their manners here in the Lone Star State."

"Guess I've been living in the wrong state all this time. You're not offended?"

"Why would I be offended?"

"Some women suggest that it means I think they aren't capable of opening their own door. To me, it's just mannerly." He reached for Kyle after Lissy got him out of his car seat. The boy nestled in the crook of his arm as if he'd been doing it forever.

Lissette held out her arms to take the boy, but Rafferty said, "I've got him."

Her quick smile warmed him from the toes up. "Jake usually forgot to open my car door. It didn't bother me either way. He was always so eager to get out of the car and get to the action that he swept me right along with him."

Jake. There he was again, the specter between them.

C'mon. Jake isn't the only obstacle.

Obstacle to what? Anything between him and Lissette was a pipe dream. He might want her, but he couldn't have her. She was vulnerable, hurting on so many levels. He would not, could not take advantage.

I could, laughed the masculine beast inside, sharpening his teeth. *Eat her up right now. Get a load of that sweet caboose.*

Go to hell.

He clubbed his baser animal into submission, and followed Lissy up the steps to the Danielses's front door. But he couldn't help cocking his head for a gander at her backside.

"Lissy!" A petite blond answered the door with a toddler on her own hip. "You came! I'm so happy. And you must be Rafferty." She shook his hand, smiled warmly. Then she glanced at Kyle in Rafferty's arms, looked hesitant. "Should I still call Kyle by name even if he can't hear me?"

"He's still got some residual hearing," Lissette explained. "Talk away."

"I can't believe how well you're adapting." Mariah shook her head. "C'mon, let's take the kids to the playroom with Ruby. Joe is out in the backyard along with Cordy and Ila and Prissy and Paul. He's grilling steaks."

"Are Brady and Annie coming?" Lissette asked as Mariah escorted them inside.

"They're not back from Monesta yet, but they'll be here for our annual Halloween bash. Will you be here for that, Rafferty? You're invited."

"Thank you, ma'am."

"The guys and Ila are in the backyard, go on out and introduce yourself," Mariah said to him. "While Lissy and I will get the kids settled." Mariah waved in the direction of the backyard.

Rafferty trod through the house, feeling out of place,

but the minute he stepped out on the porch, a tall, lanky man with work-roughened hands that looked so much like his own came across the yard to greet him.

"Joe. Joe Daniels. C'mon over and I'll introduce you."

Rafferty followed Joe over to where two men and a tall woman who bore a striking resemblance to the actress Angie Harmon stood around a big stainless steel state-of-the-art barbecue grill.

"This is Cordy Whiteside and his fiancée, Ila Brackeen," Joe introduced.

Cordy stood maybe five-foot-eight with his cowboy books on and Ila stretched well over six feet. Their Mutt and Jeff proportions made Rafferty smile as he shook their hands. Ila's handshake was as strong as her fiancé's.

"Rafferty Jones," he said. "Please to meet you."

"Jake's brother, right?"

"Yeah."

The other man turned out to be Paul Gibson. He was ruddy faced and sturdily built, with a military haircut and an army T-shirt. "Your brother was a great man. An honor to his country."

"Thanks," Rafferty said because he did not know what else to say.

"I better go see if the ladies need any help." Ila moved away from the barbecue. "Before they start badmouthing me for shirking my girlie duties."

"They wouldn't dare," Cordy said.

Ila leaned down to kiss Cordy's cheek. "Don't drink too much beer. I don't feel like driving home tonight."

"Your wish is my command." Cordy tossed his half-consumed beer into the trash.

"Nice meeting you, Rafferty." Ila waved and disappeared inside, leaving the backyard.

Cordy sighed, gazed longingly at Ila's retreating figure. "Ain't she sumpthin'?"

Rafferty immediately liked Joe and Cordy and Paul. They had a lot in common. The talk quickly turned to horses. They knew more about cutting horses than Rafferty did, so he milked them for information. Joe gave him specific tips on training Slate for cutting. By the time the brisket was ready for the table, Rafferty felt as if he'd known them all his life.

"How long are you planning on staying in town?" Joe asked.

"Through the futurity."

"Mariah said you just found out about Jake's death," Joe ventured. "We're sorry for your loss."

"I was in Australia," he said, feeling as if he owed them an explanation.

They seized on the neutral topic in the way of men and started asking questions about Australia. Rafferty was relieved to be off the hook. The tone of the conversation swiftly shifted from somber to teasing. They carried the meat indoors, laughing and cutting up.

Rafferty caught sight of Lissette, who was in the kitchen with Mariah, Ila, and Paul's wife, Prissy. Her eyes met his and they exchanged a quiet glance. Just looking at her caused his heart to skip a beat. How beautiful she was in that simple, white button-down shirt, Levi's, and pink cowgirl boots.

The couples gathered around the table. The food was delicious, the conversation witty and charming.

I could get used to this.

Don't get used to it. No matter how good it feels you can't stay. You've got responsibilities in California.

After they finished the meal, everyone pitched in to clean up and in no time, the dishes had been dispatched and they were sitting back at the table again, anteing up for penny poker. No big winnings or losses. Just for fun.

"Texas hold 'em." Cordy dealt the cards.

Rafferty had the ace of clubs and the ace of diamonds. He forced his face to remain neutral. He wasn't much of a gambler, but poker was one game you could make a little money at if you could control your emotions. When he was a kid, desperate for cash, he'd picked up a few skills from the guy who ran the stables where he'd been hired to muck out stalls.

"I'm out." Mariah tossed her cards to the middle of the table.

"Me too." Prissy sank her elbows on the table and started talking to Mariah about new wedding veils she'd ordered for the shop and how much she was loving the latest season of *The Bachelor.* She also slipped in a detailed description of the sweater she was knitting for Paul, and then complained about how she couldn't stop their new Shar-Pei puppy from peeing on the carpet.

"Crate training," Mariah threw in. "I'm telling you, it works."

"But I can't stand the thought of Miss Shoo-shoo being caged up," Prissy moaned.

Stone-faced Ila narrowed her eyes at chatty Prissy and studied her cards. She was a serious competitor. "Check."

Joe, Cordy, Rafferty, Paul, and Lissette checked as well.

Cordy dealt out the three community cards known as the flop—seven of diamonds, six of clubs, jack of hearts.

Not great potential, but Rafferty had the pocket aces.

Lissette sat up straighter.

"Garbage." Paul tossed down his cards.

"My fiancée has a killer hand," Cordy observed, his eyes on Ila.

"How do you know?" Paul asked.

"She's got a tell. See the way her—"

"Blow it for me, why don't you," Ila complained good-naturedly and pitched her cards on top of Paul's. "I'm out."

Cordy followed suit. "Me too." He got up to go around the back of Ila's chair for a cup of the coffee that Mariah had put on to perk. Ila reached out to pinch his butt.

"Turnabout is fair play," she told him. "You outed me, I goose you."

"Just wait until I get you home, woman," Cordy threatened with a wicked grin.

"Hey, hey," Joe said. "This is a G-rated game."

"G-rated?" Mariah teased. "With the way you cuss?"

"Okay, PG–13."

"So if I want to smooch on my bride-to-be—" Cordy asked from the kitchen as he poured a cup of coffee.

"Take it outside," the group chorused in unison.

"Cordy," Ila said, "you're supposed to be dealing the cards."

"Can you handle it for me, babe?"

Ila leaned across the table and flipped over the turn card.

Six of diamonds.

Now Rafferty had two pair. Aces and sixes.

Joe looked at his cards, grumbled. "Fold."

Rafferty smiled at Lissette. "Looks like it's just you and me, sweetheart."

She slanted her eyes downward in a coy gesture that made her look so damn cute he forgot to breathe. "I'm in. I raise." She tossed two more chips into the pile.

"Looks like you know what you're doing." Rafferty tipped up the edges of his cards that he had lying flat facedown on the table, even though he knew what they were. Just double checking. "Is this no limit?"

"Up to you," Joe said.

Rafferty cocked his head. "Lissy?"

She arched an eyebrow. It made him feel good to see her having such a good time. "Sky's the limit, cowboy."

"I see your raise and raise you another two chips."

"Call," Lissette said.

"Oooh," Prissy said. "Rafferty looks like he's played poker before."

"Jake was a card shark," Paul said. "You have big shoes to fill, Jones."

A hush fell over the group as everyone thought of Jake and the smiles disappeared. Mariah rushed to fill in the silence. "Anyone besides Cordy want a cup of coffee?"

"I do," Joe said. "I'll help you."

Everyone scattered back to the kitchen leaving Rafferty and Lissette dueling over the hand. Cordy returned to the table to deal the river card.

Ace of spades.

Rafferty pressed his lips together to keep from grinning. Full house. He had this sewed up. Nonchalantly, he tossed five more chips onto the pile. "I raise."

Lissette upped his raise.

"You sure you want to do that?" he asked. She had to be bluffing. He couldn't imagine what she had that could beat his full house. No chance for a straight or flush with those cards on the table.

"Let's go higher." She pushed all her chips to the middle of the table. "All in."

"Looks like you've got a tiger by the tail," Cordy said.

"I'm in all the way." Rafferty pushed his chips into the middle of the table to join hers. He knew he had this one.

By now, everyone else had wandered back over to see what was going on. They were sipping coffee and snacking on the cookies Lissette had brought and speculating on what each player had in their hand.

"Read 'em and weep. Full house." He flipped over his cards, reached for the chips, letting the grin he'd been suppressing sweep across his face.

"Not so fast, cowboy." Lissette laid out her cards. Two sixes in her hand, two on the table. "I believe four of kind beats a full house."

Cordy let out a whoop.

Prissy applauded. "Go girl."

"She got you." Joe slapped him on the shoulder.

Lissette held Rafferty's stare. "As Paul said, Jake was a card shark. Don't you think he taught me a thing or two?"

Rafferty raised his palms, got to his feet. "You got me. I'm out." He bent at the waist. "I bow to your greatness."

"As well you should." She laughed and extended her hand. "Now help me up, my foot's gone to sleep because I was sitting on it to keep myself from bouncing up and down with joy when that six of diamonds showed up."

He reached out, took Lissy's hand, and as he did he heard Mariah whisper to Joe, "Look how happy he makes her. I swear I never saw her look like that with Jake."

Chapter Twelve

On Saturday morning after the poker game, Lissette got up at her usual time and set about perfecting the recipes she'd decided upon as her new bakery offerings. She caught herself humming Maggie Walters's "Real Life Cowboy" and realized that for a few minutes there, she'd been caught up in the zone of baking bliss.

It felt nice, this flash moment of happiness.

A knock sounded on her back door. *Rafferty. I've got a cowboy in my backyard*. Her heart gave a jolt that was beginning to feel all too familiar.

She went to let him in. "What are you doing here?"

"Am I too early? I've been out to the acreage and trained Slate for a couple of hours. He's looking sharp, Lissy." Rafferty's face lit up. "I really think he's got a good chance to take a purse."

He moved forward and she had no choice but to step aside and let him in or he was going to plow right into her. He rubbed his palms together. "I'm ready to start building your Web site."

"I thought we left that up in the air."

"We did, but it's time to get moving."

Those cowboys. Once they got something in their heads it was a done deal.

"Kyle still asleep?" he asked, headed for the cabinet where the coffee cups were housed as if he owned the place.

"Yes." She wrapped her arms around herself, unnerved by just how cozy things were getting between them. "He was pretty tuckered out after last night."

"He had a good time." Rafferty's gaze met hers. "I did too. I like your friends."

"They like you."

He took out two mugs, poured them both a cup of coffee, and without even asking, put two teaspoons of sugar and a dollop of milk in hers, just the way she liked it. He'd been paying attention. That unnerved her even more. "So about the Web site. I'm thinking keep it simple."

"Me too. No wait. Stop. I haven't agreed to this yet."

"Use my skills while you have a chance. I won't be around forever."

There. That was exactly the problem. He was winning her over, charming her, and soon he'd be gone. "You're pretty good at this, huh?"

"Prepare to be dazzled."

"Now you're just being cocky."

"You like that about me."

"Oh-ho, here comes the cowboy bragging."

"It's only braggin' if you can't back it up, sweetheart."

Sweetheart.

That simple word stilled something inside her. As if a loudly ticking clock had suddenly stopped, leaving everything in mysterious silence.

"Hmm. We'll see."

"You seem skeptical."

"I know how men like to blow smoke—"

"There you go with blanket statements. Don't reduce me to a label, Lissy."

She liked it that he was no longer coddling her as he'd done the first two days he'd been here. The kid gloves were off. He no longer treated her like a victim of circumstances. Not the widow of a soldier. Not the mother of a deaf child. But a woman. He was challenging her, teasing her, showing her another side of his personality, and she liked it.

A lot.

She woke Kyle up and fed him breakfast, and then put in an Elmo DVD for him to watch. She hated using the television set for a babysitter, but they wouldn't get anything done with him crawling all over them.

"Turn on the closed captioning for him," Rafferty suggested.

"He can't read yet."

"No, but it's a good habit to get into."

He was right.

Just as when they'd Skyped Guillermo, Lissette had to sit right beside him so they could both see the computer screen. His delicious masculine scent invaded her nose, took her hostage with its pleasant potency, and his shoulder—mother of all things holy—his broad shoulder brushed lightly against her arm as he leaned over and tapped a URL into the search box on the browser.

Lissette gulped, closed her eyes, tried to fight off the heat twining through her at the lightness of his touch. It should not feel this good. She should not be making such a big deal out of innocent body contact.

"There we go," he said, and leaned away, giving her some breathing room.

Yes. That was better. No touching.

Why then did she feel robbed?

The computer screen filled with a high-tech video

of a man riding a horse. Not just any man, she realized, but Rafferty decked out in full cowboy regalia—Levi's, cowboy boots, double-yoked plaid shirt, chaps, and a lariat slung over the horn of the horse's saddle.

Seeing him like that made her heart go pitter-pat. She so loved the sight of a cowboy at work. Here was her secret fantasy, the one she'd thought she was getting when she married Jake too soon after meeting him.

Those romantic notions had led her astray before. It was nothing but a myth. Still, she couldn't shake the way he made her feel. Turned on and ashamed of it. She shifted uncomfortably on the couch, shot him a sideways glance and caught him looking at her.

His stare was steadfast, curious.

Quickly, she yanked her gaze back to the screen.

The Web site was slick and polished. It looked like a professional Web designer had done it. Rafferty's voice narrated the recording. He spoke of his techniques for training horses. How he eschewed rough training practices in favor of a gentle touch. Lissette fell into the narrative. His pitch made her long to visit the ranch. She wanted to ride horses, to teach Kyle to ride.

"You built this site yourself?" she asked in awe.

"Yup."

"How did you learn how to do it?"

"When I first started, I was on a shoestring budget. It's amazing what you can learn when you put your mind to it."

"Where did you learn HTML?"

"Self-taught. Got books from the library."

"Is there anything you don't know how to do?"

"There's plenty of things I don't know how to do, but I learn best by breaking things down to their basic components in order to reassemble them. Take things one step at a time and it will all work out."

"You're detail oriented."

He shrugged. "I suppose."

"I'm more big picture. I imagine what I want, then start making it happen. Like with a cake. I visualize the finished product, then I backtrack from there to find the steps to get to where I need to be."

"Organic," he said.

"What?"

"Your process. You're more organic. I'm step-by-step. You let things happen as they come."

Lissette dared to meet his eyes again. She was getting into this deeper with every passing moment and the thing of it was, she liked it. Liked being with Rafferty. Liked his approach. Liked the way he made her feel.

And that's what was so upsetting.

"Let's get down to brass tacks," he said. "You visualize what you want your Web site to look like and I'll get you a URL and we'll progress from there."

An hour and a half later, they were deeply into setting up Lissette's Web site. Rafferty had already completed the basic template design and they were going through the trial and error process of finding the right images and color scheme. Lissette had kept a photograph portfolio of the pastries she baked, so now it was about showcasing her work in the best possible light.

They tried out different color combinations. She'd point to the palette and he'd put it up. Then one or the other of them would shake their heads, and he would discard it.

If she were doing something like this with Jake, they would have been bickering constantly as he would have questioned every decision she made until she just gave in and let Jake have his way. But Rafferty tried out everything she suggested without offering an opinion first. He patiently allowed her to experiment and stretch her wings.

And then she went and spoiled the peace by noticing how they were breathing in tandem, simultaneously pulling in air, letting it out in slow, steady exhales. Calm. His breathing not only calmed her, but regulated hers.

The rhythm was hypnotic. Sexual. Almost like foreplay.

She was taking on his breathing pattern. Letting him lead the way, just as she always had with Jake. Rafferty's way was more subtle, but clearly more insidious. He might not be outwardly trying to control her, but she had surrendered her power to him all the same.

Disconcerted, Lissette broke the pattern. She held her breath, waiting to exhale when he was inhaling.

Rafferty stopped breathing too. He looked over at her, his stare startling, bold, and intimate. A sharp crackling of erotic energy shot from him to her and back again. The hairs on her forearm lifted. She shifted on the couch cushion, trying to put some distance between them. He was too close. Things were moving much too fast. She did not want to be on this thrill ride after all. She let her gaze drift back to the computer screen, assessing the latest mock-up.

"Looking good," he murmured, but he was not studying her homepage. She could feel the heat radiating off his body. He was studying her. "Real good."

Those last words were spoken so softly, she wasn't sure she'd heard him correctly.

Real good.

Closing her eyes, she willed herself not to shiver, but quickly opened them again. "Nice."

He reached out and put a hand on her knee. His touch seemed to burn right through her pants and she felt him as acutely as if he'd stroked her bare skin.

"I need to stretch my legs," he said. "Clear my head.

I'm getting cross-eyed staring at the computer screen. You want something to drink?"

She nodded.

He stretched, lifting his arms over his head. His shirt rose up, revealing a peek at his tanned, muscular torso, and her mouth went instantly dry. It was probably because all the moisture in her body was pooling in a fine stream of perspiration between her breasts. The room wasn't hot, but the man in front of her surely was.

The Elmo DVD had finished and the television screen was blank. Kyle had fallen asleep on the floor, his thumb in his mouth. She thought about moving him to his bed; he'd probably wake up in the process. No harm letting him finish his nap on the floor.

Rafferty came back from the kitchen with two cans of Dr Pepper. She didn't drink soda a lot, but she had it on hand because one of the offerings in her Texas-theme bakery menu was a Dr Pepper pecan praline cupcake. Dr Pepper had been invented in Waco, Texas, and made for a supremely moist cake.

He popped the pull top from the can and walked across thc living room toward her. He moved with an easy-legged lope that came across as a slow pace, but was surprisingly brisk.

The soda was cold and damp in her hand. She took a sip. It was very sweet, but refreshing, and she drank it faster than she should have. Without ever taking his eyes off her, Rafferty tilted his head and took a long swallow from his Dr Pepper.

Her gaze tracked from his lips to throat. She watched his Adam's apple work, and this time, she shivered. Perspiring one minute, shivering the next. Was she coming down with something?

Anxiously, she shifted her attention away from him,

looking for something else to focus on. She surveyed the Web site.

It looked simple and beige and . . .

Stark.

He'd used the color palette she'd selected. This wasn't his fault, but hers.

"What's the matter," Rafferty asked, coming to sit back down beside her.

"It's blah." She crossed her arms over her chest.

"I assumed you were going for the crisp, professional look—clean lines, fresh, classic. Something that will make your photographs pop when we get them all uploaded."

"The Web site looks so generic. Like it could be any Web page. I want it to be warm and welcoming and inviting."

"Like you," he said huskily. "You were playing it safe when what you really wanted was to let your personality shine through."

"Yeah." She ran her palms over the tops of her thighs. "That's it."

"No problem," Rafferty said. "I can change it in an instant. Speak up, Lissy. Tell me what you really want. I'm listening."

"You don't mind changing it?"

"Why would I mind?"

"I'm wasting your time—"

"Shh. Consider my time as your time. What do you really want?" he asked, challenge in his eyes.

She gnawed her bottom lip. "I don't know."

He took her by the shoulders and turned her on the couch to face him. He placed his hand over her heart. It thumped erratically. She was sure he could tell exactly how much he affected her. Who could miss the wild galloping?

"Listen to your instincts," he murmured.

"Yellow," she said. "I really like yellow. It's bright and cheery, but Jake didn't like it so he wouldn't let me paint the kitchen yellow. He said it was too bright. He didn't want the walls looking like one of those yellow smiley face stickers."

"Yellow it is." Rafferty tapped a few commands on the keyboard and boom.

Sunflower yellow replaced the beige. Just looking at the color made her smile.

"What contrasting colors do you want?" he asked.

"Green."

"Any particular shade?"

"Olive."

The color appeared on the page and it looked so great she hugged herself.

"Considering these colors I have a suggestion for the font, but if you don't like it, please say so."

"Okay."

He changed the font color from black to a dark, rich burgundy. The combination of those colors transported Lissette back to the Loire Valley French kitchen where Madame Boulanger had taken the students for a two-week field trip during Lissette's pastry school education. Those two weeks had been some of the happiest of her life and she'd almost forgotten about them. Now, every time she looked at her Web site, she could remember the happy woman she'd once been.

"I love it!" She put her palms together. "L. O. V. E. Love it."

"Keep in mind I can always change it if you don't."

"No. Leave it." She put a restraining hand on his wrist and instantly regretted it. Every time they touched, something deep inside her unraveled a little bit more.

"Yes, ma'am. Let me know exactly what *you* want." He

laughed, and the sound made her feel warm and toasty right down to her toes.

His grin was cocky and his eyes glistening with the same out-of-control impulses that were simmering through her blood. He leaned closer. She did not shy away.

"If we were in a romantic movie," Rafferty said. "This would be the point where I'd kiss you."

"But this isn't a movie."

Their gazes fused.

"No.

"And you're not going to kiss me."

He leaned forward until his lips were almost touching hers. "I'm not going to kiss you.

"That's very good," she said, "because it's not like this relationship could go anywhere."

"I know."

"You *do* want to kiss me," she said. "Admit it."

"Woman," he murmured, "you have absolutely no idea how much."

A thrill blitzed down her spine. His warm breath tickled her skin. He smelled so good Lissette could scarcely remember her name.

You can't let Rafferty kiss you. You mustn't let him kiss you. This cannot happen.

She raised her hands and clutched them together in front of her chest, building a barrier between them. It was weak, but it was all she could come up with.

"Please . . ." she whispered, meaning to add *don't*, but her throat was so tight and his eyes were so dark and she was caught up in the strange magic surging between them.

"You're vulnerable," he said. "I want to kiss you so much I can't stand it, but I don't want to take advantage."

Take advantage of me. Please!

"And I seem to have this need to protect vulnerable people. It's probably not a healthy situation. You and I."

"You're just as vulnerable as I am, Rafferty Jones. It couldn't have been easy for you coming here."

"I don't shirk my duties."

"And I'm a duty?"

"I didn't say that."

"Do you think . . ." Lissette paused, cleared her throat. "That if we'd met in some other way, before I met Jake, that we would have been attracted to each other?"

"Lissy." He breathed. "There's absolutely no doubt in my mind."

She touched Rafferty's shoulder.

He looked at her and their gazes merged.

She felt everything all at once.

It was like an earthquake rocking her chest, lust and chemistry, longing and yearning, guilt and loneliness. Hunger and sadness and hope. It fell in on her, heavy and warm and too much too soon, and at the same time, not nearly enough.

What had she gotten herself into?

His gaze was like a lightning strike.

Her lips tingled.

He cupped his palm under her chin and tilted her head, his eyes never leaving hers.

She stiffened. Wanting to taste him but terrified of where all this was leading.

He dropped his hand.

No! her body protested.

Compelled by a force she couldn't understand or explain, Lissette leaned in toward him. She just knew that she had to kiss him or die, but it wasn't in her nature to act so boldly. She was accustomed to finding roundabout ways to meet her needs. She couldn't bring herself to initiate the kiss, but she could make him kiss her.

Brazenly, she wrapped her arms around his waist and held on tight.

He arched his eyebrow, making sure he understood what she was asking. *Are you sure?*

She swallowed, moistened her lips. Nodded.

His eyes lighted up and a smile tipped his mouth. It was like watching a drawbridge drop, and behind the door of the fortress, hidden beneath the strong, silent cowboy persona, lurked a heartbreaking tenderness. This man cared deeply about the world, and it hurt him that he couldn't cure all the ills of it.

"Sweet Lissy," he murmured, and lowered his head.

Her pulse skipped.

The kiss was quiet, languid, and deep. He took slow opportunity to taste and smell and feel. His tongue drew a hungry response so acute that she felt like she was falling through time and space.

She threaded her fingers through his hair, hung on to him, increasing the pressure.

He kissed her harder, deeper, and more intensely.

The taste of him! Like sunflowers and rainbows and clouds on a soft summer day. It was as if she knew every part of him—a weary traveler returning home from a long, arduous journey.

While the world shrank down into the minute width of mouths, she opened herself up to possibilities as yet undreamed. She was completely disarmed. With any other man the stunning intimacy and astonishing sensuality would have unbalanced her, but with Rafferty everything was different.

Her lips shuddered against his mouth and her body molded to his.

His hands roved over her spine and she strained into him, her breasts crushed against his chest as he fell back against the couch. In his arms, she felt not only incredibly sexual, but oddly at peace. A peaceful roller coaster. Was there such a thing?

She had to ask herself some hard questions. Was she attracted to him simply because her life was falling apart and he seemed to know exactly how to put her back together again? In her need to find her way in this new chapter of her life, was she grasping at straws? Was she mistakenly reading something into these impulses that wasn't really there? Was she confusing sexual desire for something more substantial? How could she even be thinking such things about a man she'd known only a little over a week?

Lissette dithered, caught between doubt and desire. She did not like this push-pull of emotions. For years, she'd been living life on autopilot, melding with Jake's wishes, putting on a pleasant face, getting through life by putting things in soft focus. She always did what felt safe, but the power of her attraction to Rafferty drove home that she'd done so at the price of her independence. That's what scared her most. This arousal of the self buried deep within her.

Panicked, Lissette pressed a hand to his chest, pushed away from him, broke the embrace. "We have to stop."

"Yes," he said. "You're absolutely right."

But he did not.

Chapter Thirteen

Rafferty didn't mean to claim her mouth so roughly or insistently. Hell, he hadn't meant to kiss her at all, at least not initially, but when she'd taken that step toward him, his restraint had dropped away and he'd just acted.

She tasted like heaven.

He knew she would taste good, but his expectations fell far short of reality. No pastry on this earth tasted so amazing and he couldn't get enough. His arms tightened around her, smashing her pert soft breasts against his muscled chest.

She'd made a low noise of encouragement, letting him know that she didn't mind his forceful technique. In fact, she relaxed her jaw, parted her teeth first. *C'mon in, cowboy.*

Here I come, sweetheart. He'd plunged his tongue inside her.

Her arms twined around his neck.

Rafferty heard a low buzzing in the back of his head. A ravenous fever mounted inside him. Her eyes were closed and he closed his too, savoring the specialness of this moment.

He never wanted it to end.

Many kisses. He'd kissed many women. Many times.

Not that he was a player or anything, but he was a young, healthy, red-blooded male. He'd had his fair share of romances, knew a thing or two about kissing.

But this? He had no words. It was beyond any kiss he'd ever gotten or given.

That scared him. A lot.

He hadn't meant to start anything. She'd just been talking about Jake and how spontaneous he'd been and Rafferty had started feeling jealous because he wasn't spontaneous, and obviously, Lissy liked spontaneous men, and when she'd taken that step toward him, the floodgates had opened and his brain had sent a single message to his nerve endings.

Just do it.

So he'd kissed her.

Now he had to live with the consequences. He'd gone and done the very thing he'd fought against since meeting her. He had the willpower of a fruit fly.

Dammit, Jones.

He'd started this. It was his place to stop it. Rafferty pulled away, broke the kiss.

Lissette's eyes were wide. They were both tugging in equal, desperate gasps. "Wow," she said. "That was—"

"Nice," he said quickly before she had a chance to figure out she'd rocked his world.

"Yes . . . um . . . nice. That was nice."

"Bad idea, though."

"Totally."

"I promise it won't happen again."

She looked distressed. "No, no. Won't happen again."

He got up. "I should go."

"Yes." She dropped her gaze.

He forced a smile, turned around, and headed out the back door, knowing he could never undo what he'd just done. Worse than that, he didn't *want* to undo it.

He had to leave Jubilee. Now.

Because, if he stayed, he knew he was going to make love to her. She wanted it as much as he did. He saw it in her eyes. He'd tasted the strength of her desire. Making love to her was so wrong, why then did the idea of it feel so right?

He fumbled the lock, got the door open to his apartment, and tumbled into the room. He pulled his suitcase out from under the bed. He could not stay here. Too much was at stake. He'd never felt like this about anyone and he didn't know how to handle it.

You're doing it again.

Yes, he knew that. Which was why he was leaving. He was falling for a woman who wasn't ready for a relationship. Hell, he wasn't ready. He hadn't seen this coming. Hadn't thought to defend against it.

"Jake, if you were here right now, you'd punch me out for what I want to do to your wife," he muttered, rolling up his shirts and stuffing them in the suitcase.

He didn't know why he'd stayed this long. Okay, that was a lie. He did know why he'd stayed this long. Lissette. She was the reason he'd stayed and she was the reason he had to go.

Rafferty sank down on the bed, dropped his hands in his lap. He didn't want to leave, but how could he stay? If he stayed, he wouldn't be able to keep his hands off her. He would have to make love to her.

Go.

Blowing out his breath, he fell back onto the mattress, stared up at the ceiling. He wiped a hand over his mouth. Lissette. Lissy. He wanted her with an urgent yearning that would not subside.

Get out of here.

What about Slate? What about getting money for her? What about helping her with her business? What about meeting Claudia and finding out about his father? What about Kyle?

What about him? Save your hide. Get lost, cowboy. Climb into that old pickup and head west. Now.

And he would have gone too if a sudden crackling hadn't come over the intercom and Lissy's voice saying, "Rafferty, I need you. Now."

Instantly, he sprang into action. Not knowing what she wanted or needed, but by damn, he was on it. He scrambled down the stairs and crossed the backyard, almost running to get to her.

He pushed open the French doors without even knocking. "Lissy, what is it?"

Lissette was standing over the kitchen sink, clutching her left hand around her wrist, staunching the flow of blood dripping down her fingers. On the marble slab island sat a glistening sharp butcher knife and a half-cut butter yellow spaghetti squash. She turned incredibly calm eyes on him.

"What happened?" He snatched up a cup towel from the counter and rushed toward her.

"Minor kitchen mishap," she said mildly. "But I'm going to need stitches. Can you drive me to the emergency room?"

After Lissette's hand had been sewn and bandaged (it took eleven stitches to close the deep gash from the top of her thumb all the way down to her wrist) the doctor released her with the admonition to take it easy for a few days. No cooking.

The knife had slipped while she'd been chopping up the tough-skinned spaghetti squash for a new recipe she'd dubbed Tumbleweed Bread. In retrospect, she should have cooked the squash whole and sliced it up afterward.

Heck, in retrospect you should have had your mind on what you were doing instead of on Rafferty's kiss.

Feeling a little light-headed from the blood loss and drama, she made her way to the ER waiting room where Rafferty sat with Kyle on his knee, playing giddy-up horsey. Kyle was grinning and clinging to Rafferty's kneecap as Rafferty bounced him up and down.

When he spied her, Rafferty immediately got to his feet, swinging Kyle up and into his arms with the smooth movements so practiced it looked as if he'd been a dad all his life. Concern clouded his brown eyes as his gaze took in her bandaged hand.

"You okay?"

"Fine," she admitted. "Except I shudder to think about the hospital bill."

"I've already taken care of it," he said.

For a moment, she thought about protesting. She didn't want to be dependent on him, but it simply took too much energy to argue, and right now, her thumb was starting to throb again as the local anesthetic wore off. All she wanted to do was go home and take a long nap. "I'll pay you back."

"No."

"Yes, I will. I—"

"Lissy," he said in a kind but commanding tone. "It's taken care of and that's the end of it. You don't owe me. If anything, I owe you."

"How's that?" she asked as he escorted her from the hospital.

"You opened your home and heart to me without any prejudice or hesitation. You accepted me for who I am. Do you know what a rare quality that is?"

He depressed the door locks on her truck's remote control key chain and opened the passenger side door. He held out his hand to help her climb inside. "Lean on me," he welcomed.

What temptation, to lean on him.

Instead, she boosted herself into the seat, even though

she had to use her injured hand to do it. She turned her head so he wouldn't see her wince.

Was she being stubborn? Stupid? The deal was that she simply couldn't grow accustomed to having him around. He'd be leaving soon enough, she might as well get used to it. Still, he had gotten her out of a jam. It made her realize how completely vulnerable she really was, a single mom living alone with a deaf child.

"I don't know what I would have done if you hadn't been here," she said, feeling sheepishly grateful, once he'd gotten Kyle buckled into his car seat and joined her in the cab of the pickup.

"You would have called 911. I didn't do anything special."

"Thank you for being here."

He shrugged, looked uncomfortable with her gratitude.

She'd needed him and he'd been there in a crisis. He was a man you could count on, but she didn't want to count on him. All she wanted was to be strong enough to take care of herself and her son. Was that so much to ask?

Slanting her head, she glanced over at him. He was so good-looking. He stared straight ahead, concentrating on the road. Her mind drifted back to the kiss. How he'd made her feel. It had been such a long time since she'd felt wanted, cherished, sexy. Jake's affairs had made her insecure about her femininity. Rafferty's attention restored it.

When they got to the house, Rafferty insisted on carrying a sleeping Kyle inside to his bed and she didn't argue.

"Now," he said, turning to her as she shut Kyle's door after them, leaving it open just a crack. "You need to take a nap as well."

He ushered her up the steps to her bedroom, but hesitated at the threshold. "Anything I can get for you? Some aspirin? A glass of water?"

"I'm fine," she said. "They gave me a mild painkiller at the hospital." She was acutely aware of the fact that he was in her bedroom. The big king-sized bed stretched out like an invitation.

How crazy was it that she wanted him? Fantasized that he'd strip off both their clothes and join her in the bed. It was just a fantasy. They couldn't progress beyond that kiss for so many reasons, but that didn't change the fact that goose bumps fled up her back at the thought of his naked body pressed against hers.

She stared at his lips, wished he'd kiss her again. Neither of them moved.

"Sleep well," Rafferty said finally, and then turned and bounded down the stairs.

Leaving Lissette feeling hot, achy, and more confused than ever.

It was time to tell Claudia about Rafferty.

Between her aching hand and her guilty conscience, she hadn't managed to snatch more than a few hours of sleep the previous night. Rafferty was staying at her place. He'd met her friends. She couldn't keep hiding him from her mother-in-law. Claudia was going to be hurt, but the longer Lissette put off telling her about him, the worse it would be.

On Monday morning, while Rafferty had taken Slate over to Joe's ranch to cut cattle, she had called Claudia and asked her to meet her at the little park in Lissette's neighborhood at nine o'clock. She'd picked the park because it was neutral territory and Kyle loved playing there, but she'd been so on edge, she'd arrived early.

She'd paced for a while, practicing how she would break the news about Rafferty. She sat down on a playground swing, wrapped her fingers around the chain, the thick wad of the bandage on the pad of her thumb providing a barrier over the stitches.

Lissette couldn't remember the last time she'd swung on a playground swing. When she was a kid living in an upscale Dallas suburb, there'd been a neighborhood park not far from their house with tall, A-frame metal swing sets.

The seats of the swings were long and wide and made of smooth polished wood, just perfect for risk-taking girls who dared to stand up on the seats in a valiant attempt to swing high enough to flip over the top of the pole. She had never been risk-taking, daring, or valiant.

Her mind wandered to last week's merry-go-round of consultations with doctors and therapists and deaf educators, all orchestrated by her parents. She'd accepted their help because it was for Kyle, but a nugget of resentment lodged in her stomach. They didn't think she was capable of taking care of her own child.

Her brain buzzed on information overload, her mind fraught with choices and decisions about Kyle's future. There were all kinds of things to consider about educating her son. Things she'd never imagined.

Everyone seemed to have an opinion on what she should do—from the experts, to her parents, to her friends, to Claudia, to Guillermo. Whatever she decided, they all assured her it was urgent that she make a decision and make it soon.

It normally took her a long time to make up her mind. She liked to explore, consider all possibilities, weigh the pros and cons before jumping into something. The few times she had been rushed into a decision—marrying Jake for one—she'd ended up unhappy with the results. But she knew she irritated people who moved faster. Those closed-ended types who seemed to rule the world. Make a decision. Move on. Next!

Bundled in a hooded sweatshirt, Kyle was silently rolling a toy truck through the sandbox.

When she was small and let loose in a park, Lissette

would run from one piece of playground equipment to the other, never able to make up her mind which one to play on first. She'd hop on a swing, then hop off to join one of her sisters on the slide, think better of it halfway up the ladder and skip over to ride a spring horse.

"Make up your mind," her mother would holler at her, "and start having fun, Lissy."

But when she'd dig into the sand pit, the jungle gym enticed and she'd end up like a hummingbird, flitting from flower to flower, never settling in, and never filling up. She admired that Kyle knew what he wanted, made a choice, and stuck with it.

She inhaled deeply. It was the kind of morning Claudia called the dog days of autumn—those languid days just before the holidays began, when the air tasted dusty and the fields lay fallow following fall harvest, a time of stifling, stagnant waiting.

Lissette pushed with her blue-jeaned legs, kicking out, and then tucking her legs back to send the swing moving forward faster.

Higher and higher she flew, her stomach rolling up and tumbling down with the back-and-forth motion. She glanced down from her lofty perch. The playground stretched out before her like a baking sheet lined with cookies, uniform rows between the sandbox, the jungle climber, the slide, teeter-totters, spring horses, the space whirl.

She kicked higher and higher, soaring toward the sky laden with moody gray clouds. A few minutes later she was whizzing so fast she could barely see Kyle in the sandbox below her. How things had gotten so complicated so fast?

For most of her life, she'd depended on others to give her direction, tell her which way to go. She'd made a talent of ignoring her own instincts, burying her needs. The only time she'd ever rebelled was when she'd dropped out of college to go to culinary school. How had she managed to gather up the courage for that insurrection? Why did she now feel so stymied? So unable to chose a path and walk down it?

Because this was about Kyle's future, whatever choice she made now would affect him for the rest of his life.

If Jake were here, he'd listen to his gut, and then pick the path he thought was right and never look back, and Lissette would have gone along for the ride.

But Jake was not here. He could not make this choice for her. It was time to claim her power, and accept the consequences that went along with it.

Tired of her own mental machinations, she glanced at her watch. It was just after nine. A moment later, her mother-in-law's silver Acura pulled into the playground parking space. She got out.

Lissette quit kicking her legs, allowing the swing to slow. By the time Claudia had picked her way across the lawn, she had come to a complete stop, her feet firmly planted in the sand.

"I was very happy to hear from you," Claudia said, anxiously biting her lip. "I kept waiting for you to call to tell me how things went last week with Kyle's appointments."

It took Lissette a minute to realize that her mother-in-law believed she was shutting her out, and in a way, perhaps she was. Nothing personal against Claudia, but when she was around it was difficult for Lissette to find her own strength. It's why Lissette hadn't called her. That and the fact her mind was filled with Rafferty and guilt.

"Oh! What happened to your hand?"

Lissette wasn't ready to get into the details, so she just kept her explanation short and to the point. "Cut it. Had to get stitches."

"Goodness," Claudia flattened her palm against her chest. "Why didn't you call me?"

"He loves the sandbox." Lissette nodded at her son, who'd filled both hands with sand and was slowly letting the grains trickle through his fingers. "It's the first place he goes."

"Do you need help with the emergency room bill? I know you have that horribly high deductible. What are you going to do about those medical bills?" Claudia fretted.

"I've got it under control."

"If you need money, I can help. I've talked to Karen about letting me go full-time. She seemed amenable." Claudia worked part-time in medical billing for a group of OB/GYNs. She surprised Lissette by sinking down on the swing next to her. Idly, she kicked her legs, setting the swing in motion.

Lissette launched her own swing again.

They swung in opposition. Lissette going forward as Claudia rolled back.

"I remember when Jake was his age." Claudia nodded at Kyle.

The chains on the swings creaked in unison. Lissette said nothing.

"I would have done anything for him," Claudia said, "done anything to protect him." Her face turned fierce, her voice hardened. "I could have killed anyone who threatened Jake with my bare hands if need be."

As a mother, Lissette completely understood where Claudia was coming from. *Hurt my kid, and I'm coming after you.* But the ruthlessness in Claudia's voice was startling.

"I can't strangle hearing loss," Lissette mumbled.

Claudia's swing slowed. She spurred hers faster. They passed each other by, Lissette headed up, her mother-in-law sliding back.

"You need to fight this. Fight back."

"Like you fought to keep Jake from reenlisting?" The second the words were out of her mouth, Lissette regretted them.

Claudia looked stricken. "Are you blaming me for Jake's death?"

The question settled into the dark quilt of clouds hanging low over the horizon. Her mother-in-law voiced the question that Lissette had been asking herself for months.

Did Claudia blame *her* for Jake's death because she'd been unable to keep him home?

They'd avoided the topic. Avoided anything to do with war. If a movie about soldiers came on the television, or the nightly news had a special report about the Middle East, either she or Claudia would casually, but quickly, change the channel. Whenever they drove over the Brazos River bridge together, neither of them looked at the water rushing below where they'd scattered Jake's ashes.

Now, Lissette realized they'd both been feeling guilty. Each thinking the other one held her accountable, both of them afraid to broach the subject for fear of hurting the other.

Should she say something first? Should she tell her mother-in-law that she suspected Jake was having an affair? Or should she keep the waters unruffled? The boat unrocked? Keep the mutual guilt and secrets and hurt and shame hidden away?

It would be so easy just to let things go. She had enough to worry about without digging up ghosts.

Lissette glanced down from her perch, seeking her son in the sandbox.

He wasn't there!

A moment of sheer terror kicked her heart and a spurt of hot adrenaline shot through her veins as momentum swung her backward, her gaze frantically searching the playground for him.

He'd just been there. How could he have disappeared so quickly?

She jumped right out of the moving swing. Hit the ground with both feet, the hard impact jolting up into her hip joints.

She whipped her head around. Desperation gripped her. "Kyle!" she almost cried out. Then remembered that he couldn't hear her. She clamped her lips tightly closed.

The loud rumble of an approaching diesel engine reached her ears. At last, she spied Kyle, and he was toddling for the street.

"Kyle!" Claudia's scream shattered the calm of the peaceful neighborhood. Her voice echoed out loud and long.

In that moment, it struck her as odd that Lissette had not screamed too and then she realized her daughter-in-law had already made adjustments for her son's deafness and instead of wasting time and energy hollering, she sprinted for the street at a dead run. How swiftly it had happened, Lissy's practical acceptance of the thing she could not change.

Lissette snagged the hood of Kyle's sweater, yanking her son back from the curb at the same time a red pickup truck halted in the middle of the street. Even as relief and gratitude pushed through Claudia, something darker brewed inside her. Something she was highly ashamed of.

Envy.

That green putrid bile at the crux of Claudia's greatest misdeed.

She was jealous that it had taken Lissette little more than a week to come to terms with her child's deafness. To Claudia, it seemed almost callous to recover so rapidly.

The door of the pickup opened and a cowboy got out, tall, lanky, handsome as the devil.

Instantly, her jealousy evaporated, replaced by stone-cold terror. She was staring at a ghost.

Up close, Rafferty Jones looked so much like his father had at that age. A gray Stetson sat perched atop his head. He was slightly bowlegged, just as Gordon had been, and he moved with a silent grace toward Lissette. When he reached her, he lowered his head to murmur something in her ear and touched her shoulder in a tender gesture as she clutched hard to Kyle.

Claudia's baby was gone and Amelia Jones's was here. Not only here but he was looking at Jake's wife and child with incredible tenderness, as if they were *his* wife and child.

Her hands curled into fists as hard as crabapples.

And the truly awful thing was that Lissette was looking at him the same way. In a way she'd never quite looked at Jake. The same way she'd looked at Rafferty the night Claudia had seen them together through Lissy's French doors.

How long had this been going on?

Claudia knew then that she was in serious jeopardy of losing the two things she held most dear—her daughter-in-law and her grandson.

She slapped a palm over her mouth. Her entire body shook.

Rafferty lifted his head, met her gaze.

Panic was a corkscrew, twisting deep into her center. She wanted to run, but her feet were rooted to the spot as in a nightmare when the nameless monster is upon you.

Maybe that's all this was.

A nightmare.

Rafferty stepped away from Lissette, and came toward her.

Wake up, Claudia. Wake up.

Everything slowed, intensified.

In a surreal instant, she saw him how he'd been, a solemn two-year-old, wearing nothing but a diaper and staring at her with accusing eyes. The same dark eyes that were stabbing her now.

Claudia struggled to swallow the hard knot of bile blocking her esophagus, but her throat seized, froze. A thin whistle of air slipped between her lips. She wondered if this was what it felt like to be found guilty in a court of law. If even after the verdict was read, the jury's scalding eyes passing outraged and righteous judgment, you would stand there swaying on your trembling knees, your mind blank as if your body understood something your brain could not.

Guilty. Time to pay the price for your sins.

He was upon her, hand extended, his mouth curving into a smile.

A smile.

He was smiling at her.

For one brief moment joyous relief bloomed in her heart. He forgave her. She'd been forgiven.

"Hi," he said. "I'm Rafferty Jones."

And then she realized he had no idea who she was.

"This is my mother-in-law, Claudia Moncrief," Lissette said.

Rafferty's smile stumbled. Failed.

A whip of rage lashed Claudia—black and red and hot as Satan. Rage just as fierce as it had been on that day twenty-seven years ago when she'd found Amelia's letter tucked in Gordon's hip pocket as she was stuffing his dirty jeans into the laundry.

The smile was gone, but his hand stayed extended.

Shake his hand. Say hello.

But she could not. She would not!

"Mom, this is Rafferty," Lissette continued the blasphemous introductions. "Gordon's son. He's staying in my garage apartment and training Slate to compete in the futurity. He's been there for the past ten days. I wanted to tell you earlier, but I didn't know how to bring it up."

Mom?

How dare Lissette call her Mom under these circumstances when she'd blindsided her with this man?

Hold up, old gal, she didn't blindside you. This is it. Your chance for redemption. You can confess, get it all off your chest. Make peace. Make your way to forgiveness. Get whole. Get good. Straighten everything out.

But if she did that, then they'd know the truth about her. They'd know her shame and she'd be rejected. Disconnected from her loved ones. She couldn't tolerate being that vulnerable. That wounded.

"Gordon's son, Gordon's *only* son, is dead." Claudia spit out the words cold as obsidian pebbles.

Rafferty stood unmoving, that hand still outthrust.

Claudia batted it away. A smart smack. Her palm slapping against his knuckles.

"Mom!" Lissette's shocked gasp punched a hole in the dreary air.

I'm sorry. I'm so sorry. Forgive me. Please, forgive me. I've lost everything. I'm damaged. I'm hurting Rafferty because I've been hurt.

But that's not what Claudia said. Fear hardened her eyes, shrunk her heart, twisted her brain, kidnapped what she really wanted to say. "I am not your mom. And as long as you have anything to do with this man, I do not want to have anything to do with you."

Chapter Fourteen

A sick feeling, heavy and insistent, curled tight against Lissette's rib cage. Four days had passed since that awful encounter at the park but she still could not forget that hateful expression on Claudia's face and the awful things she'd said. She'd never seen this alarming side of her mother-in-law.

"Lissy?"

She blinked, looked over at her friend Mariah. They were sitting in the back room of the The Bride Wore Cowboy Boots, coordinating the details for an upcoming wedding. Rafferty had taken Claudia's reaction in stride. "You can't really blame her," he'd said. "Look at it from her point of view. I'm her worst nightmare. She thinks you've replaced Jake with me."

In a way, wasn't that precisely what she'd done? That notion unsettled her almost as much as her mother-in-law's behavior. She'd left Kyle with Mariah's babysitter because she wasn't about to call Claudia after her cold announcement in the park. She was absentmindedly doodling on a piece of notebook paper, drawing pictures of wedding cakes.

"Uh-huh?"

"You're a million miles away."

She gave Mariah a rueful smile. "I'm sorry."

Mariah laid a hand on Lissette's forearm. "Do you want to talk about it?"

Lissette sighed. "It's Claudia." Briefly, she updated Mariah on what was going on between her and her mother-in-law.

"This is a tough time for you both."

"I know."

"I can't imagine what Claudia is going through, losing a son."

"I agree, but the way she treated Rafferty was inexcusable. She slapped his hand, Mariah."

"That doesn't sound like Claudia. She must be out of her head with grief."

"I know, but she's cutting me off because I'm associating with Rafferty. I can't deny that it hurts, but Kyle is the one who is truly suffering. He loves his grandmother so much."

"Have you considered asking Rafferty to leave?"

Lissette hardened her chin. "He already suggested that, but he's done nothing wrong. She owes him an apology, and even if he left town, this rift between us isn't going to be so easily cleared up."

"You certainly don't need this on top of everything else."

"Exactly." Lissette fussed with the sheet of notebook paper, curling up one corner around her index finger.

"Still, it would go a long way to repairing the damage if Rafferty left town."

Lissette met Mariah's eyes. "He's teaching Kyle sign language and training Slate and helping me expand my business."

"It's more than just that, isn't it?" Mariah's voice softened.

Helpless, Lissette nodded. It *was* more than just that. She did not want Rafferty to leave town, and that worried her most of all.

"You like him."

"Far more than I should," she admitted.

"Wow. That's sticky."

"Yeah."

Mariah pushed back from the table and got to her feet. She was a bundle of energy and couldn't sit still for very long. "So from a purely objective view, to keep the peace you could simply hire someone else to train Slate and I could help you with your business."

"Yes, but I don't know anyone else who could teach Kyle sign language."

"You're going to send him to school for that."

"He's Kyle's uncle, and Rafferty's deaf foreman is giving me insight into the condition."

"And didn't you tell me that the foreman was pressuring you to educate Kyle the way he thinks your son should be educated?"

Lissette nibbled her thumbnail. "No more than Claudia is pressuring me to teach him lipreading instead of sign language."

"Oh," Mariah said, her eyes widening as if something had just occurred to her.

"What is it?"

"I finally get what's going on here. You don't want to keep the peace."

"What?" Lissette shook her head.

"You don't *want* to smooth things over with Claudia."

"Of course I do."

Mariah gave a delighted laugh.

She frowned. "What's so funny?"

"I think it's wonderful, Lissy. You're always so worried about what everyone else thinks that you bury your own needs and keep your opinions to yourself. I think it's a good thing that you're not letting Claudia bully you into sending Rafferty away."

"She's not bullying me. You should have seen her. She looked completely shattered, Mariah. She was just lashing out."

"The answer is easy enough."

Lissette stared at her. "And that is?"

"What do *you* really want?"

She'd struggled to figure out how she could please everyone. "I want him to stay. He's going to leave soon enough anyway."

"There you go. That's your answer."

"But—"

"No buts. Let Claudia stew or pout or whatever she's doing, and when Rafferty's gone you two can kiss and make up."

"What if our relationship can't go back to normal?"

"Maybe it will be better than it used to be."

"I don't see how."

"Perhaps by standing up for what you want she'll see who you really are, not just Jake's wife and Kyle's mother."

Mariah made a good point. "Still, I don't want to hurt her. She's very dear to me."

"I know. You're just an old softie." Mariah gave her a one-armed hug. "But I want to know more about these feelings you're having for Rafferty."

"It's nothing but gratitude. He's been a big help to me."

"And you're sure that's all it is?"

"Absolutely." But while she might be able to fib to her friend, in her heart, Lissette knew the truth. What she was feeling for Rafferty was a whole lot more than gratitude.

She wanted him.

And in the worst—or maybe it was the best—way possible.

For the next several days leading up to Halloween, life slipped into a welcome routine. She'd worked on getting the word out about her online bakery business and she'd already had several orders. A couple of days a week, she helped Mariah in her shop and she was still baking wedding cakes.

She got a book on sign language and enrolled in an online class. She worked with Kyle on signing, but she wasn't as facile as Rafferty. Never mind. She would get there. Rafferty ate alone in his room. He never came to the back door anymore. Lissette tried to tell herself that was a good thing and kept working.

On the day before Halloween, she bought Kyle a Spider-Man costume. Not terribly original, but it was the outfit he'd wanted. Probably the vivid red and blue colors were what had attracted his attention. She'd become aware over the course of the past few weeks of how much colors mattered to him. Vision was important. She considered painting his room in primary colors.

He insisted on wearing the costume the minute they got home, running through the house, climbing on things and jumping off them. His exuberance lifted her spirits.

"Now that's a superhero," Rafferty said, lounging one shoulder against the back doorframe.

Lissette's breath caught as her gaze landed on him. His eyes were soft. A smile tipped his mouth. She hadn't seen him in days and he was a sight for sore eyes.

"How are you, Lissy?"

"Good. I'm good."

"You look good." His eyes grazed her.

"Thanks. Is there something you need?"

You, his expression said. "Since Joe and Mariah invited me to their Halloween party tomorrow, I was wondering if you could help me come up with a costume?"

"Sure, sure. I can do that. What have you dressed up as in the past?" she asked.

"In L.A. I could get away with dressing as a cowboy, so I went in my work clothes. But in Jubilee, that's not going to cut it."

"That's true."

"Are you dressing up?"

"I am."

"What are you going as?"

"I'm a traditionalist when it comes to Halloween costumes."

"Something classic, huh?"

"I'm going as a vampire."

"Sexy."

"Economical too. Same costume I wore last year."

"We could always poke two holes in a sheet and call me a ghost."

"We can do better than that." She hitched Spider-Man on her hip and moved across the floor to take Rafferty by the hand.

She knew it was a mistake the minute she touched him. The jolt of electricity that passed between them had nothing to do with static electricity and everything to do with their lightning-hot chemistry. But she didn't want him to know he unnerved her, so she did not let go. She dragged him outside.

"Where are we going?"

"The storm shelter."

"The storm shelter?" he echoed. "What for?"

"You're going as a tornado."

"A what?"

"You know, those whirling things that drop out from the sky and cause lots of destruction."

"I know what a tornado is. How do you propose to whip up a tornado costume by tomorrow night?"

"I already have a tornado costume."

He pulled back at the entrance to the storm shelter. "Is it an old costume of Jake's?"

"Would that bother you?"

"I'd rather not take any more of his castoffs."

Lissette stopped, let go his hand. "What do you mean?"

The wind blew scattered leaves across the lawn and ruffled Rafferty's hair. Kyle squirmed in her arms. She turned her head to see what had captured her son's attention. A brown squirrel, cheeks full of acorns, ran up a tree.

"Could you sign 'squirrel' for him?" Lissette asked. "I haven't learned that one yet."

Rafferty moved around her so Kyle could see him and moved his hands.

Kyle grinned, settled down. How much easier it was to communicate with her son when Rafferty was around. She was going to have to seriously apply herself to learning sign language so she didn't have to depend on him.

"What do you mean, Jake's castoffs?" she asked.

There were so many skeletons popping out of closets around here. Appropriate enough on Halloween. She just wanted the damn closet door wrenched up and cleaned out. She was tired of being blindsided by the past. Tired of tripping over the littered mess of the dead. Gordon and Jake's ghosts were impacting her life far too much.

"Nothing. Forget I said anything. Let's see that costume. It sounds interesting."

"What castoffs did you get of Jake's?"

He shrugged. "It's nothing, really."

"Then if it's nothing, why not just tell me?"

Rafferty sighed, shifted. "Claudia used to send boxes of Jake's clothes and toys when he outgrew them."

That surprised her. She thought Claudia had been too resentful for that kind of generosity, and it made her feel bad that she hadn't yet tried to mend fences with her mother-in-law. She should call her. Apologize.

"Don't get me wrong. I was happy to have the clothes. It was better than walking around in high-water rags, but just once, just one time I wished I had new clothes. Something bought just for me, something that was all mine. Something I didn't have to share with an invisible big brother. Taking Jake's clothes made me feel . . ." He paused.

She didn't rush to question him. Instead, she studied his face, watching for emotions that he was reluctant to show.

He shrugged. "Unimportant."

"I'm sorry you were made to feel that way."

"Hey, we all have some kind of childhood angst, right? That was just my version."

"The tornado costume wasn't Jake's," she assured him. "It's actually a wedding prop."

"A what?"

"You know, for the cowboy weddings that Mariah puts on. One couple met because of a tornado. They wanted it in their wedding. So we have a sandwich board made up with a picture of a tornado on it. All you have to do is drape it over your head and presto, instant costume."

Rafferty laughed and she realized how much she loved the sound. "I can do that."

Halloween in Jubilee was a little different from Halloween in most places. Around the country kids went from door to door, asking for tricks or treats. Some neighborhoods organized block parties. In other towns, parents pulled their decorated cars into school or church parking lots and kids trick or treated from car to car. Others honored the tradition of fall harvest with carnivals including games of chance, face painting, dunking booths, and cakewalks.

Jubilee put its own unique spin on the holiday, merging several traditions into one. The local ranchers took turns hosting the experience. This year, Joe and Mariah Daniels opened up Green Ridge Ranch to the public.

Instead of going door to door or car to car, kids rode horses, going from cow to cow, snatching handfuls of candy from the saddlebags strapped over the wooden cut-outs painted like Holsteins, but that was just the beginning of the festivities. After trick or treating came the bonfire. Complete with weenie and marshmallow roasts, spooky ghost stories told by some grizzled cowboy, and followed finally by a late night hayride. They had dunking booths for sinking sad sack cowhands, bobbing for apples, and instead of cakewalks, there were pie walks.

Rafferty, Lissette, and Kyle arrived at Green Ridge Ranch. Ila was playing traffic cop, directing people where to park. He parked, cut the engine, and unbuckled his seat belt. "I'll get Kyle," he told Lissette, "so you can carry your pies."

"I do appreciate the help," she said, retrieving the two boxes of Giddy-up Pecan Pie she'd made for the pie walk to help advertise her expanded bakery menu.

Rafferty took the toddler from his car seat. Kyle was busily sucking on a pumpkin-shaped pacifier. Rafferty enjoyed the familiar heft of the boy in his arms. He trailed behind Lissette, feeling a bit out of place as people rushed up to her.

"Mmm," Ila said when they went past her. "Lissy's pies are the fast road to inner peace."

"Well, well," said Cordy as he came up to greet them wearing a black cape and vampire teeth, his only stab at a costume. "Let me guess. You're a real Texas twister."

"What?" Rafferty frowned, and then remembered he was dressed like a tornado. "Oh, yeah."

"I'll take the pies from you, Lissy," Cordy offered. "You might want to hurry on over to the equestrian center. They're saddling up the ponies for the kids."

"You want a beer, Rafferty?" Joe asked, nodding to a gold-plated horse trough loaded down with iced beer.

Rafferty raised a hand. "No thanks. I better help Lissette with Kyle." He didn't drink, but he realized that other men often thought him odd or unsocial because he didn't.

He followed Lissette as she joined the stream of people walking through a gateway arch with a sign above it that said: "The Dutch Callahan Equine Center."

A man in a horse costume was leading horses from the barn while ranch hands saddled them up and helped children climb aboard. Off to the side was a corral full of polled cattle.

"One group of six at a time," the man in the horse costume said. He pulled the horse head off, tucked it under his arm, and fanned himself with the opposite hand. "No one told me it was hot as hell in this damn thing," he complained with a wink and a grin.

"Brady!" Lissette exclaimed, and hugged the man in the horse costume. "You're back."

"We are."

"Where's Annie?"

"Somewhere in this madhouse." He flapped a hoof at the thickening crowd.

"Rafferty, this is horse whisperer Brady Talmadge. Brady, Rafferty trains horses for the movies."

"I'd shake hands but . . ." Brady held up his hooves. "I'm familiar with your work. You're famous."

Rafferty shrugged. "There's not many people training horses for the movies."

"We should get together. Talk shop."

"I'd like that," Rafferty said, and was surprised to realize that he really would.

He and Lissette took Kyle to the corral where the saddled ponies were lined up. A surprised expression came over Kyle's face when Rafferty set him in the saddle. He looked to his mother. She signed. "Okay."

Kyle shifted his gaze back to Rafferty. He nodded at the boy.

Lissette gave Kyle a sack decorated with pumpkins. She walked beside him while Rafferty led the horse to where the trick-or-treating cows were set up. Unique way to experience Halloween. He would have loved this as a kid. Hell, he was enjoying himself now.

After the trick or treating, they made their way over to the bonfire. Lissette had brought camp chairs for them to sit on and Rafferty went back to the truck to retrieve them. When he came back, he took Kyle from her. "So you can circulate with your friends."

She met his gaze. "I'm good right here."

He didn't know what to think. Things with Lissette could turn on a dime. They had this whole push-pull thing going on between them, and while he understood why she ran hot and then cold and then hot again, it was starting to get to him. Especially when she looked so sexy and she kept throwing those winsome glances his way.

Kyle stared at the fire, mesmerized. Rafferty bounced him on his knee while Lissette skewered a clutch of marshmallows and squatted down to hold them over the fire. Her hair gleamed in the crackling glow. The air smelled smoky.

Nearby, an old cowboy was telling a modernized version of the story of the headless horseman to a group of tweens who were trying to act like they weren't the least bit scared.

When Lissette pulled a cooled roasted marshmallow off the skewer and popped it in Kyle's mouth, Rafferty enjoyed seeing the delight spread across his face. Kyle held out a hand, wanting more.

"Let him roast his own marshmallow, Mama," Rafferty suggested.

"I don't want him getting that close to the fire. He's too little."

"The boy knows what hot is."

She looked like she was about to argue, but she then nodded, loosing the apron strings.

"Come to Mommy." She held out her arm to Kyle, and Rafferty slid him off his knee so the boy could go to her. Lissette gave him a raw marshmallow and guided his hand, showing him how to put it on the skewer.

Lissette glanced over her shoulder at Rafferty, a big grin on her face. She had one hand wrapped around Kyle's waist as her son struggled to hold the skewer over a small flame at the bottom of the bonfire. He kept turning his face into his mother's chest to escape the intensity of the heat, but when she tried to relieve him of his obligation, he would grunt, screw up his face, and determinedly go back to his task.

"He's loving being in control," Lissette said. "Thank you for suggesting I let him try."

"Hey, he's an independent kid. There's no holding this one back."

After the hot dogs were consumed and all the wieners roasted, after the ghost stories were told and the musical among them had played a few Halloween songs on guitars and harmonicas, Joe announced it was time for the hayride.

A tractor engine revved up in an adjacent pasture. It

pulled a trailer piled with loose hay. Teenagers were the first to climb aboard, jostling around to sit with a particular girl or boy. Next came the families who didn't mind staying up late. The early birds were gathering up their things, saying good night and heading for their vehicles.

"You want to go on the hayride?" Lissette asked, a hopeful note in her voice.

"Sure," Rafferty said easily. He got up from the folding camp chair, held out a hand to her.

She hitched Kyle on her hip and took Rafferty's hand. They walked across the pasture in the light of the full moon. Rafferty found them a spot big enough for the three of them. Kyle's eyelids were already sinking.

One of the guitarists sat across from them. He was picking a tune from The Band Perry, "If I Die Young." It made Rafferty think of Jake. He wondered if Lissy was thinking of him too. How many times had she and Jake ridden on a hayride just like this together?

"None," she whispered.

Rafferty startled. "What?"

"You were wondering how often Jake and I took a hayride."

"How do you know that?"

"When you're thinking about Jake you get this tense set to your chin."

"He never took you on a hayride?"

She shook her head. "He said it was too slow-paced."

Rafferty stretched out an arm around the back of the trailer's boards. Lissette's hair trailed over his hand. A jumble of emotions mixed up inside him. Desire. Longing. Sex. Things he shouldn't be thinking about. Not in regard to his dead brother's wife.

"Well, lucky for you I like slow-paced," he drawled, and immediately regretted it the minute he said it.

"I've noticed," she said in a throaty tone, "that you don't ever get in a hurry."

"You should have seen me the time I dislodged a nest of yellow jackets from a lemon tree when I was twelve. I was moving pretty quickly then."

"I'll bet." She chuckled.

"You're making fun of my pain?" he teased.

"Did you get stung?"

"Six times. On the face."

"Ouch. I'm sorry." She reached up to cup his cheek in her palm.

The soft, simple stroke was his undoing. Try as he might, Rafferty couldn't fight off his natural masculine reaction. He closed his eyes, took a deep breath, prayed it was dark enough on the ride that nobody noticed.

The guitarist switched tempo and went into Vince Gill's "Cowboy Up." That got the group—including Lissette—singing along.

The tractor toiled through the field. The moonlight played against scarecrows and pumpkins. The leaves of a corn maze rustled spookily in the wind. Lissette leaned against his shoulder. Her sweet scent carried to him. She looked so sexy in her vampire cape, dark makeup, and black fishnet hose. Some of the couples were kissing. Rafferty quelled an almost impossible urge to kiss Lissy.

It was a perfect night. The kind of special night you wish you could capture in a jar so when you opened it later you could be right back in that moment. Too bad memories didn't work that way.

"Is he asleep yet?" she whispered.

Rafferty bent his head to get a look at her little Spider-Man. His eyes were shut tightly and he was slumped in his mother's arms, completely relaxed. "He's out."

"You've made this so much easier," Lissy murmured.

"What?"

"Dealing with Kyle's deafness."

"It was sheer luck that I knew sign language."

"I don't know, sometimes I wonder if fate didn't bring us together."

Rafferty smiled. "You believe in fate?"

She shrugged. "What if you hadn't been in Australia and you'd come the minute you heard about Jake's death? You wouldn't have stayed around in July."

"Probably not," he admitted.

"What if Jake hadn't left you the money? You probably won't have shown up at all."

"I would have," Rafferty said, but he had to wonder if it was true.

"It just seemed you showed up at the right time."

"It's easy to romanticize coincidence."

"We don't want to do that, do we?"

"Do we?"

The tractor labored to a stop. They were back at the ranch house. Mariah and Joe were there to greet them. The other passengers climbed out, parents collecting sleepy children and belongings. Neighbors called to one another.

They bade their hosts good night and drove home.

"It was a wonderful evening," Lissette said. "Thank you for making it so special."

"It wasn't an effort. I enjoyed being there."

They didn't speak the rest of the way home, but the sexual tension inside the cab of Lissette's truck was thick as custard. Staying away from each other for several days had not diminished his desire for her one bit. Rather, it made him want her that much more.

The forbidden fruit.

Rafferty carried Kyle into the house for her. He laid

the boy down in his bed, kissed his head and whispered, "Sweet dreams, little guy."

Straightening, he turned to find Lissette standing in the door looking completely irresistible in her vampish costume. She'd cocked her leg at a totally seductive angle and there was a come-hither tilt to her head. Until now, he'd never understood the sex appeal of vampires. But right now, all he could think was *Suck my blood.*

Did she want him or was he reading something into her posture that wasn't there? Desire ran through him, brooding and untamable. He licked his lips.

"Rafferty," she breathed.

The sound of his name on her tongue sent a hot, hard pulsing straight to his groin, and his burning need for her, which had been growing steadily every day, could no longer be denied.

Chapter Fifteen

Lissette raised a hand to her hair, thinking how silly she must look in the vampire costume, and ducked her head. He'd already shed his tornado costume long before the hayride. They stood on opposite sides of the living room. He pulled off his cowboy boots and set them aside. She kicked off her black stilettos.

Rafferty's eyes never left hers. He studied her like she was the most precious thing he'd ever seen and she studied him right back, marveling that it was possible to feel this way about someone so soon, especially when the rest of her life was in tumult.

He traced a finger down the bridge of her nose, stopping at the tip to press down, and then he trailed a path over the ridge of her cheekbone, and followed the line of her jaw to her chin. He caressed her with reverence, marvel in his eyes as if he were a fortune hunter who'd spent his life seeking a legendary treasure he'd almost stopped believing in and had now accidentally stumbled across it.

"C'mere," Rafferty murmured, and held out his hand.

His deep tone of voice, the look of his face cast in shadows sent a sweet shiver winnowing through her bloodstream, but she did not resist. Her will had been slowly eroding since that first night in the pasture.

His hand on hers was sure and strong; his lips firm, but sweetly inviting. They'd been building toward this moment for the past few weeks. Even so, she should have resisted.

But she wanted to yield to him. Meld into him.

Was that so wrong? Was she falling back into old habits simply because he was so easy to be with? Going with the flow, letting herself be carried along by the current of sexual energy surging between them, a dandelion shedding her seeds to the breeze.

But his kiss quickly snuffed out all doubts, blotted everything from her mind except for how he made her feel. Fully, one hundred percent wanted. He wasn't demanding, but instead took his time, drawing out every bit of response in her. His body was so strong. So warm. Radiating so much masculine heat.

His tongue flirted with hers, teasing, coaxing, exploring, arousing.

She strained against him, desperate for more contact. Sensation swirled her around until she didn't know up from down. She felt like silk sliding darkly down a cascade of melted chocolate—rich and weak—and she finally understood there was no going back. She didn't want to go back.

He slipped a hand down her spine, pressed it to the small of her back. Her pulse quickened and she wrapped her arms around his taut waist, held him close. She clung to him and he kept kissing her, exploring her, tasting her. She could feel every inch of his arousal, hot and insistent.

Crave.

She craved him.

His hand slipped to her bottom, his palm cupping one cheek. Panting, aching, she savored every second. Nothing in her universe—and it was a universe of delicious tastes and scents—had ever been so scrumptious.

When he finally pulled his lips away from where he'd been doing devastating things to her throat with his tongue, she let out a noise of frustration. *Don't stop.* She'd waited so very long to feel like this. Fully and completely alive.

"You are so beautiful," he murmured.

She knew she wasn't beautiful. She had two beautiful sisters. But Rafferty made her feel beautiful.

"I know there's a lot of good reasons not to do this, but Lissy, I've never in my life wanted a woman the way I want you. Need you."

"I want you too."

"Last thing I want is to hurt you."

"I don't want to hurt *you*."

He laughed. "Darlin', it's already gonna hurt when I have to leave."

Why do you have to leave? she wanted to ask, but she knew. He had a life in California and hers was here. There were too many other complications. He was her dead husband's half brother. There was Claudia to consider. And Kyle. She could not be irresponsible with her heart.

"Shh," she said. "Let's not talk. Let's not think. Let's just—"

She never got the rest of the words out because his mouth was closing over hers again and he was kissing her like they were already joined.

It was all teeth and tongue and lips and heat and a heartbreaking bittersweetness. He ate her like she was the best tasting cake in the world, as if he could eat and eat and eat her and never get sated.

He reached to untie the strings of her skimpy costume, his fingers unexpectedly cool and a sweet relief to her blistering hot skin. She arched her back, thrusting out her chest, eager to feel his lips on her breasts.

She ran her hands along his upper arms. They were hard as concrete.

"Let me take care of you, Lissy. I want to take care of you. Just for tonight. Don't fight me on this. Give up your pride and let me take you where you need to go."

She wanted to argue because it was so easy for her to turn over the reins. She'd fought for her newfound independence and she didn't want to fall back into old habits. But her body, damn her treacherous body, wanted nothing more than to give it all up to him, let him be in charge, take control, meet her needs.

That's what was different here, she realized with a jolt as his mouth, oh his spectacular mouth, closed over one of her erect nipples, while his wicked hands worked the straps of her costume down over arms. He was looking after her needs rather than pulling her along with him in pursuit of his own satisfaction. Would it be so wrong to simply surrender?

The more he stroked her with his tongue, the more tension gathered, tightening, concentrating in one throbbing location. He seemed in no hurry, leisurely caressing and kneading and massaging her body in miraculous ways.

Time elongated, moved in glorious slow motion. She lost track of everything except him, his mouth alternating between tender and commanding. At one point she tried to get him to hurry, to put out the raging blaze between her legs, but he resisted her anxious urging.

While his tongue was occupied teasing her nipples, his hand traveled down her side to the small of her back, attuned to her every nuanced response and adjusting his pressure according to her soft noises of pleasure. He discovered erogenous zones she never knew she had.

In languid movements, he removed the rest of her clothing, slowly sliding the black fishnet over her legs as if peeling the skin from a banana. Once she was fully undressed, he dispatched this own clothing and she saw for the first time his naked body.

Her breath stilled in her lungs at the sight of him and she realized that he too was holding his breath as his gaze took her in. He was as awestruck with her body as she was with his.

His hands were on her again, sliding smoothly over her waist, and she arched into him. They both kept their eyes wide open, staring into each other, searching deeply and finding what they were both searching for. Acceptance.

Together, they sank to the living room rug.

He kissed her navel and each hipbone, then finally, with a laugh, buried his face in the V between her legs. She twined her fingers through his hair and tugged lightly.

Rafferty teased and explored until she felt like a wild, untamed horse. She bucked, begged, and arched her back. He straddled her, pinned her wrists to the comforter, and stared down at her. Her heart thumped. She should have been scared or at least unnerved a bit. But while this man was powerful, she was not afraid of him. She trusted Rafferty.

With her life.

From somewhere he produced a condom and she helped him roll it on. Then they went back to kissing for a long, sweet time, the towering pressure building higher and hotter in them both.

He made a low growling noise in his throat. "I can't take any more. I have to have you," he murmured into her ear.

She thrust her hips up at him.

He was in her then, slick and hot. She gasped at the sudden intensity of his fierce penetration. He pushed into her, stroking her body both inside and out. Filling her up. Making her whole. Making her feel whole.

Hard muscles grazed over soft curves.

Each thrust drove them closer and closer until she could not tell where he ended and she began. Above her, his face contorted as he struggled for control, fighting against the primal urge pushing him to every bit of her, trying to hold on for as long as he could.

She wrapped her legs around his waist, rocked him into her, deeper and deeper still until there was nothing left to give.

He moved his hands from her wrists, slipped his palms upward, interlaced his fingers with hers. He slowed the pace.

"No," she begged. "Faster."

"If I go faster, I'll come."

"So will I," she gasped.

He let loose then, driving himself into her hard and fast, sending silky spirals swirling through her.

They were one.

His gaze latched tight to hers and she could not look away. Never wanted to look away.

They broke together, tumbling over the crest of their simultaneous orgasm, locked in each other's rapt embrace.

Slowly, their breathing returned to normal and they lay there, arms and legs tangled. She lay with her head on his chest, listening to the crazy tempo of his out-of-control heart.

How odd, lying here with a man who was not Jake. Not just that, but Jake's half brother. It was a thought she did not want to think, so she pushed it away and concentrated on how he'd made her feel.

"That was . . . well, hell, sweetheart, I don't have any words for what that was," he murmured into her hair.

She raised her head, peered at him. He looked so gorgeous in the moonlight spilling through the window. "Right back at you, cowboy."

He lightly tickled her ribs.

"You know," she said. "If I knew you were coming I would have baked a cake."

His hearty laugh rang out. "You get the cutest expression on your face when you're sassy, like you can barely believe you're doing it."

"What can I say? I was raised to be a good girl. I feel naughty when I'm bad."

"Then you're in trouble because you've been a very bad girl."

"I know." She grinned.

"Sassiness is bad?"

"It was in my house."

"Way up there on the hill in Highland Park."

"I know I had it easy."

"I didn't say that."

"Compared to how you grew up?" She shook her head. "My childhood was a cakewalk."

"I'm glad." His voice was somber. "You've had more than your share of sorrow now."

"Things are looking up," she observed.

"If heaven exists it surely smells like you." He kissed her lightly on the forehead.

"You don't believe in heaven?"

"I'd like to," he said, "but I haven't seen any proof of it."

"That's the thing about belief. You have to believe even when there's no proof."

"And what happens if you're wrong? It's not belief at that point but self-deception."

"Your mom never took you to church, did she?"

"Hey, we were lucky if she took us to the grocery store."

"I wish I could understand what that was like."

"No you don't. Be grateful you grew up in a gentle world."

"It didn't prepare me for this."

"You're handling it very well."

"Only because you're here."

"You could make it just fine without me. If I wasn't here, Claudia would help you."

"Claudia doesn't know sign language or how to train a quarter horse."

"Is that all I am to you, Lissy?"

"No," she whispered. "It's not."

"Lissy." He sighed her name. "I've never met a woman like you. You're so strong even though you don't know it. That sassiness you've been keeping under wraps is really an asset."

All at once, melancholia washed over her. "You know this can't last."

"Look at that pretty moon." He pointed at the sky outside the window. "So big and round and yellow. You like yellow."

She burrowed against him, tilted her head up to look at the moon. "It's beautiful, but were you listening to me?"

"Every word." He squeezed her tight and kissed her gently and they lay there for the longest time just staring up at the moon.

Last night, Rafferty had been unable to deny his masculine urges. He'd lost control and made love to Lissette when he knew there was no future for them, but being with Lissy made him feel like Atlas when he shrugged. A huge weight had dropped from his shoulders. When she looked at him with those green eyes that spoke more than words, he experienced a foolish kind of hope.

You're kidding yourself.

Because of Kyle they couldn't fall asleep on the living

room rug, nor did Lissy want her son to wake in the night and find Rafferty in her bed.

"Too confusing for him," she said.

Neither did Rafferty want to sleep in the bed she'd shared with Jake. It just felt wrong.

So they'd separated in the wee hours of the morning, Lissy going to her bedroom, Rafferty hightailing it back to the garage apartment. He vowed he would not make love to her again. It would be too painful. Knowing he was going to have to leave her behind.

Utterly wretched, he dressed at dawn determined to spend the entire day working with Slate and pushing his own body to exhaustion. He didn't want to think about what crossing that line had meant, but he feared that their intimacy would invariably be the thing that pushed them apart.

When he got home, he was surprised to see Lissy waiting for him. "Hi," she called to him out the back door as he trudged up the stairs to the garage apartment. Her smile was bright and sweet. "Dinner's ready."

He wasn't expecting this. He'd anticipated that she would put up a wall, back off, keep her distance. Instead, she was waving him inside that warm house with her and Kyle.

Watch out. It can't last.

Yes, yes, he knew that but he couldn't seem to get to her fast enough.

Once he was through the door, he realized that beneath that frilly apron she was wearing a slinky blue dress with a very short hemline and four-inch stilettos that made her look like a gazelle. He stood there staring.

"Did you want to say something?" she asked.

He could scarcely clear his throat. She has the most gorgeous legs. "Nice dress," he croaked.

"I bought it today."

For him? Something unraveled in his stomach.

"Where's Kyle?" he asked.

"He's spending the weekend with my parents. They came by to get him this afternoon and they'll bring him home on Sunday."

"So we've got the whole weekend alone?" He gulped.

Her grin turned saucy. "We do."

"Is this . . . are you trying to seduce me, Lissy Moncrief?"

Coyly, she lowered her lashes. "Am I too bold?"

"Hell no, darlin'," he said, happiness lighting up his heart, and took her in his arms.

They kissed for a long time and then she pulled back. "I need to check on the meat loaf."

"You sure know the way to a man's heart." He cocked his head as she walked away, his gaze zeroing in on the hem of that dress.

They ate dinner by candlelight. Just the two of them, and it felt like a real date. Afterward, Lissy led him to the bathroom where all around the claw-foot tub scented candles sat. The room glowed romantically in the illumination from the flickering flames.

While she ran a hot bath, complete with bubbles, they did a slow striptease for each other. Lissy put her hair in a ponytail high atop her head and then got into the warm water. Rafferty slid in behind her. He wrapped his arms around her, held her against him, listening to the soft sounds of their tandem breathing as the smell of coconut scented the air. They could be on a tropical island, just the two of them. All alone and blissfully cut off from the rest of the world. It was a wonderful dream.

Lissy had gone quiet.

"What is it?" he asked, squeezing her tighter.

"I was thinking about Claudia. I haven't talked to her since that day in the park. I was going to try and call her and smooth things over, but I decided, you know what? I'm not the one in the wrong. She overreacted. She freaked out. I understand why she's upset, but this time, I'm not going to run in and try to make things all better. She's going to have to make the first overtures."

"That's hard for you. Not making peace."

Her head bobbed and her ponytail tickled his nose. "A fortune-teller once told me that it was my fatal flaw. So anxious to placate others that I lose sight of myself."

"Do you think that's true?"

"Yes, but I'm trying to change. It's why I'm not calling Claudia even though this rift is killing me."

He dipped his head to lightly kiss her neck. Her skin tasted of salt and soap, but she smelled of vanilla. "I'm the cause."

"No," she said. "I'm the cause. I've let people push me around for too long and now that I'm standing my ground, she's startled and doesn't know what to make of me. She'll come around as long as I don't make the first move. If I extend the olive branch when she was the one at fault, I'll be right back at square one, but it's hard for me to hold steady because I know how much she's hurting."

"You really do love her, don't you?"

"Yes."

"I could just . . ." He didn't want to say the word. "Go."

"No," she said. "Our time together is short enough. I only have you for a few more weeks. I've got Claudia for the rest of my life. We'll work it out, but I need for it to be on my terms."

"You're feeling guilty. Being with me like this."

"Yes. A little. But I don't want to feel guilty."

"It's hard not to when you care about someone."

"I want to thank you," she said. "For last night. It was the loveliest night I've ever had."

"Really?"

"Not just the sex." She turned in his arms to look into his eyes. "But the hayride, the way you accepted my friends, how gentle you are with Kyle." She slanted her head up to kiss his chin. "I know we probably took things too far and a psychologist would tell us that we can't trust what we're feeling considering our circumstances, but I can't regret what happened."

"Me either," he said gruffly.

"There's rough sailing ahead for us later," she said.

"I know."

"But for now? For the reminder of the time you're in Jubilee, I want to soak up every minute I have with you."

"I feel the same way."

They didn't say anything else for a long time. They just sat together in the tub, his arms wrapped tightly under her breasts. He loved the weight of them against his forearms.

"How did it go down when Jake showed up to meet you? Was he bitter like Claudia? Angry? I know you said he stayed for three months so you must have gotten past the initial barrier, but that must have been a weird conversation," she said

Rafferty chuffed out a breath. If he told Lissy the story of how he and Jake first met, he'd be giving her a window into the dark side of his soul. "It's not a pleasant story."

She paddled the water with a hand, skimming bubbles off the water. "Was he terrible to you?"

"No. Exactly the opposite."

"You were terrible to him?"

Rafferty swallowed hard. "I've never told anyone the whole story."

"It's okay," she rushed to assure him. "You don't have to tell me."

"No," he said. "I want to tell you. It's just hard to talk about."

She didn't speak again, let him have space, allowed

him to tell the story at his own pace. It was easier, telling about it this way. Her facing forward, him at her back. This way, he didn't have to see the shock in her eyes.

"It was a hot night in June, just after my sixteenth birthday. My mother had been dating this low-level guy on the fringes of the movie industry. Mostly, he was a small-time dope dealer and I'd seen the way he'd been looking at my sister, Heather." He clenched his jaw against the memory. He could see it as if it was playing out in his mind right now. As if he were back in that hellish place all over again.

"How old was Heather?"

"Eleven," he said unable to keep the hard edge from his voice. "Amelia—that's my mother—she was blind to that sort of thing. Just plowing through life, oblivious. Swinging from manic highs to the depth of despair in the course of a day."

Lissy's muscles tensed, but she remained silent.

"I came home from work around ten that night," he said, not knowing why he was going into the dirty details except that once he started, he could not stop. In an instant, he was back in that darkened stairway, his sneakers, slick with fryer grease, slapping against the cement stairs. "I was working at a fried chicken joint and I would bring home the leftovers that they were going to throw away so we'd have something to eat for the next day. We ate so much damn fried chicken that summer that I hate fried chicken to this day."

His knees were bent, drawn up on either side of Lissy's thighs. She rested her palms on his knees, squeezed gently. The candlelight threw shadows on the wall. The water had grown tepid. He'd never taken a bath with a woman before. It was real nice. A guy could get used to it, especially with a woman like Lissy.

"I came up the stairs of the shithole place where we

were living," he continued as matter-of-factly as he could. It was harder than he thought, talking about it. Even after all this time. "First thing I see is Amelia passed out on the couch in her housecoat. Dane was seven at the time and he was up way past his bedtime watching a horror movie on our busted-up old TV. It was all fuzzy but you could still see the guy with the chain saw. I made him turn off the TV and go to bed and that's when Heather screamed."

"Oh no," Lissy whispered.

"I threw that damn bucket of chicken, wings and drumsticks went flying everywhere. I ran to the back of the apartment, flung open her bedroom door." He paused because he could see it so clearly. It was something no kid should have to see.

Lissy squeezed tighter. He could hear the water faucet drip into the tub.

"Amelia's boyfriend was ripping Heather's pajamas off of her and she was sobbing hysterically. He had his pants down around his ankles, his hairy butt sticking out, and the sixteen-year-old kid that I was immediately turned into a full-grown man."

"I can't even begin to imagine what that was like."

"Thank God for that. It felt as if a knife severed some kind of tether that kept me attached to my body. It was like the real me floated to the ceiling and I was above it all, watching myself pummel the guy."

"I think it's called detachment," she said. "I've heard it often happens to victims of violent crimes."

He curled his lip. "The anger tasted like dirt and sweat and vomit. I'd never felt such rage. I grabbed that son of a bitch by the shoulders, and I spun him around." Rafferty fisted a hand, rested it on the edge of the cool porcelain tub.

Lissy leaned over and pressed her lips to his fist, a healing kiss.

"The guy stumbled and fell because of his pants being around his ankles. Heather had stopped screaming, but I could still hear her whimpers. She was pressed into the corner of the bed and when I looked at her, I could see from the terror in her eyes that she was more afraid of me than she was of him."

Rafferty paused again, took another deep breath, felt his muscles tense. His throat was dry. The dripping faucet underscored his narrative.

"You were a kid. Protecting your sister."

"I was sixteen. I knew exactly what I was doing. I started punching him as hard as I could. I took out all my rage at my mother for all the men she'd allowed to come into our house. I beat him and I beat him and I beat him. Even after he stopped fighting back, I kept hitting."

Lissy hissed in her breath. "Oh, Rafferty."

"I had no control. I couldn't stop. Then there were these arms going around me and I looked up and there was a man I'd never seen before. If he hadn't stopped me I might have killed my mother's boyfriend. Of that I have no doubt. I didn't know who this guy was or where he came from so I just started swinging at him. He raised his arms and said, 'Don't hit me kid, I'm your brother.' "

"It was Jake? Just in the nick of time?" Lissy's voice came out high and reedy.

Emotion burned Rafferty's throat, seized his chest. This was supposed to have been Lissy's seduction and he'd turned it into a confession. "That's how I met my older brother. While I was in the process of beating a man to death for attempting to rape my sister. That's the kind of life I had, Lissy."

"I can't believe you've been living with that all these years." Her breathing rasped harshly in the confines of the small bathroom. "What happened next?"

"Jake helped me get the guy out of the house. We

took him to a hospital across town and dumped him out at the ER."

"You didn't report it to the police?"

"No and neither did the guy. We never saw or heard from him again. That's why Jake decided to stay the summer. He knew how badly I needed him. He moved us out of the projects. Got us a better place to live. He took care of me and that's why I came here when I found out he died. I came to take care of you and Kyle. It's the only way I can repay him."

Lissy squirmed around in the tub, maneuvering her body until she was facing him. Hands trailing bubbles, she threaded her fingers through his hair, held his head still, and stared deeply into his eyes. "Thank you for trusting me enough to share that with me. Thank you, thank you, thank you."

He held her tight, kissed her fiercely. After a few minutes, he climbed from the tub, scooped her into his arms, and carried her into the bedroom.

Chapter Sixteen

For two glorious days, she and Rafferty stayed in bed. They made love in as many positions as they could think of and as many times as they could manage. Voraciously, they pleased each other, giving and receiving in equal amounts. They memorized each other's bodies, delighted over finding erogenous zones. They laughed and cried. Talked and hugged. Slipped from the bed only to eat, shower, and go at it again. Neither of them held anything back. It was the best weekend of Lissy's life.

She woke on Sunday morning, exhausted and sweetly sore in every part of her body. Her eyes opened and she smiled up at the ceiling, feeling like she was keeping a most decadent secret. Rafferty Jones was one helluva lover.

A strong arm went around her waist and he pulled her against him. "Good morning, dandelion," he whispered into her hair.

"Dandelion?"

"You weren't kidding when you said you were bendable. Last night . . . well, whew, let's just say flexibility is a very good thing."

She closed her eyes, savoring the moment. It was all

too beautiful to last. She knew it. Knew her vision was clouded by the way he made her feel. He'd swooped in and saved her, a stalwart cowboy coming to her rescue. In the past, she wouldn't have questioned it. Would have quietly accepted his help without qualms. But now she knew better. This was a fantasy. He was a fantasy. She could enjoy it without losing her direction.

Or her heart.

She wasn't going to make the same mistake with Rafferty that she'd made with his brother, believing that a man could solve all her problems.

At least that's what she told herself.

Eventually, he would leave and she'd be left to move on with her life. She accepted that. It was okay.

The fact that she didn't panic over the thought told her she'd already grown in significant ways. She could take care of herself and her son. She no longer had any doubt.

Her parents brought Kyle home that afternoon and Lissy was so happy to see him. While she'd enjoyed her wild weekend with Rafferty, Kyle was her anchor, the thing that kept her grounded in real life. She'd missed him so much.

"We enjoyed him," her mother, Erin, exclaimed as her father brought in the diaper bag and playpen. "Thank you for letting us keep him."

Lissette took Kyle from her mother and smothered him with kisses, then turned to introduce Rafferty, who'd been waiting in the background, to her parents.

"You're Jake's brother," her mother said.

"I am." Rafferty shook her head.

"The one he left all the money to?" Lissette's father, Charles, said.

"Yes sir."

Lissy saw the tension in her father's shoulders as he hesitantly reached to shake Rafferty's hand. She'd already explained their relationship to her folks the week she'd stayed in Dallas going from specialist to specialist, but she worried her parents would sense something more between them. She didn't want to get into that. Especially since Rafferty would be leaving soon enough.

"Lissy tells me you manage the Hyatt Regency in Dallas," Rafferty said to break the ice with her father.

"Yes." Her father nodded. "And you train horses for the movies?"

The men moved deeper into the living room, engaged in conversation, leaving Lissy and her mother still standing in the foyer.

"So how is Claudia?" her mother asked.

"I don't know."

Erin frowned. "You haven't made up with her yet?"

"Claudia started this rift. She's the one who should apologize."

Her mother's eyebrows shot up. "You didn't make any overtures?"

"No," Lissy said in a firm tone. This was between her and Claudia. It wasn't any of her mother's business.

"My, I'm surprised about that."

"What's so surprising?"

"Usually . . . well, Sug, there is a reason we called you the peacemaker. You so hate for people to be mad at you that you apologize even when you're not in the wrong."

"You can't be a successful business manager and do that," her father called from the living room, putting his two cents into the conversation.

"I'm proud of you," her mother said. "If Claudia's wrong, she should apologize. You're blooming."

"Thank you, Mom."

"I never thought you'd change. I thought you'd always be a bit of a pushover."

"Gee, thanks for the backhanded compliment."

Her mother's face colored. "That came out wrong."

She was about to say, *That's okay*, but then decided against it and said instead, "I'm certain you didn't intend to hurt my feelings."

"No, no."

Kyle squirmed in her arms, used sign language to tell her he wanted some crackers and cheese.

Her mother reached out and folded her hands over Kyle's little ones. "No, no, sweetie. You need to speak up. Say what it is you want." To Lissette she said, "We've been working all weekend to get him to stop with those crazy hand gestures."

A wick of anger lit in her. "What?"

"You know the specialists you took him to said that if you really want to integrate Kyle into society that he has to learn how to speak and if he has sign language to fall back on, he's not going to do that."

"Mom," she said, as calmly and patiently as she could. Her mother was accustomed to running over her, but she was no longer the old Lissy who drifted along on life's crazy currents. Because of what she'd been through, she'd learned she had to take a stand if she didn't want to end up where other people thought she should go. "We talked about this. I haven't yet made up my mind how I want Kyle educated. I'd appreciate it if you'd honor my wishes."

"My goodness, I had no idea you felt so strongly about this."

"Well, now you do."

A surprised expression crossed her mother's face, her smile uncertain. "I didn't mean to step on toes."

"No, you're just used to doing what you like without paying any attention to what I want. It's okay. I'm not blaming you. It's my fault for allowing it to happen."

"I . . . I . . ." Totally flummoxed, her mother moved past her to join the men in the living room.

Lissette took Kyle into the kitchen, got him cheese and crackers, and put him at the table to eat. A moment later, her mother wandered in.

"I am sorry, Lissy."

"It's all right. Just honor my wishes from now on."

"Okay."

Honestly, Lissy was amazed at how simple that had been.

"Have you decided what to do about Thanksgiving? Will you be spending it with Claudia? Both your sisters and their families are coming to our house. I was hoping you'd come too, but I don't want to step on toes if you have other plans."

Wow. That was a change. Normally, her mother would have just told her what time they were having Thanksgiving dinner and what to bring.

"I'll be there."

Her mother cast a glanced over her shoulder. "Rafferty too?"

"It would be nice," she said, "if you invited him."

"Yes, of course." Her mother turned and headed back to the living room. "Oh, Rafferty . . ."

Lissette couldn't help smiling. She felt as strong as Superwoman.

Kyle glanced up from his empty plate, cracker crumbs on his lips. He made the sign for cheese and in a hesitant, soft voice said, "Chee."

It was such a joy hearing him say something besides "da" that she couldn't help wondering if her mother was right and Guillermo was wrong. If she wanted her son to be fully integrated into society, should she be discouraging sign language in favor of speech?

After that weekend life settled into a happy rhythm. Lissette and Rafferty did not talk of the future. Both of them knew this time they had together was short and precious and they weren't going to waste it on regrets.

The weeks leading up to Thanksgiving were filled with activity. Rafferty trained Slate for three to four hours every morning, then he came home to help Lissette with her business. They cleared out a guest room and turned it into an office, painting, refinishing furniture, shopping for supplies. At one store, the clerk mistook them for a married couple and neither of them bothered to set the record straight. Rafferty got her Web site up and running. They passed out flyers and samples of her baked goods and within a few days, she had several orders.

In the evenings, they had dinner together. They Skyped with Guillermo a few more times, but he kept pushing Lissette to get Kyle involved with the Deaf community. She appreciated his input, but it escalated the pressure she was under to make up her mind on how best to educate her son. For now, Rafferty kept teaching Kyle to sign, while she worked on making sure Kyle could see her lips when she spoke to him.

On Guillermo's advice, they wore earplugs and noise-canceling headphones, trying to approximate Kyle's hearing loss to better understand what he was going through. It provided Lissy with a whole new level of understanding. When they watched television, they turned the volume down and watched closed captioning. It taught Lissette to pay closer attention to visual images and helped teach her how Kyle processed his world.

There were times when Lissy would stop in the course of her day and hug herself, unable to believe how things had turned around in just a few short weeks and it was all because of Rafferty. He'd taught her so much about herself.

One evening, Rafferty came home with an armful of tactile picture books for Kyle. The minute he opened the door, he said, "I love walking in here every day. Your baking makes a house smell like a home."

Lissette smiled at him from behind the stove, spatula in hand. "It smells like a workplace to me."

After dinner was over, Lissette gave Kyle his bath while Rafferty insisted on cleaning the kitchen. Later, they converged in Kyle's bedroom for story time.

"How do I read to him?" she asked Rafferty.

"Just read like you normally would, but put his fingers on your lips so he can feel you forming the words."

His suggestion made sense and she felt silly for not having thought of it herself. She took Kyle's hand and put it on her lips. His little eyes widened when she started reading, his gaze fixed on her face.

"Pat the bunny." She enunciated slowly, and then shifted his hand from her lips to the tactile storybook where he could run his hand over the material that replicated rabbit fur.

Kyle grinned, put one hand on her mouth and the other on the storybook.

"That boy is a quick learner," Rafferty said. "He's not going to have a lick of trouble." Then Rafferty signed, *Pat the bunny.*

She ended up reading the book to him three times. Rafferty played his role as well as or better than any biological father, but he kept staring at Lissette. She could feel the heat of his gaze. From time to time she'd glance over and he'd offer her a bright smile of encouragement. What was it about this man that made her feel more confident and secure than she'd ever felt in her life?

Don't get used to it. He won't be here forever. He'll be going back to California after the futurity. Just enjoy it for what it is. She had to constantly remind herself.

Kyle's head weighed heavily in the crook of her elbow.

"He's asleep." Rafferty got up and crossed the room. He reached down to ease Kyle from her arms.

Regret stabbed her. Jake should be here, putting his son to bed, but even when Jake had been alive, he hadn't taken much interest in domestic life. When Lissette had read to Kyle in the past, Jake had restlessly prowled the house, and then finally unable to stand being confined, he would grab his cowboy cap off the peg in the hallway and call out, "Going out to the Silver Horseshoe. Just for one beer."

Except it had never been just one beer. He'd come staggering home, singing at the top of his lungs, and then get angry when she didn't want to have sex. He hadn't been like that before the Middle East. War had changed him until he was no longer the man she married and sometimes, oh God, sometimes, she'd been happy when his leave was over and he had to go back.

She shoved those thoughts into the trunk of her mind and locked them up tight. Rafferty settled Kyle into his bed and covered him up.

"Did your mother read stories to you when you were little?" she asked him.

"Do gossip articles from the tabloids count? Or the stories in confession magazines?"

"You're serious?" She flicked off the light, leaving only the Elmo nightlight glowing in the room. Together, they tiptoed out, leaving the bedroom door slightly ajar.

"I think she was simply reading out loud to herself, but I'd curl up on the end of her bed and stay real still so she wouldn't make me go get in my own bed," he said as they walked into the living room.

"That must have been rough."

He shrugged. "Wasn't so bad. It was all I knew."

She smiled so he wouldn't think she was feeling sorry for him.

"Did your parents read to you?" he asked.

"Oh yes, all the usual upper-middle-class things."

"Let me guess. Princess stories."

"But of course."

"And your favorite was . . ." He snapped his fingers. "Sleeping Beauty."

"How did you guess?"

"You married Jake."

"What does that mean?" She sank her hands on her hips.

"Um . . . I shouldn't have opened this can of worms."

"No, I want to know."

Rafferty scratched the back of his head. "Really, it's nothing."

"Then why did you say it?"

He blew out his breath. "You sure you want to hear my analysis?"

"Absolutely." She crossed her arms.

"Jake was the kind of guy who went in for agreeable women."

"Are you saying I'm too agreeable?"

"No. It just seems to me, from what you've told me about yourself, that you sort of slept through the first part of your life, hence the appeal of Sleeping Beauty. The kiss of a handsome prince wakes you up."

"I'm nothing without a man, in other words."

"I think that on some level you've believed that about yourself, but I know you can do anything you set your mind to, Lissette Moncrief. Look what you've done with this whole cowboy-themed bakery idea."

"Damn right."

"See, no reason to keep scowling at me."

"So, of the *True Confessions* stories your mother read, which were your favorites?"

"The second chance stories."

"Made a lot of mistakes, have you?"

"I just made one tonight."

"Comparing me to Sleeping Beauty."

"I never compared you. I simply guessed your favorite princess."

He was right about everything. She'd spent her life in a dream. Until now. "How do you know so much about princesses?"

"Who do you think read to my little sister?"

"You didn't have a childhood."

He held out both hands. "It is what it is."

"You've got a savior complex."

"That's a bit definitive."

"But accurate."

"You trying to make me squirm?"

"You were pretty unflinching with me."

"I'm powerfully attracted to you, Lissette."

"Because I'm an emotional wreck?"

"You're not a wreck. You're holding it together pretty damn good if you ask me."

"Because I have no choice. I have a son."

"You're a good mother."

The earnestness in his voice touched her to the core. "I do the best I can."

"Kyle is lucky to have you. Jake was lucky to have you. I don't know why he left you in favor of war." He came across the floor toward her.

Lissette did not back up. "Rafferty . . ."

"Lissy." His arms went around her waist. He leaned down.

"Don't."

"What?"

"Just don't."

"Kiss you?"

"I'm not Sleeping Beauty."

"I know."

She leaned against him, tossed back her head. "Please."

"Lissy," he whispered.

"Rafferty."

"I want you."

Their gazes hooked and they both moved forward at once. Rafferty's hands went up to cup her head and at the same time she made the same move. There wasn't any thought involved. Just action. Feelings. Chemistry. Need. All the things that made for bad mistakes. Impulse. Rashness. She was no better than Jake running headlong into battle, tempting fate.

Rafferty's mouth was on hers and his hands were in her hair and she was drinking him up like he was lemonade on a hot summer day, drinking and drinking and drinking.

Oh God! He tasted delicious and Rafferty was kissing her like she was the only woman on the face of the earth. It was heady stuff.

He was guiding her down to the rug.

Her knees touched the ground and she was frantically snatching at the snaps on his shirt and he was kissing her like it was the end of the world. She was sinking. Sinking.

She arched her back, felt his hand skim the backs of her thighs as he peeled off her panties. Her feminine smell scented the air. She saw his nose quiver. He groaned again.

Her fingers went to the zipper of his pants. "Hurry, hurry."

She pulled down his zipper, slipped her hand inside, felt his hard erection. "Rafferty."

"Lissy."

He turned her around, pulled her up on all fours. He was behind her, knees apart. She felt a rush of moistness. She was slick and ready for him. Her breathing was coming in quick, desperate pants.

"Take me," she begged. "Just take me."

He took her legs and wrapped them around his waist. She could feel the roughness of his blue jeans against her calves. He leaned forward, pushed against her.

It was a mad coupling.

"Give me all you've got, cowboy," she challenged.

He didn't need any more encouragement than that. His body took complete possession of hers. She writhed and twisted and called his name. He filled her up, until she feared she could not take one more inch and then she took more.

Lissette felt her own body respond to the cascade of hormones shooting through her. The friction. The fusion. Beauty. Nothing like it. Heat and pressure and hard, thick thrusts. He pulled out, pushed in. Back and forth. Rhythmic and mesmerizing. Lust tasted like forbidden fruit on the back of her tongue. She smelled everything, the hardwood floor, the scent of cookies wafting in from the kitchen, their combined aromas. It aroused her even more. The way they smelled together.

"Rafferty," she gasped.

He gave one last hard desperate thrust and buried himself inside her.

They collapsed at the top, falling together in the bliss of each other's arms.

The futurity started the Monday before Thanksgiving. The competition comprised a series of elimination events in various divisions. It stretched out over three weeks from the end of November into the first week of December, culminating in the Triple Crown of cutting.

For Jubilee, it was the Super Bowl of the cutting horse world. In most places people were gearing up for the holidays, but here, they geared up for the Fort Worth futurity.

Lissy had managed to get a vendor's permit to sell her

Texas-themed pastries at the event. Because of Texas law, she'd have to bake the goods she sold at the event in a commercial oven, but she had a friend with a storefront in Twilight who'd agreed to let her use her bakery for the task and Mariah was helping her run the booth. She'd had business cards, flyers, and pamphlets made to hand out. Her parents had taken Kyle to Dallas. Rafferty and Lissette would pick the boy up when they went for Thanksgiving.

Rafferty was amazed at how quickly Slate had become a first-class cutting horse. Of course, Joe and Cordy had given him specific tips, but ultimately, it was the quality of the horse. Jake had picked a good one.

Maybe, just maybe, his scheme was going to work.

He'd already opened a bank account at the First Horseman's Bank of Jubilee with half of Jake's money and put the other half in a trust fund for Kyle. When the time came, he'd invent a fake buyer for Slate and pay Lissette with the money from the account. She never need know he was behind the purchase and she could accept it with her pride intact.

Damn, he was proud of her. She'd grown so much in just a few short weeks. He considered himself lucky that he'd been there to watch her blossom. Plus he'd grown mighty fond of little Kyle. Leaving them was going to hurt far more than he cared to admit.

Lissy's not the only one who's changed.

If someone had told him six weeks ago that he would be in Texas, longing to leave his old life behind and start a new one with his brother's widow, he would have called him a liar. But here he was. Wanting what he couldn't have.

Never mind. He'd been gone soon. Although Slate was a great horse, he was young and still in training. He might win a small purse, but there was little chance he'd go the distance. It didn't matter. His entry had all been an excuse. At first, it had been an excuse to save Lissette's pride while still keeping his promise to Jake, but it quickly had become an excuse for Rafferty to spend more time with her.

Hell, he needed to get back to California and get his head on straight. He'd been away from his ranch for far too long. Soon enough, he'd be back on the road and Jubilee would be nothing but a sweet memory.

Chapter Seventeen

"Swanky," Rafferty said when he saw Lissette's parents' Highland Park home. He had an autumn flower bouquet he'd picked up at Searcy's. "You grew up in a palace."

"You exaggerate." She tucked the cake box she carried underneath one arm and leaned over to ring the doorbell. She wore a red skirt, black tights, white fluffy sweater, and looked like a Christmas package he couldn't wait to unwrap.

"You underestimate."

"Don't be jealous. It's illusion. They're up to their chests in credit card debt."

"Now I don't feel so intimidated."

The door opened and they were immediately overwhelmed by Erin's embrace. He awkwardly thrust the bouquet at her. "These are for you."

"How sweet of you, Rafferty." She lightly kissed his cheek and ushered them inside.

The house smelled of roasting turkey. Lavish decorations included horns of plenty, flower arrangements, and flickering candles. It was the kind of home you saw in the movies. When he was a kid, he would have given his right arm to be invited to a Thanksgiving dinner like this.

Erin escorted them into a dining room packed with people. Walking into a room full of strangers was never easy but everyone welcomed him with smiles as big as Dallas.

"Gramma Jean," Lissette exclaimed, delight in her voice. "I didn't know you were going to be here."

An elegant older woman, dressed in black except for a bright orange scarf around her neck, wrapped her arms around Lissy. "Your aunt and your mom swapped me Thanksgiving for Christmas. Judy and her family are going skiing in Aspen and invited me along and you know how I love to ski."

Ski? The woman was at least seventy. Rafferty was impressed.

"Gramma Jean was in the 1960 Olympics in Squaw Valley," Lissy told him.

"I didn't win a medal," she explained. "I came in sixth."

"Gramma Jean," Lissette continued the introductions. "This is Rafferty. Jake's half brother."

"Ah," Gramma Jean said in a friendly tone. "The mysterious bastard."

Everyone in the room gasped at the same time.

But her bluntness didn't bother Rafferty. In fact, he laughed, happy that it was all out in the open. "That'd be me."

"Another cowboy. Lissy has a thing for cowboys."

"Gramma!" Lissette's cheeks turned pink.

Gramma Jean winked at him. "Honey, no one is blaming you. There is something compelling about a handsome cowboy. I'm very pleased to meet you, Rafferty."

"Pleased to meet you as well, ma'am." He shook her hand.

"Where's Kyle?" Lissette asked her mother. "I've missed him so much."

"I put him down for a nap an hour ago," Erin said.

"I'll go wake him up for dinner." Lissette popped out of the room, leaving Rafferty alone with her family.

Erin introduced Rafferty to Lissette's two sisters, Brittany and Samantha, and their husbands, Tim and Heath. Brittany had two children, Zeke and Ella, who were eight and ten. Samantha had a four-year-old daughter named Spice. He made small talk the best he could with people he didn't know.

"Sit beside me." Gramma Jean sat down at the table and patted the seat beside her. Everyone else was standing, the women bustling around putting food on the table, the men in the corner talking about the Cowboys' chances for making the playoffs. "I want to hear all about you."

Not knowing what else to do, he took the chair beside her.

"My daughter tells me you're from California," Gramma Jean commented.

"Yes, ma'am."

"You seem very polite for someone from California."

"Must be the cowboy thing," he said.

"Manners and all that." She smiled. "I see the appeal. I do have a special fondness for California."

"From being there in the Olympics?"

"From meeting my husband there."

"He was Californian?"

"Heavens no. Dust bowl Okie. But I met him while I was competing in the Olympics. He was a ski patrol medic putting himself through medical school."

"That's something to be proud of."

"It wasn't conducive for romance. Him going to medical school in California. Me living part-time in Texas, part-time in Colorado. It was a crazy time."

"You've led an interesting life."

Gramma Jean looked pleased. "Thank you."

"I bet you've got a lot of colorful stories to tell."

"Yes, I do, so don't encourage me or I'll bend your ear all day, when the one you need to be giving all your attention to is my granddaughter. This is her first Thanksgiving without—" She broke off. "Would you like a drink? You don't have a drink. Charles," she called to Lissette's father. "Bring the man a drink."

"Scotch okay?" Charles called from across the room.

"Glass of water is fine."

Gramma Jean arched an eyebrow. "You don't drink?"

"My mother was an alcoholic."

"Ah," she said. "Explains some things."

Where the hell was Lissy? He glanced toward the door, willed her to walk through it. Amid the dinner preparations, no one else was paying any attention to them. It was as if he and Gramma Jean were on their own stage. He wished he were on a movie set waiting for the director to holler, "Cut" so he could get out of this scene.

"That was rude, wasn't it? I apologize."

"Nothing to apologize for. The truth is the truth."

"It's good that you don't drink." She patted his arm. "Jake drank too much. Not an alcoholic, but you know how drink can sometimes make people do stupid things." Gramma Jean glanced at the cake box on the table. "Ooh, did Lissy bring that?"

"Yes."

"What kind is it?"

"One of her new cowboy cake recipes."

"She's a very talented baker."

"She is."

"Unfortunately, she also wants to please everyone. You can't do that and be a successful artist. And she is an artist with pastry. You have to have a vision and stick to it."

"She's got vision."

"I know. It's the sticking to her guns that's the hard part for Lissy. She's always been afraid to take a stand."

"I don't see her that way at all."

"No," Gramma Jean pulled a surprised face. "Maybe she's changing." She paused a minute to size Rafferty up. "Maybe you're changing her."

"Lissy doesn't need any help from me. She does just fine on her own." He was beginning to see where some of Lissy's self-doubt had come from. If the people you loved kept telling you that you were a certain way, you tended to live up to their expectations.

"Loyalty. It's a good quality in a man." Gramma Jean took a sip from the tumbler of Scotch that her son-in-law put at her elbow. Charles passed Rafferty a glass of water. "I approve."

"Thanks."

"You know, I really am glad I got to meet you," she said. "Lissy is special. As a girl, she was so easy to be around. Not like those other two." Gramma Jean inclined her head toward the kitchen were Brittany and Samantha were arguing over who had the best haircut. "She might not be as pretty as her sisters, but she's got substance."

"I think she's beautiful."

"There's that loyalty again. You, Rafferty Jones, are a keeper. But it's got to be odd. Her having been married to your brother."

"Nothing odd about it," he said smoothly, even though the old lady was messing with his head.

"If you say so." She met his gaze. "Just don't hurt her. She's been through enough."

"Never," he said staunchly.

Gramma Jean canted her head. "You're very different."

"From what?"

"Jake. Oh, the exterior is similar, that cowboy walk and talk, but inside, you're night and day."

He didn't know what to say to that.

"I've been worried about her for a long time. Even before Jake died."

"Why?"

"That she's too swayed by influences. That she'll never live up to her potential because others keep her under their thumbs. But when I see her with you, well . . ." Gramma Jean straightened. "I feel encouraged."

"Like I said before. It's got nothing to do with me. Lissy is coming into her own. She's going to make a huge success out of her bakery. You just wait and see."

"Loyalty," she mused. "It's a rare trait."

Lissy came into the room carrying Kyle. She smiled at him like a rainbow and Rafferty was never so glad to see anyone in his entire life.

Rafferty jumped up from the table and hurried toward her. He put a hand to her back and kissed Kyle on the cheek. Immediately, her son put out his arms to him. Rafferty swung the boy up on his shoulder and Kyle's happy laugh rolled around the room.

"So Gramma Jean had you on the grill, huh?" she murmured.

"No, no."

"C'mon. She's really protective."

"She told me that you were an easy child but that it trips you up as an adult."

"Hmm, that's not exactly a newsflash."

"I don't see it that way."

"No?"

"I think having the ability to see both sides of an issue is what's going to take you to the top."

"I didn't know I was interesting enough to be the topic of an entire conversation."

"Dandelion," he said in such a masculine tone that it sent a shiver down her spine. "You're interesting enough for a lifetime of conversations."

Lissy's face flushed at his compliment. She was getting too accustomed to him. Enjoying his company too much.

The family sat down for dinner. Rafferty ended up sitting across from her, Kyle in his high chair at the end of the table between them. The older children were seated at the kids' table. She was very aware that everyone was watching Kyle, but things went smoothly until her mother began serving dessert.

"I've got pecan pie, pumpkin pie, and Lissy's Dr Pepper cake. Who wants what?"

"So, Lissy," Gramma Jean said. "Have you made up your mind yet how you're going to educate your son? Your mother told me you're seriously considering teaching him sign language. I went online and did some goggling—"

Brittany's son, Zeke, giggled. "Great-Gramma Jean, it's Googled, not goggled."

"Goggle, Google, same thing." Gramma Jean waved a hand. "The upshot is that if you want to fully integrate Kyle into society, you have to teach him how to speak and read lips. If you teach him sign language, he'll only be able to communicate with other people who know sign."

"I'm well aware of the issues, Gramma." Lissy smiled sweetly. "I'm still trying to figure it all out."

"Well," her grandmother said, and tapped the face of her watch. "Time's ticking. The longer you wait the further behind he's going to get. It's bad enough that he's going to be at a disadvantage his entire life, but with your tendency to drag your feet . . ."

"Thanks for your input," she said as calmly as she could, even though the anxiety she'd felt on that day she'd had a meltdown in Searcy's was back, knotting her up inside. She wanted to keep the peace, please her grandmother, but she couldn't go back to being the placid woman she'd once been. Things had changed. She'd changed.

"Pumpkin, pecan, or cake?" her mother asked Gramma Jean, clearly trying to derail her.

"I'll have dessert later." Gramma Jean waved her away. "Lissy and I are having a philosophical discussion."

Underneath the table, she felt pressure on her foot. She looked up. Rafferty caught her eye, held her gaze steady. Just knowing he was on her side made her feel better. The tension in her belly eased.

"Rafferty?" her mother asked, holding the tray of desserts.

"I'll have a piece of Lissy's cake."

Kyle started bopping up and down in his high chair at the sight of the desserts. He made the sign for cake and then signed pie.

"Is he using sign language?" Gramma Jean asked.

"He is."

"You've started teaching him sign language? You've already decided to condemn him to isolation in the Deaf community?" Her eyes widened and her mouth pulled tight. "Oh, Lissette, I think that's a mistake."

"Gramma Jean has a point," Brittany put in. "I think you should listen to her."

"I haven't made any decisions," Lissette said. "Rafferty knows sign language and he was generous enough to teach Kyle a few simple signs to help me communicate better with him. It's not going to hurt anything for him to know some rudimentary sign language."

"Slippery slope," Gramma Jean muttered.

Kyle kept signing. *Cake. Pie. Cake. Pie.*

"Lissy, what's he saying?" asked her mother.

"That right there. That's what's wrong with letting him sign instead of learning how to speak," Gramma Jean said.

"He's saying he wants cake and pie," Lissy told her mother.

The pressure on her foot increased. She caught Rafferty's gaze again. He winked. *Gonna be okay.* His eyes sent the silent message. *Don't let 'em bulldoze you.*

"Which is it, Lissy? Pie or cake?" Her mother squatted to Kyle's left and slowly mouthed, "Pie or cake?"

Kyle moved his hands at a furious pace.

"Which is it?" her mother asked, sounding exasperated.

"I want cake!" hollered Lissy's niece Spice from the kids' table.

"He wants both," Lissy told her mother.

"We want cake too," chimed in Ella and Zeke.

"I'll have some cake myself," her father threw in.

Her mother looked confused. "What do you mean, Lissy?"

"He wants them both. He wants a piece of pie and a piece of cake."

"Well, honey that's an awful lot of dessert for one little boy."

"Give him small slices, Mom."

"Well, which kind of pie? Pumpkin or pecan?"

"Give him a piece of each."

"You mean give him three desserts?"

"I want three desserts!" Spice was out of her seat and twirling around the dining room. "Three desserts. Three desserts. Three desserts."

Her mother made a noise of irritation. "Look what that stirred up."

Why was this turning into a major thing? "Just give him one spoon of pecan pie, one spoon of pumpkin pie, and one forkful of cake. Problem solved."

"He can't have three desserts, Lissette," her younger sister, Samantha, said.

"Why not?"

Kyle was wailing and making grabbing motions at the dessert tray.

"See what you stirred up?" Brittany said. "Mama, just give the kid a bite of something so he'll settle down."

Okay, that hurt. Mainly because she was always the one in the family to smooth things down, not stir them up, but then suddenly, Lissette realized that if you wanted to get what you needed, sometimes you had to kick up a fuss, even if other people didn't like it. And why on earth couldn't Kyle have three desserts? Why did he have to choose?

If Jake had been here, he would have already told them all off. He would have done the dirty work for her, rescued her from having to ruffle feathers, but in doing so, his will would have been done, not hers.

Rafferty, on the other hand, was sitting there, one hundred percent in her court, encouraging her with his eyes, letting her know he was on her side, but letting her handle it on her own.

It hit her then, the answer to her dilemma on how to educate her child, and the frustration she was feeling just fell away. She didn't have to choose right now whether to teach him sign language or lipreading. She didn't even have to make a choice. She could teach him both methods, no matter what anyone else thought. She would allow her son to be her guide. She would give him what he needed when he needed it and not be swayed by the opinions of others, even the experts. She could allow everyone to be unhappy if they didn't like her decision. How they felt was not her problem.

Lissette pushed back her chair, planted her hands on the table and proceeded to tell her family exactly how she felt. When she was done, they stared at her slack-jawed. The room had gone silent. Across the table, Rafferty gave her a thumbs-up.

"You know, Erin," Gramma Jean said. "I think I'd like three desserts too."

"Claudia, what's the matter?" Stewart asked. "You're more nervous than a long-tailed cat in a roomful of rockers."

"Lissy never called me over Thanksgiving. I haven't spoken to her in more than a month. We've never gone that long without speaking. She didn't even call me to say happy Thanksgiving. If it hadn't been for you inviting me over for Thanksgiving dinner with you and your kids I would have been all alone." Listlessly, she poked at her pork chop with a fork.

Stewart had invited her out to Cracker Barrel for the Monday fried pork chop special and she'd gone because she didn't want to be alone. No, that wasn't completely true. She'd also gone because she was hoping things might progress between them. They'd been dating since that night he'd taken her out on his motorcycle, but he'd done little more than kiss her. She wanted more, but she didn't want to mess up the good thing they had going. His company was the only thing that had gotten her through the past month, but she wasn't quite ready to tell him stuff like that yet.

"Have *you* tried calling her?"

"I can't do that. I'm the one who . . ." Claudia trailed off. She was the one who'd given Lissy an ultimatum and Lissy had chosen Rafferty over her. Leading her to believe that Rafferty had told her what Claudia had done all those years ago in California. She'd been stricken with anger and grief when she'd made that ultimatum, and she sorely regretted it, but fear kept her from apologizing now, fear of being rejected and disconnected.

You're already disconnected. What have you got left to lose?

"Lissy has a lot to deal with," Stewart said gently, and reached across the table to lay his hand over hers. "I bet she'd been too busy to call you. Don't fret. She'll come around. Eat up. Your pork chops are getting cold."

She didn't argue with Stewart because she hadn't told him about Rafferty because she didn't want him to think less of her. She was enjoying their deepening friendship and she didn't want to upset the delicate balance.

Too late. Once he finds out what you're really like, you'll lose him too.

Why was she even here? She knew this relationship wasn't going to last. How could it? When he found out the truth, he wouldn't want her.

Stewart cleared his throat. "Claudia, there's something I've been meaning to tell you. Tonight probably isn't the best night since you're so down in the dumps, but there's something I need to say."

Great, he was going to dump her before they were even officially going together. She straightened, met his gaze, and braced herself for the worst. "What is it?"

"We're too old to play games. That's for the young ones who've got plenty of time to dither and mess around."

Her heart leaped into her throat. "Stewart—"

He raised a palm. "Hear me out. I know you've been going through dark times and that's why I've taken things slow so far. It pains me to see you struggling. I've known dark times too. But you don't have to struggle alone. I'm here to lighten your burden. I want to see you smile the way you used to smile before Jake died. I want . . ." He pulled his palm down his face, chuffed out a breath. "I want to make you happy again, Claudia. I want to be happy with you."

She shook her head. She pushed her plate away, picked up the old-fashioned peg game they kept on the tables at Cracker Barrel to entertain yourself with while you waited on the food, and started moving pegs around. She'd never been able to successfully remove all the pegs through strategic jump moves. Inevitably, she stranded one lone peg.

"Claudia?"

She shook her head harder, blinked away the tears pressing at the backs of her eyelids, concentrated hard on the peg game. Six months ago she would have been giddy over Stewart's attention. She'd always admired and respected him and it didn't seem unnatural for that respect to turn to something more.

"Is it me?" He lowered his voice. "Are you not attracted to me?"

Let's see, if she moved this peg over that one, then . . . No, dammit, that wouldn't work. She'd leave one peg isolated without a way out of the corner.

"That's it, isn't it?" His voice cracked. "God, I was so dumb. I thought that day we kissed at the lake—" He broke off.

She didn't look up. Couldn't bear to gaze into his soulful eyes. "It's not you."

"What is it then? Linda? Is it loyalty because of your friendship? Believe me, I understand. Linda is the reason I haven't made a move earlier. I loved her deeply and I didn't want to do anything to tarnish her memory, but, well, I had a wonderful dream about her the other night."

Claudia moved pegs around, blue one over yellow, green over blue. She didn't dare glance at Stewart or she would come completely unglued.

"Linda told me how much she loved me. How much she loved you. She wanted us to be happy again. She wanted me to be with you. Does that sound crazy?"

"Wish fulfillment."

"What?"

"Your dream. It wasn't Linda. Just your subconscious giving you permission."

"So Linda is the reason you're hesitant? Because when I kissed you the other night, it seemed—"

"It's not Linda." Red peg over blue. Yellow over red. Yes, yes, she was getting it. She was going to make it this time. Finally. Success at something.

"If you're attracted to me too and it's not guilt over Linda, what is it?"

Three pegs left. It was going to work. She was going to do it.

"Claudia, please look at me."

Almost there. Yes, yes! She removed all the pegs from the board, clutched them in a triumphant fist. One thing in her miserable life had gone right.

"I did it," she said, finally raising her gaze to meet Stewart's.

He looked confused. "What."

"The peg game. I beat it."

Slowly, he shook his head. "You haven't heard a single word I said."

She couldn't avoid it any longer. "Yes, Stewart. I did. I heard every word you said. It's not you. You're sexy as hell and I'd love nothing better than to jump your bones. It's not Linda. She was my dear friend, but she's gone. I don't think she would hold a grudge if you and I hooked up."

"So what *is* it?"

"It's me. I'm messed up."

"I know, but it's okay. You'll heal. I want to help you heal." He reached across the table for her hand, but she scooted her chair back before he could touch her.

"You wouldn't want me," she said, "if you knew the truth about me."

"I've known you for over thirty years. You were Linda's best friend. You're a wonderful person. Smart, loving, generous. When I had to go to work you were there with Linda after every round of chemo, holding her hair back for her when she got sick. I see you for who you are, Claudia. I'm not blind. We all have flaws."

"It's not just a character flaw, Stewart. I'm damaged in a twisted way."

He frowned. "You're not twisted or damaged. You've just been through a lot."

"There are things about me you don't know. Terrible things."

Stewart laughed. "What? You shoplifted some lipstick when you were fourteen?"

"You don't believe I can be terrible?"

"I do not."

"You want to sleep with me?"

His eyes glistened with desire. "More than anything in the world."

"Before we take that step, I have to tell you what I've done. It's something I've never told another single living soul, but I need to confess, I need to clear my soul. And if you still want me after I tell you what I've done . . ." She shook her head. "Well, you won't want me. It will take that look right out of your eyes."

Stewart straightened. "Nothing you could tell me would make me turn my back on you."

She didn't believe him. Not for one second. "You say that now."

"Do you really think so little of me? You have to take a chance, Claudia. Risk it. For anyone to connect with another human being we have to allow ourselves to be fully seen and heard for who we are."

"You got that from Linda."

"I did," he admitted. "She was a very wise woman. If

it helps any, I'll go first. When I got called out to my first fire I was so terrified that I hid in the chaos."

Claudia's eyes widened. "You? But you're so brave."

"I wasn't brave that night, but I was brave the next day when I went in to see my boss, ready to resign over my cowardice. You know what he said?"

"What?" she whispered.

"He said bravery isn't the lack of fear, but the ability to feel the fear and do it anyway. He said every single man in the stationhouse was scared every time we went out on a call. He said he didn't want a man who wasn't afraid. Bravery without fear is nothing but recklessness."

Like Jake.

She closed her eyes and let all the air leave her body before she opened them again. She couldn't keep it inside any longer. She had to confess to someone or implode.

"Feel the fear, Claudia, and tell me anyway."

She glanced over her shoulder. They were alone in the far corner of the restaurant, no one within earshot.

There, in the Jubilee Cracker Barrel, over the peg game she'd finally won and a plate of uneaten pork chops, Claudia began to tell him about the awful thing she'd done.

Chapter Eighteen

After Thanksgiving a change took place. The mood between Rafferty and Lissette thickened, waiting to be shaped into something more.

But what was going to happen? Time was running out for them and she didn't know what to do.

Nothing. Do nothing. What can you do? You always knew this was temporary.

California awaited him. He had responsibilities just as she did. Her bakery business had sprouted legs after she'd passed out samples at the futurity and around town; new holiday orders were coming in every day. She could barely keep up. No time for spinning romantic what-ifs. She'd done far too much of that in her life. She was no longer afraid of reality. In fact, she felt freed. Powerful.

Rafferty had helped her get here. She would forever owe him for that great gift. They would exchange cards at Christmas. She'd e-mail him pictures of Kyle. He might send presents for Kyle's birthday and Christmas. She would call and congratulate him on the big events in his life. When he got married, had children, but that's all their relationship would ever be. All it could ever be. Because she didn't dare hope for more.

To the surprise of everyone except Rafferty and Lissette, Slate kept winning events and progressing in the futurity. Jubilee was buzzing not only about Jake's amazing horse, but about the California cowboy who'd made it possible.

Then on the third day of December, Slate's luck finally ran out.

Lissette hadn't ridden to Will Rogers Coliseum with Rafferty that day. She'd had orders to bake and deliver before she could get away to man her booth at the exhibit hall. Since she and Claudia still weren't speaking, she'd dropped Kyle off at the babysitter's and headed toward Fort Worth at three P.M. It took everything she had in her not to be the one to mend the rift, but her mother-in-law was in the wrong and Lissy had spent too many years apologizing for things that were not her fault.

On the drive, the cloudy skies darkened and the snow that the meteorologists had been predicting for days began to fall in a slow, thick tumble. The experts had warned that this promised to be an especially cold and precipitous winter, so she'd made sure to bundle up.

Before she went to her booth, she rushed to the John Justin Arena where the competitors were getting ready for their upcoming events. Rafferty was competing at seven P.M. She found him with a crowd of other entrants, including Joe, Brady, and Cordy.

The minute his eyes found hers, Rafferty's face broke into a welcoming smile that sent her heart reeling. He took her by the elbow and escorted her to an out-of-the-way corner. Even so, it was still difficult to have a conversation amid the sounds of mooing cattle, nickering horses, and joking cowboys and cowgirls.

"I just wanted to wish you good luck."

"The competition is getting stiffer."

"Still, you have a good chance."

Rafferty nodded. "Listen, Lissy, I just wanted to let you know I've had an offer on Slate."

"Already?"

"Yes."

"Who's the buyer? How much did they offer?"

An enigmatic expression flicked across his face. "The buyer is from California. He's offering to purchase both Slate and his horse trailer for two hundred thousand dollars."

Lissy gasped. "Really? That's amazing. I had no idea we could get that much for him."

"He's done well."

"It's all because of you." Joyously, she threw her arms around his neck, squeezed him tight. "You've saved my life."

"No, Dandelion, you saved your own life."

"I don't know what I would have done if you hadn't shown up when you did."

"You would have done just fine."

"Don't be so humble."

"Don't be so scared of your own awesomeness."

They stared at each other. If people hadn't surrounded them, she knew he would have kissed her.

"I'm going to write you a check for the two hundred thousand," he said. "So you can have the money now."

"There's no need for that. I can hold out until the buyer sends the money."

"Let me do this," he said. "While your bakery business is taking off, that means you're going to need more capital fast to keep expanding. I've already made out the check." He took it from his shirt pocket and passed it to her. "Please take it."

He was right. She had exhausted most of her money on the business and while she did have more income coming in, in order to grow, she needed to spend more. The two hundred grand was a godsend.

"Please."

She realized she'd refused Jake's check from him because she'd felt hurt and betrayed, but this was different. For one thing, it was money from the sale of Jake's horse, which he had left to her, so that seemed okay even if it was Rafferty's training that made Slate worth so much. For another thing, she'd fully let go of the pain and resentment. She forgave Jake and released those negative emotions.

"All right." She smiled.

He looked so incredibly relieved that it made her feel a little guilty that she'd caused him anxiety over this.

"Thank you, Rafferty."

"You're welcome."

"Well," she said. "I better get to the booth and spell Mariah. Give you a chance to get psyched up for the match."

"See you afterwards?"

"I'll be here." She raised a hand in good-bye, and scurried from the arena, feeling more secure and at peace than she'd felt in a very long time.

Rafferty tried his best to win the event. Coaxed as much out of Slate as the horse had to give. If he won, he could stay at least a few more days in Jubilee, but if he lost, there was nothing holding him here any longer. He had to get on the road. Go home.

He felt a bit bad for not coming clean to Lissy about the sale of Jake's horse. He hadn't lied exactly. The buyer was from California. He just hadn't told her that *he* was the buyer. If he'd been honest, he was certain that she would not have taken the money. She had so much stubborn pride, but he admired that about her. She was an exceptional woman and he was happy that his plan to preserve her pride had worked. Not only had he gotten her to accept the check, but he'd also been able to spend two great months getting to know her and his nephew.

Too bad it was almost over.

Slate gave the challenge his all, but in the end, the horse was still too young, still too green to keep winning. He was an amazing animal and he'd be a nice addition to Rafferty's stables.

When the scores were tallied, one of Joe Daniels's horses won. Rafferty congratulated his new friend and meant every word, but he couldn't help tripping over his own disappointment.

It was time to go home.

Joe clamped him on the shoulder. "You did a phenomenal job with Slate. Much better than Jake could have done."

"Thanks."

"Will you be back next year to compete?"

Rafferty shook his head. "Probably not."

While the idea was appealing, it was probably best he make a clean break from Lissy and Kyle. They had their own path to follow, and if he kept popping in and out of their lives it would only confuse things. For the first time, he understood why Jake hadn't kept in touch over the years. It was simply too hard on the emotions. Better to relegate Lissy and Kyle into a tidy box in his head and just get on with it. He'd kept his promise to Jake. He'd made sure they were okay, he could move on knowing he'd done his duty.

Why, then, did he suddenly feel so damn empty?

Lissette closed her booth at the trade show and slipped off to watch Rafferty compete. He'd given it his best shot, but he'd come in second to Joe's first place.

It fully hit her then that Rafferty's time here was done.

She left the stands and hurried down to the floor to search for Rafferty. The events were over for the day and everyone was loading up the animals. She found him currying Slate in one of the horse stalls.

"Hey," she said.

He stood, set the currycomb aside. "Hey."

"You were awesome out there."

"Thanks."

"I'm proud of you," she said. "Gordon would have been so proud of you too."

"That means a lot," he said, and she could practically see the weight that had been burdening him for far too long roll off his broad shoulders. All his life he must have felt inferior to the father who never acknowledged him. "I do feel like I proved myself."

"I'm going to just go break down the booth and we can get out of here." She forced herself to sound perky.

"Let me help you. I can load Slate up later. It'll be easier anyway after most everyone else has thinned out."

She didn't turn him down. They cleaned up her booth and carried the supplies to her truck.

Rafferty shut the pickup door and turned to face her. The night air was crisp and cold. A fine dusting of snow covered the ground, but the skies had cleared.

"It's cold," he said. "Let's get back inside." He took her by the hand and led her to the empty arena. There, small pockets of people were dotted throughout the arena, but for the most part they were alone.

Lissette took a deep breath. Tried to think of the right thing to say, but Rafferty was the first to speak.

"I've trained a lot of horses for the movies," he said. "It's my favorite thing in the whole world, but I've never enjoyed myself the way I've enjoyed being here with you and Kyle."

"Your entire visit has left a mark on me. I can't look around without seeing evidence of you," she said.

Silence fell, lingered.

"If I were a superhero you know what kind of powers I would want?" he murmured.

She laughed. "What's that?"

"The ability to freeze time. You know, when there's a perfect moment that you want to preserve forever, wave a hand and stop the clock from ticking and just revel in it? Stay in that one spot for hours, weeks, months, years if you wanted."

"It's a nice dream." She nodded.

"But . . . ?"

"Only one problem."

"What's that?" he murmured, wrapping a hand around her waist. His touch felt so good that she wanted to cry. "You don't approve of my imaginary superpower?"

"Everyone else would be frozen in the moment too, and what if in the moment of your bliss, they were clutched in the moment of their greatest despair? You couldn't do that to other people just so you don't have to face the next imperfect moment."

"You're right. That would be terrible." He pulled her up against him with both hands. She felt the pressure of his belt buckle against the small of her back. She tipped her head back to rest against his shoulder. "The two of us locked in selfish bliss."

Lissette closed her eyes, felt his warm, pepperminty breath against her neck. What if he did indeed have superpowers? They could stay right here forever and ever. But that wasn't the way life worked and they both had responsibilities. Hers were here. His were in California. She sensed he was about to say something, so she beat him to the punch. "Please, don't say anything. Let's just stand here."

"I have to leave soon," he said.

"Shh."

He turned her around in his arms so that she was facing him, and using sign language said, *I will miss you.*

She mirrored his signing. What would she do without him? Better question, what would Kyle do without him?

You'll be fine, he signed, reading her mind. *You're strong.*

He was off to rescue someone else. That's what knights in shining armor did. Rescue people. He'd rescued her, but his work here was done. He was off to find someone more needy.

I'm needy, she wanted to say. *I need you most.*

But she could not put that burden on him. She would not add to his pressure. She'd already kept him away from his home for too long. Besides, she had good friends here. She had her son. Eventually, she and Claudia would repair their relationship. She would survive.

A cowboy climbed down from the control both. "You folks need something?"

Lissette realized then that they were the only ones left in the arena. Empty soda and nacho containers lay scattered on the floor along with popcorn, beer cups, and ticket stubs. An event program with a boot print on it lay facedown in the mix.

"We're fine." Rafferty raised a hand.

"I need to shut things down."

"We're moving on."

Moving on.

Rafferty tucked her against him, ushered her to the door. They stepped out into the cool night air. Christmas lights twinkled from the streetlamps surrounding the coliseum.

"I have to go load up Slate," he said.

"I can come with you."

"Kyle's waiting."

"I have pastries to bake too," she admitted. "Christmas rush. Too bad we had to come in separate vehicles."

"I appreciate that you took time out to come watch me compete."

"I wouldn't have missed it for the world."

They paused at the exit where the last remaining competitors were leading their horses out to the trailers in the parking lot.

"Superpowers sure would be nice." Rafferty reached up to brush a strand of hair from her forehead.

"We have to live in the real world."

"Why?"

"Because neither one of us are slackers."

"I should have cultivated a lazy streak, but I had too much to do." His gaze never left her face.

"I've been thinking about it. Developing a lazy streak." She cocked her head.

"You can't."

"I know. Family. Obligations. Roots. That's what we've both got, with several states in between us."

"And that's not even counting guilt and shame and grief."

"Not even," she echoed.

He nodded. Somewhere a horse nickered along with the sound of trailer doors clanking closed and cowboys in muted conversation.

Gone. This was it. Their time together. Gone forever. It had blown by so fast.

She whimpered. No. Not more loss.

Rafferty gathered her to him and kissed her for a good long time—at least a solid minute without stopping to take a breath. She unzipped his jacket, slipped her hands up underneath his shirt. His skin was so warm. He wrapped the edges of his down jacket around her, pulled her as close as two people could get with clothes on. They huddled together enveloped in the down cocoon.

His supple mouth went back to hers. He tasted so good. Like Christmas. Too bad Christmas came and went so quickly. She felt drugged, dizzy with the flavor of him, like a kid jacked up on a sugar cookie high.

This had to stop. It was torture dragging out a long good-bye. "Rafferty—"

He cut off the rest of her words with his lips. She sagged into him. His hands rose to thread through her hair, holding her in place while he kissed her thoroughly, letting his mouth carry his feelings.

They delved into each other, sending messages through their nerve endings, a physical love letter. Communication empty of words, yet deeper, richer because of it.

Finally, they both parted at the same time, in mutual agreement, but although their mouths were separate, their gazes stayed fused. They stood enthralled, trembling, and deeply melancholy.

"Do you think selfish people are happy?" he asked.

"No doubt. They're selfish. They don't worry about what other people think or need from them."

"I'm jealous. I wonder if there's a vaccine you can take that cures you from caring about others."

"Don't think so."

"Maybe I should add that to my superpowers wish list." He pantomimed pulling an invisible list from his pocket and jotting that down.

"If you were selfish, Rafferty Jones, I wouldn't admire you the way I do."

"Ditto, Lissy Moncrief."

"We're damned," she said woefully.

"Pretty much."

"This stinks."

He laughed, but his eyes were sad. "In the words of my mother. Sucks like an Electrolux."

"I think she stole that from Stephen King."

"Actually, it was a failed advertising campaign slogan put out by Electrolux themselves. My mother said it so often—usually in regards to something I wanted to do, but couldn't because I had to watch my brother and sister—that I looked it up."

"Look at you. All bookish and everything."

"I'm more cerebral than I look," he teased. "Got books on my MP3 player and everything."

"*Hank the Cow Dog*?"

"Now you're just giving me a hard time."

"Louis L'Amour?"

"You know me too well."

"Easy to figure. You have a romantic soul. That book of poems you checked out from the library was a dead giveaway."

"And look where that's gotten me. Lovesick in the Lone Star State."

Lovesick?

He might fancy himself in love with her, but this wasn't love, Lissette told herself. They had compatibility, yes. They made good friends. And certainly the sex with him was amazing, but neither one of them was in a place where they could evaluate whether they were really in love or if this was simply a stopgap relationship.

They filled each other's needs for the time being. It wasn't enough to base a long-term relationship on, and there were so many complications. Easier to pretend this was nothing more than mutual attraction. You didn't change your life and upset the people you already loved for something you couldn't be sure of.

"You have to go get Slate," Lissette said, spoiling the moment.

It had to come to an end. Unfortunately, Rafferty couldn't freeze time. From the Tex-Mex restaurant down University Drive wafted the scent of cumin, chili powder, and garlic. The aroma mingled with the horsey smell clinging to Rafferty.

"And you have to get home so you don't have to pay the babysitter overtime."

"Jones!" Cordy called from the back entrance. "You comin' to get your horse?"

"Be right there." Rafferty raised a hand but never glanced at the man. His eyes were full of Lissette.

"You better go."

"I don't want to."

"I know, but once you're home things will go back to normal again and Jubilee will be nothing but a memory."

"No," he said loudly, causing Lissette to jump. "That's not true. You and I, we will *always* be connected."

"Because of Jake," she murmured.

"And Kyle. He's my nephew."

Were those the only reasons? *Don't play mind games with yourself, Lissette. It's counterproductive.* She stepped away from him, stuck her fingers in the pockets of her blue jean jacket, and curled her hands into fists.

"Jubilee will never be just a memory. What we have—what we did—will never feel wrong."

"That's a sweet thing to say, Rafferty, but you can't make me any promises and I can't make you any either. We don't know how we'll feel once we're away from each other. Once everything returns to normal."

"Nothing is ever going to be normal again."

"Out of sight, out of mind."

"Absence makes the heart grow fonder."

"Familiarity breeds contempt."

"Are you trying to chase me off?"

"I'm trying to give you the distance you need to make an informed decision."

"I get it. You're scared. I am too. We'll do it your way." He reached for her hand. "Let me walk you to your truck."

Reluctantly, she took her hand from her pocket. This was just dragging things out. "I can't take another good-bye."

"It's not forever."

"It might be. It could be. We have to step away from this foggy cloud we're under. Let our heads clear before we know if this is something substantial or just the effects of losing Jake and digging up the past and—"

"Shh. Stop explaining." He kissed her again, then took her hand and led her across the parking lot to her truck. "Give me your keys."

She pulled the keys from her pocket. He opened the door. Stood there while she got inside and started the engine. He kissed his fingertip, and then pressed it to her window. He gave her a lonesome smile, just before he turned and walked away.

Chapter Nineteen

It took everything Rafferty had in him to walk away from her. This was killing him. Tearing him into two pieces. He wanted to stay here, but he had a ranch and employees that he'd already been away from too long and he was homesick for his horses.

But here were Lissette and Kyle and the promise of a whole new kind of future. Except Lissette didn't believe in the feelings he had for her. Jake had gotten everything Rafferty had not. A father. A functional mother. A beautiful wife. A son. A home. A prizewinning horse.

And here was Rafferty with castoffs again. Jake's cast-off horse, his cast-off wife . . .

No. He did not think of Lissette that way and he was ashamed of that passing thought.

He had never intended on starting a relationship with his brother's wife. Staying out of her bed had been his central goal and he'd failed. Miserably.

But once begun, however, he wanted more. Much more. A simple fling would have been easy. Keep it quiet until it burned out. A secret that brought a smile. But that wasn't enough for Rafferty. He needed more.

Except Lissy didn't.

She couldn't say it to him. He'd seen it in her eyes. She didn't want to hurt him, but she was still grieving. Still sorting out her life. Still learning to deal with Kyle's disability. She didn't have any room in her heart for a complication like him. So he was going home. He would not go to her on this last night as he'd planned. He would spend the night in the garage apartment. Would not slip into her bed one final time, and in the morning, he would head back to where he belonged.

Because it was the only option that his conscience would allow.

Lissette left the back door unlocked, hoping against hope that Rafferty would join her when he got back, but he did not come to her.

She never slept.

Finally, she got up at four A.M. and spied his truck parked in the driveway. So he was still here, but he had not come into the house. She understood why he had not come in, but understanding did not soothe her.

Might as well get to work. Nothing calmed like the reassuring act of measuring sugar and sifting flour and rolling out dough.

She'd been working for about an hour when the back door opened.

"Lissy?"

She glanced up. A strand of hair had fallen across her face. She tossed her head to get it to move. Her hands were dusted with flour. "You didn't come in last night."

"No." Rafferty looked more handsome than ever in his Stetson and cowboy boots. "I thought it best not to string things out."

"So," she said. "I guess this really is good-bye."

"I wish—"

"You don't have superpowers, Rafferty." She stiffened, fighting everything inside her to keep from running across the kitchen, wrapping her arms around him, and begging him to make love to her on that marble amid the muffins.

"Let me finish."

"Go ahead."

"I wish there was some way to know if what's going on between us was the real deal or just a consequence of losing Jake."

"There's no way to know for sure without separating."

"I realize that."

"Here," she said, slipping muffins into a Ziploc bag. "Have a Mockingbird Muffin for the road."

"Mockingbird Muffin?"

"It's my newest pastry. It's like a hummingbird cake but with a secret Texas ingredient. So good it will have you singing like a mockingbird."

"Your bakery is going to be a huge success, Lissy." He picked up the muffin bag, turned to leave, stopped, and then came back. "I almost forgot," he said, "that I got you a good-bye present."

"You didn't have to do that."

"It's a Christmas cactus. It's supposed to bloom on Christmas Day. I left it in the apartment."

She smiled and her heart clenched.

"I'm gonna miss the hell out of you." He came over and pressed his lips against her neck. Hot. Blistering. Masculine lips. Not soft, but tender.

Rafferty!

And then he was gone, his feet padding away. Lissette stood at the counter, the spatula curled in her fingers, tears streaming down her cheeks. This wasn't fair! She wanted him. Wanted him more than she'd ever wanted any man and that included her husband. But she couldn't claim what she wanted.

She was in love with him.

No, no. She was not in love. She was mixed up. She was lonely. She had needs and Rafferty was a sexy man. She didn't love him. She couldn't love him. Yes, he was kind to her son. Yes, he had made her heat up in places she had no business heating up in. Yes, he helped her in the way of a real helpmate. But that did not equal love. Gratitude, yes. She could not mistake this for something it was not.

She slung down the spatula, spun around, ran after him. "Rafferty!"

Lissette could see him through the window inside the back door, the blinds partially pulled up.

He stopped.

So did she.

Lissette reached out a hand, clamped down on the knob.

Rafferty shook his head, and then he was moving again. Running now. Running away from her, across the yard toward his truck.

She flung open the door. "Rafferty!"

He stopped. His back was to her. His shoulders went down and he slowly turned around. That's when she saw the mist of tears in his eyes.

"Your feelings are probably going to change once you get to California," she said. "But just in case they don't, then let's make a pact."

"What kind of pact?" he asked.

"If you want to be with me, then be back here by Christmas Eve. If you're not back by midnight on Christmas Eve, then I'll know you got home and had a change of heart. No harm. No foul. How does that sound?"

A faint smile curled his lips. "Wasn't there a movie like this?"

"*An Affair to Remember*, but pay attention. This is important."

"I saw it a long time ago. Amelia used to love old movies. I don't remember much about it except that it didn't have a happy ending."

"What do you mean? It had a happy ending."

"No it didn't, the woman he loved ended up in a wheelchair."

"You're missing the point. They ended up together."

"But she was in a wheelchair."

"This from the man who taught me that deafness isn't a handicap."

"You're right. I'm looking at this the wrong way."

"So we have a deal? Midnight? Christmas Eve? If you don't show we never mention it again. No hard feelings."

"Deal," he croaked. "I've got to go."

"I know."

A slice of dawn shone down on her. *Nah-nah, lovesick fool. He's never coming back.*

She watched him drive away, pulling Jake's horse trailer behind him. He waved. She waved. Good-bye.

For the longest time she stood there, willing him to come back to her. She stood until the smoke alarm went off, blasting an ear-splitting shriek, and the smell of burning muffins singed her nostrils. At least it wouldn't wake Kyle up, she thought ruefully.

Finally, she went back inside. Dumped the burned muffins in the sink, pulled the battery from the alarm until the smoke dissipated, and then she started all over again. Because these days, that was what she did best.

Start all over from scratch.

Claudia couldn't stand it any longer. The guilt was too much to bear. After she'd confessed her sin to Stewart, he'd told her she needed to forgive herself, but she couldn't do that until she asked Rafferty for forgiveness. Then Stewart had told her he loved her no matter what she'd done in the past and he took her to bed.

She heard through the grapevine that Rafferty had been training Jake's cutting horse and entered him in the futurity and that he'd been winning. She'd been trying to work up a head of courage to go apologize to him, but it was so difficult. What if Rafferty refused to forgive her? What then?

When she heard that one of Joe Daniels's horses had won the amateur division, she knew Slate had finally lost. This was her opportunity to go to Rafferty and congratulate him on a good showing and then confess everything.

She got dressed that morning on December 4 and faced herself in the mirror. She had to do this. It was the only way to move on. More than anything, she wanted to see Lissy and Kyle, and this was her ticket back into their lives.

Unless they didn't forgive her either.

But Stewart had forgiven her. He understood.

Yes, but he wasn't the one she'd wronged.

Finally, before she chickened out, she got into her car and drove to Lissette's house.

She parked in the driveway and she was more than relieved to see the red dually with the California plates wasn't here.

You're not getting off that easy. Go find Lissy and ask where he is.

She forced her legs to move, and started around to the back door. Her heart pounded as she remembered the last time she'd been here. When she'd peeked through the French doors into the kitchen and seen Lissy and Rafferty together. Her hand pressed against his heart.

Her stomach roiled and she almost turned and ran, but

then she saw that the door to the garage apartment was open. Was Rafferty up there and his truck was simply closed up in the garage?

This was it.

The time had come.

Drawing on whatever little courage she had left, Claudia forced herself up the stairs. A vivid green Christmas cactus in a bright red planter was sitting on the landing. She hesitated at the threshold, curled her fingernails into her palms, braced herself and peeked inside.

There was Lissette bent over, stripping sheets off the bed.

Claudia's gaze darted around the room. No sign of Rafferty. The air seeped from her lungs, hissed through her clenched teeth.

Lissette's head shot up.

Their gazes met. Stuck.

"Lissy," Claudia said.

Her daughter-in-law smiled sadly. "Mom."

Mom! Hope lifted her spirits. She'd called her Mom. "Is Rafferty here?"

"He's gone."

"When will he be back?"

"He's gone for good. Home to California."

Claudia's knees almost gave way with relief. Rafferty was gone, but that didn't absolve her. She had to set things right and confessing to Lissette would be a start. "Can I . . . can we talk?"

Lissy dropped the sheets to the floor, sat down on the bare mattress, and patted the spot beside her.

Her legs moved toward Lissy, but she was barely aware of the journey, her mind busy with how to begin.

"I've missed you," Lissy said.

"I've missed you too."

They sat there looking at each other.

Claudia's bottom lip started to tremble. "Lissy, I'm so sorry."

"I know you didn't mean to hurt me," Lissy said.

"I didn't! I didn't!"

"I know you were just hurting. That's why you lashed out at Rafferty."

"I was." Claudia plastered a palm to her forehead. The ache in her heart was so acute that she had to stop and catch her breath. She gulped, desperate for more oxygen. Lissy looked so calm, so put together in a simple sweater and black slacks. She was such an elegant woman. "Where's Kyle?" she asked, suddenly desperate to see her grandson.

"He's at Mother's Day out. I had to get some baking done and while the bread was in the oven I thought I'd come clear out the apartment."

"You're in love with him, aren't you?" Claudia's voice came out high and reedy.

"Who? Rafferty?"

Mutely, she nodded.

She glanced away but not before Claudia saw the mist of tears in her eyes. Lissette didn't answer her question, instead she said, "This is the way it has to be."

"Because of me? Did you send him away because of me?"

"Only partially." Lissette picked at imaginary lint on the knees of her slacks. Finally, she raised her head and her gaze locked with Claudia's. "The last thing I want to do is hurt you, but I'm not going to apologize for anything I've done."

She knew then that Lissy had slept with Rafferty. "You love him more than you loved Jake."

"He's different than Jake," Lissy said. "Kinder. More understanding."

Claudia pressed her lips together, fighting back the

tears. She considered jumping up and running from the room so they did not have to have this conversation, but she made herself stay rooted to the bed. "I know."

"Jake and I—"

"I know."

Lissy put a hand to her nose. "He gave me Kyle."

"Uh-huh."

"Because of Jake I have you." A single tear rolled down Lissy's cheek.

"Lissy, before you say anything else, there's something I have to tell you."

Lissy's face paled. "I'm listening."

"It's about Rafferty. About what I did to him when he was young. That's the reason I lost it when I met him in person. Not because I was jealous that he was with you. It's because I was so ashamed of what I'd done."

Lissette put a hand to her mouth. "What did you do?"

Claudia's shoulders slumped. She felt as if her bones were shrinking. "It was at Christmas time. Jake was six years and I was putting Gordon's jeans in the laundry. There was a letter in the back pocket. I took it out and instantly smelled perfume."

"It was from Rafferty's mother?"

She nodded. "Amelia Jones. In the letter, she told Gordon that he had a two-year-old son and she wanted him to come to California for Christmas to see him."

They sat there in the awkward silence.

"What did you do?"

"Well, at first I was hurt, betrayed, but then I started thinking what would happen if Gordon went back out there? Would he leave me for her? What would this do to our family? What would it do to Jake?" She paused. "I knew what I had to do to protect Jake. I couldn't let my son's life be unraveled by his father's indiscretions. You're a mother. You know what I'm talking about."

But Claudia could see by the look in Lissy's eyes that she didn't fully understand. "I got on a plane and flew out to California. I was so full of self-righteous rage. I was going to make this woman suffer for bursting the bubble of my life. I'm not proud of what I did, but at the time, I thought I had the right, but I've regretted my actions every day since then."

"What did you do?" Lissy's green eyes were wide.

Once she said the words there would be no taking them back. When Lissy learned the truth about her, would she stop loving her? "Did Rafferty ever say anything about me?"

Lissy shrugged. "Other than his mother wasn't a fan of yours, no. But that's understandable."

What if she just didn't say anything else? What if she clamped her mouth shut and never said another word? But she couldn't do that. Her life wasn't worth living if she couldn't face herself in the mirror every morning with an unburdened conscience.

"I flew out there to confront her."

"That was brave of you."

"It wasn't bravery that drove me. It was pure jealous rage. How dare this woman try to disrupt our lives? She was demanding money from Gordon. Money we didn't have. Money that would take food from the mouth of *my* child." Even now, as ashamed as she was of herself for what she had done, she could still feel the ghost of that old rage haunting her. Jealousy was a terrible, terrible thing.

"But Rafferty was Gordon's child too," Lissy murmured.

"I know, I know." Wretched misery seized hold of her. "What I did was unforgivable, inexcusable, and I've regretted it every day of my life since. But you have to understand. Jake was my primary concern. What I did, I did for him. It was wrong. It was misguided. It was awful."

"Claudia." Lissy's voice was small. "What on earth did you do?"

"I tracked Amelia down to some squalid apartments in a very rough part of town. But I didn't care. I was so angry that I was afraid of myself. I barged up those steps, went down that dark ugly corridor, and slammed my fist on that door. I could say that I was temporarily insane, but that would just be an excuse. I'm not making excuses."

Lissy's hand was soft on her shoulder. "You've been torturing yourself a long time over this."

"It's so hard telling you this. I'm so very ashamed. I'm worried that you'll hate me."

"Claudia, I could never hate you."

She closed her eyes, clenched her jaw, and breathed deeply through her nose. "The door opens and there's this tiny boy standing there wearing nothing but a diaper so soggy the bottom is sagging halfway down his legs."

"Rafferty?"

"Yes," she whispered. "He was just about Kyle's age. So young. So vulnerable.

"I asked him if his mama was home and he pointed at the couch. There she is, slovenly in a ratty pink housecoat, passed out. I storm across the room and grab her up by the hair of the head and yank her out of her stupor. She's blindsided of course, but the boy comes over—"

"Rafferty," Lissy reiterated.

"And he was pummeling the back of my legs with his little fist, yelling at me to leave his mama alone. I swear it should have broken my heart but all I could think was *This kid can't be Gordon's. No way.*"

"Denial."

She opened her eyes, cut a sharp glance over at Lissette to see how she was taking it. Her daughter-in-law's face was serene. That kind expression was what gave Claudia the courage to continue.

"She started fighting me back and we had a knock-down, drag-out bitch fight. I won." Claudia notched up her chin. "God help me, I wish I hadn't won because I lost myself in that triumph. I told her that if she dared try to bilk money out of Gordon again I would call child protective services and make sure that baby was taken away from her. I made her pick up the phone and call Gordon and tell him that it was a lie. That he wasn't the father of her child and she'd had a sudden attack of conscience. I wanted to make sure he wouldn't come back to California looking for her and the boy, and if he thought the kid was really his, I know he would have done that."

"It wasn't your finest hour," Lissy said, making excuses for her. "But you were young and hurting. It wasn't a nice thing to do, but you're not that person anymore."

"But Lissy, I turned and walked away. I left that apartment . . ." She stopped speaking, her nose burning. She gulped back the tears and continued. "That apartment was littered with empty booze bottles and marijuana roaches in the ashtray. I left that baby boy alone with her. Knowing what she was. I abandoned him, and that's something I can never ever forgive myself for."

The tears she'd been trying not to shed came in a hot rush of shame.

Lissy wrapped an arm around her shoulder. Warm and comforting. She rocked her gently. "Shh, shh. It's okay. Rafferty survived. He's a strong man, a great guy. He turned out just fine."

"He turned out to be a better man than Jake." The sobs wracked through her, shaking her bones. "Oh, Lissy, can you ever forgive me?"

"There's nothing for me to forgive. Rafferty is the one you wronged."

"I know, but I had to tell you too. I had to make you understand why I acted the way I did that day in the park."

Lissy waved a hand. "Water under the bridge."

"I thought . . ." Claudia drew in a shuddering deep breath and accepted the clean tissue Lissy pulled from her pocket. When she was a young mother, she'd kept tissues in her pocket at all times. Little boys could get so messy.

"You've been beating yourself up for years. There's no need for me to do it too."

Claudia dabbed at her eyes. "So what happened between you and Rafferty?"

"He had to go home." Lissy's voice was light, but Claudia could hear the pain in those words.

"I thought . . . I heard . . . You seemed . . ." It was tough for her to say this. "Happy with him. You haven't been happy in a long time."

"Things with Jake and me . . ." Lissy shook her head. "It started good but turned out bad."

"I know. I'm sorry for that too."

Then they were both crying and hugging each other and in that moment of grief, they accepted their losses, forgave each other their mistakes, and made way for future tears of joy.

Home looked strange.

Rafferty hadn't realized how arid the ground was here. How barren and desolate. He thought of Jubilee. Of the cowboy-friendly town and the warm people he'd met there. His stomach contracted. He thought of Lissette and Kyle, and a rare homesickness, unlike anything he'd ever felt, crept over him.

He tried to shake it off. Lissette had told him that he couldn't trust what he was feeling. That their attachment was nothing more than the very human attempt to douse their sorrow in each other's bodies.

It sounded logical. Rational. And life had made Rafferty a practical guy, but he couldn't help wondering,

What if she's wrong? What if what they were experiencing was a true, honest, and enduring love?

His chest tightened as he turned into the driveway. Horses galloped in the field, following his truck. The pain in his chest intensified, pushed into his throat. The ranch hands were going about their daily chores. One cowboy was hitching horses to the circular walker. Another was saddling a high-spirited mare. A third was unloading sacks of oats from the bed of a pickup.

Home.

Loneliness blew through him. He took a deep breath, trying to center himself. Yes, he was home.

Why, then, the utter desolation rolling around his heart?

He pulled to a stop, surveyed the ranch house. Wind eddies stirred the dust. He got out. The sun beamed down on him. December in Southern California was almost as warm as August. He'd never missed the changing seasons before, but now his mind strayed to Jubilee and the coming snowstorm that had been predicted as he'd driven out of town.

Winter should be cold, he decided, at least now and again. It didn't have to be Montana cold, but a little weather, like the kind they had in North Central Texas, seemed just right. A pleasing blend of winter and warmth. Not the constant, unchanging temperature of Southern California.

Guillermo came across the yard, moving his hands a mile a minute in greeting. *Boss! You are back!* he signed.

I've got a new horse, Rafferty signed in return, and walked around to the back of the trailer.

Cutting horse? Guillermo's hands questioned.

Rafferty met his ranch foreman's eyes and spoke as he signed. Normally he didn't do that with Guillermo but he'd gotten into the habit of it with Kyle. "What else? I've been in the cutting horse capital of the world."

Guillermo rubbed his palms together like a hungry man about to dive into a banquet.

Rafferty opened the back door of the trailer.

This is good, Guillermo signed. *Robert Redford is directing a new movie about cutting horse cowboys. Just got a call from the studio.*

"Hear that, Slate?' Rafferty told the stallion. "Sounds like there's a good chance you could become a movie star."

Slate nickered as if it sounded like a good idea to him.

How's business? he signed to Guillermo as they unloaded Slate.

Good. Good. His foreman proceeded to give him a full accounting of what had gone on in his absence. One horse had been sick, but recovered. He'd had to put one of the trucks in the shop and it ended up costing less than expected. The ranch dog, a beautiful golden retriever named Lacey, had had her puppies six weeks ago, and the seven unruly puppies were getting into everything.

Once they finished getting Slate settled in, Guillermo led him into the house and showed him the books. Under Guillermo's management over the past six months, with only minor long distance input from Rafferty, the ranch had turned a significant profit. Much more than what Rafferty usually coaxed out.

"How?" he asked.

Guillermo informed him of some ingenious cost-cutting methods he'd instituted. He'd also worked with a director to create a video trailer about training opportunities to coincide with the latest movie one of Rafferty's horses appeared in. It was a smart move. They'd had a tenfold increase in the amount of people asking to have their horses trained at Harmony Ranch.

"Looks like you don't need me at all," Rafferty said, feeling a little taken aback. Honestly, he thought he'd find things in a bit of shambles since he'd been gone for so long. Of course, he'd known Guillermo was more than competent. What he hadn't expected was that his foreman would do the job better than he did.

How was Texas? Guillermo asked in sign language. *How is the boy?*

"He's doing well."

Guillermo nodded, signed, *You helped him and his mother.*

"If it weren't for you I wouldn't have been able to offer them anything."

You're the one who took the time to learn sign language, Guillermo messaged with his hands.

That was true, but if he hadn't learned how to sign, would he have been able to get so close to Lissette? Maybe in this case, his skill at sign language was a liability, except he couldn't regret being able to draw the boy from his shell. Kyle had bloomed while Rafferty had been in Jubilee.

He exhaled. Time to let Lissette and Kyle go. His place was here. "How are Heather and Dane?"

Guillermo shrugged.

"They haven't been around?"

Guillermo pulled a computer printout from the desk, passed it to Rafferty. It was Heather's grades from medical school and Dane's grades from his sophomore year in college for the fall semester. Straight A's. Both of them. He'd have to take them out for a big celebratory dinner.

Things were changing on the ranch, and damn if Rafferty didn't feel like he'd been left behind.

Chapter Twenty

Lissette tried to tell herself it was going to be okay. Once she got Rafferty out of her head, her life would finally be in balance again. She and Kyle would develop a new routine. Her business was going well. Her son was happier. She had two hundred thousand dollars in the bank, and it was all due to Rafferty. She owed him a debt of gratitude. It felt good standing on her own two feet. She felt strong.

But she missed him.

Several times, particularly when Kyle did something noteworthy, or she learned a new word in sign language to practice with him, she wanted to call Rafferty and share the good news. She managed to squelch the impulses. She did not want to stoke hope. If he got home and realized—as she feared he would—that what they had was really nothing more than a sweet illusion, she would not be crushed. This was the best way. If it was meant to be, then he would come back, and if it wasn't, she might as well start the separation process now.

She kept her head down and stayed busy. It wasn't difficult. Mariah was putting on three weddings in December. Plus she had plenty of holiday rush orders for her pastry business. Her Web site was getting over a hundred hits a day. Kyle had gotten accepted into a deaf school in Fort Worth, where he'd start classes in January, attending three days a week. Things were good.

Even so, she couldn't stop thinking about Rafferty. Every time she glanced out the window at the garage apartment, her heart would catch.

Let it go.

Easy to say. Hard to do.

The days sped toward Christmas. She tried not to think about it. Tried not to wonder if he'd show up for Christmas Eve or not. She wondered why she'd set up an *Affair to Remember* time clock. Yes, it was one of her favorite movies, but she didn't need to relive it in her life. It had been dumb to set a time limit on love.

But that was just the thing, wasn't it? Was it really love? Or was it nothing more than raw emotions? She'd needed someone and he'd been there. Rafferty needed to feel useful and Lissette had needed someone to fill the void in her life. It had worked for a while, giving them both what they required, but it wasn't something they could base a long-term relationship on.

Two days before Christmas, another snowstorm hit. She and Kyle holed up in the house together. They'd played games and communicated with sign language and then her son signed, *Rafferty?*

Gone, she signed back.

Like Daddy?

That had knocked her down. He had understood that his father wasn't coming back. She thought he hadn't been affected by his father's absence. He was young and Jake had been away so often. She hadn't imagined that he ever remembered Jake.

No, she signed. *Not like Daddy. Daddy died.*

Kyle had looked hopeful and signed, *Rafferty* and *home*.

He went to his *home*, Lissette explained.

Kyle's face clouded and he shook his head.

Rafferty's home is in California. She got out a map. Pointed out Texas, then California, even though she knew he was too young to understand the concept.

Her son's eyes narrowed. "Home," he spoke. "Here."

That got to her. Her son understood far more than she'd given him credit for. She shook her head. "No."

Kyle had thrown a tantrum then. A normal boy, almost three now. She'd let him cry it out. What else was there to do? She couldn't make promises she couldn't keep.

After his tantrum, Kyle fell asleep on the couch. Lissette got up and went into the kitchen to make pastries. She had orders piling up, but even so, she put aside time every day to work with Kyle.

She made piecrust dough with ice-cold apple cider vinegar instead of water, her secret weapon for the perfect piecrust. She sprinkled flour over the marble slab kitchen island, her mind flashing with memories. She thought about the day he'd first shown up at her door. The first time Rafferty had kissed her. She reached up to touch her lips and closed her eyes.

Rafferty.

She could taste him now as she'd tasted him then. Robust. Rich. Real. Except he was gone. She'd sent him away because if he stayed he would never know if it was for the right reasons or not. She'd had no options. No choice.

She washed her hands at the sink, wondered where he was. She rolled out the pie dough, pressed it into a nine-inch Pyrex baking dish, preheated the oven, got out the ingredients for the filling of Giddy-up Pecan Pie. It had become her top-selling pie.

Once the pies were assembled, she put them into the oven to cook, stepped to the faucet to draw a glass of water. She cast a glance out the window and saw in the gathering darkness the Christmas cactus that Rafferty had given her. That day after Claudia had come to confess what she'd done, Lissette had hung the cactus from the branch of the pecan tree. She'd intended on bringing it into the house once she'd seen her mother-in-law off, but she'd forgotten about it.

"It will bloom at Christmas," Rafferty had said. "And you'll remember me."

Except she'd left it out in the snowstorm. Emotion pushed her from the kitchen and out into the backyard shadows.

The cold wind hit her, blowing snow up her apron, but she scarcely noticed. Her attention was focused on the potted plant hanging from a low branch of the tree. She ran toward it, her pulse pounding, but she knew before she ever got there what she would find.

The cactus had frozen.

It was dead. Stiff. The leaves brittle and darkened.

Tears sprang to her eyes.

Oh, this was dumb. Crying over a plant.

Except it wasn't just any plant. It was the plant Rafferty had left for her. The plant represented their relationship. It was supposed to have flourished and bloomed by Christmas. But she'd neglected it. Allowed it to die, just as she'd severed the precious connection between herself and Rafferty.

Don't give up hope. Don't give up hope. He could still come back.

She clenched her jaw, blinked back the tears, and cradled the Christmas cactus in her arms. She'd lost so much. What was one more thing?

Lissette.

Her name throbbed through Rafferty's brain.

Lissette.

He had to have her. No obstacles mattered. She was the one he wanted to be with. He loved everything about her. Her smile. Her bravery. Her work ethic. The way she mothered her son.

Lissy.

His love.

It felt as if he'd just been waiting for her all his life. Wasting time until he could find her. Why had he walked away? He couldn't begin to imagine why he had ever gone, but he couldn't wait to get back to her.

He pulled his cell phone from his pocket, almost called her, then put it back and smiled to himself. No, no. He'd surprise her. It would make for a romantic moment when he walked into the house on Christmas Eve. He had the back of his truck stocked full of gifts. For Claudia and Joe and Mariah and Jonah and Cordy and Ila and the rest of his new friends. For Kyle he had a golden retriever puppy in a crate beside him. A puppy to whose collar he was going to tie a big red bow on Christmas morning.

And Lissette.

He had a very special gift for her. Anxiety bit him then. Was it too soon? Offering her an engagement ring?

What if she'd changed her mind? What if she decided that what they had was ephemeral?

Except it wasn't ephemeral. It was true and deep. Yes, it had happened fast. It had happened amid tumult and turmoil. Yes, she had been his brother's wife. Yes, she had a child with special needs. But when you found the right one you could not allow fear to hold you back. You had to seize life with both hands and take a chance.

And this trip back home had shown him what he hadn't been able to see all these years. His siblings were no longer children and he no longer had to assume the parent role. They were fine without him. He could let go of the need to be needed. He could expand fully into himself. He wouldn't be able to do it without Lissette. She'd accepted him for who he was. She never saw him as a castoff. That was a label he'd put on himself. He could let it go. It was all past, and the past no longer had the power to define him.

He was free.

He could start fresh in Jubilee.

Rafferty threw back his head and laughed out loud. Too bad there were so many miles between them. He should have flown, but he'd loaded up his possessions and he was pulling them in a trailer behind him. Ready to take the leap, make the move.

He pressed harder on the accelerator. If he got a ticket for exceeding the speed limit, he'd pay it gladly. What was a speeding ticket when the most wonderful woman in the world was waiting for him in Texas?

He was going to give her the very best Christmas Eve ever.

The miles rolled by.

He crossed the border, entering Arizona at eighty miles an hour. He had Christmas music on the radio and he was singing along with "I Saw Mommy Kissing Santa Claus" as loud as he could sing.

Lissy. His sweet dandelion.

The more he thought about her, the wider his smile grew. He could smell her. That sweet, yeasty aroma of baked goods. The undeniable scent that spoke of home and hearth and love.

"I'm coming, Lissy. Don't give up on me."

It was dark outside now. If he drove straight through, stopping for nothing but gas, he would be there in time to read Kyle a bedtime story before tucking him in bed on Christmas Eve. He'd never felt so happy in his life.

The moon shimmered off the road. He wondered if Lissy was looking up at the same moon that was guiding him home to her. He liked to think that she was.

"I'm coming, Lissy. I'm coming."

It was one A.M. on the day of Christmas Eve and he was about fifty miles outside Phoenix when he saw the car on the side of the road. A beat-up old Ford sedan. A haggard young woman was leaned against it. She had a baby on her hip. His headlamps caught her and she shaded her eyes. She waved, flagging him down.

Rafferty slowed.

If you stop, you might not be able to get to Jubilee in time. You'll have to give her a ride or try to fix her truck.

But how could he not stop? What if that was Kyle and Lissy broken down on the side of the road? What if it was an Amelia and her little Rafferty?

That got to him. He remembered all the times one of Amelia's shabby vehicles had given up the ghost. More times than he could count. He remembered how scary it had been. Broken down. Not knowing who or what was going to stop and offer you a lift.

He had to stop.

Disappointment pinched his stomach. It was okay. It would be all right. He would call Lissy when he finished helping this woman. It might take the edge off the surprise, but he couldn't bear the thought of her watching the clock, waiting to see if he was going to show up in time to keep his promise. He would not hurt her like that. He'd call and tell her that he was on his way and he'd be there by Christmas Day.

It would be all right. She would understand. She was an accepting woman. It was one of the things about her that he liked most. She accepted things as they were and went about dealing with them to the best of her ability. Admiration for her replaced disappointment.

He pulled his truck and trailer over onto the shoulder of the road and stopped behind the forlorn-looking woman. He took off his Stetson, ran a hand through his hair, and got out. "Evening, ma'am," he called. "You having trouble?"

"Yes, please, thank you so much for stopping. I think it's the radiator. It started smoking underneath the hood."

Radiator. That might not be so bad. A little water in the radiator and he could follow her to the nearest gas station.

"You should have Triple A, ma'am," he said, walking closer. "Seeing as how you have a young one and all. It can be dangerous out here in the desert alone."

"I can't afford no Triple A. Don't even got a cell phone."

She kept shifting her weight, edgy, nervous. The baby looked thin and gaunt. The outside of his diaper was covered in dirt, and from the smell of it the inside was dirty too.

Apprehension rippled over him. The woman was painfully thin and she had dark circles under her eyes. It was hard to determine her age. She might be thirty, but she could just have easily been a hard-living twenty. She forked fingers through her matted hair. Her thin cotton dress was torn. She kept sniffling, and when she spoke he noticed she was missing teeth.

"Let's just take a look," he said, alarm running through him. Could he really let her drive off even if he got her engine running? Clearly, the baby was being neglected. Maybe he should call the cops. Call CPS. Call somebody. "Pop the hood."

"Yeah, okay." She ran the back of her hand underneath her nose, opened the car door, sat down behind the wheel, and pulled a latch that released the hood.

Rafferty raised the hood. The car was so old it had one of those thin metal braces to hold the hood up. He propped it open. The radiator was bone cold. He scowled. "Ma'am, you sure you saw smoke?"

A noise sounded behind him. Boots on rocks.

Before Rafferty could turn around, he felt something

smash hard against his head and he stumbled into abject darkness.

Claudia and Stewart puttered in the kitchen, making eggnog. Lissette knew they were in there sneaking kisses. She didn't mind. She was happy for her mother-in-law. It was long past time that she found happiness.

Lissette was also happy that she and Claudia had mended their rift. But Lissette just couldn't help feeling a little sorrow for herself. She didn't have anyone.

Snap out of it.

Through knowing Rafferty, she had at least learned one thing. She was far stronger than she'd ever given herself credit for. No, that wasn't giving him the credit he deserved. He'd taught her so much more than that. He'd shown her how to speak up for herself. To express her needs instead of burying them. She recalled the things he'd taught her in the bedroom and felt her face flush. The way he'd explored her body! He'd given her a life-changing gift of her own sexuality.

A smug smile curled the edges of her lips. Kyle saw her smile. He picked up a storybook from the stack on the coffee table and brought it over to her. She put down her knitting, opened her arms, and welcomed her little boy into her lap.

He nestled in the crook of her arm and opened the book. The fire crackled in the fireplace. Stockings hung from the mantel. Lights twinkled from the real Christmas tree that Stewart had cut down and set up for her. She and Claudia and Kyle had decorated it. Their first Christmas without Jake would have been a sad affair if not for Stewart and all the friends who'd been dropping by all day.

Kyle pressed one hand to her mouth and tapped on the book with the other.

Slowly, she started reading *The Night Before Christ-*

mas. Kyle's gaze fixed intently on the pictures as his fingers gently combed her lips. How quickly he'd learned. The child had an amazing adaptability. She was a bit jealous. She wished she could navigate life as quickly as Kyle.

When she finished the story, she glanced up at the clock. Nine P.M.

Not that she was looking or counting the hours.

Liar.

He's not coming.

It's okay if he doesn't come. You'll be fine. Stop looking at the clock.

When she finished the story, Kyle opened it back at the beginning. Lissette started the story all over again.

Stewart and Claudia came into the living room, giggling like teenagers, their socked feet padding softly against the hardwood floor. The air smelled of cinnamon and nutmeg. Claudia settled a glass of eggnog on the end table beside Lissette, along with a small plate of cowboy Santa cookies.

"He's asleep," her mother-in-law whispered.

"What? Oh?"

Claudia reached for Kyle. Lissette shifted and allowed her to take him. "I'll put him to bed for you."

"Thank you." She smiled.

Stewart sat down on the chair across from the sofa where Lissette was sitting. "She appreciates your forgiveness," he said when Claudia was out of earshot.

"I know."

"It's torturing her to think that she broke you and Rafferty up."

"It wasn't Claudia's doing," she said. "We didn't break up because we were never really together. It was just one of those things."

"Two ships passing in the night, huh?"

"You're good for her," Lissette told him. "She's happy again."

"Only because you forgave her. It had nothing to do with me."

"Don't sell yourself short, Stewart." Lissette shifted her gaze to the clock. Nine-thirty. Two and a half hours left. If Rafferty wasn't here by midnight, it meant he realized that she'd been right, that their feelings for each other weren't real. Just illusion, a result of bonding during a difficult time. She drew in her breath.

Don't think about it.

"Are you expecting someone?" Stewart asked. "You've been looking at the clock all evening."

"Waiting on Santa." She forced a smile.

"Why don't you just call him?"

"Santa?"

"You know who."

She glanced away. "Can't."

"Too much pride?"

"It's not that."

Rafferty had to make his own decision. He had to come back to her on his own. If she called and he came back she would never know if it had been fully his decision or if he returned simply because she called him. She would not break down. Would not give in. And if he did not come, well, then at least she would not have made a fool of herself.

"Pride means less the older you get," Stewart said. "You realize your time here on earth is extremely short and it's not worth losing out on love just to save face."

"Would you excuse me?" she asked, getting up from the sofa.

He nodded. "Certainly."

She picked up the afghan from the back of the sofa and

tugged it around her shoulders, plodded to the kitchen, then stepped out onto the back porch. A half moon hung in the sky. The air was frosty, and when she exhaled, her breath came out in a puff of white.

"Rafferty," she whispered. "Where are you?"

She swallowed hard, remembering what she'd told him. *Be back here by Christmas Eve. If you're not back by midnight on Christmas Eve, then I'll know you got home and had a change of heart.*

Why had she drawn a line in the sand? Of course he would feel pressured as Christmas Eve ticked away. By setting a ticking clock she'd closed off all other options.

Chapter Twenty-One

Carolers showed up on Lissette's doorstep singing, "Hark! The Herald Angels Sing" just minutes after Claudia and Stewart left at ten P.M. Lissette stood on the porch, tolerating their bright, smiling faces and cheerful voices. It wasn't their fault that the clock was ticking and Rafferty had not appeared. They had not set up this arbitrary deadline. They were not the ones with conflicted hopes and dreams.

What was wrong with her?

Once the carolers left, she shut the door and wandered into the kitchen. Bake. It would keep her occupied.

She baked cowboy cookies. She sifted flour and scooped sugar. It calmed her. These measured details.

She'd told Rafferty that she was a big-picture person, but that wasn't true. She was just as detailed oriented as he was. She liked the comfort of measuring and weighing. A baker needed instructions, rules.

A cook was another matter A cook could throw a handful of this and a handful of that. A cook could eyeball something, guesstimate. Jake had been like that. Not bound by rules. She, on the other hand, needed a recipe to follow.

The cookies would not turn out if you just tossed in whatever came into your head. Baking was more of a science, cooking more of an art. She and Rafferty had more in common than she imagined. Where had she gotten the idea that she was an organic artist? Did it come from being with Jake? She had a tendency to take on the characteristics of the people she was around. Tofu. She was tofu. Not any flavor on her own. She tasted like who or what she mixed with. No personality on her own.

Bullshit.

It was Rafferty's voice she heard in her head.

You have plenty of personality. You just tuck it away because you're afraid to go out on a limb and express who you really are. You're not tofu, Lissette. You just pretend you are because you're scared of your own power. Be bold.

Lissette looked down at the dough she was stirring. Which was she? A structured baker or a daring cook or a little of both?

Really, deep inside? It was okay to be a baker if that's who she really was. That was the question. Who was she?

She wiped her hands on her apron, wandered over to the pantry.

Be bold. Be strong. Feel your power.

Blindly, she began grabbing up ingredients. She was going to find out precisely who she was.

She started tossing things into the batter, measuring nothing, a palm full of chocolate chips, a sprinkle of cinnamon, a capful of vanilla. She stirred it all in. Held her breath.

Who are you?

The batter seemed the right consistency, the recipe unknown. It felt scary. Forbidden. The same way she'd felt when she made love to Rafferty.

A part of her sang, *Do it. Do it.*

She spooned batter on a cookie sheet and slipped it into the oven. Soon the delicious smell of baking cookies filled the house. She heard a noise from the bedroom and went to check on Kyle. He was sitting up in bed. He looked at her. Signed *cookie*.

"Cookie," she said slowly so he could read her lips.

It was late. She should put him back to bed, but she didn't. She'd had enough of doing what she should do. No harm would come of allowing him to stay up late on Christmas Eve. She bent and scooped him from his bed. He nestled his head against her neck.

Her baby. Her boy.

She thought of Claudia and in that instant understood her. Once upon a time Claudia had felt like this over Jake. Lissette hugged Kyle close. Kissed his head and briefly closed her eyes, inhaled his scent, savored the moment. It was a beautiful moment she would never have again. Her heart tightened.

Precious.

All the minutes of the day, every single one of them, even as they ticked away.

"Cookie," she whispered as the timer on the oven went off.

She carried Kyle to the kitchen table and seated him on his booster seat. She went to the oven and took out the cookies. While they cooled, she poured him a glass of milk in his sippy cup, and then came back for a cookie. She broke off a piece and settled it into her mouth. It dissolved hot and melty.

Heaven.

It was the best damn cookie she'd ever eaten. As she put two on a plate for Kyle, a smug smile tipped up the corners of her lips.

She glanced at the clock. Midnight. Christmas Eve.

Rafferty wasn't coming.

Lissette couldn't sleep. She lay in bed staring at the ceiling. Rafferty had not come.

She had to deal with that.

He was gone, but he'd left her with a precious gift—the knowledge that she was strong enough to survive. He had listened to her. He had heard her. It was time to put the past behind her and move forward.

Their relationship had served its purpose. He'd helped her deal with Kyle's deafness. He'd been the right person at the right time. She had to accept that the small time they'd had together was all that it was meant to be. She could let go now, and that meant dealing with Jake's personal effects that she hadn't had the heart to deal with before.

Restlessly, she threw back the covers, got up, and padded to Jake's closet on the left side of the bedroom. She hadn't touched his things since he'd died, but cleaning out the closet would be a symbol.

An act of bravery.

She was accepting her losses and moving on. She opened up the closet door and switched on the light.

One by one, she pulled his clothes off the hangers, sorting them into piles. Salvation Army or Goodwill for the clothes in good shape. The trash bin for the worn-out clothes he'd liked to lounge around the house in. The peace that fell over her was comforting. This was the right thing. She felt confident.

An hour passed. Then two. The closet was almost empty. Clothes were piled on the bedroom floor.

She moved a duffel bag that was on the floor behind his accumulated shoes. Beneath the duffel bag was a metal lockbox. Lissette held her breath. Jake kept a lot of secrets. Did she really want to know what was in that box? Maybe she should give it to Claudia. But what if he had pictures of naked women in there or something? Claudia didn't need to deal with that.

Tell you what. If it's unlocked, you can look in it. If it's locked, then stick it in the attic and leave it there for twenty years.

Solid plan.

Lissette took the lockbox to her bed and sat down on the end of the mattress. She ran her fingers over the cool metal. "How many secrets did you have, Jake?"

Gingerly, she touched the lock, pushed on it.

The lid sprang open. If there were deep secrets in there, wouldn't he have locked it?

In it was a video camera she'd never seen before. She turned it on. Surprisingly, the battery was good. There was a disc in the camera. Should she watch it?

Holding her breath, she turned it on.

Jake's face filled the screen. He was dressed in military fatigues and wearing his dog tags, but he was sitting on their bed. On the quilt his mother had made. Her heart lurched at the sight of him.

"Hey Lissy," he said. "If you're watching this I guess that means I'm dead because I know you don't snoop in my things."

Oh God. She splayed her palm over her chest. Did she really have the strength for this? In the wee hours of Christmas morning?

"Damn you, Jake. Why did you have to make a video?" she said out loud.

"I'm screwed up. We both know that. I was screwed up before the war, but since I've been over there"—he fisted his hands on his knees—"I can't feel things the way I'm supposed to feel them. Not love. Not happiness, Not joy. I'm numb. I play at it. I try to pretend, but I don't feel anything. Not when I look at you. Not when I look at Kyle. I want to love you. I used to love you, but I can't anymore.

It's not your fault. The only thing that makes me feel alive is war. The adrenaline. It's like a drug. I gotta have it. Knowin' that each step, each breath just might be my last, well it's the only time I feel alive. It's fucked. I know that. I wish it wasn't this way, but it is."

He'd been so tormented. She wished she could have helped him.

"Babe, you deserve better than I can give. Kyle deserves better. I can't be what you need. I can't be a normal husband. That's why I reenlisted after I promised you I'd get out of the army. If I'm dead and you're watching this, then don't cry for me, Lissy. I'm finally at peace."

Her entire insides iced up, until she was completely numb. She wanted to turn off the camera but her fingers wouldn't move.

"You're probably cussin' me out right now and I don't blame you. I deserve it. I know you have one burning question on your mind. Why the hell did I leave my life insurance money to Rafferty instead of you and Kyle? Call it my lame attempt to make amends."

"Did you go completely off your rocker, Jake?" she asked him.

"One thing that ate at me for years is the fact that I had a brother I could not recognize. My mother wouldn't hear of it and I understand her position. After my dad died, I went to California to meet him. Well, shit, I get there and there's this amazing kid who got all of our old man's good traits and none of his bad. Unlike me. He was only sixteen and working two jobs and raising his younger brother and sister and cleaning up his wack job mother's messes and he was so damn happy to see me. I felt ripped off for not being able to know him and for the fact our old man completely turned his back on the kid."

Jake paused in the video, ran a hand over his head. "This feels weird, recording my final words. Anyway, it ate at me that Rafferty was never recognized as a Moncrief so I made him beneficiary on my life insurance policy and death gratituity benefits. It was the best I could do for him. We got married right after that. I thought about changing the policy, but I didn't. Then we had Kyle and I still didn't change it. I was gonna change it and then it hit me. If I didn't change it, I *knew* Rafferty would come to Texas to give the money to you. He's that kind of guy. And once he was here, he would make sure you were taken care of. Sorta underhanded I know, but both of you got a lot of pride. It was the only way I could think of to get you two together. Anyway, if you guys end up hooking up, and I kinda hope you will, you've got my blessing."

And then Jake got up and turned off the camera.

Stunned, Lissy sat there, trying to wrap her head around what she'd just seen and heard. Jake had been playing matchmaker from the grave.

One last time she cried for Jake and what had happened to him. Then she got up and destroyed the disc, burning it up in the fireplace. She never wanted Claudia to see this. When she was done, she fell exhausted into her bed, only to be awakened a short time later by a little boy who wanted to see what Santa Claus had brought.

Christmas morning was chaotic. Friends coming in and out of the house. Her parents showed up. No one wanted Lissette to be alone on her first Christmas as a widow. It was nice that everyone cared, but with the combo of Rafferty being a Christmas Eve no-show and Jake's bizarre video, Lissette was on edge and she wished everyone would go home and leave her and Kyle to themselves.

"What's this doing in the trash?" Mariah asked, rooting around in Lissette's garbage.

"What?" Lissette dried her hands on her apron.

"This Christmas cactus."

"I forgot to bring it inside and it froze."

"Just because it froze doesn't mean it's dead." Mariah plucked it from the garbage, started breaking of the dry, dead limbs.

"It doesn't?"

"Christmas cacti are hearty."

"It'll come back?"

"It never left. Took a beating, yes, but it'll put out new leaves. Not in time to bloom for this Christmas, but it'll live."

"Really?"

Mariah moved to the sink to add water to the plant that now looked completely horrible stripped of all its limbs. Just the core of the plant remained. It looked naked, stark, hopeless.

"Are you sure?" Lissette eyed the cactus skeptically.

"Positive. My mom used to keep a Christmas cactus. I have one. It's blooming."

"If I hadn't neglected it, if I hadn't left it out in the cold, this one would be blooming."

"It would." Mariah acknowledged. "But don't assume that just when something looks ragged that it's dead. If I hadn't come by and you'd thrown it out with the trash, it would have been all over, but now . . ." Mariah smiled. "There's hope."

She settled the cactus on the windowsill beside the aloe vera plant. "Aloe vera heals. Maybe it will rub off on the cactus. Actually, aloe vera is a cactus too. So birds of a feather . . ."

"Belong together." Lissette blew out her breath.

Mariah settled her arm on her shoulder. "It's going to be okay."

"How do you know?"

"Because you're strong."

"I feel weak. I feel crazy."

"You're neither," Mariah said staunchly.

Just then a thin wail issued from the living room.

"Boys," Mariah called to their sons. "Play nice." She slapped a hand over her mouth. "Oh, I'm sorry, I forgot that Kyle can't hear."

"It's okay to speak to him. Don't treat him any differently. That's what the therapist said." *What Rafferty said too.*

Rafferty. Maybe there was still hope there. Maybe she should call him?

While everyone else was gathered around her table eating and drinking, Lissette took her cell phone and went outside to call Rafferty. Her heart thumped as erratically as it had the first time she'd dared call a boy.

It rang and rang and rang. When the call finally went to voice mail, she felt too stupid to leave a message so she just hung up.

Two days after Christmas, the phone rang at midnight. Bolting awake out of dead sleep, Lissette grabbed for the phone. Her first thought was *Rafferty.*

"Is this Lissette Moncrief?"

"It is."

"My name's Heather Jones. I'm calling to tell you that Rafferty is in a coma in a Phoenix hospital."

"What happened!"

"He's been there since Christmas Eve. They didn't know his identity at first, so my brother and I just found out this afternoon and we arrived in Phoenix a couple of hours ago. Rafferty was found unconscious on the side of the road in the Arizona desert. The police believe he was ambushed, beaten, and robbed. His truck was stolen and he was left for dead. If a passerby hadn't found him when he did . . . In fact, the passerby wouldn't have even seen him if it hadn't been for the golden retriever puppy."

"What puppy?"

"Rafferty's foreman Guillermo Santo told me that he was bringing the dog to your son for a Christmas present. Apparently whoever took the truck tossed the dog out too. The puppy was sitting on Rafferty's chest and that's what caused the motorist to stop. Someone from the hospital staff took the dog home for safekeeping until Rafferty's better. Everyone around here calls the puppy Hero," the young woman was chattering a mile a minute, obviously stressed. "Guillermo also told me you and your son were very special to my brother."

"Thank you for calling, Heather. I'm on my way to Phoenix."

"We'll be here."

Lissette hung up. Rafferty had been headed for Texas on Christmas Eve. He'd been coming to see her. She would have been joyous except for the fact that he was in a coma. He'd been beaten and robbed. She bundled Kyle up, put him in the truck, and drove over to Claudia's. Her mother-in-law answered the door in her nightgown.

"Lissy, what is it?"

"Rafferty's in a coma in a hospital in Phoenix."

Claudia paled. "I'll keep Kyle. Don't worry. Go to him."

"Thank you." Lissette grabbed her mother-in-law's hand. "Thank you."

Claudia held on to Lissette, gripping her strongly. "I'm so sorry. I still have to apologize to him."

"Later. You can tell him later when he's well."

"I'll drive you to the airport."

"I can drive myself. Please, just keep Kyle. He needs stability."

"Yes, yes, okay."

"I'll drive her."

Lissette turned to see Stewart standing in the doorway of Claudia's bedroom. He was buttoning up his shirt.

Claudia looked at him with pure love in her eyes.

"Thank you," Lissy said. "Thank you both so much."

By the time her plane landed in Phoenix, Lissette was shaking all over. Rafferty had been coming home to her. For three days, she thought he wasn't coming back. She had struggled to put him out of her mind and get on with her life, but how could you forget a man who'd branded you in the way Rafferty had branded her?

She took a taxi from the airport to the hospital. Once she stepped through the doors and the antiseptic smell washed over her, it was all she could do to put one foot in front of the other. What if he never woke up from the coma? Fear was a boulder in her throat. She walked to the front desk and asked about him.

"ICU hours are restricted," the receptionist behind the desk told her. "But you can stay in the waiting room."

"Thank you."

The woman told her how to find the waiting area.

Each step felt like a million miles as she moved across the waxed floor to the bank of metal elevator doors. She punched the button and waited. "Please be okay. Please be okay," she prayed.

When she got to the waiting room, it was filled with a cluster of families and she had to sign in at the front desk. "Name?" the woman asked.

"Lissette Moncrief."

The woman crinkled her nose. "Are you family? Because only family is allowed in."

"She's family," said a voice behind her and she felt a hand on her shoulder.

Lissette turned to look into the eyes of a pretty blond

woman who resembled Rafferty a bit. They both had the same cheekbones. "Come sit with us," she murmured, and guided Lissette to a corner of the waiting room. "I'm Heather, by the way. Rafferty's sister. And you're Kyle's mother."

Lissette nodded and wondered what Rafferty had told Heather about her.

"This is my brother Dane."

The young man was on a tablet computer. He had a California surfer dude look to him—blond, brawn, and bronze. He put the tablet aside, stood up, and shook Lissette's hand. "Hey."

She forced herself to be calm and tolerate the introductions. It was good to meet Rafferty's siblings and know that Rafferty hadn't been here alone, but she felt desperate to see him for herself. "How is he?"

"He's going to be okay," Heather said. "I told him you were on the way. Whispered it in his ear and I'll be damned but if two hours ago he didn't wake up."

"Really?" Tears misted her eyes.

"He's bruised and battered but he's going to be okay," Heather reassured her.

"Visiting hours," announced the woman from behind the desk. "But only two may go in at a time. Fifteen-minute limit."

"You go on in alone," Heather said. "We saw him the last time."

"Are you sure?" Lissette asked.

"He was driving fourteen hundred miles to be with you on Christmas Eve. You must mean the world to him." Heather gave her a little push. "Go on."

Lissette didn't have to be told twice. She followed the other visitors through the double doors into the intensive care ward. She searched for the room with his name on the little placard outside. Smoothing her hands over her hair, she stepped into the room.

It was a shock to see him looking so pale, hooked up to all that machinery, but she schooled her features. "Hi," she whispered.

"Lissy," Rafferty croaked, his voice scratchy. "Is that really you or am I having another one of those fantastic morphine dreams?"

She sat down on the edge of his bed. "Don't try to talk."

"I was trying to get to you in time for Christmas Eve. I would have made it too."

"What did I just tell you? Your throat must be sore."

"I heard you," he said. "I want you to know that I heard you. I always hear you. I will always hear you. Even if I go deaf I will hear you."

"Shh, Rafferty, shh."

"I know you don't want me to talk, to save my energy, but I have to tell you."

"You don't have to say anything."

"Don't make this easy on me. You make things too easy on people. I need this."

"Okay." She settled her hands in her lap. "Say what you need to say."

He reached out for her hand and she sank it in his. "Look at me."

She raised her gaze. Met his dark eyes, felt something important soften inside her. "Yes?"

"I love you." He brushed his thumb against her knuckle. She couldn't have looked away from him if someone had walked into the room with a bomb strapped to him. "I know you're going to insist it's not real. It's too soon. All those arguments you built up against your feelings, but I'm not going to be denied. I love you and I think you love me too."

"I do," she said helplessly. "That's precisely why I sent you away."

"I went home. I found out everyone was doing fine

without me. And who am I to think that I have to take care of everyone?"

"You have the biggest heart of anyone I've ever met, Rafferty Jones."

"I care about you, Lissy. I care about Kyle."

"You care about your family too. Your brother and sister are out in that waiting room because they love you too."

"Yes, but I've been holding them back by watching over them too much. Holding on too tightly. I was afraid."

"What were you afraid of?"

"That if I let them learn on their own they'd get hurt."

She rubbed the back of his hand.

"But I figured out you've got to get hurt to grow. Look what happened to you after you lost Jake and found out about Kyle's deafness. You took charge of your life. You expanded your business. You came into your own as a woman. If I keep holding tight to the reins, my family will never find their own power."

"That whack on the head really got to you."

"Yeah," he said. "It did."

"There's nothing wrong with looking out for those you love."

"It's a balance," he said. "Between taking over and taking care. You've taught me the line of balance, Lissy. If I'd never met you, I would never have been able to get to this point."

"Sure you would have."

"I screwed up."

"You didn't."

"I didn't make it to you in time. I hurt you."

"It doesn't matter now." She leaned down to kiss him and he cupped the back of her head in his palm, pulling her closer to him.

"All that matters now is that we're together. Are you ready to take that step with me?"

She nodded. "I'm ready now."

"What changed?"

"The coma thing was a biggie," she said.

He smiled. "If I'd known that's what would convince you I would have gone into a coma a long time ago."

She chuckled. "You could have picked a less dramatic way to get your point across."

"You are a magnificent woman."

"You are given to superlatives." She stroked his cheek.

"Around you, it's a necessity."

"I found a video Jake made just before he left for his last deployment."

His face grew serious. "Oh?"

"He told me about the demons."

"Was it bad?"

"I hated that he felt like he couldn't talk to me. I hated that I couldn't save him."

"Me too."

"But he wanted us to be together."

"What do you mean?"

She told him about the entire contents of the video. "He knew you would come take care of me and Kyle if anything happened to him. That's a lot of confidence. Jake didn't put a lot of trust in people. You convinced him."

"I wished I'd known him as well as he felt he knew me."

"Me too."

"I'll take this as slow as you want, Lissy, but I want you. I'm moving to Jubilee. I'm turning the ranch over to Guillermo to run and I'm letting my family live their own lives and I'm going to start living mine."

"I'm happy to hear that."

"And I hope you want to share it with me."

"Well, if you're going to be rattling around Jubilee, what choice do I have?" she teased.

"We'll have to have a Christmas redo. I have something I want to give you."

"A present?"

"A present."

"Rafferty, the only present I need is your recovery." She traced his dear face with her index finger. He was the best thing that had ever happened to her and she wasn't about to let him get away. She was going to do what Jake told her to do. She was going to open her heart and let love in. The love she saw shining in Rafferty's eyes. "Claudia and I made up. She's got something to confess to you."

"I never blamed her for anything."

"I know, but she needs your forgiveness."

"I'll give it to her."

They stared at each other. Poignancy gripping them in the exhilarating embrace of emotion, joy and sadness, relief and tension, sorrow and love. Lots and lots of love. Life was complicated, scary, exquisite, so many things, and from here on out they were going to share it together. They would weather all the ups and downs—the births, the deaths, the weddings, the funerals. Life was complicated and grand and glorious, and Lissette didn't want to waste one second more without him.

Epilogue

Two weeks later, Rafferty pushed the grocery cart through Searcy's grocery store, past the sale items in the middle of the store. Marked-down Christmas items that hadn't sold before the holiday. Candy canes and garlands and candy mistletoe. At this hour of the morning, the store was almost empty. A few senior citizens shopped the aisles.

"Got the list?" he asked Lissette.

"Right here." She held it up for him to see.

He leaned over, picked up one of the candy mistletoes, and held it over their heads, and then he bent to kiss her sweetly on the lips. She absorbed his warm flavor with a heartfelt sigh. They turned onto the baking goods aisle. Kyle was in seated in the cart and he was busy turning the pages of *Pat the Bunny*.

"What's first?" Rafferty asked.

"Flour."

"Shouldn't we buy the fifty-pound bags at Costco?"

"We should," she said, proud that she now had someone to lift the heavy fifty-pound sacks for her. But his handiness wasn't the only reason she felt proud. Rafferty had chosen her. He'd come back. Bruises still lingered under his eyes, but they were fading. He caught her studying him, slipped an arm around her waist, and whispered, "I'm doing fine."

"You have an irritating habit of reading my mind."

"You love it and you know it."

"How do you do it?"

"I know you, Lissette. As well as I know myself."

"That's a bit cocky, don't you think?" she said, but inside, she felt very happy. She rested her head against his shoulder. Three months ago if someone had told her she would feel like this she would never have believed it. In such a short time, she'd gone from shattered to complete.

"You can trust it." Rafferty ran his hand up her spine. "I'm here. This is real."

"Stop that!" She chuckled.

"I can't help it, Lissette. When I'm attuned to a woman, I'm attuned to her."

"I've never had that with anyone."

"Get used to it."

Once upon a time, she'd been madly in love with Jake. When she'd first met him, the chemistry had swept her away, but then the passion had ebbed, she'd been left with a stranger. That was not going to happen with Rafferty. The passion she felt for him grew stronger, more fortified with each passing day. He was a cowboy she could count on.

This was the cowboy the fortune-teller had told her about on that long-ago day.

He reached for her hand, laced it through hers, and they strolled down the baking goods aisle. A woman was pushing her cart in their direction. She saw their joined hands, smiled, and moved over to the side so they didn't have to separate in order to get past her.

"Thank you," Lissette whispered as they went by.

"Been there." The woman smiled.

Lissette realized this was the first time she'd been there. So head over heels with a man that she didn't want to let go of his hand to traverse the baking goods aisle.

"Here we go," Rafferty stopped in front of the flour and bent down to pick two sacks off the bottom shelf. He set them in the cart.

Kyle looked up from his picture book, turned his head to see what Rafferty had put into the cart, then he shifted his gaze to Rafferty's face.

"Flour," Rafferty mouthed, enunciating clearly so Kyle could watch his lips, and then he signed the word.

Cookie? Kyle asked with his hands.

Rafferty grinned, ruffled his hair. "Yes, little man, your mother uses flour to make cookies."

Joy split Lissette in two. She was going to have to double up on her signing lessons to keep up with these two. Kyle had come into his own since Rafferty had started communicating with him in sign language. She hadn't known before what a wonderful sense of humor her son possessed. He'd accepted what was happening to him. As Rafferty had told her, this was Kyle's world. To him it was normal. She was the one who'd had to change her view of what deafness meant. None so deaf as those who will not hear.

"Why hello, sweetie!" A chirpy voice drew Lissette's attention behind her.

It was the diminutive blue-haired great-grandmother she'd met in Searcy's on the day Kyle had been diagnosed.

"Good morning." Lissette beamed.

"It's good to see you again."

"You too."

"You run a bakery."

"How do you know?"

"It's on your T-shirt."

"Oh, so it is." The T-shirt had been Rafferty's idea. Not

in the least, he'd said, because it made her breasts look rockin' sexy.

The elderly lady's eyes twinkled. "Bakers have a special place in heaven because they bring so much happiness to the world."

"What a sweet thing to say."

"You look a lot different." A secret smile lit the woman's face as she took in Rafferty signing to Kyle. "You look a lot healthier."

"I feel healthier."

"I can see that." Her smiled deepened. "I also see you took my advice."

It took Lissette a moment to realize what she was talking about, and then she remembered what the woman had told her that fateful afternoon. *Accept your losses and forgive your mistakes, then you can embrace a happy future.*

The woman nodded to Rafferty. "I approve."

"Thank you for saying that. Can I get you something off the top shelf?"

"Not today, sweetie. I was just walking by and saw you and I remembered how sad you were the last time we talked. I wanted to come over and say hello."

"Why, thank you. Any other words of sage advice?"

The woman glanced at Rafferty and Kyle again and shook her head. "I think you've got it covered."

"Oh, I thought you'd tell me to live each day as if it were my last or something equally profound."

"I can see you already figured that out for yourself."

Lissette smiled because it was true. She had indeed.

RECIPES

When things go wrong, Lissy takes control of her life by getting in her kitchen and baking her heart out. She feels there is nothing like creating delicious cakes and cookies and pies to take your mind off your troubles. When she's feeling especially down, she loves to whip up her famous Mockingbird Cake. One delicious bite will put a smile on your face and have you singing like the state bird of Texas.

Mockingbird Cake

1 plain yellow cake mix
1 can (8 ounces) crushed pineapple, undrained
2 medium ripe bananas, peeled and mashed
½ cup shredded coconut
½ cup water
½ cup vegetable oil
3 large eggs
1 teaspoon almond extract

Directions

Preheat oven to 350 degrees F (175 degrees C). Grease and flour two 9-inch cake pans. Place cake mix, pineapple with juice, bananas, coconut, water, oil, eggs, and almond extract in large bowl. Blend with mixer on low for 1 minute. Increase mixer speed and beat for 2 minutes. Blend until fruit is well incorporated. Pour batter evenly into pans.

Bake until golden brown (30–32 minutes). Cool before icing with your favorite frosting recipe. (Tip: Lissy believes cream cheese frosting works best with Mockingbird Cake.)

Rafferty Jones loves Lissy and everything she bakes, but he thinks these Cowboy Brownies are absolutely addicting.

Cowboy Brownies

½ cup butter
1 cup white sugar
2 eggs
1 teaspoon vanilla extract
⅓ cup unsweetened cocoa powder
½ cup all-purpose flour
¼ teaspoon salt
¼ teaspoon baking powder

Frosting

3 tablespoons butter, softened
3 tablespoons unsweetened cocoa powder
1 teaspoon vanilla extract
1 cup confectioners' sugar
½ cup chopped pecans
½ cup Texas wild red plum jam (may substitute jam of your choice)

Directions

Preheat oven to 350 degrees F (175 degrees C). Grease and flour an 8-inch square pan. In a large saucepan, melt ½ cup butter. Remove from heat, and stir in sugar, eggs, and 1 teaspoon vanilla. Beat in ⅓ cup cocoa, ½ cup flour, salt, and baking powder. Spread batter into prepared pan.

Bake in preheated oven for 25 to 30 minutes. Do not overcook.

To Make Frosting: Combine 3 tablespoons butter, 3 tablespoons cocoa, 1 teaspoon vanilla, and 1 cup confectioners' sugar. Frost brownies while they are still warm. Garnish with pecans. Heat jam in the microwave for 10 seconds. Drizzle over brownies.

Sometimes Lissy's mother-in-law, Claudia, can be pretty prickly, but Lissy understands her, and when Claudia is in a blue mood, Lissy whips up her favorite—Cactus Cake.

Cactus Cake

⅓ cup soft butter
1¾ cup flour
1⅓ cup brown sugar
3 teaspoons baking powder
2 eggs
½ teaspoon cinnamon
½ cup milk
½ teaspoon grated nutmeg
½ cup peeled and chopped prickly pear cactus

Directions
Preheat oven to 350 degrees F (175 degrees C). Mix all ingredients in a bowl and beat for 3 minutes. Grease and flour a 9-inch square baking pan. Pour into pan and bake for 40 minutes.

Lissy's two-year-old son likes to help in the kitchen. He loves baking with his mama and he has lots of fun molding these tasty delights into the shape of armadillos in Lissy's tangy Texas take on the popcorn ball.

Tangadillos

2 cups white sugar
1 cup light corn syrup
½ cup butter
¼ cup water
salt to taste
1 tablespoon barbecue sauce, original flavor
(add 2 tablespoons for a stronger flavor)
5 quarts popped popcorn

Directions

In a saucepan over medium heat, combine the sugar, corn syrup, butter, and water. Stir and heat to hard-crack stage or 300 degrees F (150 degrees C). Remove from heat, add barbecue sauce; mix well. Add salt to corn before popping. Pour mixture slowly over popped popcorn while stirring. Wait 5 minutes and shape into armadillos. Form the best you can. Makes one dozen.

If you missed the two other books
set in Jubilee, Texas

THE COWBOY TAKES A BRIDE

THE COWBOY AND THE PRINCESS

by *New York Times* bestselling author
Lori Wilde,
then take a look right here!

The Cowboy Takes a Bride

Chapter One

> Good sense comes from experience, and a lotta that comes from actin' like a damn fool.
>
> —Dutch Callahan

The naked cowboy in the gold-plated horse trough presented a conundrum.

In the purple-orange light of breaking dawn, Mariah Callahan snared her bottom lip between her teeth, curled her fingernails into her palms, and tried not to panic. It had been a long drive down from Chicago, and jacked up on espresso, she hadn't slept in thirty-six hours. There was a very good chance she was hallucinating.

She reached to ratchet her glasses up higher on her nose for a better look, but then remembered she was wearing contact lenses. She wasn't seeing things. He was for real. No figment of her fertile imagination.

Who was he?

Better question, what was she going to do about him?

His bare forearms, tanned and lean, angled from the

edges of the trough; an empty bottle of Jose Cuervo Gold dangled from the fingertips of his right hand. Even in a relaxed pose, his muscular biceps were tightly coiled, making Mariah think of hard, driving piston engines.

Like his arms, his legs lay slung over each side of the trough. He wore expensive eelskin cowboy boots. She canted her head, studying his feet.

Size thirteen at least.

Hmm, was it true what they said about the size of a man's feet?

She raised her palms to her heated cheeks, surprised to find she made herself blush.

Question number three. How had he come to be naked and still have his boots on?

Curiosity bested embarrassment as she tracked her gaze up the length of his honed, sinewy legs that were humorously pale in contrast to his tanned arms. No doubt, like most cowboys, he dressed in blue jeans ninety percent of the time.

She perched on tiptoes to peek over the edge of the horse trough. The murky green water hit him midthigh and camouflaged his other naked bits. Robbed of the view, she didn't know if she was grateful or disappointed.

But nothing could hide that chest.

Washboard abs indeed. Rippled and flat. Not an ounce of fat. Pecs of Atlas.

A rough, jagged scar, gone silvery with age, ambled a staggered path from his left nipple down to his armpit, marring nature's work of art. The scar lent him a wicked air.

Mariah gulped, as captivated as a cat in front of an aquarium.

A black Stetson lay cocked down over his face, hiding all his features, save for his strong, masculine jaw studded with at least a day's worth of ebony beard. His eyes had to be as black as the Stetson and that stubble.

Mesmerized, she felt her body heat up in places she had no business heating up. She didn't know who this man was, or how he'd gotten here, although she supposed that drunken ranch hands came with the territory. If she was going to be a rancher, she'd have to learn to deal with it.

A rancher? Her? Ha! Big cosmic joke and she was the punch line.

Less than twenty-four hours ago she had been standing in line at the downtown Chicago unemployment office—having just come from a job interview where once again, she had *not* gotten the job—her hands chafed from the cold October wind blowing off the lake, when she'd gotten word that Dutch had died and left her a horse ranch in Jubilee, Texas.

She didn't call him Dad, because he hadn't been much of a father. The last time she'd seen Dutch, he'd been hovering outside her ninth grade algebra class, battered Stetson in his hands, his sandy blond hair threaded through with gray, his blue eyes full of nervousness, remorse, and hope. Horse poop clung to his boots and he wore spurs—*yes, spurs*—against the polished maple hardwood floors of her Hyde Park high school. His Wrangler jeans had been stained and tattered, his legs bowed, his belt buckle big. He'd smelled of hay, leather, and horses.

The other students had stared, snickered, pointed.

"Where's the rodeo?"

"Who's the hick?"

"How'd the cowboy pass security?"

"He smells like horseshit."

"Hillbilly freak."

Dutch had stretched out a hand nicked with numerous scars, beseeching Mariah to come closer. "Flaxey? It's me. Your pa."

How many times had she fantasized that he would come back to her? Be a real dad? Love her the way she'd always loved him? But now that he was here, she didn't want him. Not in her high school. Not among her friends. Not dressed like that.

Shame flushed through her. She'd walked right past Dutch as if she hadn't seen him, and when he called her name, she started running in the opposite direction as fast as she could, schoolbooks clutched tight to her chest, heart pounding.

Not only was she ashamed of him, but also she was still mad because he had disappeared a week before her seventh birthday. He told Mariah's mother, Cassie, he was going to see a man about a horse, and he just never came back.

They'd been living in Ruidoso, New Mexico, at the time, and Cassie waited three months for him to return while she cleaned rooms at the Holiday Inn and cried herself to sleep every night. When one of the wealthy Thoroughbred owners in town for a race offered Cassie a job as his family's live-in housekeeper, her mother snatched the opportunity with desperate hands. They packed up their meager belongings, moved to Illinois, and didn't look back.

Dutch never missed a child support payment and he phoned a few times over the years, usually when he was drunk and feeling maudlin; the conversation generally ended with Cassie hanging up on him. Once in a while he sent Mariah gifts at Christmas or for her birthday, but they were always inappropriate. One year, a lasso. The next year, a lucky horseshoe engraved with the words "Make Your Own Luck." Another year, a pair of purple Justin boots, two sizes too small, as if he thought she stayed forever seven.

As she waited in line, Mariah's cell phone rang playing Wagner's Bridal Chorus. She fished it from her purse at the unemployment line and checked the caller ID.

Randolph Callahan.

A strange mix of anxiety, hostility, and gratitude lumped up in her throat. Why was Dutch calling her after all these years? If he was broke and looking for money, he'd certainly picked the wrong time to call. On the other hand, it would be good to hear his voice again.

The weary woman in line behind her, holding a runny-nosed kid cocked on her hip, nudged Mariah, and then pointed at the poster on the wall. It was a symbol of a cell phone with a heavy red line drawn through it.

"Hang on a minute," Mariah said into the phone, and then smiled beseechingly to the woman, "This'll just take a sec."

The woman shook her head, pointed toward the door.

"Fine." She sighed, never one to ruffle feathers, and got out of line.

A blast of cold air hit her in the face and sucked her lungs dry as she stepped outside. It was the first of October, but already cold as a Popsicle. She liked Chicago in the spring and summer, but the other six months of the year she could do without.

"Hello?" Head down, hand held over her other ear, she scuttled around the side of the building to escape the relentless wind.

No answer.

"Dutch?"

He must have hung up. Great. She'd gotten out of line for nothing. Huddling deeper into the warmth of her coat, she hit the call back button.

"Hello?" a man answered in a curt Texas accent. It didn't sound like her father.

"Dutch?"

"Who's this?" he asked contentiously.

"Who is this?" she echoed on the defensive.

"You called me."

"I was calling my father."

A hostile silence filled the airwaves between them.

"Mariah?" the man asked, an edge of uncertainty creeping in.

"You have the upper hand. You know my name, but I don't know yours. Why are you answering Dutch's cell phone?"

He hauled in a breath so heavy it sounded as if he was standing right beside her. "My name's Joe Daniels."

"Hello, Joe," she said, completely devoid of warmth. "May I speak to Dutch please?"

"I wish—" His voice cracked. "I wish I could let you do that."

A sudden chill that had nothing to do with the wind rushed over her. She leaned hard against the side of the building, the bricks poking into her back. "Has something happened?"

"Are you sitting down?"

"No."

"Sit down," Joe commanded.

"Just tell me," Mariah said, bracing for the worst.

"Dutch is dead," he blurted.

Mariah blinked, nibbled on her bottom lip, felt . . . *hollow.* Hollow as a chocolate Easter bunny.

"Did you hear me?"

"I heard you."

Joe's breathing was harsh in her ear.

So her father was dead. She should feel *something*, shouldn't she? Her heartbeat was steady. A strange calmness settled over her, but she didn't realize that she'd slowly been sliding down the brick wall until her butt hit the cold cement sidewalk.

All she could think of was how she'd cruelly run away from Dutch that afternoon fourteen years ago.

"Mariah?" A whisper of sympathy tinged Joe's voice.

"Yeah?"

"You okay?"

"I'm fine. It's not like my life is going to change," she said quickly.

"I know you weren't close. But he *was* your father." Joe's tone shifted, barely masking anger.

Oh, who was Mr. High-and-Mighty Joe Daniels to judge her? He didn't know her. "How did it happen?" she asked, ignoring her own shove of anger.

"He'd had pneumonia for weeks. We tried to get him—"

Jealousy ambushed her. "We?" she interrupted.

"The cutters in Jubilee."

Cutters.

She'd almost forgotten the slang term for people involved in the training and raising of cutting horses.

"We tried to get him to go to the doctor, but you know Dutch, mule stubborn and set in his ways," Joe continued.

No, she didn't know Dutch. Not really.

"He just kept working. Workaholic, your dad."

That Mariah knew. Dutch lived and breathed horses.

"We were at an event, Dutch swung off his horse, staggered, coughed. I could tell he was suffering. His face was pale and sweaty. He looked me in the eyes and said, 'Don't call Mariah until after the funeral.' Then he just dropped dead." Joe's voice cracked again. "He died with his boots on, doin' what he loved."

A long pause stretched out between them. Chicago and Texas in an uneasy marriage over the airwaves.

"Joe," she murmured, "are *you* okay?"

"No," he said. "Dutch was my closest friend."

Joe's words finally hit her, a hard punch to the gut. Her head throbbed, and she felt as if a full-grown quarter horse had squatted on her chest. Dutch was dead, and the last thing he said was *Don't call Mariah until after the funeral*. Her father hadn't wanted her there.

"You've already buried him?" A soft whimper escaped her lips.

"At Oak Hill Cemetery in Jubilee. It's what he wanted."

She turned to stone inside. Iced up. Shut down completely. "I see. Well then, thank you for calling to let me know."

"Wait," he said. "Don't hang up."

Her hand tensed around the cell phone. "What is it?"

"Dutch left you his ranch."

Dutch left you his ranch.

The words echoed in her head, breaking the thin thread of memory and bringing Mariah back to the present.

The morning sun pushed free of the horizon, bathing the ranch in a butter-and-egg-yolk glow. The joyous twitter of birds greeting the dawn, filling the air with song. How long had it been since she actually paid attention to birds singing? She blinked, seeing Stone Creek Ranch clearly for the first time in full daylight.

It was a country-and-western palace.

The main house sprawled over acres and acres of rolling grassland. On the drive up in the predawn, it had looked like a fat dragon sleeping peacefully after a heavy meal of virgins and villagers. In the daylight, it appeared more like a lazy but handsome king lounging on his throne. Not unlike the lazy cowboy draped insouciantly over the horse trough.

Constructed from limestone and accented with wood finishes, the cowboy mansion boasted a Ludowici clay tile roof, an elevated stone porch, and an accepting veranda. It had to have at least five bedrooms, but probably more like six or seven. A circular flagstone driveway swept impulsively up to the house.

Mariah had parked just short of the main entrance, pulling her rental sedan to a stop by a planter box filled with rusty red chrysanthemums. Numerous other buildings flanked the house. Horse barns, sheds, garages, all well maintained.

Dutch owned this?

She now owned this?

All these years her father had been living in luxury while she and her mother scrimped every penny. The emotions she kept dammed up flooded her—hurt, anger, sorrow, regret, frustration.

Yes, frustration. She had no idea how to run a ranch. She was a wedding planner's assistant, for crying out loud.

Correction. She used to be a wedding planner's assistant. "Used to" being the operative phrase.

What was she going to do with the place? And on a more immediate note, what was she going to do with the man in the horse trough?

Tentatively, she inched closer.

He didn't move.

The shy part of her held back, but the part of her that had learned how to slip into the role of whatever she needed to be in order to get the job done—and right now that was assertive—cleared her throat. "Hey, mister."

No response. Clearly, it was going to take cannon fire to get through his stupor.

You've got to do something more to get his attention. Hanging back and being shy has always put you in hot water. Take the bull by the horns and—

Okay, okay stop nagging.

She reached out and poked his bare shoulder with a finger. Solid as granite.

No response.

Come on. Put some muscle into it.

She poked again. Harder this time.

Not a whisper, not a flinch.

What if he was dead?

Alarmed, Mariah gasped, jumped back, and plastered a palm across her mouth. Dread swamped her. She peered at his chest. Was he breathing? She thought he was breathing, but the movements were so shallow she couldn't really tell.

Please don't be dead.

In that moment, the possibly deceased naked cowboy was the cherry on top of the dung cake that was her life. Three months ago, she'd lost her dream job working for the number one wedding planner in Chicago, and then her vindictive boss had blackballed her in the industry. And now Dutch was gone too and she'd been left a ranch complete with a dead naked cowboy.

Be rational. He's probably not dead.

Maybe not, but clearly he was trespassing, and she couldn't have him thinking that it was okay for him to go around stripping off his clothes and falling into other people's horse troughs during his drunken stupors.

Be bold, do something about this.

Bolstered by her internal pep talk, she stepped up to flick his Stetson with a thump of her middle finger. "Yo, cowboy, snap out of it."

She was just about to thump the Stetson again when one of those sinewy arms snapped up and his steely hand manacled her wrist. The tequila bottle made a dull pinging sound as it fell against the ground. Big fingers imprinted into her skin.

"Eep!" Oxygen fled her lungs. Panic mushroomed inside her. So much for being bold.

"Never thump a man's Stetson," he drawled without moving another muscle, his voice as rich and luxurious as polished mahogany. "Unless you've got a death wish. You got a death wish?"

"N-n-no." Mariah stammered.

She tried to pull away from the Clint Eastwood clone, but pushing against his grip was like trying to bully marble. In fact, struggling only seemed to ensnare her more tightly.

With a lazy index finger, he slowly tipped the brim of his cowboy hat upward, revealing eyes as black as obsidian, and he studied her with a speculative scowl, like he was the big bad wolf just aching for a reason to eat her alive.

Oh man, oh wow, oh just kill me now.

He was one hundred percent alpha male, the kind who staked a claim on a woman with one hard sultry stare and who would fight to the death to hold on to her. The kind of man whose self-confident arrogance had always unsettled her.

She shivered.

His gaze lasered into her as if he could see exactly what she looked like with no clothes on, his intelligent eyes full of mysterious secrets. He didn't seem embarrassed in the least. In fact, he had an air of entitlement about him. As if he had every right to sleep off a berserk bender in her fancy horse trough.

Strangely enough, he made her feel as if *she* were the naked one.

Who was this man? Did he live here? Was he one of Dutch's cowhands?

Even though he was sitting up and she was standing, he seemed to tower over her. He would tower over her when he was on his feet. Of that she was certain. Almost everyone towered over her.

The steady pressure from his strong fingers stirred a

bizarre fluttering inside her. Her stomach quivered. Unnerved, Mariah marshaled her courage, gritted her teeth. "Please let go."

His smile exploded, exposing straight white teeth. This cowboy possessed serious star quality. "What if I don't?"

"I'll dunk your Stetson in the water."

His devilish eyes narrowed. "You wouldn't dare."

Her knees wobbled. She was scared witless, but she learned a long time ago to hide her fears behind bluff and bravado and act brave whether she felt it or not. Ignoring her sprinting pulse, she swept the cowboy hat off his head with her free hand. A thick tumble of inky black hair, two months past the point of needing a trim, spilled out.

"Try me," she said as tough as she could, hoping her voice belied her trembling legs.

His hard laugh clubbed her ears as he slowly released her. Mariah slapped his hat down on his head and snatched her arm back, held it across her chest. He hadn't hurt her at all, but his sizzling body heat had branded her.

"What's the deal?" She glared. "You don't have indoor plumbing?"

"You're funny," he said. "And I don't mean ha-ha. Who are you?"

His ebony voice unnerved her. That and his big, lean, bare body. It occurred to Mariah that she was completely alone here with this stranger. If this were a slasher flick, she'd be in deep trouble.

She swallowed hard, notched up her chin, and silently repeated the mantra her mentor and former boss, Destiny Simon, had taught her. *Never let 'em see you sweat.* Then again, Destiny had been the one to put her in the sweatbox, so what did she know? "I should be asking you that question."

"Oh yeah?" An amused smile played at the corner of his mouth. "Why's that?"

She drew herself up to her full five-foot-one. "Because my name is Mariah Callahan and this"—she swept a hand at the land around them—"is my ranch."

"Oh yeah?" he repeated.

"Yes, and you're trespassing."

"Am I?" He lowered his eyes half-mast. Bedroom eyes the exact color of the cup of strong coffee she'd snagged at the Starbucks drive-through in the last big town she'd passed.

"You are."

He studied her as if she was the most comical thing he'd ever seen. As if he wasn't lying naked in a gold-plated horse trough looking as sexy as three kinds of misdemeanors.

Not that she cared. Not really. She had no room in her life for men—especially those of the cowboy persuasion. She knew just enough about cowboys to know she never wanted one.

"You sure about that?"

His words gave her pause, but, determined not to let him intimidate her, she plunged ahead. "I just inherited this ranch from my father, Dutch Callahan, and I'd appreciate it if you'd remove yourself from the premises immediately."

"Okay." He made a move to hoist himself up.

"No wait." She shielded her eyes with her hands. "I don't need to see that."

He chuckled, clearly finding her amusing, and sank back in the trough. But beneath the incongruous smile, she spotted the shadows that dug into the hollows beneath the angular blades of his cheekbones.

"Your father, huh?" he said.

"Yes."

"That's funny. I don't ever recall you coming to visit him."

Was that an intentional dig? Or just an innocent observation? Mariah glanced over at him. There was nothing innocent about this guy. "You knew my father?"

He crossed his middle finger over his index finger. "We were like that."

She felt envious, melancholy, and irritated. "We were estranged."

"And yet he left you this impressive ranch. I wonder why?"

Sarcasm. From a naked cowboy. The guy was cocky.

Mariah shifted her weight, feeling like she was being indicted or mocked. "I didn't say it made any sense."

"That's because it doesn't."

"Look," she said. "Could you just go?"

He shook his head. "I'm just not buying it."

"Buying what?"

"That you own this ranch. Perfect hair. Perfect makeup. Perfect fingernails." He waved a hand at her. "You look like a Barbie doll."

"I'm not tall enough to be Barbie."

"Barbie's sidekick then."

"Sidekick?"

"I don't know what they call Barbie's sidekick. Tonto Barbie. Doc Holliday Barbie. Sundance Barbie. Pick one."

"Are all your references movie cowboys?"

"Pretty much. Except the Barbie one. I could call you Calamity Jane instead if you prefer symmetry."

Seriously annoyed, Mariah sank her hands on her hips. "Do I have to call the cops?"

"Do you?"

What a jerk. "I'm calling the cops," she threatened, pulling her cell phone from her purse.

"Are you always this friendly?"

"Whenever I find a naked cowboy in my gold-plated horse trough I am. I'm pretty sure there's laws against public nudity, even in this backwater place."

"First off, I'm not naked," he said.

She couldn't stop herself from raking a gaze over his amazing body. "You look naked."

"Appearance can be deceiving. For instance, you look stuck-up."

"Sometimes appearance can be deceiving, but on the whole, I've found that generally what you see is what you get."

"So you're saying you *are* stuck-up?"

"I'm saying you look like a drunken derelict."

"Hungover derelict," he corrected. "I'm not drunk anymore."

"Excuse me for missing the distinction. I'm sure your mother is so proud."

"I have underwear on," he offered.

"How comforting." As if a little strip of soaking wet cotton cloth hid anything. Why she should find that even more tantalizing than full nudity, she had no clue, but she did.

And that bothered her. A lot.

"Secondly, this isn't public," the cowboy continued. "It's private property."

"I know," she said. She couldn't believe this conversation was happening. Had she driven down a rabbit hole when she wasn't looking and ended up in Wonderland? She half expected to see the White Rabbit pop up at any moment, muttering about being late. "*My* property."

"Thirdly, it's not your horse trough."

Her finger hovered over the keypad. Should she call the cops? By challenging him, was she making things worse? Maybe she should just walk away and let him get out of the horse trough at his own pace. She was thirty-six hours without sleep and hungry and sad and strung out from the road and she wanted to find a place to curl up and take a nap, but first she had to set things straight with this cretin.

Before she could make up her mind whether to call the cops, a sheriff's cruiser motored up the road.

"Ha! Apparently someone else has already reported you," she said. "Nice of them to save me the trouble."

"I wouldn't gloat too hard," he observed. "The deputy will be on my side."

"Why's that? Just because you know each other? The good old boy network in action?" Mariah clenched her teeth. She'd had enough of cronyism in Chicago.

"Nope. The deputy is a woman."

"Then why are you so sure she'll side with you? Did you sleep with her?"

"Does that bother you?"

"Why should it bother me? I don't care who you sleep with. Why would I care about who you slept with?"

"You tell me."

"Tell you what?"

"Why you're upset at the idea that I slept with a lady deputy."

"I'm not!" She snorted.

"You look upset."

"I'm upset because you're naked in my horse trough."

"This conversation is going around in circles."

"No kidding."

"It's not your horse trough."

"It is."

"Nope, because it's not your ranch."

"It is and I can prove it."

"It's not and here's the reason why. My name's Joe Daniels, this here is Green Ridge Ranch, and I have a sneaking suspicion you're looking for Stone Creek."

The Cowboy and the Princess

Chapter One

You might be a princess if . . . you have to ditch your bodyguards to get some "me" time.

Brady Talmadge had five unbreakable rules for leading an uncomplicated life.

One stormy June night in Texas, he broke them all. Starting with rule number five.

Never pick up a hitchhiker.

He'd honed the rules through twenty-nine years of trial and error, most of them compiled while towing his vagabond horse trailer from town to town, and as long as he stuck to his edicts, life flowed as smooth and simple as the Brazos River ambling to the Gulf.

In regard to the hitchhiker rule, he learned it the hard way. He had a permanent whup-notch on the back of his skull from a pistol-whipping meted out by a wiry, goat-faced thief who'd taken him for thirteen hundred dollars, his favorite belt buckle, and a pair of ostrich skin cowboy boots. Never mind the four-day hospital stay that drained his savings account to zero because he'd had no health insurance.

On the satellite radio, the weatherman warned of the fierce line of unrelenting storms moving up from Hurricane Betsy. "It's gonna be a wet night, folks. Find someplace warm and dry to hole up with someone you love."

Brady took the exit ramp off Interstate 30, heading for the parking lot of Toad's Big Rig Truck Stop on the outskirts of Dallas. His headlights caught a lone figure huddled on the road shoulder, thumb outstretched. Automatically, his hand went to his occipital bone.

No dice.

Lightning flashed. Thunder crashed. Rain slashed. The hitchhiker shivered violently.

Sorry about your luck, fella.

The eighteen-wheeler in front of Brady splashed a deluge of water over the skinny stranger. Small, vulnerable. Been there. Done that. Lived through it. The fella raised his face and in a flash of fresh lightning, from underneath the hooded sweatshirt, he saw it wasn't a guy at all, but a woman.

No, a girl actually. Most likely a runaway.

Don't do it.

Trampas, his Heinz 57 mutt—who, come to think of it, was a hitchhiker of sorts as well—peered out the window at the dark night and whimpered from the backseat. A year ago, Brady had found the starving puppy, flea-bitten and tick-ridden, on a long stretch of empty road in the Sonoran desert.

He was already driving past her. He'd almost made it. Then hell if he didn't glance back and meet the girl's eyes.

Please, she mouthed.

Aw, shit.

He didn't mean to do it. Hadn't planned on doing it, but

the next thing he knew he was slowing down and pulling over. And that's when he broke rule number four.

Avoid damsels in distress.

That rule came to him courtesy of a short-skirted cowgirl broke down off Route 66 in Flagstaff. She thanked him for changing her flat by inviting him back to her place for a home-cooked fried chicken dinner and rocking hot sex, except she neglected to tell him she had a grizzly bear–sized husband with a high temper and a hammy fist.

Brady rubbed his jaw. He wasn't going to give the runaway a ride. Just get her inside the building and out of the storm. Maybe buy her a meal if she was hungry. He would toss her a few bucks for one of the cheap bunk-and-bath motels attached to the truck stop and advise her against hitchhiking.

Meddling. That's meddling in someone else's business.

Yeah, and where would he be if Dutch Callahan hadn't meddled in his life fourteen years ago?

Prison most likely. Or the bone orchard.

He hit the unlock button, knowing it was a bad idea, but doing it anyway. The hitchhiker ran for his truck. She was short enough so that he couldn't see anything but the top of her head from his perch behind the wheel without peeping into the side view mirror, but he heard her fumble the door handle on the passenger side.

The howling wind snatched at the door, ripping it from her pale, trembling hand and throwing it wide open.

Brady glanced down.

The hitchhiker looked up.

Her eyes were a dusty gray, too large for her small, narrow face, and she stared right into him as if she knew every thought that passed through his head, yet didn't hold it against him.

He tried to take a deep breath, but to his alarm, discovered that he couldn't.

For one brief moment, they dangled in suspended animation. Their gazes meshed, their futures strangely entwined.

Drive off!

Of course he didn't, couldn't. Not with her standing there looking like a soaking wet fawn who just lost her mother to a hunter's gun. But the impulse to run, Brady's instinct to avoid complications at all costs, fisted around his spine and wouldn't let go.

"Thank you for stopping," she said in a voice as soft as lamb's wool. Looped around her shoulder she carried an oversized satchel. "Your kindness is much appreciated."

The breath he'd tried to draw finally filled his lungs with a swift whoosh of damp night air. He nodded.

Somehow, she managed to plant her feet on the running board, grab the door in her right hand, and then swing up into the seat in one long, smooth, ladylike movement. Her satchel rustled as she tugged the heavy door closed behind her, and with a solid click they were cocooned inside.

Alone.

Her scent, an intriguing combination of rain and talcum powder and honey, filled the cab, vanquishing his own leather, horse, and beef jerky smell. The sweatshirt hoodie was tied down tight under her chin so that he couldn't see her hair, but her eyebrows were starkly black in startling contrast to skin the color and texture of fresh cream. She possessed the cheekbones of a Swedish supermodel, as high and sharp and cool as the summit of Mount Everest, but in spite of that barrier of heartbreaking beauty, there was something about her that had him yearning to toss an arm around her shoulders and tell her everything was going to be okay.

Maybe it was because she was so ethereal—pale and slender and wide-eyed.

She wore dark blue jeans with a sharp crease running down the front of the legs. Plain, brown, round-toed cowboy boots shod her petite feet. In spite of being drenched, both the jeans and boots looked brand-new.

Trampas leaned over the seat, ran his nose along the back of her neck.

"Oh." She startled, laughed. "Hello." She reached out a hand to scratch the mutt behind his ear. He whimpered joyously. *Attention hound.*

"Down, Trampas," Brady commanded.

The dog snorted but reluctantly settled, his tail thumping against the backseat.

The hitchhiker turned to snap her seat belt into place, the satchel now clutched in her lap.

"I'm not going anywhere," Brady said. His words hung like a curtain in the air between them, not making a lick of sense coming from a traveling man who dragged his home behind him.

She raised her head and met his gaze again. "I beg your pardon, sir?"

Speech eloped. Just ran right off with his brain. On closer inspection, her eyes weren't simply gray, but loaded with tiny starbursts of sapphire blue. He motioned toward the gas pumps. "I was just . . ."

She canted her head and studied him as if every word that spilled from his mouth was golden. "Yes?"

"Gonna get some gas."

"That is acceptable." She folded her hands over the satchel.

Huh? As if she were giving her permission? "And supper. I was gonna have supper."

"Here?"

"Yes."

"Then why did you stop to pick me up?"

Beats the hell out of me. "You looked cold. And wet. You looked cold and wet."

"I am," she confirmed. "Wet and cold."

He reached over to turn on the heater, angling the air vents toward her. He had never turned on the heater in June in Texas. First time for everything. "Why didn't you go inside the truck stop?"

She shrugged as if the gesture said it all.

"No money?"

Her slight smile plucked at him.

"You hungry?"

The shrug again, accompanied by a shy head tilt. She licked lips the color of red honeysuckle, and for no good reason at all, he thought of caramel—sweet, thick, chewy. If he kissed her, she would taste like caramel. He just knew it.

You're not going to kiss her. Get that idea out of your head right now. You don't need the hassle.

But the more Brady tried not to think about kissing her, the more her lips beckoned.

"You got a name?" he asked.

"Do you?"

"Brady. Brady Talmadge." He put out a hand.

She looked at his palm as if shaking hands was an alien concept, then finally took it for a brief second, smirked like someone enjoying a private joke, and said, "Annie."

"No last name?"

She paused. "Coste."

"Well, Annie Coste, you can join me inside for a meal, my treat, or you can find yourself another ride and be on your way. It's up to you." Damn, he hoped she chose the latter option. She had trouble scribbled all over her. Yeah, so why had he broken his own rules? Because he was a sucker for doe-eyed damsels.

Sucker.

That was the operative word.

"I am hungry," she admitted.

"Great," he said.

Great as a busted axle. Why had he picked her up? Stupid. Glutton for punishment. Misguided sense of chivalry. Dumbass. What a total dumbass. What was wrong with him? But come on, how could he have left Bambi shivering by the roadside when some unscrupulous son of a bitch could have given her a ride instead? Things had been humming along just dandy and now he was stuck with her. If he'd kept driving—which he couldn't have because he was almost out of gas—he would be in Jubilee within ninety minutes. Jubilee. The closest thing he'd ever had to a real home. He didn't want to take her there.

She's not your problem. You can't save everyone, Talmadge. It's not like you're a paragon yourself.

The thoughts loped through his head as he fueled his truck underneath the protective awning and put Trampas into the trailer. The dog curled up on his bed in the air-conditioned living area and gave him a look that said, *I like her.*

"Only because she scratched your itch," Brady grumbled, and shut the door.

He climbed back inside, pulled the truck around the rear of the building with the semis, and looked over at Annie. Raindrops still clung to her long eyelashes and the hoodie of her sweatshirt. Was it weird that her eyebrows were dark, but her eyelashes were light?

As they walked into the restaurant, the big red digital clock on the wall over the door flashed 9:15. The place was rowdy busy. A port in the storm. Truckers in baseball caps and cowboy hats lined the red and chrome swivel stools at the counter up front.

Several men craned their necks for a better look at

Annie. Brady took a step closer toward her, rigging himself up in that she's-with-me strut that came naturally to a cowboy in the company of a good-looking woman. The hum of voices and clang of silverware drifted to the vaulted rafters. The air smelled of diesel exhaust, chicken-fried steak, and yeast rolls.

Brady stood back to let Annie go in front of him.

She hesitated, resistance in her eyes as if uncertain how to proceed. C'mon. Surely she'd been in a truck stop before.

"This way." He held out his arm as a guide and ushered her past the front counter on their left and the clear glass refrigeration units chock-full of homemade pies, spread high with meringue, sitting on rotating shelves. She stopped to stare at the pies, as awestruck as a five-year-old.

"We'll get some for dessert," he said.

Her beaming smile heated him up like an electric blanket on a cold winter night. "Really?"

"You can have two slices if you like." Brady escorted her past the "Seat Yourself" sign to an empty booth in the back of the room situated underneath the head of a mule deer buck.

Eyeing the taxidermied animal, she slid across the red vinyl seat, untying the string of her hoodie as she went, and then she slipped the satchel from her shoulder. She cleaved to the thing like she had gold bars in it.

Brady secured the seat across from her.

She tugged off the hood, revealing black hair chopped short and spiky. It looked as if she'd taken a pair of jagged-teethed pruning shears and hacked it off herself, but he supposed it was probably some hip salon cut that cost a hundred bucks or more. The harsh hairstyle, paired with her wide gray-blue eyes and pale skin, gave her the appearance of an anime cartoon heroine—waifish and innocent—accentuating the whole damsel-in-distress thing.

Next, she wrestled out of the sweatshirt, revealing a simple white blouse with cap sleeves, showing off toned arms that knew their way around a biceps curl. She was not the typical truck stop hitchhiker. No piercings (not even her ears), no tats (at least none he could see), no skimpy, too-tight clothing flaunting too-big breasts. She was like a daisy sprung fresh in the garden. No, that was too common. Not a garden daisy, but a rare buttercup growing on a mountaintop. Sunny, sweet, lustrous. Unexpected. Special.

Special?

What the hell? Where was that coming from?

If he were smart, he'd pass her twenty bucks, get up, and walk out. Clearly, he was not smart because instead of doing that, he took off his straw Stetson, settled it on the bench seat beside him, and ran a hand through his hair.

The right side of the booth butted up against a thick, rain-painted plate-glass window. Outside, the vapor lamps glowed ghostly in the rumbling storm. Inside, someone with a sense of humor set the jukebox playing "Let it Rain" by David Nail.

Annie harvested a napkin from the red and chrome dispenser on the table and started polishing the Formica surface, whisking away crumbs left behind from a slapdash busboy's one-swipe attempt at cleaning the tabletop.

A waitress, dressed in a retro pink dress with a white bib apron and battered sneakers, bopped over with two menus tucked under one arm and two glasses of water in her hands. "Here y'all go," she said. "I'm Heather and I'll be back in a minute to take your order." Then off she went.

Brady shifted his attention back to Annie. Her head

was bowed over the menu. One dainty finger slid down the list of offerings.

"What is chili?" she asked, raising her head to meet his gaze.

He startled again, just as he had when she climbed into his truck. Something about those eyes unraveled him in a way he'd never been unraveled and Brady was no stranger to peering into the eyes of gorgeous women. "You've never eaten chili?"

She shook her head.

"You're not from Texas."

"How do you know?"

"Texans cut their baby teeth on chili."

"I am not from Texas," she admitted.

"Where you from?"

She rested one hand on the satchel beside her. "What is chili exactly?"

"It's ground or shredded beef cooked in a tomato-based sauce."

"And served cold?"

"No. It's hot. Both temperature and spice wise."

She looked puzzled. "If it is hot, then why do they call it chili?"

Something was decidedly off about this one. "Dunno. Sarcasm maybe?"

"Sarcasm?"

"They don't have sarcasm where you're from?"

"May we get some?" she asked.

"Get what?" Brady asked, his mind rambling to all possible meanings of the phrase "get some." "Sarcasm?"

"Chili."

"Okay," he said, just like that. So much for rule number three.

Never order chili at a truck stop.

That rule was self-evident. No unsavory details

needed, but when the waitress came back, Brady handed her the menus. "Two bowls of chili. I'll have a Coors and the lady wants . . ."

"Might I have a cup of tea?" Annie asked.

"You mean hot tea?" The waitress gave her a strange look. Probably not too many truckers ordered hot tea.

"Yes, please. Thank you." Annie sat like she had a ruler implanted in her spine. Straight. Proper. "Earl Grey if it is available."

"I'll see what we got." The waitress pivoted and scooted off.

Annie hugged herself, grinned. "This is so enjoyable."

Brady cocked his head, trying to detect some kind of accent, but her speech was as plain as a Midwest newscaster. Sometimes her word choice was a little formal, a little stiff, which didn't quite jibe. Who was she? Her inscrutable gray-blue eyes revealed no secrets. "What is?"

"Ordering chili in a truck stop with a real-life cowboy."

"Are you from another country?"

"Are you?"

"No," he said.

She spread her hands, delicate and smooth, against the Formica tabletop in a prim gesture. She wore no rings, no bracelets. No jewelry at all. Her nails were short and painted with clear polish. Simple. Understated. Elegant. No adornments needed. "And there you have it."

What was she talking about? He felt as if he'd missed a step or two in the conversation. She looked so young. Not a single wrinkle on her face. No blemishes either. Flawless complexion.

"How old are you?" he asked. What if she was underage? This could be the beginning of a major snafu.

"How old are you?"

"Twenty-nine."

"I'm twenty-four."

"Naw." He shook his head. "You can't be twenty-four. I'd say twenty at most."

She raised both palms out from her head, shrugged. "It is true."

"You have some great genetics."

She glanced around the room at the other diners. "This place is quite interesting."

Interesting? Furrowing his brow, Brady followed her gaze. Nothing special as far as he could see. Asking her where she was from wasn't getting him anywhere. Clearly she didn't want to talk about her past or why she was on the run. He understood that impulse. He tried a different track. "Where are you going?"

"Where are *you* going?"

"Jubilee."

"Where is Jubilee?"

Dammit, here she was doing it again, running the conversation in circles. "About eighty miles southwest of here."

"Is that where you live?"

"No."

"Why are you going there?"

"A job."

"What kind of job?"

"I work with horses."

"You are an equine veterinarian?"

"Not exactly."

"What exactly?"

"You could be a reporter, you know, with all those questions. Are you a reporter?"

"No, I am just naturally curious about people," she said quickly. "What exactly?"

"I work with horses who've been emotionally traumatized."

"Oh!" She broke into a big smile. "Like the Horse Whisperer in that dramatic novel by Nicholas Evans."

"It's not as glamorous as Robert Redford made it out to be in the movie, but yes, I do rehabilitate horses who've been injured or harmed or developed phobias."

"How did you get started in that line of employment?"

"I just sort of fell into it."

"Is it a difficult job?"

"Not from my point of view. But horses are sensitive, highly intuitive animals. You have to know how to handle them."

"How is that?"

"With a gentle hand and a loving heart."

"I like that." She leaned forward. "What an exciting profession."

"It's just what I do." He paused. "But I do love it."

"Where do you live when you are not healing horses?"

"In my trailer."

Dejection flickered across her face. "You do not have a home? You are a homeless person? I have never met a homeless person. Is it truly terrible? Being without a home?"

Beam me up, Scotty. I don't know what planet I've landed on, but the hitchhikers in these parts are freaking nuts. "I live in my trailer. That's my home."

"Traveling from town to town?"

"Living on the road is the ultimate freedom. Footloose and fancy-free. I can go anywhere I want, any time I want to go. No limitations. No expectations."

"I cannot imagine such circumstances."

"No roots, nothing holding me back."

Annie pressed the fingertips of both hands against her lips. "It sounds so sad."

Brady blinked. Something dark and uncomfortable

slithered across the back of his mind. Something he couldn't capture or name, but it slithered all the same. Swift and heavy, scraping his brain. "What's so horrible about freedom?"

"It is lonely."

"No, no. Not lonely at all. I have my dog, Trampas, and friends all over the country, and there's the horses and . . ." He trailed off, trying to think of all the wonderful things about his life.

"No one special," she finished for him.

Brady snorted. "Hey, if you're so happy and your life is choked with special people, what are you doing hitchhiking in the rain on a Friday night?"

She pulled herself up on the edge of her seat and looked down her nose in a stately expression of the highborn. "I am out for an adventure."

"Yeah? Got away from the zookeeper, did you?" Now, that was tacky. He shouldn't have said it, but his gut poked at him.

"Pardon me?" The regal expression vanished and the vulnerable girlishness was back—hurt, disappointed.

Brady shook his head. "Never mind."

Thankfully, the waitress showed up, interrupting the weird conversation. "Toad's chili twice." She sat two blue bowls of steaming cinnamon-colored chili, swimming in the glistening grease of too much cheddar cheese, in front of them. She plunked down Brady's beer with barely any foam, and then she slid a small metal pitcher of hot water in front of Annie, along with a tea bag. "No Earl Grey. All we got is orange pekoe."

"Thank you." Annie graced the waitress with a smile as if bestowing a title upon her. "May I have an additional spoon, please?"

"Sure thing." The waitress grabbed an extra spoon for her.

Brady peered into his bowl and accepted his fate. That's what you got when you broke rules. He dug into the chili. Just as he feared, it was deceptively delicious.

He tried to blank his mind and focus on eating, but then the satchel on the seat beside Annie moved. Huh? Was he seeing things? He narrowed his eyes and noticed the sides of the satchel were made of braided mesh.

The satchel moved again.

"Whoa!" Brady jumped. Which wasn't like him. Usually he was laid back, not the least bit jumpy, but things just kept getting weirder.

Annie looked up. "What is it?"

He pointed. "Your bag moved. Twice."

"Oh." She put a dab of chili on the end of her spoon and reached for the satchel.

A little brown head popped from the side corner of the bag, and a tiny black button nose twitched.

"What the hell is . . . *that?*"

Annie laid a finger to her lips. "Shh, this is Lady Astor. My best friend in the whole world."

Shiny black eyes fixed on him.

"Seriously? That's a dog?"

"Lady Astor is a Yorkshire terrier. She is one year old and she weighs six pounds." The Yorkie lapped chili from Annie's spoon.

"You brought her with you on Annie's Big Adventure?"

"Of course. I could not, in all good conscience, leave her at the pal . . ." She trailed off, got a strange look on her face, and finished with "leave her home alone."

"Ever heard of a kennel?" Did they have those in whatever la-la land she was from?

Annie glared as if he had suggested she run the dog through a blender.

"Hey, you're the one who carries her around in a satchel."

A distraught furrow creased her brow. "She is comfortable in it. The mesh sides let air get in. It keeps her dry in the rain and I bought the most expensive one they had and—"

He raised a palm. "You don't have to justify it to me."

"Do you really think it is a bad thing that I keep her in a satchel?" She worried a paper napkin between her fingers.

"Why do you care what I think?"

"I am not—" She shut her mouth.

"You're not what?"

She tilted her head back and gave him that condescending glare again. "Disregard that."

"C'mon, you can tell me." Brady hated secrets. Had since he was a kid and he'd learned—well, there was no point going *there*—but whenever he was around someone who was obviously hiding something, he couldn't resist nudging for full disclosure. He'd discovered a lot of unexpected things about people that way. "It's not like you're ever going to see me again. Your secret is safe with me."

"I have no secret," she insisted, but her earlobes pinked and she did not meet his gaze.

"None? Nothing? Not even a tiny white lie you want to confess?"

Her eyes widened and she seemed even paler than before. Did the woman ever go out in the sun? "No."

Brady's lie-o-meter went off. Big time. He did not know who or what Annie Coste was, but she spelled complication in capital letters.

Lady Astor finished licking the spoon, and then burrowed back into the satchel. She did seem to like it in there.

Annie picked up the second spoon that the waitress had brought her and daintily dipped it into the chili. Brady couldn't help watching her bring the curved stainless steel up to her full pink lips. When they finished their meal, they ordered banana cream pie and Annie attacked it with gusto.

"I am not allowed to eat like this at home." She moaned a soft sound of pleasure and put a hand to her stomach.

"Allowed to?"

She ignored that, flicked her tongue out to lick a spot of frothy meringue from her upper lip, laughed. It was an airy sound that had real joy behind it, a gleeful laugh that embraced life in a hard hug. If he never saw her again, he would always remember the sound of her laughter, because it sounded like freedom.

For some reason, just hearing her laugh made him laugh and they both sat there underneath the mule deer, the smell of grease in the air, the taste of banana cream pie on their tongues, laughing and looking at each other and having a high old time together. It was the most fun he'd ever had at a truck stop, bar none.

Slowly, her laughter drained away.

So did his.

They were left with just the looking.

Mesmerized, he pulled a palm down over his mouth. He couldn't figure out what compelled him more, his attraction to her or his curiosity about her.

The healthy, masculine part of him was already toying with the idea of seducing her. She was sexy in an unusual way and it had been months since he'd taken pleasure in the company of a willing woman. But his gut was saying back off. Something wasn't right. All was not as it seemed.

To distract himself, he turned and peered out the window. The rain was still washing down in angry torrents. Through the dark night, a long black limousine emerged and pulled up to the gas pumps.

"Now there's a sight you don't see every day at a truck

stop in this neck of the woods unless it's prom night," Brady said. "But prom was two weeks ago. Unless it's a school with a late prom."

"What is that?" Annie asked in her slightly prissy, nondescript tone.

It drove him nuts that she had no birthplace-identifying accent. Who was she? Where was she from?

"Limo."

The chauffeur got out to fuel the vehicle. The rear door opened and two other men emerged. They were dressed in expensive suits tailored to perfectly fit their bodies. One man was tall, the other squat, and they both wore sunglasses at night and jaunty fedoras pulled down low over their foreheads.

Who were these guys? Mobsters? Secret Service? The Blues Brothers?

Then he remembered that former president Franklin Glover's daughter, Echo, was getting married this weekend and the president's ranch, where the nuptials were being held, wasn't far from here. It had been all over the radio for days.

Most likely they were Secret Service. But in a limo? He would have expected a black Cadillac Escalade with bulletproof glass.

Brady felt movement beside him, turned his head to see Annie had gotten up to come peer over his shoulder. He swung his gaze back to the window. Her warm breath tickled the hairs on the nape of his neck.

A fierce craving hammered down his spine and drove to his groin. He swallowed hard, fighting off the reaction. Yes, okay, she got a rise out of him, but he did not have to do anything about it. In fact, a smart guy would get the hell out of here as fast as possible. Unfortunately, Brady had never been particularly smart when it came to women. He always seemed to go for the troublesome ones.

The two guys from the limo broke into a trot, rushing to get out of the rain, and headed for the front door of the restaurant.

Annie made a noise of distress.

Brady jerked his head back in her direction.

She stood clutching his cowboy hat in her hands, her head raised expectantly. "May I sit here?"

"Um . . . sure."

She set his straw Stetson on the table and sank down beside him, her gaze coddling his. She did not look out the window. Did not glance around the room. Her eyes were on him and him alone.

Unnerved, he scooted as far across the seat as he could, his shoulder bumping up against the cool glass window.

At that moment, the Blues Brothers came into the seat-yourself dining area, scanning the room as if searching for someone.

Annie leaned in closer.

There was nowhere else for Brady to go. This development took him completely by surprise. He didn't know if he liked it or not.

"You are very handsome," she said.

"Um . . . okay."

"I want to kiss you."

Stunned, he blinked. "Huh?"

"Kiss me."

"What?" Had he heard her correctly?

"Kiss me."

The Blues Brothers were talking to Heather, the waitress.

Do not kiss her. Something is not right. Warning! Whatever you do, do not kiss her!

"Kiss me now!" she demanded, and puckered those honeysuckle lips.

He held up a palm like a stop sign. "I don't think so."

"Why not?"

"I don't like being bossed around."

"Please," she wheedled.

"Well, when you put it like that," he drawled. "No."

"You do not find me desirable." She reached out to stroke his chin with an index finger. He caught a whiff of her talcum powder scent.

"Quite the contrary."

"So why not?"

Brady peered into those big gray-blue eyes and he was a goner. Ah shit. What the hell? Why not? Illogically, he pulled her into his arms and proceeded to dismantle rule number two.

Always trust your gut.

Her lips were heated satin, melting Brady's self-control like cotton candy dunked in hot soda pop. She tangled her slender arms around his neck, tugging him closer, but she did not loosen her jaw.

Mystified, he lightly rested the tip of his tongue against her bottom lip. Was she going to let him in?

"Hmm, mmm." Annie increased the pressure of the kiss, but she did not part her teeth.

Okay, this was the first time he'd ever had a woman beg him to kiss her and then not let him fully do the job. Brady didn't like to brag, but he knew he was a good kisser. Many a woman had told him so.

Kissing was his second favorite part of lovemaking. He loved to taste things. Explore. Savor. Push limits. And he'd been right. Annie did taste like caramel. He wanted more.

She loosened her arms around his neck, broke the liplock, rested her forehead on his. "Are they still there?" she whispered.

"Who?"

"The men in the suits and fedoras."

Once more, Brady shifted his gaze to the dining room. The Blues Brothers were gone. He glanced back at Annie. Took in her glistening lips. Inhaled her innocent fragrance. Heard her soft intake of breath.

Right then and there, he trifled with his number one rule for leading an uncomplicated life. The rule that had kept him safe, satisfied, and single for twenty-nine years. The rule he was about to shatter into a million little pieces.

Never tell a lie.

"They're still here," he said. "You better keep kissing me."